WITHDRAWN
FOR SALE

WHAT SHE LEFT BEHIND

WITHDRAWN
FOR SALE

WITHDRAWN
FOR SALE

Also by Emily Freud

My Best Friend's Secret

WHAT SHE LEFT BEHIND

EMILY FREUD

QUERCUS

First published in Great Britain in 2022 by

Quercus Editions Ltd
Carmelite House
50 Victoria Embankment
London EC4Y 0DZ

An Hachette UK company

Copyright © Emily Freud 2022

The moral right of Emily Freud to be identified as the author of this work has been asserted in accordance with the Copyright, Designs and Patents Act, 1988.

All rights reserved. No part of this publication may be reproduced or transmitted in any form or by any means, electronic or mechanical, including photocopy, recording, or any information storage and retrieval system, without permission in writing from the publisher.

A CIP catalogue record for this book is available from the British Library

PB ISBN 978 1 52942 181 1

This book is a work of fiction. Names, characters, businesses, organizations, places and events are either the product of the author's imagination or used fictitiously. Any resemblance to actual persons, living or dead, events or locales is entirely coincidental.

10 9 8 7 6 5 4 3 2 1

Typeset by CC Book Production
Printed and bound in Great Britain by Clays Ltd, Elcograf S.p.A.

Papers used by Quercus are from well-managed forests and other responsible sources.

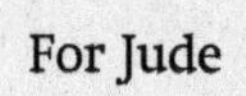

For Jude

PART ONE

CHAPTER 1

'Here she is, telling us what to do again.' Paul's eyes shine as they leave the road for a moment to enjoy my reaction. Grinning, he calls over to the back seats, 'I mean, imagine if we didn't have Lauren here to enlighten us, guys? We might actually make the right turning occasionally.'

A giggle runs through me like a train. I hit his shoulder playfully, and he grabs the spot feigning pain. 'Paul. Come *on*. Don't be such a shi . . .' Smacking my hand across my mouth, I whisper, 'Sorry,' before checking his features for signs of annoyance. His jovial demeanour doesn't waver and I'm relieved. At least I caught it in time. I keep accidentally letting them drop. Like little red flags waving, giving me away.

I hear a soft rumbling snore from behind and twist myself to peer through the letter-box gap in the headrest. They weren't paying attention anyway. Margo, who is still partial to the occasional afternoon nap, is fast asleep. And Jesse is staring out the window looking at the scenery thinking God knows what. For a four-year-old he sure is pensive. Satisfied, I rest back in my seat. We are shuttling through the countryside at speed, and I watch as fluctuating tones of green blur past. I've not seen another car since we left the motorway, and the contrast to the city is jarring, where the natural state of our four wheels was far more likely to be stationary than in motion. We overtake a petrol station and I turn to catch it. It must have the smallest forecourt I've ever seen with only two rusty pumps. For a moment I think it must be abandoned, but then I see the silhouette of a man behind the grungy glass.

For the millionth time I wonder if moving to the countryside was the right thing to do. This is such a big step for us. We've barely known each other a year, and for half of that we weren't exactly official. My aunt described the decision as a huge leap of faith. But then, she conceded that her very happy marriage was conducted after knowing my uncle for a mere three months, so really, I think she understands.

Paul reaches across and cocoons my hand in his. I glance at him with a knowing smile. That potent feeling I've grown to know well over the last twelve months washes over me. It *was* the right thing. I'm right where I'm meant to be – here with my new family. They are the centre of my universe now. I can't help looking at the kids again. My eyes rest on my happy place: Margo. The cutest darling in the whole world. Dark bobbed hair, green eyes, chunky arms and big rosy cheeks. I could blow raspberries on her rotund tummy all day. Tightly welded under her elbow is her grey toy cat which is never far out of reach. A mini explosion of happiness within, like one of those effervescent tablets you plop into a glass of water. Since joining Paul's family, I've felt as though I'm leaking bubbles of joy wherever I go. I suppose when what happened to me happens, it's difficult to take anything for granted again. You must grab what you want with both hands and run as fast as you can. Paul taught me that.

I turn back to face the front with a bounce and lean forward, adjusting the air conditioning, pointing the filter directly in my face. I look at the heat shimmying off the bonnet. It's late May, barely summer; it feels wrong somehow that it's so hot. As if we are enjoying something we'll have to pay for later. Like binge drinking on a Sunday night.

'Do you think the house will be unbearably stuffy with all that glass?' I ask.

Paul shakes his head. 'It's in the middle of a forest. The trees protect it.' His hand lands on my thigh and squeezes. 'Stop worrying. It's a big change, I know. But as Heraclitus says . . .' I roll my eyes and join him in saying, 'the only constant is change.' He looks at me with a grin. 'Those Greek philosophers really know what they're talking about.'

I rest back in my seat. He's right, of course. I worry too much. Paul always says that worrying is like riding a stationary bike: it's never going to get me anywhere. He's skilled at flipping me back into the present again – where everything is perfect. *I am so lucky I found them.* My heart sings. Before, my hands and arms were empty, desperate for something to hold on to.

I can't have children. And I lost my parents at a young age. Destined for nothing above or below. How sad is that? Until Paul. My friends tell me relationships were never my strong point. But I can't have ever really been in love before. I'm sure I would remember something as intense and all-consuming as this.

Paul clicks the indicator, and we take a sharp turn. 'Finally. We made it,' he says, relieved. The smooth tarmac makes way for a bumpy grit surface. The corner has brought us in direct line with the sun, and I raise my hand to shade my face before pulling the visor down, then I squint to find the house.

My 'friends' are all shocked that I've left London with him. They never liked the idea of Paul and felt because of how we met that he took advantage. But they don't understand. Sometimes you must break the rules to fight for the one you love. In the end they ganged up against me and left me with an ultimatum. They're *sort of* still talking to me. Just. Paul thinks they're all incredibly immature. He's right, of course: they were totally useless when I really needed them. To be honest, I'm finding it hard to care about their antics – my new family is all I need and I'm sure they'll come round once a fun weekend in our incredible new home is up for grabs.

We slowly creep up the mile-long drive. Weeds poke through the coarse surface and the bushes that surround it are scraggly and unkempt, giving the whole preamble a dilapidated energy. But this does not erode the impressiveness of the building.

I've been here before. About a month ago we visited before making the final decision to move. The sight of the house has the same effect it had on me then. The grandeur spanks me right in the face. Built in the 1950s by a noteworthy architect, it looks more like something found in the Catskills, New

York, rather than rural England. Black planks of wood clad the frame of the house which is otherwise composed of clear plate glass. The glistening surface boldly stretches across the whole of the downstairs, and then repeats between planks for the upper floor. There, one side holds the master suite, while the other is just a void, which cases the epic high ceilings of the living quarters downstairs. At night, it is like a spaceship soaring through stars. It takes my breath away. Can I really live in a house like this? Can I live up to it?

In a short amount of time, I've progressed from a lonely, broken girl to a mother of two with a detached house in the countryside. One that readers of design magazines and modernist aficionados would drool over. *How did I get so lucky?* I ask myself again as I tingle with excitement for this next chapter. It just shows: life can hit you with a curve ball when you least expect it. I swallow against the enormity of responsibility which has grabbed me by the throat.

As we swoop to a stop the sun jolts off the glass frontage right into my eyes, leaving a harsh sunspot. I blink it away. It hangs on for dear life before melting back into my veiny recesses. I wonder for a moment if it will bring on a headache – or worse. But to my relief, nothing surfaces.

Paul turns the engine off, and we sit there in silence for a moment. The air between us convulses with anticipation. As if we are nervous to begin. 'Are we really home?' I whisper, reaching out my hand which he takes.

'Yes. For a while anyway.'

Opening the car door, the cool air rushes outside, colliding with the balmy heat. I begin to get out, but Paul calls, 'Wait!' and dashes around the front of the car and catches the door, pulling it back the whole way. He then leans forward and offers a hand. The gesture is sweet. Romantic. I can't help thinking as he stands there waiting for me how attractive he is. He looks rugged with the new beard he's been growing – his 'lumberjack look', I've been affectionately calling it. It's quite jarring against his usual preppy style, but it suits him. His kind eyes and thick dark hair make him seem far less jaded and worn-down than his circumstances should allow. He'd be forgiven for letting himself go, having raised two small children practically single-handed for the last few years.

I take his hand, and get out. 'I can't believe they're letting us stay here.'

Paul laughs. 'Jack is an old friend. He owed me.'

'I hope we don't break anything,' I say nervously, almost to myself.

He pulls me over and hugs me to his side. 'It's not like you to be nervous about something . . .' he jokes, touching my face affectionately. 'Anyway, I told you, they're really laid-back.'

His friends have let us stay here for a year while they're overseas working. It's perfect: we get to road test a rural life before we commit, and they get free home security.

He pecks my lips. 'Don't ruin this for yourself, darling.'

I smile softly and nod. I'll try.

A murder of crows call from above and I pivot on the spot, watching them cross over and dive into the canopy of trees behind the house.

'Lauren!' Margo shouts and I turn quickly to the car. She is looking at me in that gruff way she does when I've forgotten something. Her lower lip stuck out in disdain. Exasperated by my inexperience. I open the passenger door and undo her buckle and help her down. Her grey cat tumbles to the floor and I crouch to pick it up. Jesse has undone his own belt and has joined his father as he sorts through a cluster of keys, looking for the right one. 'This is our new house,' Margo states grandly. Lisping in that cute way she does.

'Yes, for a bit.' I stand behind her and pull out her hair bobble which has come loose. While her head tilts back her big green eyes watch me. She does this frequently. As though she's checking I'm still there.

'I've got my own room?' she checks.

'Yes, I told you.' I move some stray strands from her face. She grins gleefully. I love making her happy.

A handful. That's what I thought when Paul told me he had two kids. She's on her way to four, and Jesse will be five at his next birthday. Was I crazy? But then he introduced me to them and there was something so instant about my love. When her chunky, soft arms went around my neck for the first time, I couldn't ever think about letting her go. This was my chance to be a mother. And I wasn't going to let what people thought of me, or us, get in the way of that. Jesse has been harder to win over. But that's just his personality. He's less trusting. That's fine. It will take time and is completely understandable under the circumstances.

I am, after all, option B.

I hold Margo's hand and we walk over to join the boys. As the four of us stand there looking at our new home I feel an excited flutter in my chest. What memories will we make here?

Paul throws the correct key up in the air. 'Hurrah!' he says, slotting it in and striding inside.

Our new start, and the beginning of my life as a mother. 'Come on. Let's do this.' I squeeze Margo's hand and we follow Paul in, trying to ignore the thing that is always there loitering in the background. Hovering above me, refusing to leave me alone.

Her.

Always watching. Always judging. I have this instinct deep inside that because I wanted so badly to be a mother, I should feel guilty. Much like the recipient of an organ from a donor. I know the only reason I am here is because she is dead. And I am nowhere near as good a mother as she was. I shake her from my mind, refusing to let her ruin this for me. Letting a smile spread across my lips, I tell myself that the hard banging in my chest isn't fear, it's excitement. I'm sure of it.

CHAPTER 2

Jesse is sitting cross-legged next to my feet on the kitchen floor. He leans into the cardboard box, pulls out a mug and holds it up to me. Crumbled newspaper sloppily hangs off, and I take it from him quickly. I'm unsure the contents of the box will survive Jesse's clumsy little hands stumbling through it. But I'm negating the risk as he's enjoying it so much. And it's rare to find a way to spend quality time in the same space. He's usually two feet away preparing to take another step back. But he's enjoying methodically handing pieces of crockery up to me which I then rinse, and place on the stainless-steel worktop with a clink.

Besides, a few broken bits of IKEA tat is a price worth paying if it diminishes the cloud of agitation that's been hovering over him. The simplicity of the task seems to have taken his mind off the enormity of what we've just done.

'I thought there were four of these,' I say, holding up a ceramic blue mug. He rustles through the pieces nestling in yesterday's paper.

'Here you go, Lauren,' he replies, holding up the fourth.

'Thank you. Best helper ever,' I say, taking it from him with a wink. His cheeks flare up at the compliment, but I can tell he's pleased. Jesse is a shy boy who does not cope well with change. Paul and I had many conversations about how he'd handle leaving London. Paul seems to think there will be a period of adjustment and then Jesse will simply be fine, that it'll be a journey and we'll just need to support him through it. *We'll* – I love it when Paul says things like that. It means so much to me that he includes me within the family unit.

I glance over to check on Margo, who I set up at the dining table. Her pens are scattered around, lids enthusiastically discarded and her colouring book open. Her elbow holds down the page with her head resting on her palm as she scrawls. She is humming the tune to 'Wind the Bobbin Up' as the felt tip makes a scratching noise. Content. Completely unconcerned by the fact she's left the only home she's ever really known. The two of them are like chalk and cheese. But there is a reason for that: being the eldest, Jesse was more aware of what was going on at home.

From across the shiny stainless-steel kitchen island, I look out into the vast space of the living area. It almost feels limitless with the transparent double-height ceiling and glass bi-folding doors which lead onto a sweeping lawn surrounded by towering pine trees. The sky is still blue even though evening is closing in – with a hazy looseness hovering around us. I'm looking forward to later when it's pitch black. I'll be able to lie back on the sofa and stare up at the stars.

I still can't believe I live in a house like this. The downstairs is dissected by a contemporary black wood burning stove which hangs down from the high ceiling like a big black club hammer. The soft furnishings are muted browns, beiges and blacks. On the far side is a long twelve-seater dining table with wooden chairs Paul tells me are called 'wishbone' because of the 'Y' shape of their back. They look very expensive. As does everything. The cushions, the rugs, the paintings on the walls.

On the other side of the wood burning stove is the hallway that leads to the kids' rooms, their bathroom and Paul's study. Along that way too are the stairs that go up to our master suite at the top of the house. Instead of bannisters there is a glass wall that lines the edge of the steps.

The owners have left a scattering of belongings that they must have decided were easily picked up at their new location and not worth shipping. As soon as we arrived the children gravitated to a wooden shaker-style toy kitchen residing in one corner of the living area. I had to brush it down and rinse off the red pots and pans before they got their mitts on it – everything seems to be covered in a fine layer of dust, more than I would have expected from six months of abandonment. What with all the cleaning on top of the unpacking, it is going to take me a while to feel completely relaxed here. I keep telling myself not to overdo it. But I'm so ready for all of this and it's my job to make it feel like home, after all.

Outside, I notice a bird hopping across the lawn picking at something in the grass with its beak. I have no idea how we'll ever get used to living within solid walls again. Being here will spoil us when we downsize to something we can afford to buy. Paul had just sold the home he shared with Emma when I moved into his rented flat in London. So, he has the money to buy somewhere, but I don't want to pry and ask how much, unsure if that would be overstepping the mark. People can be funny about personal finances, and I feel terrible that I can't contribute and rely on him so heavily in that sense. As well as all the other senses too. And he's so generous. Always buying me expensive presents. Hopefully it won't be like this forever, and I'll be able to pay his kindness back. I can't dwell on it too much right now, it makes me feel useless. Yet another thing I can't bring to the table.

'Mummy . . .' Jesse begins, but then he realises his mistake and stops himself. He looks mortified. 'Lauren, I mean . . .' he mumbles, head down, staring at the floor. Hands shaking.

I crouch next to him and squeeze him to my side. 'It's okay,' I say gently. He lost Emma in such a horrible way. Cancer. She literally withered and died in front of their eyes in a matter of months. He was so young, and still is. She just exists as fragments to him now. Moments he cannot decipher. The trauma so appalling, and he was so small – he can barely remember her at all. And Paul rarely speaks about her – well, not in front of me. The pain so raw for him, and harder still to face his children's. Margo doesn't take much notice as she was only one when it happened. She has no idea anything is missing at all. But Jesse feels it. The weight he carries around is visible to me. Grief when you can't quite recollect the person belongs to other people more than you.

My parents both died when I was very small. I was brought

up by my aunt and uncle who moved to Australia as soon as I finished school. I don't blame them for going. They were more than sixty when they got lumped with me. I was due to travel to Sydney just before my accident but obviously couldn't go once it had happened. My uncle is too old to make the trip back now, and my aunt would never leave him. We email, and they send the odd postcard, which is very sweet. I'm so grateful for all they've done for me. They really should have been relaxing and enjoying life when I came along, and I certainly don't want to be a burden to them again. Maybe, one day when the kids are a bit older, we could go out there. I'd really like to see them with my own eyes after everything I've been through. Paul agrees it would be nice, although the twenty-four-hour flight with two kids is quite a horrendous thought. Thank goodness for iPads.

'Sorry,' Jesse says, still unable to look up.

I squeeze him again and kiss the top of his head. 'It's fine, Jesse.' To be honest, I'd quite like them to call me Mummy one day. But I know it will take a while to work up to that. And I have no idea what Paul will think of it. It's a big step and one that is very loaded. I'm not trying to replace her. Anyway, it's something the children can decide much further down the line. He's not even asked me to marry him yet.

We continue our teamwork. Jesse unwrapping as I wash and organise.

'Sorry we're having such a boring day,' I say.

He shrugs. 'Only boring people get bored.'

I break into a smile. 'That is very smart, Jesse.'

The whole production of unpacking is taking a while longer than I was hoping. Mainly because I don't really want to use any of Paul's friends' things in case they get damaged. So, I've found myself clearing all of them into our empty boxes to store in the garage.

Paul pauses as he walks past, taking in what I'm doing with a bemused smile. 'They said they didn't mind if we use their kitchen stuff.'

'Kids break everything, Paul. I'd prefer it this way.' He shrugs and lets me get on with it. I know he thinks I'm being overly cautious. But from what he's told me of his friends, I can tell they're the kind of people who'd appreciate my vigilance. And there is no way I can spend the next year stressing over every little breakage. I bet Emma would have done the same. No, that's wrong actually. Emma wouldn't have got all het up about it in the first place; she'd be in complete control the whole time.

'It's too hot,' I say, walking over to the bi-folding doors and yanking them open with a heave. It doesn't make much difference. In fact, I think I've just let more hot air in. I look longingly out to the garden. Like the front, it's completely overgrown. Nevertheless, I'm looking forward to carving out a few hours away from unpacking to spend in the sunshine with the kids tomorrow. I think Paul said he spotted a sprinkler in the garage. I must order a paddling pool now we have a garden. I imagine what it will look like all pruned and mowed. I think of myself in a floaty cotton dress handing out pieces of watermelon for Jesse and Margo to crunch on. The sticky pink liquid pouring down their forearms as they rush back under the sprinkler squealing. The image stalls me. I forget what I'm doing for a moment.

'Lauren?' I jerk my head in surprise. Paul is standing next to me. 'Are you okay?' he asks, frowning.

'Yes, fine.' I smile broadly, wanting to remove his worry.

'Why don't you stop and take a break?' he suggests. 'You seem to have doubled the workload with the system you've cooked up. Tell me what to do, I'll take over.'

I shake my head. 'No, I'm fine, honestly. Full of beans. And I've got the best assistant here helping me.' I smile down at Jesse who nods proudly.

'Okay, well, don't worry about sorting Jack's study, I'll do it. He said he's happy for me to use it, but he'd prefer me to lock away his things now people will be coming and going, as he's got all his important paperwork in there.'

I nod as I reach to open another cupboard. I find it jam-packed with colourful plastic beakers and plates and a couple of baby bottles too. I pick up a beaker and stare at it. It's well worn. I run my finger over the daily-use scratches. It could be any cup in any family house anywhere. I look out at the sophisticated setting. It really looks too pristine to have had children living here.

'They've got a little girl Margo's age,' Paul reminds me. 'I'm sure they wouldn't mind if we used their stuff. She'll have grown out of it all by the time they get back. We could use that booster seat I saw in the garage instead of ordering a new one to replace the one that broke?'

I shake my head forcefully, annoyed he doesn't understand. 'No, Paul. It will just get disgusting with food all over it. I'm sure they wouldn't like us to.' I tut. 'I'll see if I can get one delivered out here.'

'It's not Mars,' he replies, laughing at me before noting my displeasure and coming over, arms open, ready to hug. My irritation melts.

'Are you sure it isn't?' I reply into his chest.

'Come on, isn't it great? I feel like I can breathe again.' He squeezes me tightly and sways me from side to side in that way he does. I can tell he's thrilled to be here. I am too – just slightly more tentatively. Paul has the ability to jump into something with confident gusto in a way I'm obviously not programmed to muster.

'It's amazing,' I reply, not wanting to put a downer on things.

I empty the cupboard of children's items into the box I've already unpacked and then close the lid and tape it shut. Picking up the full box, I walk towards the internal door that leads to the garage which is set back from the main house. It's not heavier than the others, but I begin to feel light-headed. En route something on the ceiling catches my eye and I stop. A black shiny dome, like a CCTV camera in a shopping centre, but smaller.

'Hey, let me take that,' Paul says, rushing to take the box from me. I look down and realise my hands are shaking.

'I'm fine,' I murmur, but let him remove it from my grasp. 'Is that a camera?' I nod towards it.

Paul looks in the direction I'm looking. His brow furrows and he presses his lips together. 'I'm not sure, possibly. Looks like one. I don't know where it's connected to, though.' He puts the box down and goes to a plush-looking panel on the wall. 'I can't see anything,' he says as he taps on the device. He glances around again before adding, 'It's most probably connected to an app. It won't be turned on.'

'You don't think . . . they're watching us, do you?' I suddenly feel very self-conscious. I've been going through all their belongings.

'No, of course not, Lauren.' He laughs. 'They've probably disconnected it. I can ask how to make it work if you want? We can use it?'

I shake my head. 'Weird to have a security camera inside a house instead of outside, isn't it?'

'They're wealthy, and wealthy people have a lot to lose.' He comes over to me, having to quash my concerns yet again. 'Please don't worry about it, okay?' He pulls me in for another hug. 'The last thing I want is for you to be stressed. The whole point of getting out of the city is so you can rest and recover.'

'I'm not stressed,' I whisper. *Suck it up, Lauren. Why can't I just enjoy something? Why am I constantly looking for negatives?* I watch as he leans back down to pick the box up with a slightly weary look. Poor Paul. After everything he's done for me. He's going to get sick of having me around if all I do is poke holes in everything. I sigh, irritated with myself. I grab the fabric of his sweater sleeve, and he puts the box down, allowing me to direct him up, to my lips. 'Sorry,' I whisper.

'Are you happy we came?' he whispers into my hair.

'Infinitely,' I whisper back. 'I love you.'

'I love you more than you could ever know,' he tells me, and my eyelids flutter as I enjoy the feeling the words give.

A loud smash from the kitchen breaks us up. We look over, startled. Jesse is standing there with blood running down his hand.

'Sorry . . . sorry . . .' he stammers.

'Don't move,' Paul says firmly, rushing towards him. I follow to help.

'Ewwwww,' Margo cries, sitting up in her chair.

'Don't move, Jesse, you don't have any shoes on,' Paul reminds him. Jesse looks down at his bare feet and begins to cry. 'It's okay, it's okay,' Paul says sternly and reaches down to pluck him from his spot on the cold, hard tiles and puts him back down away from the smashed item.

'Paul!' I shout. He's put him straight down on the cream carpet. He gives me a cross look as he moves Jesse off. 'Sorry, I . . .' I mumble. Feeling bad my first concern was for the soft furnishings rather than his son.

'I'm sorry, Daddy, I'm sorry,' Jesse says, crying. He looks up at his dad, with a nervous expression.

'It's okay.' Paul rubs his son's back for reassurance. Then he cups Jesse's hand in his, inspecting the wound as though he is holding an injured bird. Jesse looks the other way, too scared to see. 'It's not deep. We'll clean it and find a plaster and you'll be as good as new,' Paul says.

'It's my fault, Jesse. I should have been helping,' I tell him.

Paul looks up at me from the embrace with his little boy. The glance has a note of dissatisfaction embedded. *Sorry*, I mouth. And he shakes his head slightly. Margo comes marching over still clutching a pen in her fist.

'Hospital?' she lisps, trying to get a good look.

'Not this time. Just a plaster,' I say, putting an arm around her.

'My doctor's kit?' She turns to face me. 'Where is it?'

I laugh lightly. 'Are you going to bandage him up?'

'I should,' she says sincerely.

'Come on then. I think it's in one of these boxes over here.' I look back at Jesse and his father. Jesse has moved away from him and Paul is checking something on his phone. Their relationship has always confused me. Paul is sometimes dismissive in a way he isn't with Margo. Are all fathers harder on sons than daughters? I suppose Margo is so easy to love, which means people give her that love more readily. I tell myself I must try harder with him. Jesse deserves attention and love just as much as his sister, even if it isn't reciprocated so easily.

My hand is pulled by Margo. 'Come on,' she orders. And I enjoy the feeling of being needed. It reassures me that even though I wouldn't be her first choice, I am still the one she wants now.

CHAPTER 3

It's a few days later, and I'm feeling slightly more settled after a hectic weekend organising the house. I've not exerted myself this side of normal and I'm feeling it. There is still a lot to do, but at least it's Monday, so I'll have a few hours without the constant guilt of whether the kids are suitably entertained. Margo is starting at the school nursery. It's all she talks about. 'Will I have after-school play dates?' she asks, more desperate for a social life than me. Jesse, on the other hand, is sulking; he doesn't want to go. He hated school in London and was always pretending he had a tummy ache, so he'd get to stay home, causing Paul a lot of stress.

He is due to join the reception class halfway through the summer term, and I do feel for him having to slot into group dynamics where relationships have already been formed. It was one of the factors that made us think twice about the move. In the end, the rationale was that we'd have to sign up for another year on the lease at the flat and we didn't want to wait that long. Besides, it's not as if Jesse liked his current school anyway – maybe he'd be a better fit in the smaller village variety? The offer of this amazing house rent-free really spun it, and Paul wanted to nab it quick before they changed their minds.

He keeps saying how great being here will be for my recovery – to get out of the smog and into the fresh air. So, we decided to go for it. Sometimes a baptism by fire is the best way to go, Paul said.

It takes ages to get out of the house this morning – I can't find the kids' water bottles or Jesse's black shoes which were delivered before we left and then I packed somewhere 'special' so I wouldn't forget.

My memory isn't what it used to be. Paul jokes he should leave Post-it notes around and I laugh along, but really it gives me that sinking feeling that it's another way I'm failing. I don't want him to know how incapable I really feel most of the time. I try to hide my low days as much as possible.

The school run is something I'm really looking forward to. Back in London, Paul was so busy with work he said it was the one thing that kept him tied to the kids. But now most of his work will be at home, he's happy to hand over the reins. I've only recently felt strong enough to take on this sort of responsibility. Looking after two little kids at home is one thing; outside it is a whole new overwhelming scenario. But now, here, in our fresh start, I'm excited about meeting other parents and doing all the mummy things you're meant to do at this stage of their lives. Birthday parties, PTA meetings and tantrums in shopping aisles – all of it. The good, the bad and the ugly. I shake off the familiar feeling that I'm an imposter.

As if someone has handed me an access all areas pass, just as I was told I couldn't come in.

The drive to the village takes about twenty minutes of nearly isolated roads. Not a house in sight, I note. It really brings home how far away we are from anyone else, and I'm surprised at how relieved I am when we get to the outskirts of the village. I click the indicator, remembering the turn from when we took a look the same weekend we viewed the house.

The tiny red-brick school sits on the edge of a large green, where, the head teacher told me, the fathers play cricket on Saturday mornings. My imagination ran away thinking of Paul dressed in grass-stained whites. Now we have more time, maybe he'll become a bit more sociable. He was always too busy in the city. And I wasn't exactly in the position to be on form for dinner parties and gatherings. He always said what a pity it was he couldn't get more involved in school activities, for Jesse's sake.

The rubber surface of the playground curves around the back of the structure. Snakes and ladders and hopping games are colourfully laid on the floor. A wooden climbing frame with monkey bars, hanging ropes and a silver metal slide is visible from the front. It all seems very small and rustic compared to the towering school complexes I've seen in London.

Paul had a conflicting work call this morning, and felt terrible he couldn't join us to drop them on their first day. I was secretly pleased, honoured, to be trusted with such an important event on my own, as it says so much about Paul's belief in my position within his family.

Once parked, I look over at the cluster of parents dropping off their children. Nerves trickle through me and I close my eyes momentarily. 'Are we here?' Margo asks impatiently from the back seat.

Once out, I hold their hands and we snake through the pockets of enthusiastic conversations and kids charging at friends squealing with morning energy. I look around feeling lost, wondering where we're meant to be. The bell goes and attention is refocused. Teachers come out and wait patiently for parents to kiss children goodbye. I look down at both of mine. They look so small clutching their tin water bottles, residue of sun cream on their faces, which I didn't get the chance to rub in before they squirmed and ran away.

See, I'm useless. Especially when they're really determined or on their way to a meltdown. Added to that I'm never sure if it's my place to discipline or be strict. Plus, I always feel like I'm on a mission to make them like me . . . okay, love me. How silly is it to be ruled by a three-year-old and a four-year-old? They probably know I'm under the thumb. I sigh. *I'm not doing a very good job at this.*

Emma, after all, was the perfect mother – she breastfed both children exclusively. She wouldn't allow them to go to nursery, as she wanted to do everything herself. She cooked every meal from scratch and wouldn't let them have any refined sugar.

Paul lets these little morsels of information drop, as if by accident, as I stir through ready-made pasta sauce, or suggest they don't need a bath every night.

Recognising the teachers I met the other month, I crouch down to the kids' level. 'Have a brilliant day, Margo,' I say, giving her a hug and kissing her soft cheek. 'I will!' she shouts, running off. Jesse loiters and I grab him by the shoulders. 'Remember what Christopher Robin says to Winnie-the-Pooh?' I say, repeating a line from the book we recently read together. It was about being brave and was something he picked up on and we talked about. He looks down at the floor, before nodding and wandering over to the other children in his class.

Well, that piece of wisdom went down like a lead balloon. A little flutter of anxiety rises in my chest.

How will I know when I'm doing it right?

I stand with my arms folded watching them in their respective lines. Margo drops her water bottle, and it lands with a clink. I take two steps forward before the young teacher rushes over and picks it up for her. The second bell goes, and the teacher leads the untidy queue of children into the school. Margo turns her head back to check I'm still here, and I wave enthusiastically. She grins. Then Jesse's teacher claps his hands together and turns to march his own class in. I wait for Jesse to look back at me, but he doesn't. My expectant hand falls to my side in disappointment.

These 'maternal instincts' I hear about – do you only get those with your own children? I often imagine Emma watching me as I deal with Margo crying on the floor, or as Jesse refuses to come out of his room for dinner. Her tuts of disappointment practically reverberate around the whole room.

I occasionally eke out information about their past lives – it's quite masochistic really. I have to be careful not to upset Paul, as he is easily overwhelmed when he talks about Emma. And seeing that pain, and how much he loved her, only reinforces my own inadequacies. I've learnt to limit the collection of these crumbs, not just for his sake, but mine too. Because I'm scared he will finally see how much I'm lacking in comparison. But something inside is keen to know more.

It hurts, but I crave it.

Emma would have dealt with this morning's struggle brilliantly. Margo's hair would be French plaited, something I've never managed. I've watched YouTube tutorials trying to learn but honestly her hair just slips through my fingers. She'd be wearing those white socks with the frills around the edge inside her black patent Mary-Jane shoes instead of a pair of Jesse's blue ones with trucks on – I couldn't find a matching set of her own. Paul says I'm doing a brilliant job, but I know he is just trying to be encouraging. I sense when he's noted me doing something wrong, but tries not to nag or seem condescending by pointing out my faults.

'Hi.' I turn at the sound. A woman probably five years older than me is standing there. Blonde hair tied back in a messy bun, wearing a Breton striped T-shirt and tiny gold hoops. 'You're new,' she accuses in a pushy sort of way that I like.

I smile, I've been waiting for this moment, I gulp a breath before I launch in. 'Yes, I'm Lauren. We moved here over the weekend.' I feel her eyes glide over me. I wonder if she'll notice I don't really belong at the school gates. I have reached them with none of the usual preamble: no sleepless nights, no pain of childbirth. I've cheated the system.

'I'm Isobel – welcome! So nice to have some fresh blood,' she jokes warmly. 'What year?' She nods in the direction of the school, and it takes me a moment to realise she is talking about the kids.

'Margo is in nursery and Jesse's in reception.'

'Gosh, you didn't hang about!' I have no idea at what point I should say I'm not their mother. She continues before I have the chance to decide. 'Saskia is in the nursery too! We must get them together for a play date.'

I get a feeling of lightness at the invitation and can't help but grin at the floor before looking up. 'That would be lovely. Have you lived here long?'

'We moved about eight years ago. We got the sudden urge to renovate an old mill and leave smoggy Camberwell. Did you come from London too?' I nod and she continues: 'We've had a few recently. Suddenly the rural life has become very appealing. Where are you living?'

'Off Layton Road. It's in the middle of nowhere really, in the woods. We're just renting it for now . . .'

'The glass house?' she says quickly, eyebrows raised with intrigue. 'I've never seen it myself. It's a bit of a mystical beast around here, you'll see. There's been all sorts of gossip about when it was going to be filled.' She leans in and whispers, 'The last lot that lived there were very secretive. None of us ever met them and then before I knew it, they were gone!'

I smile politely, surprised by the intensity. 'They're letting us stay there while they're abroad,' I explain.

'Oh, that's what happened.' Her shoulders fall, a bit disappointed by the simple explanation. As if I've shattered some sort of illusion. She fishes in her bag and removes her phone. 'Here.' She hands it to me, open on a fresh new contact page. 'Type in your number and I'll add you to the PTA WhatsApp group.'

I take it from her and type in my details before handing it back, pleased. 'Great – yes, do add me. I'd love that.' Her head cocks to one side in amusement and I feel as though I may have seemed too keen. Maybe I'm meant to find it all an annoying added obligation to an already busy schedule.

'I'll remember that when there are cakes to be baked and stalls to be manned,' she chuckles.

I laugh along, self-consciously.

We say our goodbyes and I walk back to the car. Shutting the door, I turn the engine on with a sudden burst of excitement to get back to Paul. It's been a few days since we've had a chunk of time without the kids. I wonder if he's got a packed day. His last job, in London, meant he was attached to a unit within a hospital and was often on call, having to dart out at a moment's notice. It was a nightmare with childcare; he said he had a string of useless nannies before he met me. I can't believe I now get him all to myself at home most of the time.

Pulling up outside the house, I get out and snap the car door shut. An excited skip is involuntarily added to my step. As I walk to the front door, I extract my keys from the pocket of my denim shorts. I stare at them in my hands; these are the old ones, from the flat. I was meant to leave them on the kitchen counter with Paul's. Will I always be this forgetful? Tutting to myself, I press the doorbell. A loud *ta-da!* sound surprises me and I take a closer look. It's one of those hi-tech models with a pinhole camera. Again, I think about Paul's friends, getting notifications to their phones about our whereabouts. I don't like the idea of being watched. It gives me an uneasy feeling.

Paul opens the door. His arm curls around my shoulders, pulling me inside, 'Hey. Were they okay? I feel awful I couldn't be there. I tried my best to get out of that call.'

'Don't worry,' I reassure him. 'They were fine. There wasn't a scene or anything!'

He kisses the top of my head. 'Thank you – I know none of this is easy. Such a big change and they can be hard work,' he says knowingly.

I shake my head. 'They're great. I love them. Tantrums and belly laughs and all.' I look up at him and he kisses me on the mouth. The kiss becomes less tender and more passionate. We pause for breath and he cups my face. 'Wasn't this a good idea? No rush hour or noisy neighbours. Or bosses demanding things from me. We're free!' I nod happily, and his lips lean into mine for more. As we connect the CCTV camera catches my eye. His tongue works its way into my mouth and my eyes focus on a little red dot which has appeared on the camera. I feel his hand slide up my jumper into my bra. My head begins to throb. I push him away.

'What is it?' he asks.

I look back up at the camera. But the red dot has gone. Did I imagine it? 'Nothing,' I murmur.

CHAPTER 4

The next day I sit back on the sofa exhausted and satisfied. The glass of ice water makes a clinking noise as I raise it to my lips. I've done it – there is not one box left to unpack and I've hoovered and dusted the place squeaky clean. I need to take a much-deserved break and relax for a bit. My eyes creep over to the garden and my fleeting contentment fades. Weeds clutter the beds, creeping forward into the overrun lawn. Clusters of ivy skulk forward unabated. I blink a few times. *You don't need everything to be perfect*, I say to myself. *Stop it. Rest. Enjoy the moment.* The trouble is, there isn't anything I can do about the black holes in my past – but there is plenty I can do to determine my present, and my future.

A few minutes later I decide to rummage around the garage for gardening tools.

It smells of damp and old paint. I couldn't find the light switch, so instead rely on the streams of daylight shining through the gaps in the retractable metal door. It's just enough to pick my way through without falling. Blue-painted metal frame shelves carry the cardboard boxes filled with Paul's friends' belongings, and a dusty old baby jungle gym lies discarded on the bottom rung. Various tools hang above a workbench, and an axe and a shovel caked in mud dangle from a beam. In the centre of the room is Paul's boxing bag, which he uses to let off steam. I duck to get around it, moving towards a basket full of what I'm looking for. I bend down and pull out a trowel and fork along with some pruning shears. Pleased with my discovery, I place them back and lift up the basket, along with an old battered bucket that will be perfect for discarded weeds.

The light snaps on and I turn towards the door. It takes a moment for my eyes to adjust.

'It's here,' Paul calls over.

'What?' I walk to the punchbag and move it to one side so I can see him.

'The light switch.' He laughs. 'What are you doing creeping around in the dark?'

'I couldn't find it.' I shrug. 'Just grabbing some gardening bits. I can't look at that view any longer.'

'You need to take a break, you've been non-stop.' The lecturing tone of his voice fills me with insubordination. 'I'm fine.' I nudge the punchbag away and walk to him, kissing him on the lips. He cradles my face, and we smile at each other. 'How am I ever going to get any work done around here?' he muses, shaking his head, turning back towards his study.

I collect the gardening things and walk to the door, flipping the light off with my elbow. Before I leave, I hear something clatter to the floor.

I turn.

The hanging axe sways from side to side and the shovel lies helplessly on the bare concrete like a murder victim. Placing the bucket and basket down, I wander over and pick it up. Then I step onto a concrete slab to give myself that extra height needed to loop the handle back through the hook. As I come back down, I notice something on the lower shelf. It looks like a tennis racket cover, although it isn't the correct shape. Intrigued, I move my hand over to it and bring it down to the floor with me.

Whisper Sniper 2.2 Air Rifle is printed on the black material in white. I unzip the cover to see the barrel of a gun. I swallow. It makes me feel a bit sick, even though I know it isn't a proper gun. We're in the countryside, I'm sure most homes around here have something similar for pests. Even so – I don't like the sight of it, and I don't like the idea of one of the kids finding it.

I reach back up and place it on the top shelf. Pushing it as far as I can away from the edge. I walk back over to the door and take one last look. The strap of the rifle bag has slipped back down off the shelf. 'Lauren!' I hear Paul call urgently, and I walk out of the garage and into the main house. Wondering what he could want.

The hot sun follows me as I work my way around the circular drive, wrestling with weeds I then unceremoniously slap into my bucket. Mid-afternoon I wave at Paul as he hops into the car to collect the kids. I'll usually be the one ferrying them around, but he wants to collect them this afternoon. I watch the boot of the car trundle down the drive, and sit back and cough, feeling dizzy. I blink up at the cloudless sky and wipe the sweat that has collected on my chest away. My head is throbbing, and I curse myself for ignoring my body, listening instead to the excited chatter of my head promising a future unhampered by all that stuff I've left behind. I throw my trowel down and give into the need for rest.

The house is pleasantly cool and I kick off my muddy worn sandals. Lying back on the sofa, I stare up through the ceiling at the sky. Taking a deep breath, I close my eyes, letting myself fall.

Sleep comes to me so easily these days.

In the dream I thrash around, screaming so loud my throat feels raw. Begging someone to help me, crying out for the pain to stop. But no one comes. My chest convulses, my fingers reach out for a hand to hold. The pain is so overwhelming I feel as though I am being ripped in two and gutted. And the blood – so much blood. And then it is gone and the euphoria comes. The white light and the calm stillness of peace which is so perfect I know I must have reached somewhere holy.

I gasp a breath as I snap awake. My view is of the sky. I sit up and look around the living room, trying to place myself. I'm in the glass house. In the woods. We just moved here. I'm with Paul, Jesse and Margo. My new family. Our fresh start. Everything is okay. Relief sweeps through me. It was a dream. My heart is still racing when I hear the sound of the keys in the front door.

'Jesse, just calm down, okay?' Paul sounds frustrated. 'As I said before, you can't have an ice lolly until you say sorry to Margo. It's very simple.'

I get up quickly, eager not to seem as drained as I feel. I pad through to where they are gathered by the front door.

'It's not fair,' Jesse cries, rushing to his room.

'Jesse! Shoes!' Paul shouts after him, staring down the hallway towards his son's room, rubbing his beard in frustration. Margo is curled around his legs, and he strokes her back. I look at him questioningly.

'Today was not a good day,' he states, with a stiff smile. 'He hit another kid and then threw Margo's drawing out of the car window on the drive home.'

'Oh dear.' I chew my lip and look towards Jesse's bedroom door. 'Maybe things will get worse before they get better?' I try. Paul grimaces. 'Do you want me to speak to him?'

Paul shrugs and nods as if to say, *be my guest*. Poor Paul. He looks tired. He's got so much on his shoulders, what with work, worrying about the kids, the move. And, of course, me. I need to step up. He can't hold everything together all the time.

'I'll talk to him,' I confirm, and he looks relieved. I hug him tight and Margo loops an arm around one of my legs too.

'Thank you,' he whispers. I remind myself that Paul needs to get used to our new surroundings as well. It's not just the children who have been through it. Paul has been through the wringer as well.

*

I knock before pushing Jesse's door open. The floor is littered with books, building blocks and miniature dinosaurs. 'Hey,' I say gently. He looks up, briefly acknowledging me before turning his attention back to his giant plastic insects. I swallow thickly. They make me feel a bit sick. I'm not a fan of spiders and I know there is a large one in his collection that turns my stomach. When I first moved into the flat, Jesse used to leave it lying around and I'd get the shock of my life. Paul said it wasn't malicious, but I couldn't help thinking the little boy knew the reaction it evoked and did it for kicks. I considered throwing it in the bin while he was at school, but I can't even bring myself to touch it.

I fight the squeamish feeling and stride over to sit next to him on the floor. Picking up a large black beetle, I lay it out next to the others in the queue he's formed. 'That doesn't go there,' he says, knocking my hand out the way. He picks it up and places it back in the tub.

'Oh, right,' I mutter. 'Did you have a good day?' I try to make the question sound as unloaded as possible. 'Anything you want to talk about?'

His hand jerks at the question and he looks up at me remorsefully. 'No,' he whispers.

'Did you get upset with one of the other kids?'

He swallows before answering; his voice shakes. 'I hit one of the girls.'

I frown. 'Well, that's naughty. You know that, don't you, Jesse?'

Jesse nods. A moment later he quietly admits, 'I felt bad afterwards.'

I am relieved at the admission, and I shuffle over and put

my arm around him. 'It's okay to make mistakes. As long as you say sorry and don't do it again. Okay?'

He nods thoughtfully. 'Okay.'

'The real reason I came was to see if you'd like to get an ice cream with me after school one day this week?'

Silence. Another insect is removed and added to the line. 'I'd really like pancakes,' and then more softly, 'My mum used to make me those.'

'Oh,' I reply, winded. 'We can do that.'

He considers the offer for a moment. 'With whipped cream?' His eyes edge up, looking into mine, and I nod. 'Yes. Lots of whipped cream,' I confirm and he smiles happily before flying the wasp in his hand through the air, pretending to buzz. I squeeze his foot before standing up to leave him to it.

Something out the window distracts me. A movement in the distance at the bottom of the lawn. I walk over to the sheet of glass which faces the back and fold my arms as I squint forward to see. It was as though there was someone waving. I blink. It happens again and I realise it isn't a person at all. Just the branch of the bush swaying in the breeze. When it moves, the beginning of a path is revealed.

'Don't go into the shed.' The sound of Jesse's delicate voice is eerie, and a shiver runs through me, as though a cold draft has found its way into the room.

'What?' I turn to look at him. He shakes his head and goes back to his insects. 'Nothing.'

'What shed? There isn't a shed?' I look back over the garden to check. But I was right. It is empty.

CHAPTER 5

I shut Jesse's door and stand for a moment. The light-headedness that caught me unaware earlier lingers. I step towards the wall, and rest back on it. 'Lauren?' Margo's voice echoes. I turn towards the sound. Her head is poking out from the living room. As I try to focus, the hallway elongates, turning on an axis, as though I'm peering down a telescope the wrong way.

'Can you help me?' she asks.

Licking my dry lips, I croak, 'Sure.'

My hand drags along the wall for balance as I follow her. She is wearing a miniature red gingham oven glove and holding a wooden spoon in the other hand. She gestures for me to sit on the floor next to the toy kitchen. And I watch as she removes a pan from inside the 'oven'. She sniffs it. 'Do you think it's ready?' Her head cocked to one side as she shoves the pan under my nose.

'It smells lovely, Margo,' I whisper.

She pretends to spoon it into a plastic bowl. 'Here you go.' She hands it over with a sigh.

'Mmm, yum. Thank you.'

'It will make Lauren better,' she says, staring at me intently. My heart tugs and I try to sit up a little straighter. God knows what the trauma of a sick mother must have done to her. The last thing I want to do is replicate that worry.

'This pasta is cooked perfectly.'

'It's soup,' she corrects.

'Oh . . . it's lovely.' I pretend to take another spoonful and she watches my reaction carefully.

'The cake isn't ready,' she says, looking down at a non-existent watch on her wrist. 'Three-two.'

I try not to laugh. 'Can't wait. Maybe we can have it after dinner.' I look over to the real kitchen and wonder what to cook.

'Are you feeling better now?' Her eyes check me cautiously. Her oven glove is clutched between her fingers. I hope I haven't frightened her.

'I'm fine.' I put my arm around her and pull her close, stroking the back of her hair. Staring at her, I am reminded how beautiful her mother must have been. My eyes wander up to the clock on the wall. 'I'd better make dinner. You'll have to tell me the recipe of your soup, Margo, it was delicious.' She looks pleased and I kiss her one more time before pushing myself up off the floor with a groan.

I end up making Jesse's favourite: shepherd's pie. He's never said he likes it better than anything else, but he always cleans his plate. I take another swig of cool water. I'm feeling much better. I don't know what came over me. 'Jesse!' I call down the hallway, wiping my hands on a tea towel. A few minutes later he wanders through, holding on to the large black plastic tarantula. I swallow. An acidic taste trickles down the back of my throat.

I help Margo into her booster seat as Jesse climbs onto a chair. He looks down at the food and, to my great pleasure, digs in. His mouth is full of potato and mince as he licks a smear of gravy off his top lip. I wink at him and smile down at Margo chewing away.

As I grate them extra cheese Paul comes through from the study to join us.

'What a day!' he exclaims, coming over and kissing me tenderly before turning to the kids who seem bemused by our affection.

'Daddy!' Margo cries, spoon in the air.

'What have you lucky kids got for dinner?' He bends down and steals some off Margo's plate. 'Delicious! I hope you leave me some.' Margo grins at her daddy. Then he strides over and ruffles Jesse's hair; the action makes Jesse duck slightly, as if he doesn't like it. Paul doesn't notice. 'I was thinking. Our first weekend out here is nearly upon us. We should do something fun as a family.'

'The zoo!' Margo suggests. Her little legs swinging off the chair. She loves animals, and her bed is so cluttered with the stuffed variety there is barely any room left for her.

'Oh, Margo, honey. I don't think we're near a zoo. We could go to that activity farm? The one I saw the sign for on the motorway? They might even have a little petting area. That would be fun, wouldn't it?' I say, knowing how desperate she is for a pet guinea pig. Her eyes widen as she nods.

'It'll be rubbish and she'll get bitten and scratched,' Jesse spits.

Margo's lip starts to wobble and tears threaten. 'No, I won't.' Then she turns to me. 'Will they hurt me?' Her voice tremors.

I shake my head. 'No, definitely not. Jesse, that isn't very kind.' I give him a look and he squirms back into his chair.

'Come on, Jesse. We've talked about this,' Paul says firmly. Jesse looks down, red-faced.

Paul leans across the table and holds Margo's hand. 'If one of those fur balls hurts my little Margo, do you know what will happen?' Margo shakes her head. And Paul crashes his fist down on the table. 'Bang!'

Margo giggles. 'Daddy so silly,' she says.

I look over to Jesse whose features have darkened. Then he whispers, 'I hate it here.'

Paul gives him a warning look. 'You'll get used to it,' Paul tells him flatly. As if he's lost patience with Jesse's behaviour. I try to catch the little boy's eye, but he sits there, still, his head bowed, as if he's crushed.

In bed later that evening I stare at the paragraph I've reread three times and place the book down with a sigh. I can't stop thinking about Jesse. I look across at Paul who is tapping away at his phone. He has a very hands-on approach with his clients, and tells them they can message him day or night. I've said a few times it's too much, and he needs boundaries. But apparently, I don't understand.

'Are you worried about Jesse?' I ask.

Paul pauses before placing his phone down and giving me his full attention. 'A little – I mean, I worry about them both all the time. It's my job. But kids go through phases – and you need to remind yourself stuff doesn't slot into place straight away, or you'll go mad.'

'But I've never seen him like this, he seems . . . different.' I want to say depressed, but I stop myself.

He nods slowly a few times, his lips pursed in thought. When he speaks the words come out in a slow, patronising tone that makes me feel thick. 'Lauren, you need to let things run their natural course. He is going to feel uncomfortable while he makes this transition. We always knew this was going to be tough. You need to accept, Lauren, that sometimes things aren't easy. And that's okay.' I feel his irritation fester from the other side of the bed. I don't want him to think I am meddling. That I'm moving into a space that doesn't belong to me. He obviously knows what he's doing, far more than me.

'You're right,' I say quickly. 'We haven't even been here a week.' I must remember not to fuss so much; Paul doesn't like it. 'Is there a shed in the garden?' I ask, changing the subject, remembering the peculiar comment.

'A shed?' He thinks. 'Erm . . . I haven't seen one. Why?' His tone is distracted, and he picks up his handset and begins to tap away again.

I shake my head. 'It doesn't matter,' I whisper, remembering the sinister quality to Jesse's voice. 'I couldn't see one,' I mutter. But he isn't paying attention.

CHAPTER 6

The next morning, I have the beginnings of a headache. I almost ask Paul to take the kids to school, but after knocking back a few paracetamols I feel much better. Relief. I really didn't want to cause him any hassle and ruin his morning. I look out at the rich blue sky as I pull on my shorts. Another sunny day. I'm desperate for a storm to come and move the oppressive heat along. Being in this house seems to have magnified all my aches and pains. It's so bright and open, but there are no cool shadows to escape inside to find relief.

As the children squabble behind me in the living room, I pull the back doors closed and snap the lock. 'Come on, let's go. Jesse! Where's your water bottle?' I ask, turning to check they have everything they need.

'I'm not going,' Jesse says, crossing his arms and sitting on the floor in protest.

I glance up at the clock. We're late. 'Come on. It'll be fun once you get there! And it's the weekend soon.'

He shakes his head defiantly. I finally coax him into the car by bribing him with a chocolate biscuit. I glance at the rear-view mirror and see his smug face covered in melted chocolate. I feel the chalk draw *Jesse 1, Lauren 0*.

Watching as they join their class lines, I feel exhausted already. The whole morning has felt like one long obstacle course.

'Morning!'

Isobel waves and I call, 'Morning,' back, happy to have a friendly face to swap pleasantries with. I nod in understanding as she makes a hurried gesture before dashing up the road.

Once back, I stare out of the windscreen at the posturing house, enjoying the quiet. It is beginning to feel familiar coming back here. I wonder if I'm starting to feel at home. It's been so long since I belonged anywhere, I'm not entirely sure I remember what it's like. The hospital, the unit, and then Paul's rented flat – they all felt so transient. I suppose this house is just a stopgap too. Paul teased the other day that maybe his friends won't want to come back, and we could buy *this* house. There was something about the twinkle in his eye that made me think there could be some truth in that. But would I want to live somewhere so remote forever?

I get out the car and walk to the front door, removing the keys from my pocket. As I push it open my keys fall onto the porch with a jangle. '*Shit*.' I collect them off the stoop. Once inside I slip off my Birkenstocks and enjoy the feeling of the cool polished concrete floor. I call out, 'I'm back.'

I hear a crash from inside. As I walk into the kitchen, Paul is hurrying something into the bin with an edgy manner. He looks up at me and his anxious demeanour is quickly covered with an easy smile. He rubs his beard in the way he's taken to. I look out to the garden; the doors are open slightly. Paul's trainers are on. 'I went for a run.' He coughs. 'Were the kids okay?'

'Yes,' I sigh, 'Once we got there.'

'Great. You're doing such a brilliant job, Lauren.' He comes over and puts his arms around me. Usually, when he holds me, I feel a sense of relief. But this time, there is a gnawing feeling. After a run he's normally slimy with sweat, and I'd usually hit him playfully to get away. But his T-shirt smells of detergent, and the fabric is dry against my cheek.

'I've got an appointment – I should log in,' he says, breaking free.

As he walks towards his study, I realise he doesn't have a diamond-shaped sweat patch on his back.

'Shoes!' I call as he approaches the cream carpet.

'Oh . . . right!' He slips them off. The rims are covered in moist shards of nipped grass.

I stand there for a moment after he leaves. There is something odd about the haste in which he was fiddling with the rubbish. As well as the lie about the run. Chewing my lip, I walk over to the pedal bin. *You're being silly*, I think, before pressing down and releasing the lid. Inside are discarded toast ends and the kitchen roll I used to clean up a cup of milk that Margo spilt. I remove my foot from the pedal. But something stops me from walking away. I press down again and use my fingers to dig inside, trying not to touch the left-over sloppy Weetabix I spooned in after breakfast. My hand hits something hard below that I don't remember putting there, and I pull it out. It is the outer casing from something, which looks as though it has been moulded around something square with a U-shaped top – just like a padlock. I put it back, stuffing it down where I found it. Then I look out at the garden. Where there is a freshly trodden path through the long grass which snakes down to the bush at the bottom of the lawn.

Taking my bucket and basket, I heave back the doors, slip my sunglasses from the neck of my T-shirt and place them on the bridge of my nose. The back garden needs about three times more work than the front and I almost feel too intimidated to begin.

I step off the patio and onto the unruly lawn. The grass reaches the top of my ankles. I've asked Paul a few times to get the mower out, but he hasn't had time. Leaving my gardening things on the slabs, I look down at Paul's matted path, and I decide to explore before beginning the mammoth task.

Digging in my pocket, I take out my wireless earphones. A present from Paul. He gave me them to help with all the guided meditation work he'd given me. Removing my phone, instead of choosing one of those recordings, I turn to a music streaming site and search for Kate Bush. I don't know why, but she's all I feel like listening to recently. There is a kernel of something there, as if she is trying to pull something out of me. Like a one-sided game of tug of war. I wish I knew what it meant. I stop myself from getting into a wormhole about it. I've taught myself, with Paul's help, to be grateful for everything I have: I'm alive, and I found him and the kids. Who cares if I can't remember a few details? I mustn't dwell on what was lost. Only what I've found. And who knows where I'd be if it had never happened? I doubt I'd be as happy as this. When I woke up a doctor told me I'd only been given a five per cent chance of survival. If that's not lucky, I don't know what is.

The music fades in, and her breathy, clear voice caresses my ears. After briefly closing my eyes to enjoy it, I begin my walk.

Apparently, the house sits within six acres of woodland. I'm interested to find out how big that is, as I'm not sure. It's weird not knowing the limits of something, where the line is you shouldn't cross. I march down to the waving branch I saw from Jesse's bedroom. I touch the rich pink petals that clutter the entrance to the path. Soft and delicate like lamb's skin. Moving the rogue branch away, I begin to walk through the passageway created by the undergrowth.

The music brings a whole new level of intense otherworldlyness to the escapade, and I hum to myself and stretch out my arms, twirling on the spot and enjoying the sense of freedom the music brings. I press the button on the side of my phone to bring the volume up. Then the sound dulls, and I pull it out to see what the notification is.

I smile when I see the message from Claudia: *Hope the move went okay x* Tears leap to my eyes, and I bite my lip. *Stop it. You're cross with her*, I remind myself. She was so cold and quick to judge. *Get a grip*, I think. *You don't need them. This is your life now with new friends to be made. Better friends, stronger friends. Friends who won't dip out at the first sign of trouble.*

I still can't believe they can be angry with me for falling in love. Maybe I handled it badly. I do wish I hadn't blurted it out the way I did. But they took it completely the wrong way, twisted it into something it wasn't.

We can't be the first patient and doctor to fall in love. And I'd know if I were being taken advantage of. I'm not a child. None of them even gave him a chance. They wouldn't even meet him, for God's sake. It's so easy to take the moral high ground, isn't it? The weight of anger around the whole thing stings and I feel wrought with angst again. I look at Claudia's message. A glimmer of hope? Maybe I don't need to completely close the door on my old life.

I think about the photograph of us all together. I nearly threw it away, but in the end, I didn't have the guts. It was taken on a night out when we were in our late teens. We're showing off our tiny waists in tight jeans and crop tops. Big hoop earrings and dark crimson lipstick. The happiness radiating from our faces makes me long for that connection again. I love Paul and I'm so lucky to have found him, but I do think I'm lonely for female friendship. I think about Isobel and the other mums at the school, and wonder if I'll find my new tribe there. But they probably won't let me in once they find out I'm not a proper mother.

I come out of the bush into a clearing. And there, to my surprise, is a shed. Just like Jesse said. It looks more like one of those fancy garden offices than an old-fashioned tool shed.

I walk over to it and peer inside. The large glass wall across the front has become cloudy with moist morning dew, and a layer of moss cakes the edges of the pane. I put my face up to the surface and my breath flashes against it. I move back and wipe it away before having another look. There's not much there, apart from a sink on the back wall. The floor, like parts of the house, is formed of thick poured concrete. In the centre is a wooden hatch with a big fat shiny padlock. Just the same shape as the packaging I found in the bin. I swallow. How strange.

I try the handle. It's locked. Moving my hand away, I realise there isn't a keyhole. Stepping back, I turn on the spot and look up at the sun shining through the green leaves, creating a dappled effect on the floor. It would be lovely to use this as a reading shed, or to listen to my meditation tapes. I'll discuss it with Paul later.

Noticing another trail, I decide to keep going. The music is swirling in my ears, and I feel like I'm in a bubble. Light streams through cracks in the undergrowth highlighting tiny drifting particles of dust in the air.

A few minutes later I come out to a field with long grass that rises nearly to my waist. About ten metres ahead is a thick wooden post and rail fence. I walk through the grass, skimming my fingers on the tips of the blades. When I get to the fence I stop and hike myself up onto the bottom rung. The fencing holds a perfect square of land with patches of earth and balding yellow grass. In one corner is an old metal trough, and a discarded white and green striped horse jump is collapsed on the floor. On the other side of the fenced area is a neglected cottage.

Sun beats down on my face and I wince up at the sky. Not a cloud. I lick my dry lips. I should head back. I might get a juice and lie in the sun with a book instead of tackling those weeds. Walking slowly, I notice movement by the stile on the boundary fence to my right. Two shining eyes, a long nose and a dark chestnut coat. A horse. I freeze. We stare at one another for a moment and it moves its snout over the fence to get closer. I take tentative steps towards it, but it doesn't move. I stop about a metre from it. 'Hello. What are you doing out here?' I ask, my head to one side as we stare.

In the distance a car backfires and the horse snorts, before jumping back a few steps. Distressed, it runs away and I watch as its black tail sways from side to side, disappearing between the trunks of tall, uniform trees.

Turning, I continue my walk back to the house. I take a fleeting last look at the cottage before bending into the passageway and up through the narrow path. I begin to dance as I come out of the tunnel and through the clearing with the shed. My arms wide open, my hands fluttering like doves.

I feel free.

I turn and turn – up through the next passage. I mouth the words with my eyes half closed . . . I sing, twirling as I reach the top of the undergrowth and head out past the pretty flowers. I continue to turn, lost in the music. A smile spreads across my face. I put my hand up to wipe my face and am surprised when it comes back wet with tears.

I am lost, and I swallow, feeling something powerful circulate around me. A charge of a tangible thing which is just out of reach.

I stop suddenly, clutching my head. What is it?

Then I look up at the house from my position halfway up the lawn.

Paul is standing on the other side of the glass doors. His arms are crossed, and he has a sort of lopsided grin on his face. I'm embarrassed, and I smile bashfully over at him. He claps and I curtsy.

And the strange moment is lost.

CHAPTER 7

A few days pass. I dust my hands together and throw my trowel into the basket, ending another session in the garden. I step a few feet back to appreciate my hard work. My smile fades when I see the small dent I've made, and I sigh and sit down on the patio step to absorb the wildness of it all. The forest twitches with hidden energy, and the sound of birds calling echoes from one side of the canopy to the other, as if someone is talking about me behind my back. Hopelessness overwhelms me. *Stop being silly.* I sniff. My chin wobbles. How on earth will it ever look right? By the time I've finished one section, another will need redoing. It is a never-ending task.

I'm surprised the owners haven't organised for anyone to keep on top of maintenance. It sounds, and looks, as though they can afford it. I walk through the back doors and pull off my stinking vest, wiping my sweaty chest with it. Kicking off my sandals, I wander through the living room and traipse up the stairs to the master suite. Balling up the offending item, I throw it into the wash basket and turn to the en suite. Turning the shower on, I check the water is warming before undoing my shorts and shaking them down my legs. W

the bedroom, I stare down at the untamed

drawn to it, as though it has infected me and I

I hear footsteps and turn.

Paul is standing there. Grinning.

'How's work?' I ask, enjoying the way his eyes are lingering on my sheer knickers and chest. He takes a few more steps towards me. 'What work?' he murmurs, and I laugh.

'Don't you have a meeting now?'

He shakes his head. 'There is something wrong with the Wi-Fi, the whole house is down,' he says, gesticulating with his hand. A cheeky glint forming in his eye.

'That's weird, it's working for me.' I lean back on the glass. He shakes his head, removing his T-shirt with one hand. Paul looks after himself: he has a six pack and big arms I love to nestle my face in as I breathe in his manly scent. I almost shudder when he touches me. His fingers pulling down on my bra straps, hands moving down to find my hardening nipples. As he kisses my neck, I moan. I can feel he is already stiff, and I move my hands to quickly fumble with the buttons of his jeans. He pulls me up and carries me over to the bed, sliding my knickers to one side as he takes me.

Later, I rush to pick up the kids, and arrive just as the bell goes. I grin as Margo toddles out with the rest of her nursery class. She's happily waving a piece of paper in the air and as she gets close, I crouch and take the flapping card from her hand.

h Margo, is it for Daddy?' I ask, looking at the riot of plattered colours on the mauve sugar paper.

'No – I made it for you, Loz!' she replies, throwing her arms around me.

I kiss the top of her hair, the smell of her orange-flavoured shampoo flooding my senses. 'Best present ever. I love it!' I say, looking down at it again.

I stand to check whether Jesse's class has been dismissed. A few moments later they file out the building. Jesse is the last one and dawdles a few metres behind the orderly line. His book bag drags along the floor. I chew my nail, before pulling it out and replacing it with a big smile and a cheery wave. He looks up but his expression is desolate and gloomy. He wanders over still staring at his shoes.

'How was it?' I ask brightly.

He shrugs. 'Fine,' he replies unconvincingly, kicking his shoe against a railing. 'Can we go?'

His teacher comes rushing over with a note and to my surprise Jesse's hand finds mine, and holds it tightly. I squeeze it back supportively.

'He locked one of the children in the stationery cupboard today,' the teacher tells me with a heavy sigh.

'Oh.' I look down. Jesse's whole body is attempting to lean into mine and vanish. 'Jesse, that's terrible. Why did you do that?' I say. 'I'm so sorry. He's never done anything like that before.'

The teacher shakes his head. 'Well, there was the incident the other day too.'

I forgot about that; my mouth clamps shut.

'We're trying to be as supportive as possible. You aren't going to do that again are you, Jesse?' he asks sternly, and Jesse shakes his head. 'He was very upset when he was told off. Hopefully that will be the last of that sort of behaviour. Tell Mr Bloom to call me if he wants to discuss anything,' the teacher says, handing me the note and walking away.

We stand there in silence for a moment. I crouch next to him. 'Jesse, why on earth did you—'

'Don't know,' he mutters quietly. 'Can we please go?'

'Come on,' I whisper, taking them back to the car. I notice Isobel staring over at us, and she gives me a sympathetic smile. I hope she didn't hear what was said. I hurry them inside the car and turn the engine on. I just want to get away from the prying eyes and groups of parents chatting.

I glance up at Jesse in the rear-view mirror. It's not his fault, I remind myself. This is a big change. He's bound to act out. *The only control you have over a situation is how you react to it.* Paul taught me that. We whizz through the country roads and Margo begins to clap her hands and sing. Jesse is staring painfully out of the window. His nostrils are flared, and his mouth is set in a grimace.

'What do you want for tea?' I ask.

Jesse looks up, suddenly startled. 'But what about the treat? You said we'd go for pancakes after school.'

'Pancakes!' Margo roars, lifting her arms in the air.

'I'm not sure you've been well behaved enough for a treat.' His face crumbles in devastation.

Margo screws up her mouth. 'I didn't do anything naughty,' she sulks. 'Not fair.'

'You promised,' Jesse whines.

'I didn't do nothing,' Margo says dismally, crossing her arms.

'Please can we have pancakes? Pleeeaaseee!' Jesse asks, squeezing his hands together.

I bite my bottom lip. I should say no – if I backtrack now, then what sort of precedent does that set? 'I just don't think . . .' I glance back up at the look of desperation in their eyes.

And I give in.

'Okay. But only because I promised.' I sigh. They cheer. Urgh. Useless. But I'm not rewarding bad behaviour. This is separate. I promised them this trip, and Margo shouldn't suffer because of Jesse. My mind shifts involuntarily over to what Emma would do. She would have handled this transition seamlessly. But I suppose that's the problem. Jesse wouldn't be acting out if she were here. A few pancakes isn't going to change that.

Margo whoops again, and a small smile appears on Jesse's lips. I click the indicator and take us in the new direction.

This morning after drop-off, I had a google to see where we could go for pancakes in the area. It's not like London where everything is available at the touch of a button. I found a farm shop with a café called The Meadows, and I'm just praying there's something sweet and exciting on the menu. And if they're really set on pancakes, I can always buy the ingredients there and we can make them at home.

I softly tell myself not to panic. *Shhh*, I tell my inner voice as it babbles on and on about the fact I'm not qualified to help these little people navigate through this fresh start away from everything they've ever known. Paul should have chosen someone more capable to fall in love with, not me.

'Loz!' Margo shouts and I shake the dark thoughts and join her in a rendition of 'Old McDonald Had a Farm'.

Once we arrive, I help the kids out, and we hold hands as we cross the gravel car park. I am nicely surprised as we walk into the large, converted barn. Fresh produce spills out of rustic wooden crates and smartly packaged deli goods line the walls. On the other side are about six tables and chairs with a corner set up with children's furniture, books and toys. In the centre is a counter with cakes and pastries enclosed in glass domes.

I notice a few other parents with kids in Jesse and Margo's uniform, and I realise this is bit of a local hub. I imagine myself at the large six-seater table laughing with new friends over coffee. The children run ahead and decide on a table closest to the children's play area and jump onto seats. Margo grabs an old tin with coloured pencils inside.

'Loz!' she calls to me, shaking the tin, alerting me to the fact there must be some sort of fun activity paper.

'I'll get it,' I assure her with a nod as I walk to the counter, almost tripping over a big grey cat who's curled itself around my leg. I bend down to stroke it and it purrs into the palm of my hand.

'Lauren, don't forget!' Margo calls, shaking the tin again.

'I won't,' I reply with a laugh.

Her assured demeanour jars with Jesse's despondency. She shrugs things off that disarm him completely. Sometimes I watch as he attempts to articulate a memory but gives up halfway through, too confused to know where to begin. Like a dream that begins to trail off as soon as you wake up.

I approach the counter. There is a smiley man in his early forties who turns and wipes his hands on his apron. 'Good afternoon. What can I get you?'

'Hi. This is a long shot, but you don't do pancakes, do you? There is a very solemn little boy over there, and I think it might just pull him out of his sulk,' I ask, hopefully.

The man laughs and scratches the back of his head, thinking. 'Erm . . . I'm really sorry, we don't – but we do sell Dutch pancakes.' He points to the rows of groceries behind me. 'I could warm some up and top with cream and strawberries?'

My voice fills with gratitude. 'That would be perfect, thank you! I'll take two.' I turn to find the packet he suggested. I order a tea for myself and apple juice for the kids and pay. Then I pick up a colouring sheet and hold it pressed between my lips as I balance the drinks precariously.

Putting them down, my tea spills into the saucer. Margo claps her hands together at the sight of the paper and I place it in front of her with a wink. She grabs some pencils and gets scribbling. 'Jesse, they have pancakes, isn't that great!' He nods with a soft smile. He holds the red and white paper straw between his fingers and pulls it to his lips. The grey cat that nearly floored me earlier jumps onto his lap. Jesse sits back in shock as the feline makes itself comfortable, padding around. Jesse tentatively puts his hand on the animal's back, amazed.

'That's Rocky, he likes you,' the man says as he places the pancakes down in front of the children. Their eyes become saucepans at the sight of all the whipped cream and fruit.

I smile at him and mouth, 'Thank you.'

'Rocky,' Jesse whispers as he strokes his back, and for the first time since we arrived, he smiles broadly.

I bring my tea to my lips and blow. 'How are you feeling about the move, Jesse?' I ask, settling in for an awkward and frustrating conversation. 'It's hard moving to a new place. New school, new home – everything.' *New mother*, my mind taunts.

Jesse shrugs. 'I've been here before,' he says, stroking the cat.

I lean in, putting my elbow on the table and resting my chin on my palm. I nab a strawberry off his plate and pop it in my mouth. 'Well, yes . . .' I say, chewing, remembering the day we drove down to see the property. 'But it's different packing up and moving away. Starting a new school and having all these new people in your life. It can feel a bit overwhelming until you get used to it. I know I feel like that.'

He eyes me in that way he does. 'It's okay. You wouldn't understand.'

'Understand what?' I ask. 'Try me.' I lean in further. Maybe I'm getting somewhere.

'Do you believe that after you die you come back to life as someone else?' he asks.

I cough in surprise. His cheeks flare red and his eyes avert again. I place a hand on his arm and nod, wanting to show I'm listening, and I'll take whatever he says seriously. 'You mean reincarnation,' I say and he mouths the word silently as though he is trying to remember it. 'Well . . . it's not really something I've ever thought about. But some people do.'

He takes another sip of his juice and continues to stroke the purring cat. I can see it's having a relaxing effect on Jesse too. He looks up to me, his eyes staring into mine with a directness that I've not seen before. 'I used to be someone else. I was re-in-car-nated,' the word trips from his mouth, and his neck bobs as he gets out the complicated word.

My mouth opens and closes. Unsure what to say. Then the cat jumps from his lap and Jesse runs off after it. Leaving me sitting there, completely perplexed.

CHAPTER 8

The rest of the day flies past in a blur. I get the kids home, and cajole them into eating as many vegetables as possible even though I've filled them with pancakes (I'm never making that mistake again) and they hardly touch a thing. Undress: 'No, you can't wear your socks in the bath'; bathe: 'Come on, why do you think you can't drink the bathwater?' and teeth: 'No, Margo – you have to do the top ones as well. Come back. I said, *come back*. You haven't finished.'

And then finally, Paul comes out of his study after a late call, and I feel relieved to hand over the reins. I stand in the doorway, resting against the frame, watching the three of them cosied up together. A book is open on Paul's lap with the children leaning into it. The warm orange glow from Jesse's dinosaur night-light illuminates their faces. It is the sweetest thing I've ever had the privilege of witnessing. Nothing makes Paul more attractive than moments like this. I leave them to it and settle back on one of the patio chairs with a glass of red wine.

It is a warm summer's evening; the heat gives the garden a

moist, exotic quality, more akin to the Mediterranean. Right here and now, with my warm bare legs, it is impossible to imagine what it will be like during winter.

I pull out my phone, remembering something I've not had a chance to do all afternoon. I type *reincarnation* into Google. Strange-looking ancient illustrations jump out at me, and words like *transmigration*, *metempsychosis*, *rebirth* float in front of my eyes. I click onto videos and scroll through – *10 creepy reincarnation stories*, and another promising to teach *the REAL science behind reincarnation*. Ignoring the less credible options, I play a clip from a documentary. A concerned mother describes the first conversation she had with her four-year-old son when he told her he was murdered as a little boy, and that he missed his real mummy. The penny drops. This is all a muddle in Jesse's mind. He must be so confused.

My eyes begin to twitch and my ears ring lightly. I close my eyes, begging for the throbbing not to turn into a headache. I dash my phone onto the table, irritated. I shouldn't have looked at it for so long. The bright light always brings on the worst kind of pain. I've been lucky recently, and although the odd funny turn has caught me out, I haven't had a full-on migraine for weeks. I'd started to hope they were a thing of the past. *Please, no. Please, please, no*, I whisper to myself.

The throbbing dies away and I open my eyes. The garden shifts in front of me before settling. And poof. It's gone.

Paul steps through the door and onto the patio and walks out onto the edge of the paving stones. He sips his wine before taking a deep breath in and out. 'Man, I love it here. There is something about being so isolated that makes me feel so plugged in. Do you know what I mean?' he asks, turning back. I nod, even though I feel the reverse. 'This really is a dream come true, Lauren. A gorgeous partner, two beautiful kids, a new beginning in this incredible house. I really feel like I've made it.' He grins, and I smile at the scene he's created. Thrilled to be part of his vision.

'Are they down?' I ask.

He nods, walking towards the table. 'Only twenty minutes of requests for water and extra toilet trips.'

'You got off lightly,' I joke.

He pulls me to my feet, and we hold each other, enjoying the silence. 'I just can't believe we made it. Just us. Isn't this perfect?' He moves to kiss me. His eyes search my face. 'Are you okay? You look pale.'

Swallowing, I lick my dry lips. 'I'm just tired.'

'Is it your head?'

I cave in and nod, admitting to it. 'Just since we got here. Only a few dizzy spells.'

He looks thoughtful. 'You've been non-stop since we arrived. I'll have the kids most of the weekend so you can rest. I'll get you some pills.'

He stands up and goes inside, re-emerging a couple of minutes later with a few white tablets in his hand. I toss them into my mouth and gulp them down with wine.

'Thanks.' I smile gratefully at him. He leans over and pecks my lips, his beard rough on my smooth skin.

'Are you ever going to shave that thing off?'

'Don't you like my new look?' His hand moves up and strokes it instinctively.

'I do . . . when it's tidy.'

'I'll try out the barber in town next week.'

'Not that I don't love the dishevelled lumberjack look,' I tease.

He stares back at me. There is something cool about his gaze, and I hope I haven't offended him. I take another sip of my drink and look out at the garden.

'What do you think?' I say, pointing at my handiwork.

He looks ahead and considers his answer.

'I think for an invalid you make a pretty good gardener.'

I hit his arm. 'I'm not an invalid any more.'

He strokes my arm with a finger and looks up. 'No, you're right. You definitely aren't any more.' I enjoy the moment of recognition.

'Can I tell you something weird?' I whisper.

'Oh yes, please do.' He smiles. He looks so relaxed I hate to bring something he may see as a problem to his door. 'This afternoon while we were out, Jesse told me he's been reincarnated.'

Paul leans forward, almost spitting out his drink. 'What?' He turns to look at me. 'Are you serious?' I'm surprised when he laughs.

'I'm worried about him, Paul. You saw that note from the teacher – he locked a kid in a cupboard . . . That's a worrying development, isn't it?'

Paul waves his hand, as though batting my fear away.

'Look, Lauren, he probably heard about reincarnation somewhere. Kids his age – they get obsessed with the idea of something and their imaginations run wild. And as for locking that kid in the cupboard, I mean, come on, it was probably a prank he took too far.'

Jesse isn't exactly a born prankster, I think. 'I'm just worried about how confused he is. Don't you think he could be acting out as a misguided way of trying to show how he's feeling?' I remember Paul pointing that out about me, a while ago. 'Do you think he should see a therapist? A grief counsellor? Just to help him—'

'I *said*, it's nothing to worry about. It's just going to take him a few weeks to settle here, that's all. I don't want to add anything else that may stress him out.'

I'm taken aback by his firm and unremitting tone. 'I don't want to stress him out either,' I whisper, feeling misunderstood.

He paces across the patio. 'Maybe believing that reincarnation exists . . . maybe it's easier for him to think of his mother . . .' His voice cracks and something plunges in my stomach. I wish I hadn't said anything. To my horror, his eyes fill with tears, the way they do whenever he talks about Emma. The love he feels rages against raw grief, and the frustration that he can never have her again is visible.

How can he possibly love me when he so clearly wishes she was here instead?

'Of course,' I whisper. Getting out of my seat, I go to him. 'I'm sorry, Paul.'

He accepts the hug. We stand there, holding one another, listening to the early evening sounds of the forest. My chin is firmly pressed against his shoulder.

'There is a shed,' I whisper.

I feel his embrace faulter. 'Hmm?'

'Remember Jesse said there was a shed? And he was right. There is.'

'I saw it too.' His voice croaks and he lets me go and sniffs.

Taking his glass, he moves to the edge of the patio and stares down the lawn. I join him and slip my hand into his, hoping it won't be rejected.

'I was thinking I could do it up and use it as a reading room or as somewhere to meditate? It would be nice to have a little space just for me . . .'

He's looking the other way. He raises the glass to his mouth and takes a big gulp of his drink. 'I haven't seen a key for it,' he mutters.

I bite my lip, thinking of the brand-new padlock attached to the hatch on the floor. How could he have put it there if he can't get in?

'I'll ask Jack, but he never mentioned it, so maybe it's out of bounds.'

'Oh, right . . . well, it looked empty . . . so I don't see why—'

His hand breaks from mine and he stalks towards the back door. Before entering, he looks back. 'Lauren. I'll try, okay? But don't you think they've given us enough? I don't want to have to keep going to them and asking for things.'

I nod. 'Of course. Sorry, I should never have asked,' I say, feeling foolish.

And with that he strides into the house and stalks through the living room, disappearing into the hallway. I feel winded. I'm being too needy, and that isn't attractive at all. What if he goes off me? What if he realises I'm not a touch on his dead wife? What if I lose Paul and Margo and Jesse? I'll be all on my own again.

It suddenly dawns on me how much I've got to lose.

CHAPTER 9

Finally, the weekend arrives. Somehow we've managed to unpack our life into this extraordinary house and make it through the first five days of our new routine. From now on, the only way is up. Paul even managed to mow the grass this morning, and much to the children's glee he gave them each a turn up and down the rolling lawn on the back of the large ride-on mower. The orderly stripes make the whole plot feel less haunted, and more lived in, and my head feels instantly clearer.

After a pyjama-heavy morning, we decide to get our act together and venture out to the local activity farm. Margo is extremely excited. She's already chosen which soft animal is coming along – her fluffy sheep – and she's been chatting away about the petting area I've seen on their website, and the ice cream we've promised them both. Jesse has been harder to negotiate out of the house, but I'm hoping once we arrive, and he's distracted by all the fun activities, he'll have a good time.

I'm really looking forward to doing something as a family outside of the perfunctory morning and evening rituals that always feel rushed. We never managed it in London: Paul was working loads and liked to relax on weekends, and once I'd got my energy back, they were taken up with countryside recces, and packing up the flat.

I've been trying to get Margo dressed for ages but she's refusing every item of clothing I suggest, wanting instead to wear something more suitable for ten degrees cooler. 'It's very hot, Margo,' I try to explain. But she shakes her head firmly. 'Margo, please!' I cry in frustration. Possibly too harshly. She stares at me, shocked.

'Everything okay?' Paul asks, poking his head into the room.

I nod. 'Yes.' My cheeks are red, and I wave a hand in front of my face feeling nauseous. He looks at me suspiciously. 'Are you sure you want to come? You could have the morning off and relax?'

I shake my head. 'No, no. I want to come. I'm fine.' I jump to my feet. We gather by the front door. My head is throbbing lightly, but I'm sure it will pass. To be honest, I'm desperate for a change of scenery.

This house . . . It's so open and vast in some respects, but there is something about being inside an open box in the woods which feels disorientating. The quiet unnerves me. The hard, sharp sheets of glass, although transparent, feel oppressive and stifling. Especially when I'm minding my own business, and I hear the whirring noise of the CCTV camera.

Paul said he asked his friends about it, and I shouldn't worry. It's on a motion sensor but the feed isn't programmed to go anywhere any more. His friends were planning to switch it off, but it's wired into the mains, and it's easier to just leave it running, and I'm so silly to obsess about it.

As always, Margo sings in the car. I look out the window quietly as I listen to her jubilant voice. My phone buzzes and I glance down to see a message from Isobel. I open it quickly, excited.

'Who's that?' Paul asks.

My eyes track the message and I reply, 'Just a mum from school. She's invited us over for tea this afternoon!' I say, thrilled. 'Won't that be lovely? We could go on the way back from the farm . . .'

'I don't think we'll have time, Lauren,' he says briskly.

I blink. 'Really? But . . .'

I sense him close off to the idea and he shakes his head. 'Sorry, Lauren, but the kids will be knackered after this and it's just not fun trying to squeeze stuff in. You wouldn't understand.' Silence permeates as I shove my excitement back down. 'She hasn't given us much notice. It's quite rude really,' he says, and I lower the phone onto my lap, disappointed.

The drive takes about half an hour, and as we pull into the car park, I realise this isn't the quaint little country farm with a few goats and a cow I'd been imagining. Parked cars fill out two fields and we're directed into one called 'overspill' by a woman in a hi-vis jacket. There is a dual entrance and *Wind in the Willows* themed paintings on the welcome signs in the distance. Margo is already wriggling around in her seat desperate to get out. 'I'm coming,' I say as I flick the handle of the door. Paul gets out the driver's seat and stretches.

Once Margo is on the ground I grip the back of her top to stop her rushing into the dangers of the car park. Suddenly she stops. 'Uh-oh.' I follow her gaze down to her tights where a wet patch has appeared. Then she begins to cry, 'My tights!' and I crouch down.

'Don't worry, I've got a change of clothes in the bag.' I notice Jesse looking over with a sigh, knowing this will involve some sort of boring detour. 'Come on, I brought a lovely cool sundress.' I try to take her hand to sort her out, but she resists.

'My tights!' she howls again, refusing to come with me.

Paul appears and picks her up swiftly. He whips her around to the boot of the car and efficiently undresses her before she can stop him and pulls the spare over her head without a thought. *See, Lauren, that's how you deal with kids. Just get on with it, not your namby-pamby pathetic soft touch which doesn't get you anywhere.*

'There,' Paul says, placing her on top of his shoulders. 'What's up?' Paul asks, noticing my downtrodden expression.

I realise I'm chewing my thumbnail and I remove it. 'Nothing. I'm really looking forward to this.' I don't want him to notice how inadequate I'm feeling and quickly plaster on a smile.

We queue for a while before being admitted and once we're on the other side of the gate we loiter, gaining our bearings. There seems to be a trail through to the animals and then another towards some amusement rides.

'What does everyone what to do?' I ask and Margo points from her perch on Paul's shoulders and cries:

'Animals!'

Jesse just shrugs. 'Don't care.'

We walk past stables first. The names of the horses are painted on little wooden plaques on the front of their half-open doors: Rocket is lying down on a bed of straw; Angus and Dover both stick their noses out, chewing, unphased by their guests.

'Horsey-horsey-horsey,' Margo says, her little hand out. 'Neigh, neigh.' Paul grimaces slightly at the weight of her bouncing a little too enthusiastically on his neck. Jesse climbs up the door of the stable and dangles over the top, peering down at Rocket before jumping off in disgust. He kicks the door and then walks away.

'Jesse?' I question.

'I want to go back to the house,' he says impatiently.

I look up at Margo who is in pure bliss as she chats away. 'Let's just stay a bit. Margo is having such a good time,' I try, walking over to him, attempting to coax him back. He shrugs me off and then charges past me to the door and rattles the lock in its place. 'I want to get them out.'

'Jesse!' I pull at his shoulder, hoping no one has noticed. Glancing around at the various pens and barns and all the families milling about enjoying their day. 'They have a nice life here.' I think back to the horse I saw the other day in the woods, how its coat glimmered with iridescence against the shards of light escaping through the trees, and how its mane danced freely in the air as it cantered away. I know what Jesse means. It is sad to see them locked away like this.

Margo runs over, having dismounted from her father, and shouts, 'Mooooo!' into another pen. The large cow returns the greeting and Jesse glances over in disdain. Next, we walk into a barn called 'The Wind in the Willows Village'. Inside is a miniature indoor play area with a grocery shop and a hairdresser's and baker's for the kids to play make-believe. Margo claps her hands together and hurries off. Finding herself a small plastic shopping basket, she begins wandering the grocery aisle, ticking off an imaginary shopping list as she goes.

Parents relax back on benches, taking advantage of a few moments' rest.

'This is stupid,' Jesse says, huffing.

I notice a make-believe post office, and kids are crawling up onto a mezzanine level and sending parcels and letters down a shoot. 'Why don't you go and play over there? That looks fun,' I say, pointing. He crosses his arms and sits on the floor next to Paul on one of the benches, who is tapping away on his phone, most probably to a client having a bad day. Jesse is determined not to enjoy himself; I mustn't get frustrated. Margo is having the time of her life – one out of two ain't bad.

'Petting area, Lauren?' Margo asks, looking up at me, both her hands clasped together in excitement.

'Sure.' I take her hand. I call over to Paul. 'Paul' – he looks up – 'she's desperate to go to the petting area.' He nods and stands. I watch as he crouches down next to Jesse, trying to coax him up.

Holding Margo's hand, I walk out the entrance and wait for them. I wasn't expecting it to be so crowded and shift my head around the people flooding through the pathway to see if Paul's managed to get out. Finally I see him with Jesse, reprimanding him for something. Paul catches my eye and motions with his hand for us to just go. 'We'll see you over there,' he calls.

A few minutes later we join the queue. Margo whines. 'Come on, Margo, we need to wait our turn,' I say. I dig around in my bag and hand her a container of sliced apple to distract her. I watch through the mesh wire fence as a smiley young woman in wellies and a green wax jacket helps a little boy stroke a small ball of fur. It's very sweet, Margo will be in her element. She pulls at the corner of my jacket; her big eyes look up at me. 'Won't be long,' I reassure her. The woman next to us looks down at Margo, 'What a gorgeous little girl. You look just like your mummy.' Margo looks at me and I squeeze her hand; neither of us want to own up.

The sound of a carousel drifts over and I look above heads to see the amusement area with a turning carousel and dodgem cars. I can just about make out the garish colours and frozen faces of lions, horses and dragons which jar against the straw floors and wooden fences of the farm. People sat on the ride cheer and wave at family members taking photos from the sidelines. The music is sickeningly sweet. The same chords repeat over and over.

Margo is stomping her feet impatiently, whispering, 'My turn, my turn, my turn,' with each foot.

Another child goes in, and I assure her it's, 'Not long now.'

Then I hear a horrific scream and my head whips towards it. Then a shout. This time I recognise Paul's voice. A group of people obscure my view, and I can't see what's happened. Picking up a protesting Margo, we flee the queue, much to her alarm.

I duck through the gathering crowd. 'Excuse me, excuse me,' I say, pushing past shoulders. Then, at the stables, I see Jesse yanking on one of the doors. The horse that had been resting earlier is up on its hind legs, snorting in distress.

Paul looks up and sees me – his face pale. Jesse's teeth are clamped together as he screams. His chest hyperventilates; the sound is guttural and distressing. The gathered crowd look on in horror. Margo turns her head into my shoulder, scared. Finally, Jesse falls to the floor. I kneel next to him and begin to stroke his back, calmly shushing. 'It's okay, Jesse, it's okay.' I look over at the horse, it seems to be calming; a farmhand has climbed over and is patting its neck and whispering to it soothingly.

Jesse's his face is muddy and red. Paul looks at me, his eyes haunted. He seems quite helpless in the face of chaos. 'Jesse, Jesse, you're okay,' I repeat over and over. His jaw slackens, and he scrambles up and charges into my arms next to Margo, almost pushing me over. I rub his back again and he begins to sob. 'It's okay. It's okay.' His cries become soft whimpers, and I whisper, 'Jesse, what is it? What happened?'

'The horses. She loved horses,' he rambles. 'We have to let

them out,' he says between gasps of breath. 'We have to get her out.'

I look at Paul. He shrugs, shakes his head. Blinking in shock at the scene.

'She loved them. My mummy loved horses! You hate them!' he accuses Paul with a stiff pointed finger. People around us stare solemnly at the boy, and then at us, looking for answers.

'Jesse. Stop it,' Paul says firmly. My lips part in surprise at his aggression. I'm not sure it's the best way to deal with this. Before I know it, he's pulling Jesse away. His fingers grab at me, not wanting to leave my arms. I want to hold him and keep him safe. But I can't. He's not my son. 'This is not on,' Paul is frantically hissing to Jesse. 'You've ruined a perfectly nice day out.'

I stand, lifting Margo with me, and watch Paul thrust through the crowds clinging to the boy who is frantically pushing him away. The nauseating sound of the carousel tinkers. I turn to look and see the frozen face of a horse on the ride. The gold pole shafted through its centre. An ugly, startled, red-painted smile.

Margo's sobs snap me out of it. I whisper, 'Everything is okay,' as she bemoans her chance to hold a rabbit. I follow Paul, feeling ashamed as prying eyes watch us flee the scene. And for the first time I think, *Is there something more to know about his perfect relationship with Emma?*

CHAPTER 10

The journey home is filled with stunned silence. Margo doesn't sing a note. Once back, Jesse runs into his room. I open my mouth to begin a discussion with Paul but he marches past and rushes up the stairs, two at a time. I walk down the hallway and gently push Jesse's door. He's hiding under his duvet.

'Jesse? Can I get you a drink or a biscuit or something?' I ask. The cover shakes a no. A sniffing sound, as though he's crying. 'Jesse, are you sure?' I sit on the edge of the bed and put my hand underneath the duvet searching for part of him to comfort. His foot kicks it away.

'Leave me alone,' he cries.

'Jesse.'

The mound shifts back into the wall. 'Go away,' he says fiercely.

I decide to let him cool off. I walk back to the hallway just as Paul comes dashing back down in his running gear. Without a glance, he is out the front door, slamming it behind him.

Wincing, I go into the kitchen and begin to prepare lunch. The soggy sandwiches wrapped in foil I prepared for our outing aren't very appealing now we're home. I glance at the front door, frustrated. This is what Paul does when he has a personal problem. He removes himself from it. He is more than capable of wading through other people's issues but as soon as it's his own he completely shuts down and focuses on distracting himself. *Maybe he took you on to distract himself from the pain of losing Emma.* The thought hits me in the chest and I quickly turn to open the fridge. My head throbs, and I pour some water and glug it down.

Lowering the glass, I breathe out in relief. I get lost watching Margo who is happily playing on the rug. She seems unaffected by the scene at the farm. I wonder when the ability to stay constantly present and in the moment ends. As I prepare our lunch Margo begins to lay a fake table in front of her kitchen. Our processes mimic one another. Her eyes follow me as she copies. She has the pan on the hob, just as I do. And has laid a table for four, just like me. I get out the wooden spoon and carefully stir the pasta, and she does the same. A few minutes later I prick a piece with a fork and put it in my mouth to test. I turn to see she has done it too.

'Is it ready?' I ask.

'Nearly,' she replies earnestly, and I nod, agreeing.

I lean around the partition wall and call the boys, and a few minutes later Paul comes through. 'Are you okay?' he asks, kissing me on the cheek. 'You're still pale,' he says, frowning as his fingers draw along my jawline. The run must have sorted him out. He seems relaxed compared to earlier. I wonder if now is the right time to talk about the scene at the farm.

'I'm fine.' My voice comes out in a croak. I cough and repeat myself in a sturdier tone. 'I'm fine.' He pulls an arm around me so I'm winched in. He smells good, he must have showered. It's funny, I don't remember hearing him come in.

'Are you okay?' I feel him break away from me. He begins to hum.

'You've asked me that five times,' he says, bemused.

I touch my chest. 'What?' I haven't had the chance to talk to him yet. 'Paul, do you think we should talk about what happened today? I've never seen anything like it. We really need to . . .' The look on his face causes me to stop. He laughs.

'Lauren, that's all we've done since we got back. Look, I've got a call, let's go over it again, if you really feel we need to, tonight.' Leaning over, he pecks my cheek as I stand there, confused.

'But lunch,' I say, pointing at the laid table as he leaves. To my surprise the table is empty and wiped down. I gasp and raise my hand to my mouth. 'What the . . . ?' I whisper.

The sound of the television causes me to look over at Margo who's lying on the sofa watching *Peppa Pig* and cuddling her grey cat. The kitchen is now full of our lunch things, dirty and used. I look up at the clock. An hour has passed. My brain feels like it has expanded and is pressing painfully into sharp corners of my skull.

'Loz, can you play with me?' Margo calls from the sofa.

I nod and walk through, sitting on the floor amongst her

things. She hops down and joins me. I don't have the energy to instigate a game, and I think she senses this and opens her doctor's kit and begins to check my forehead for a temperature. I put a cushion behind my back and lean against the foot of the sofa. She scoops the stethoscope around her neck and presses the diaphragm against my arm.

My eyes burst open, and I gasp. I had the dream again, the pain circular and dagger-like. It grips me to the core and twists. Then the white light and the burst of pure bliss. Did I die? The doctor said I nearly did. Panting, my eyes flutter around the living room to gain my bearings, telling my brain I'm not there, I'm here – safe. My beating heart settles, and I raise my arm, where a loosely applied bandage hangs.

Standing, I look around for Margo, but she's not behind the sofa or in the kitchen. Just as I'm about to call her name, I hear her infectious giggle coming from the hallway. I gingerly walk towards the noise. The door to the study is open, and she's sitting on his recliner holding a packet of Post-it notes, slowly peeling them off. Paul's headset is around his neck, and there is a half-written Word document up on his screen. He transcribes meetings with clients so he can think about their concerns outside of sessions, and files them away, for his records.

'Hello.' The word escapes like a soft puff of air, almost as if my voice belongs to someone else.

'We thought we'd leave you to rest, didn't we, Margo?' She nods happily. 'Honestly, Lauren, you seem exhausted, is there something you're not telling me?' He looks concerned.

'I'm just tired,' I whisper. He nods, eyeing me up cautiously. This is the last thing I wanted, to be the cause of more stress.

'Have you checked in on Jesse?' I ask.

'I just poked my head in, he's fine. You saw him at lunch – he seems to have bounced back. Kids,' he says with a shrug. I nod, not wanting to admit to the strange gap in my memory. The idea of it causes a panicky flurry in my chest. That's never happened before.

'I've been thinking about our chat,' he says, crossing his legs and placing the palms of his hands together. 'And you're right, we do need to make some adjustments around here.' I nod. Thank God, he's taking the issue seriously. He strokes his beard. 'The outburst was a classic reaction to overstimulation after a big change. I think we should stay home while they get used to it here. You know you're meant to keep cats inside for a month after your move so they settle and feel secure in their new surroundings? Imagine that, Lauren. And Jesse is far bigger and more complex than a house pet, isn't he?' His voice is calm. His eyes bore into mine and I nod, wondering if that really is the best thing to do. But Paul knows more than me, I suppose.

'What was that about the horses?'

He shakes his head. 'I honestly have no idea.' Paul sighs. He seems tired, and I realise how worried he is.

'I really think he should see someone, Paul . . .'

Paul's demeanour changes and his eyes dart up to mine fiercely – I regret it instantly. 'Lauren, don't you think I know what's best for *my* son?' I take a step back in shock. He's never said anything like that before. He's never placed me outside the box like that.

'I wasn't . . . I didn't mean . . .' I stumble.

'I have a lot to do. Can you just leave worrying about Jesse to me, please?' He waves his hand and turns to his daughter, who's lying back in a bed of yellow squares. 'Margo, why don't you go help Lauren? Daddy needs to finish some work.' And with that he turns back to his screen and snaps his headphones back over his ears, finishing the conversation.

I stand there for a moment, stung. Then I smile over at Margo and hold out my hand. She hops off and takes it. 'Let's go check on Jesse,' I say, and we leave the study and push open his bedroom door. He's lying on his front, watching Paul's iPad. He looks up at us and smiles at Margo.

'Hello.' She hops into the space next to him and mimics his position.

'Come on, guys, a few more minutes on that and then let's play a game.' I get closer. 'What are you watching?' I plonk myself down next to them. *Spirit*. It's a cartoon about horses on the American Frontier. One of his favourites and I don't mind him watching it too much as it's one of the more relaxing, innocent options for kids, it seems.

He looks over at me with hesitation, as if he is deciding whether to ask me a question.

'Do you like horses, Lauren?'

I think for a moment. 'Yes, I do. They're beautiful. I don't think I've ever ridden on one before.'

'She did,' he whispers proudly, a small smile creeping onto his lips.

'Your mummy?'

He nods intently. 'She loved horses.'

He sits up and I put my arm around him. 'Well, I'm not surprised. They are magnificent creatures,' I say. He doesn't reply. He is staring out of the glass into the garden with a faraway look.

Sunday passes quickly. It's a beautiful day, and I spend it in the garden with the kids. Jesse even dares to enjoy himself; he laughs hysterically as they run naked under the sprinkler. Shouting, and egging each other on. Paul doesn't join in. He has too much work to do. Whenever I pass through the hallway, I look longingly at the study door.

The rest of the week is mostly uneventful. Each day I drop the children at school and come back to the house. After tidying, doing the washing and ordering the shopping, I find myself in the garden with my weeding tools. I'm not sure I'm going to be a very good housewife. I don't seem to gain any self-worth or satisfaction from the role I am in. It is monotonous and thankless. Then I feel ungrateful and imagine Emma in an apron smiling sweetly as she patiently irons out creases in Paul's shirts.

One afternoon just as I'm on my way out for a walk, I notice a large grey cloud looming. Spots of drizzle become fat blobs, and I sit back on the sofa and stare into space. I'm starting to understand why Jesse says he hates it here.

Hearing the noise of wheels on the grit drive, I stand and walk to the door, waiting expectantly for the doorbell to ring. Instead, a package flops through the letter box. Opening the parcel, I find a picture frame I ordered online. Holding it, I go over to the kitchen drawer full of random bits and bobs and pull out the envelope holding the photograph I had printed. Unpicking the fastenings at the back, I slot it into place behind the glass.

A passer-by took it of the four of us at a local park in London at the beginning of spring. Paul organised the picnic as a surprise. I'm trying hard to smile in the photo; I found the excursion a bit much. I replace the wooden backing and refasten the clips down. Walking to the partition wall, I place it on an empty hook.

I cock my head to one side and admire it. In it, we are the perfect family. You would never know there are a series of sad stories linked to each of us. I glance towards Paul's study. He has distanced himself from me since the trip to the farm. I feel a change. A leak in our boat.

It occurs to me then that out of all the belongings his friends left, they didn't leave one family photo. They must have taken them all with them to the States.

That is the only explanation.

CHAPTER 11

A couple of weeks later I hear Margo calling as my brain engages with reality. My night was fitful. I tossed as dreams attacked me. Debris settling from that fateful night. Flashbacks of the harrowing violence have pulled me into a dark place. I preferred it when I didn't remember a thing. I should talk to Paul. He'd know how to make me feel better. But Paul's method is very invasive, and the horror of it is indescribable. I'm not sure I'm ready to tackle this, and I know he'd force me to confront it.

I push myself up as Paul presses the button, releasing the blinds. A wet, grey vista emerges. Gone are the panoramic blue skies and puffball clouds, and I watch the damp branches shake vigorously, as though we are sailing through a raging storm. I grab my robe off the back of the door and pad down to Margo, whose little voice has become more urgent and distressed. 'Coming,' I say gently as I enter the room. She jumps out of bed and bolts towards me. I collect her up and hold her as she snuggles her head under my chin. 'Morning, darling,' I whisper and my harrowing dreams are banished away.

While the kids have breakfast, I watch the rain. A memory comes to me then, slamming into me as I take a sip of coffee. I am so struck by it I freeze. A bright red anorak and yellow wellies – running through a park jumping and laughing. Tights soggy with brown sludgy water. Someone calling my name . . .

'There'll be lots of puddles,' Margo says thoughtfully between chews. 'Can I wear my Peppa Pig wellies?' she lisps, and I nod, wondering if they'll still fit.

'It looks cold,' Jesse says as he takes a sip of milk.

'It might be a shock after all that heat. But I don't think it will be too cold,' I reply.

'My other mummy really liked the cold,' he says.

I frown. 'Really?'

'She used to say she did.' He nods, spooning up some Weetabix.

I wonder if that's true. I can't think of anyone saying they enjoy being cold. He must have misunderstood, or it could have been a dream? But then again, maybe Emma did like the cold. I pause, picturing her in a windbreaker, a bobble hat and tough boots. A big grin and rosy cheeks as snow falls around her. Again, I try to work her out. All the little titbits I've heard make her sound impossibly perfect. But that's to be expected, I suppose. Losing someone wipes away their defects. Especially when they're ripped away like that. I understand how memories can fall in the wrong landing spot. The ones I have of my parents are so contorted – I have no idea what's an assumption, or a photo, or a dream. Some of them must belong to me. The fear of the unknown grabs me once again and I lean down and kiss Margo's head to deflect it. Her big eyes check me, and she smiles. Jesse grins over too. And I try to ignore the uneasy feeling that I'm stealing again.

In the end, time runs away from me. Rushing them out the door, I leave the breakfast things to tidy when I get back. Hopefully Paul won't mind. I shield them one by one under an umbrella into the car. Finally, I slam the driver's door, and put the key in the ignition, beginning the journey down the glistening mist-filled road.

Some things come back to you so easily, as if the blueprint is embedded like a tattoo onto my brain. I remember the long hours at the hospital regaining the confidence to walk, but this is easy. Driving is so liberating after being cared for by other people for so long. I try to remember my first car. Was it black? No. Dark blue?

After exiting the drive, we crunch to a stop, before joining the country lane that then takes us to the A-road. I never felt brave enough to drive in London. I didn't understand the one-way systems and the heavy traffic put me off. But I insisted Paul let me drive on our weekend excursions to the countryside, so I could prove ferrying the children around would be more than manageable once we began our new life.

On the A-road a big truck turns the corner behind us. It's driving faster than necessary and before I know it, it's right up behind our car. His speed forces me to press down on the accelerator, causing me to go faster than I would like in this downpour. I click the wipers up a few notches, and they rock back and forth at full throttle, making a whiny noise with each swipe. My heart beats quickly, and my breath becomes shallow. I don't know how to work the ones at the back, and my hands search around trying out various options while still trying to focus on the road.

'Lauren?' Jesse asks quietly.

'Yes?' I reply, distracted.

'Why can't cars fly?'

'Erm . . .' I look up at the mirror. He's always asking me random questions at the worst possible moments. 'I guess helicopters are flying cars,' I say, preoccupied with the huge vehicle on our tail. My head pulses and I clench my jaw.

'They don't have wheels,' Margo interjects, with a lisp.

'That's cos they're in the air, silly,' Jesse tells her.

'At least they don't get in traffic jars,' she replies.

'Jams,' I correct her, still distracted by what is happening behind.

'Like when Daddy got cross,' she says.

I glance in the rear-view mirror again. Margo's remembering the time Paul threw a fit when we were stuck in gridlocked traffic trying to get into the Blackwall Tunnel. He was so enraged it took ages to calm him down. I'd never seen him lose it before. The kids were terrified.

The truck is still behind us. I swallow as I push down against the brake, hoping that the sight of my lights will encourage him to do the same. The space between us contracts as the rain pelts down, and the back of my neck covers in anxious sweat. We fling forward faster and faster. Visibility isn't great, with the heat inside the car, and I hunch and lean forward to wipe the inside of the windscreen. Feeling out of control, my knuckles whiten as I squeeze the wheel tightly.

Then to my relief, suddenly the truck turns off the road, and the space behind us is empty again.

'Daddy got very cross,' Margo lisps.

'He gets very angry sometimes,' Jesse adds, agreeing. 'Mummy always said not to be scared,' he tells Margo, and I glance up and notice him pat her arm reassuringly.

'What?' I ask, zoning into their conversation properly for the first time.

'He doesn't when you're around,' Jesse tells me.

'What do you mean?' My head begins to throb, and I indicate, noticing a good place to pull over to the side of the road. Coming to a stop, I remove my hands from the wheel and squeeze my fingers into my palms, surprised at the rigid force I was hanging on with.

'Why are we stopping?' Jesse asks.

I open the bottle of water I have in the cup holder and glug it down. 'Just need some water,' I reply, wiping a little stray liquid from the side of my mouth. Watching their little faces in the rear-view mirror, I wink. 'Before I crash the car,' I joke.

'Is it your head, Lauren?' Jesse asks. Margo's eyes widen.

'I'm fine,' I reply quickly.

'Daddy says we need to look after you till you're better,' Jesse says stoically.

'Are you going to die?' Margo asks.

I laugh. 'Absolutely not!'

'*She* did,' Margo says quietly, pulling her toy cat into her chest.

'I'm fine, guys. I'm going to be here for you forever. Okay?' They both nod in unison. I put the engine on, and we get back on the road.

Just as I pull into the small school car park, the rain stops, and the clouds make a hasty withdrawal. Blue sky is revealed, reflecting back at us from newly formed puddles that we dash through to make the bell. After waving goodbye, I turn back to the car, and decide to go for a coffee at The Meadows. I still feel full of adrenalin from the truck earlier. It scares me how out of control I felt. I imagine for a moment what would have happened if I'd crashed. The police would have gone to the house taking off their hats out of respect, before telling Paul that I was dead and I'd killed his kids as well. A widower twice over and now . . . I realise there is no word for a parent who loses children. The thought too unbearable to name.

Walking into the barn, I enjoy the familiarity. The same man is behind the counter. He smiles and waves.

'Hello,' I say cheerily.

The café area is empty, and I decide on the ledge at the window. I look out onto the pretty meadow recovering from its onslaught, shimmering in the sun.

'Coffee?' he calls over and I turn and nod vigorously.

'Three shots.' I hold my fingers up and he laughs as he turns to the machine.

'I'll bring it over.'

I smile gratefully and slide onto a stool.

I put in my earphones, and I select some calming music to drown everything out and remove my Kindle from my bag. A few minutes later I mouth *thanks* as my drink is set down next to me. Steam rises from the mug. All is well. I can relax. I feel calm and content for a moment. Then I stare at the screen, enjoying the simple pleasure of getting lost in a book.

It's a psychological thriller, my favourite genre. I always want to shout at the lead character, usually a girl stuck in a situation she can't quite see from where she is entrenched within.

When I next check the time an hour has passed. I remove my earphones and look around in amazement. The shop which had been completely deserted is busier now. A few people mill around with shopping baskets and a small queue has formed at the café counter. And a new florist section has opened by the entrance doors.

I put my things inside my bag and check my phone. My lips part as I notice a new message from Claudia. *Just wanted you to know even though we didn't leave on good terms, I'm always here for you x* I smile, pausing before deciding on a reply. *Thank you.* I add, *And you'll be the first to know if it all goes tits-up *laughing face emoji** I take the last sip of my cold coffee and wait for her to reply. *Well . . . I'll be waiting here for you if it does.* My thumbs hover. Before I would have protested, I would have shot back a message of undying love for Paul. But something stops me. I simply reply, *Thank you x*

Before exiting, I pause at the flower stall to admire the bouquets. They are rustic, simple and very pretty. I pick up a bunch, thinking the house could do with brightening up – aside from the kids' plastic crap, it's all greys, browns and creams.

'How much are these?' I ask the woman standing nearby wearing a leather apron with pockets full of undyed string, ribbon and scissors. Her cheeks are rosy, as if she's spent a lot of time in the elements, and her hair is wiry and grey. She didn't hear me and I step forward and ask her again. 'Excuse me, how much are these?'

Startled, she looks up. 'Oh, umm.' She stares at the bouquet, trying to remember. 'Ten pounds, please.' But then she corrects herself with a jolt. 'Oh, wait no, those are fifteen. Sorry.'

'I'll take them.' I bring them up to my nose for a sniff as the payment goes through. 'They're lovely.'

'Ah, thanks, love. You visiting someone?'

'Actually, we just moved here. Renting until we find our feet.'

'Well, welcome. Staying in the village then?'

'No, we're pretty isolated actually. It's down Layton Road – it's a mid-century house . . .'

She nods briskly, her friendly smile fading. 'Ah, yes – the glass house.'

I nod.

'We used to live just the other side of there.' She looks sad and distant. 'I moved last year. I got an offer on the land I couldn't turn down; I couldn't keep it up on my own. And business sort of . . . dried up. Think they're planning to knock down my old cottage,' she says briskly. Her eyes avert from mine. She sniffs and turns away, upset. 'Well, it's good the house is filled with new people who can make happier memories,' she whispers, as if consoling herself.

'The owners have relocated to America for a while,' I explain.

She sighs uncomfortably. Then finally she looks up at me properly. 'That's where they scurried off to.' The bitterness in her voice catches me by surprise.

My phone vibrates before I can find out more. Paul's name flashes on the screen – I mouth *sorry* to the woman as I answer it. 'Hello, darling,' I sing, preparing to tell him about my morning.

'Where are you?' His reply is flat.

'I'm at The Meadows.'

'Oh, right.' There is an annoyed tilt to his voice.

'Sorry, I just stopped for a coffee.'

'I've taken a long lunch and cooked you this nice meal that I wanted to treat you to. I wasn't expecting you to be so long . . .'

'Okay, well, I'll come back right away,' I reply.

He hangs up without saying goodbye. I say, 'Bye,' anyway, embarrassed that the woman may think that I've been hung up on. 'I'd better go. Thank you again,' I say, feeling rushed, striding out the doors and back to the car.

CHAPTER 12

As soon as I walk through the door, he's there. His arms around my neck, leaning in for a kiss. Having spent the whole journey catastrophising, I'm floored with relief. Of course he isn't angry with me! I'm surprised at how emotional I feel. Tears spring to my eyes. What was I imagining? That he was going to chuck me out for being late for lunch? Absurd! This is Paul. Wonderful, incredible Paul.

Throughout the meal he fusses over me, refilling my glass and admiring the flowers I bought. He's made delicious Turkish eggs for brunch, and I feel spoilt. Rain begins a new assault and it's romantic sitting at the dining table, as chaos unfurls around us.

'This was lovely, thank you,' I say, and he leans in for another peck on the lips. 'Next time give me a heads up and I'll make sure I'm not late,' I say lightly.

His finger traces along my jawline. 'You're crazy,' he whispers. 'I did tell you!' he adds with a laugh.

I think back to the rushed morning. I'm sure I would have remembered, something like this wouldn't have been brushed off easily. Would it? I touch my head.

'I'm going to have to start leaving you those notes around after all,' he jokes, and then he adds more seriously, 'I moved an appointment to spend time with you, Lauren.'

A burst of guilt. 'I'm sorry.' He's right . . . sometimes I get muddled. I should have checked with him before deciding on the detour. Next time I'll ask before changing plans. That's what partners do. And you have to bring everyone into your actions when part of a family. *You can't just think about yourself any more.*

'I'm sorry,' I say softly, 'I'll double check next time.'

He looks pleased. Then he pulls me from my seat and onto his lap. 'That's okay. I think you forget it's not just you against the world any more. You've got me, you've got all of us.'

I nod. 'You're right. It's a big change.'

'You are doing a great job.' He moves my hair out of my face, studies my features intently. 'I should get on. These people aren't going to get better on their own.'

'Can I bring you a coffee or something?' I say, getting off him.

'No, I'm fine, thank you.' He squeezes my hand before walking away. 'And thank you for apologising. It makes me really happy.'

I grin at him and watch as he disappears into the hallway. My smile fades quickly. I hate the feeling that he may have been harbouring resentments against me. After everything he's done for me. *You're not good enough for him.* The thought chokes me. I need to be better. I slip up. I do stupid things. There is no way I can hold this together and be the wife and mother they deserve.

One of the great things about Paul is he helps me see things as they truly are. Take my friends, for example. He said they'd act a certain way about us and look – they did. I wonder what he'd do if he knew I was in contact with Claudia again. He'd be upset, and I suppose he'd have a right to be. They tried their best to tear us apart – even threatened to go to the police. But I stood firm, and luckily, they didn't take it that far.

Paul has put everything on the line for me. His job, his family. Everything that matters. I bite my lip. What if he decides he's made a massive mistake?

The beginning of our relationship was intense. It felt like the only thing I could believe in. I was petrified when I woke to my new reality. All alone with only transient people in white uniforms to reassure me. The paralysing pain shooting through my head and the throbbing agony down my legs. Events, past and present, felt like an assembly line of objects in a memory game. I'd stare and stare, repeating them over and over, hoping they'd stick. Even back then, I was hiding how bad it was. Slowly I recovered, the machinery keeping me alive dwindling as I progressed.

I don't remember much about the high dependency ward; my brain was still patchy at forming new memories. But everything began to clear up when I met Paul. Aside from the doctors, Paul was there to monitor my well-being and counsel me through the difficult transition. The memory of our first meeting is still so vivid. Under his NHS lanyard he wore his trademark shirt with his sleeves rolled up and thin tie. My pointing finger slowly raised to where his pen had leaked, leaving the bottom of his pocket coated in black ink. He'd followed my gaze to see what I'd found so amusing and jumped up in such a comical way that I'd laughed. The shock of the vibrant sound rushed through the stale air.

Throughout that period, I'd tried my best to dress for the job I wanted – which, at the time, was to be me. I'd rolled my eyes and made jokes with the nurses, and they all told me I'd be on the stand-up circuit in no time. My humour was coating my very real fear that I was going to be stuck there forever. I was drowning in fear. When they moved me down to the assisted care facility, I thought I was destined to be forgotten about. But Paul arranged to continue seeing me. And cracks of light began to pour in. The nurses at the unit would all coo over him when he arrived. 'Oh, Mr Bloom is here to see you, Lauren,' they would say with a blush. And I'd rush to the mirror to check my face.

I walk over to the sheet of glass facing the garden and place my forehead on it. How will I fill my days here? They are starting to feel as empty as those I left behind. I think about my prospects. I used to be a freelance graphic designer. At the hospital my old laptop was delivered to me, and I looked through and played with the software but just couldn't get my head around it. Quickly the bright lights of the screen made my head ache and I shut it scornfully.

'Well?' Paul asked the next day, feeling pleased he'd helped locate it. I'd swallowed and shrugged.

'Looks like I've missed a few deadlines,' I said dryly, and

he laughed. I was too embarrassed to tell him there was yet another thing to add to the list of my incapabilities. I desperately wanted to be someone he deserved.

Here, now, I feel swallowed up by the isolation. This new life isn't the one I'd imagined at all. Maybe I'm being ungrateful. I think back to the decision to move. Paul was full of it after the viewing. He manically listed the positives: the school, the incredible grounds, the space – the space!

'It's amazing, Paul,' I agreed.

'I feel a "but" coming on,' he laughed, prodding me playfully.

'I just think . . . are we rushing this? It is such a big step; we haven't been together that long.'

He'd winced at that, and turned away, bruised. My regret was instant. My words rushed out trying to fix it. 'I'm just scared we're stretching ourselves too thin too early. When everything is so perfect.' I stumbled towards him, my hands against my chest. But his contorted face didn't soften. In fact, it became harder.

'Are you telling me I've risked my livelihood, and my children's well-being, and you aren't even sure you want to be with me?' he asked, sounding incredulous.

'Paul – that's not what I meant. I'm sure about us. About everything, I swear . . .' The words came out with a horrible pleading quality.

'I can't deal with this right now.' He stormed off, slamming the door. Leaving me standing there, full of remorse.

Finally, when we spoke again, he apologised. He told me he was scared that I was going to leave him . . . just like Emma did. I'd only been thinking about myself, but it wasn't all about me. I realised I had two choices: move or lose him.

Of course, I chose him. Of course, I chose Margo and Jesse.

Later, hearing the key in the front door, I sit up on the sofa. Paul cajoles the kids softly, their little feet pattering on the concrete. Usually, there is a litter of moans and chatter when they return – but they are shrouded in silence, and I wonder if there was a telling-off in the car. I swing my legs to the floor and stand. Jesse and Margo poke their heads into the living room. I smile but they give me strange guilty looks before turning and running back towards their bedrooms.

'Hi,' I say as he walks into the kitchen.

But he ignores me, and bangs around noisily, putting a few dirty mugs I'd left on the side, pulling out the bin and tying it up. His movements are erratic and rushed.

'Are they okay?' I ask, stepping forward, feeling a wash of unease.

He shakes his head. His eyes reach for the ceiling before landing back on me. The scorn there rushes at me, and part of me withers. Stomach churning, I wonder, *What have I done?*

'Lauren, what happened on the way to school?'

'What?' I ask, breathless.

'Margo said you nearly crashed the car!' he whispers furiously.

I shake my head, realising the mistake. 'No . . . I think she is a little confused.'

I walk towards him, but he brushes past me, holding the

bin bag and marching to the front door. I wait a few ghastly moments for him to return. He pulls the door shut with a swift slam. The fabric of his shirt damp on his shoulders from the rain.

'Paul, listen.' I go to him, but he brushes me off. 'We just stopped for a moment. I needed some water.' I laugh at the absurdity of it. 'I was joking because there was this truck and it was right up behind us.' I gesticulate as I try to explain. 'There was never a moment we could have crashed.' Heat builds as I feel the weight of the truck behind me, pushing me on faster and faster as the rain bashed down upon us. Paul runs a cloth under the tap and begins to wipe down the kitchen surface.

'Hey – I'll do that . . .' I say, trying to take it from him.

He throws the cloth down on the stainless-steel surface with a splat. 'Lauren. I just don't know if I can trust you driving the kids.'

'What?' I whisper.

'I know you've been having headaches and not telling me. I know you're painted over cracks in your recovery. You're putting my kids in danger, Lauren, can't you see that?' He looks at me tearfully. And I feel paralysed. Unable to stand up for myself.

'I'm fine!' I cry. I am, aren't I? I think of the strange patches of memory loss and the dull shooting pain inside my head.

'Don't you think I've lost enough already?' His eyes plead and I feel terrible.

'Oh God, Paul . . .' I try to hug him, but he backs away.

Sniffing, he leaves the room, calling, 'I don't want to hear it right now. Let's talk later.' As he storms away.

Then Jesse and Margo appear from behind the partition wall holding hands. 'I tried telling Daddy, but he got all cross . . .' Jesse whispers.

'Hey, hey. It's fine, guys. Just a misunderstanding.' I open my arms and they come to me for a hug. Holding them tightly, I realise Jesse is shaking.

My eyes blink open. I cannot see a thing. It must be the dead of the night. Paul came to bed separately, and turning, I feel the duvet rise and fall on his side of the bed. After a while I decide to get up. Holding my arms in front of me so I don't bang into the wall, I find the door, and step out of the room.

The house is drenched in moonlight and as my eyes adjust, I make out the hard lines of walls. My reflection mimics me against the black glass, and I have to remind myself there is nothing to be scared of. Horror stories aren't real. My bare feet press down on the cold concrete of the hallway, and then the thick pile carpet in the living room. I pull my long T-shirt down as I reach up to the kitchen cupboard for a glass. The sound of it being placed on the counter pings up into the high ceiling. Glugging some milk, I peel a banana and take a bite, before turning around.

I freeze. Jesse wandered in while my back was turned. I step forward and utter his name, 'Jesse,' but notice his glazed look. I watch his journey through the space to the back doors. Putting down the banana, I move towards him. His little hand reaches up above his head and clasps the handle. It makes a squeaking noise as he turns it up and down. *Squeak-squeak, squeak-squeak.* I shudder.

I get closer. *Squeak-squeak, squeak-squeak.* Gently laying my hands on his shoulders, I say his name again. 'Jesse, love.' But he continues. I kneel to his level and put my hand over his and try to carefully peel it off the handle. He resists; his fingers are firmly wrapped around it. 'Come on, Jesse, let's go back to bed,' I whisper, but he only pulls on the handle ever more frantically.

'I need to get her.' His voice sounds different: coarse and heavy. Layered with emotion.

'Jesse,' I repeat softly.

'She's out there,' his voice grates, and I look into the darkness.

'Jesse,' I say again with more authority, trying to calmly wake him. I pull him to me, and he growls as his hand loses contact with the door.

'That is not my name,' he spits. The power of his voice knocks me back.

My jaw clenches. He must be having a bad dream. 'Jesse, come on. Let's go back to your room. I'll wrap you up in your nice cosy bed.'

'I need to get her. I need to get her.' He rushes to the handle again before I can stop him, his balled-up fist banging on the glass. The handle twisting furiously as he becomes more distressed.

'Jesse.' I shake his shoulder. 'Jesse?'

Then he turns and looks at me, suddenly spark awake. 'I'm not Jesse. I'm not Jesse, I'm not Jesse,' he repeats, falling into my arms, crying, banging my chest. I hug him as tightly as I can.

'Who are you then?' I surprise myself with the question.

He sobs a little more, and then sniffs. 'I can't remember. I can't remember my name.'

'It's okay. It's okay.' I get up off the floor, lifting him with me. Once inside his bedroom I gently lay him down, and pull the covers up to his chin.

'Can you stay with me a bit?' he asks. And I nod and slip inside with him. His arms go around me.

'It's okay,' I whisper. 'We'll work it out. Don't worry, I'm here.'

The next morning, after I get out the shower, I sit on our bed. The ferocity behind Jesse's admission has shocked me. Something isn't right. I think of mentioning grief counselling to Paul, but he was so against it last time that I don't feel confident bringing it up again. Especially with how things are with us. The last few weeks I have begun to monitor myself around him in a way I've not done before. Running things over a few times, worried he might take something I've said the wrong way.

It seems so obvious to me that Jesse is suffering from trauma. I can't believe Paul, the big hotshot psychotherapist, can't see that. Maybe he's built a wall so he doesn't have to witness his own child's pain. I google *trauma in children* and see that art therapy is a good way of communicating what's wrong to adults. Both Jesse and Margo love to draw. Maybe this could be a good outlet for whatever he is harbouring.

Once ready, I go downstairs. I hear Paul helping them get dressed as I walk through the hallway. I pull out some paper and the Tupperware box of colouring pens and place them on the dining table. A few minutes later Paul enters the room holding Margo. Jesse trails behind looking tired and subdued. Paul puts Margo in her booster seat at the table, and pulls the paper and pens towards her. 'Want to do some colouring?' he asks.

'I do,' Jesse says, clambering into the chair next to his sister.

'Ah, great, coffee.' Paul joins me in the kitchen and kisses my cheek. I'm relieved he wants to be near me again.

I go to the children, hunched over their white sheets of paper. Paul is resting against the kitchen counter, scrolling on his phone sipping coffee. I lean over Jesse. 'Why don't you draw something about your dream? When you were the other little boy?' I whisper. Jesse nods, his hand hovering over the colours before selecting a bright pink pen. His hand shakes as he connects pen to paper, frightened by the prospect for a moment.

Paul walks towards the front door. 'I'm going to go out to get the papers. Want anything?' I shake my head, enjoying the look of concentration on Jesse's face. His tongue sticks out one side of his mouth as he scrawls. I rub the boy's back and follow Paul.

'Paul, Jesse was sleepwalking last night.'

He doesn't look surprised. 'Right. He does that sometimes.' He bends down and slips his trainers on.

'Oh.' He's never mentioned it before, and he certainly hasn't since I've lived with them. As if reading my mind, he adds, 'He used to a lot. After . . .' His eyes leave mine. 'After Emma.' Paul rubs his beard and sniffs. 'I'm sure it's nothing.' I open my mouth to tell him what Jesse said. But Paul looks crushed by the memory of his late wife and I close it again. He pecks my lips sadly and I watch as he gets in the car. I wave as he drives off.

Turning into the house, I close the door and join the children around the table. Sitting next to Jesse, I ask, 'Can I see?' He nods and I turn the paper towards me.

To my disappointment he's drawn this house. The angular lines come down like bars on a prison cell. To one side are the flourishing flowers on the pink bushes in the garden. I pick it up and smile, and try not to show my disappointment. 'This is this house,' I say, and he nods. 'I was here. With my other mummy.'

'With Emma?'

Then he whispers, 'Please don't tell Daddy.'

'Why?' I ask, putting my arm around him.

'He'll get cross.' His voice wobbles.

Wanting to pacify him, I say, 'Don't worry. I won't tell Daddy.' I watch as he continues his task, wondering where this has come from.

CHAPTER 13

A few days later I'm staring out the window in a daze. The rain has left behind impenetrable grey clouds which hold down a lingering heat I feel trapped beneath. It is nearly July; the children haven't even broken up from school. I spin on the kitchen stool to face Paul as he dusts his shoes on the mat and enters the living room. My coffee mug is cupped in both my hands.

'Jesse seemed fine at drop-off this morning,' he says as he approaches. 'He ran in. I told you it was just a matter of time.'

He takes the cup out of my hands and kisses the side of my mouth in the softest, most delicate way which makes my heart flutter.

'That's great,' I murmur.

He holds me for a moment and adds, 'It's okay, Lauren. You're still learning. I can't expect you to wake up overnight with the tools to be a good parent.' The little morsel of pleasure I felt disappears. And the comment confirms all my fears. He thinks I'm a terrible substitute.

His phone beeps and he steps away to bring it out of his

back pocket. I see the name *Amanda* flash on the screen. I've heard the name a few times. He's been spending a lot of extra time with this patient. My interest is piqued. He used to spend a lot of extra time with me.

Paul would bring things to the hospital for me. Treats – flowers, nice hand creams and special food. When someone knocked on my door, I'd get a rush of pleasure at the expectation it might be him. Soon he was all I could think about. An obsession. Possibly, yes. He became tactile, a touch here, a touch there. My eyes would follow these tiny micro-movements compulsively and all my senses heightened when he walked into the room.

When he held my hand, it was like a thousand fireworks going off. I'd think about him all the time. Imagining how it would feel if he kissed me, if he touched me. Paul became my favourite preoccupation. I loved how I could simply close my eyes and no longer be in my terrible predicament. Instead in a world that was only inhabited by him and me. I was embarrassed by how childish my crush was. But I couldn't help it.

And then one day he leant forward and pressed his lips onto mine. I cannot put into words how electric that was. All those hours of anticipation culminating in that one perfect kiss. I kissed him back, pressing my tongue into his hot mouth and grabbing his face before he could push me off.

Which he did. As he apologised profusely, begging me to forgive him. Asking me to promise not to tell anyone as he walked backwards towards the door, knocking over a chair in the process.

I was left sitting there ashamed. I asked the next nurse who came in when he was coming back, and she shrugged. 'Your guess is as good as mine, love,' she said. I decided no good could come of it anyway. I asked for more drugs – because everything hurt again. The pink cloud that had been getting me through was now out of reach. And I spent days staring at the wall.

I was moved to the unit, and I thought that was that. I'd resigned myself to never seeing him again. But then, a few weeks later, he turned up unannounced. I almost couldn't believe it when he walked through the door accompanied by a little girl. He was deeply sincere as he apologised and explained he'd had to take a bit of annual leave because of childcare issues. My eyes drifted over to her clutching a grey cat; she was wearing a pink dress with little flowers embroidered on the hem. 'We were in the area, I thought you might like to say hello.'

'Hello, Lauren,' Margo lisped coyly.

'This is my daughter, Margo.' I was struck by her. Utterly struck. And the sight of Paul standing with this gorgeous little girl made me fall even further down the rabbit hole. 'Her brother is at school.'

The next time he came to see me he held my hand and told me he was in love with me. And that as I was no longer under his care, he'd like to continue seeing me, if that was what I wanted. I couldn't have ever been happier.

Thinking of Amanda, it occurs to me that most of his private patients are women. I don't think I've ever heard him on the phone to a man. 'Is she okay?' I ask tentatively.

'Who?'

'That woman. Your patient.'

He sighs. 'Not really. She's at a crisis point. I'm trying to get her to the other side.' He flips his tie out of the way over his shoulder as he butters his toast.

'Are you worried about her?' I ask, trying to eke out more information.

The lines around his eyes crease, and he looks across at me. 'Of course. It's my job to make her better.'

'Like it was your job to make me better,' I murmur, trying to make it sound light but failing terribly. I regret the comment immediately.

He looks up, surprised. 'What did you mean by that?'

I shake my head. 'Nothing. Sorry.'

He places the knife down carefully. 'No – say what you mean, Lauren.' He approaches me calmly and places each hand on a shoulder. I feel cornered. 'We can't just let that go, can we?' he says, and I swallow.

My eyebrows pinch together. 'It's just that we met through your work. And . . . I mean . . . I've never asked you. Is that something that's ever, you know, happened before?' My voice loses its power as I trail off.

He shakes his head. 'I can't believe you're asking me that.' Oh God, I shouldn't have said that – how rude, how ungrateful, after everything he's done for me . . . 'After everything I've done for you!' he exclaims.

'I'm tired and emotional and I should never have asked,' I say, quickly thinking of excuses for my behaviour.

'Of course I haven't,' he implores, kindness flavouring his tone. The hands on my arms begin to stroke and my body slackens. 'We have something more special than anyone else could ever appreciate or understand, don't we?' His eyes bore into mine in such a punishingly intense way that I avert my gaze. 'Look, I know you've been lonely. How about we spend some proper time together soon? Really hang out, like we used to. Not just a quick drink before bed and the chaos around the kids.'

I nod, staring at the floor. 'Yes. I'd love that.'

He uses his finger to raise my chin, so our eyes are forced to lock. 'Lauren, how we met – that's what makes us so special. I know everything about you. Every thought process, every insecurity. You still aren't one hundred per cent and I get that. It is going to take time. I'm patient, Lauren, I can wait. I love you anyway.'

I feel drained. My head begins to pump. I feel breathless too. 'I'm sorry,' I muster. 'I don't want you to ever think I'm not grateful for everything you've done for me.'

He looks pleased by that. 'I'm lucky too, Lauren. You're a great girl with some amazing attributes. And I know after everything you've been through there's going to be residue. You know, your controlling tendencies – born out of fear and anxiety – I've tried to unravel the source of it for you, and help develop healthier coping strategies but . . . it's harder for some. I understand you can't help it because I understand you in a way no one else ever could.'

'Controlling?' I whisper. I've never really thought of myself in that way.

'And all this lying about your health – and trying to be perfect. And the kids – how you're so desperate for them to love you it overrides everything else.'

My cheeks flare up and I feel seen in the worst possible way. 'I . . . I didn't mean to take over. I just want them to be happy,' I stammer, wondering if it's true.

'It's okay, Lauren, I get it, it's okay.' He pulls me in for a claustrophobic hug and I stop myself from wriggling away. Then he releases me suddenly. 'I should call Amanda back.' And I am left standing alone feeling as though someone has chipped away at me. Wondering if he thinks he's made a terrible misjudgement bringing me here, while also wondering the parallel – am I the one who's made the terrible mistake?

Paul is gentle for the rest of the day. Whenever we cross paths he squeezes my hand, and kisses my forehead. He brings me cups of tea and rubs my back sympathetically. He is a big believer in 'processing', as he calls it. Feeling the feelings. Owning pain to get to the other side of it. *You need to feel the feelings, Lauren. Life isn't meant to be happy all the time. Stop chasing something that doesn't exist.* All I am is lost and scared, but I don't want to admit it.

I don't know which parts of me are okay to voice, and what is better to hold on to tightly. Air muffles as I stand in the empty cavity of the living room staring through the ceiling at the tumultuous sky. I want to be cocooned within a smaller space. I want to be amongst clutter and warmth. In the end I take myself upstairs and lock myself in the bathroom, one of the only spaces with thick opaque walls. My hand shakes as I attempt a call to Claudia. It rings and rings, but then connects to her voicemail. I hang up, disappointed. She's probably at work. She's a really busy person, unlike me. I sniff as I peel off a piece of toilet paper to wipe my nose, biting my lip in an attempt not to break into a full-on sob. To my relief my phone vibrates in my hand. She's calling me back! Her voice is rushed. 'Loz, I'm at work, can't speak. I'll message you,' she whispers furiously and then hangs up.

Loz!!

Claudia!

Sorry, nightmare boss on the warpath. How are things?

I try not to read too much into it, but I can't help but think she doesn't want to speak directly, so that she can be measured in her responses. I type a long paragraph about how I'm really feeling: unsettled. Out of place. Homesick for somewhere I fit in and where I don't have to apologise constantly.

Then I delete it all. And send:

Great ☺ Miss you.

I was thinking about you yesterday. I wonder how she's getting on in the sticks. It's so rare these days for someone to just vanish off the face of the planet.

I've only moved a few hours away.

Usually there are Facebook updates and a million Instagram stories about how wonderful someone's new life is. But not with our Lauren . . . Lauren runs off to the countryside and we don't hear a whimper.

You know I find all those sites soul destroying.

I think of how Paul hates anything like that. He's never even had a Facebook page! He encouraged me to let him delete mine; he doesn't like the idea of social media being around the kids and wants us to set an example. I don't really care, I never got my head back into it. Besides, I don't really like looking at my phone for long, my head begins to spiral and it's just not worth it.

Is it amazing?

The house?

Well, yes! I mean, it sounds epic. When can I pop over for the day? I need to get out of this city – it's driving me mad. I'd love a trip to the countryside. We can do a pub lunch and a long walk. Is it near the sea?

I'll suggest it to Paul, I reply, already worrying about how he'd react. I'm not sure he'd allow it. He took a real dislike to that whole friendship group after what happened.

Are you okay?

Do you think I'm controlling? I type and send quickly. Before I change my mind.

There is a long pause. I see her typing and then stopping and then typing some more.

Loz . . . none of us are perfect, are we? . . . I'm a massive tart who falls for bad boys. Don't beat yourself up. She hasn't refuted it. The wretched feeling within knuckles down.

I've been thinking that maybe I've made a mistake. My hands shake as I type the message. *I feel quite lonely out here*, I admit. It feels good to say it to another person.

I can see she is typing something, and my face heats up as I wait for the response.

Then I hear someone on the stairs. *Creak, creak, creak.* My eyes dart to the doorknob. *I'll try to call you later, Claudia.*

Okay babe. I'm sure whatever it is you'll sort it out. You really do love him remember! Love you xxxx

'Lauren?' Paul calls through the door, knocking. 'Are you okay?'

'I won't be a minute!' I call back, quickly deleting the thread of messages. I'm not sure why.

'The food delivery is here. I've been shouting for you. I've got a meeting.'

'Coming. Sorry!' I shout as I dash my phone into my pocket.

CHAPTER 14

A few dragged-out days pass. Napping has become my favourite pastime. Waves of lethargy cover me, and I find myself in various spots around the house, huddled in a ball allowing sheaths of slumber to encase me. On our bed, I turn after a particularly deep doze. As if far off in the distance, I hear someone call my name. It takes every ounce of willpower to leave the warmth and I pull off the blanket topper to take with me.

I sway on the spot, testing my legs. I remember the first time I walked to the bathroom on my own in hospital. They caved beneath me, and I fell to the floor, hurting my arm quite badly. I still don't quite trust my body. I'm aware it could turn on me at any moment. Light-headed, I stumble back and sit on the edge of the mattress and cough.

Why am I deteriorating again? My confidence seems to be ailing. That lightness of touch I had, where's it gone? I need it desperately. It holds within it my confidence to be here fully. I feel myself retreating into a dark place.

Hearing my name again, I force myself to take tentative

steps out of the room. My hand leaves a streak on the glass wall as I make my way down the stairs and into the hallway.

Paul is in the kitchen. He looks up. 'Hey,' he says, before continuing to chop something with his favourite extra sharp Japanese knife. 'I've been calling you.' I pull the blanket around my shoulders and hug myself as I wander across to the kitchen island. He walks over, and plants a kiss forcefully on my lips, holding on to my wrist at the same time. He lets me go and I stagger back, before hiking myself up onto a stool.

I watch, mesmerised, as Paul expertly slices through various pieces of fruit and vegetables. The motion so rhymical my lids weigh down as I stare. Then he loads the food processor, grabbing the piles with both hands and decanting them into the vessel. He flicks the switch and the loud whirring noise fills the space, sparking me back to life again.

I watch the sludgy dark green liquid as it slops into a glass. Revolting bubbles pop as air escapes from the thick goop. He takes a sip and turns to me, asking, 'Want some?' I shake my head. He takes another glass off the shelf and pours and pushes it towards me. 'Go on. You'll love it once you try it,' he says, looking pleased with himself. I take a deep breath before I let any of it enter my mouth. Just as I'd imagined, the taste is putrid, and I cough.

'You should start looking after yourself a bit more,' he says, watching me. 'Your head is playing up, and you're sleeping a lot during the day again.' I nod. His disappointment is clear, I'm letting him down. 'You're getting through the paracetamol.' I think of the empty pill packets in the cupboard above the sink. 'And all this junk food and buckets of wine every evening needs to stop.'

'Buckets of wine . . . ?' I repeat, I think of the one glass once the kids go to bed. 'I don't drink that much.'

'It all adds up, Lauren. You know Emma was a nutritionist?' My jaw clenches. Yes, I did know that. He tells me often enough. Mainly just as I'm putting some fish fingers in the oven for her kids. I picture her staring down, wailing at the second-rate life they now lead with her gone. 'I picked up a lot,' he says. 'How about I do a bit more cooking so we really start packing in the nutrients? It will be good for all of us, not just you.'

'I think my diet is quite good,' I stammer.

He looks at me intently. 'Let me do this for you. Take one thing off your plate – as it were?' He laughs at the accidental pun, and then adds more seriously, 'If you really want your recovery to have longevity, this needs to be a priority. I'm here to help you. Remember?'

'Okay,' I stammer. His eyes are full of concern, and I wonder how obvious it is that I'm struggling.

'Great. I enjoy cooking far more than you anyway.'

I nod. He's right. Although I try my best, I'm not great at it like him. I feel bruised that the task has been taken from me. Has he been pretending to enjoy my food while wondering how he can get me to stop? The thought makes me feel anxious. Maybe there are a multitude of things he's realised that I've been underperforming in.

'I'll go grab the kids,' he says, checking his pockets for keys.

'I'll get them?' I ask, straightening up. I can't remember the last time I left the house. It must be over a week at least. Paul has driven them to and from school ever since the incident with the truck. It's happened so organically, it's only now I realise this, too, has been removed from my responsibilities.

He taps the key on the counter, thinking, and then says, 'I'm a bit nervous of you driving with the kids.' There. He admitted it. I was right. He doesn't trust me with them any more.

I stand up and the blanket falls from my shoulders. 'Nothing happened, I told you . . .'

He looks at me, pondering the thought. 'Well, all right then. I suppose I can't stop you driving forever, can I?' He laughs.

Although it's clear that would be his preferred option.

I triple-check mirrors, my speed is carefully moderated not to be too fast or slow, and my hands are positioned perfectly at ten and two. Arriving at school, I sit in the car, and I look out at the small groups of gathered parents near the gates chatting away animatedly to one another. I bite my thumb as I finally pluck up the courage to join them and stand on the outskirts, alone, looking for someone I recognise. It is as if the knit of the community is tightening around me, forcing me out. Suddenly a waving hand. I blink and see Isobel making her way towards me. I move a strand of hair behind my ear self-consciously.

'Lauren – how are you? I haven't seen you for a while.' She smiles warmly.

'Oh, yes . . . I've not been that well,' I explain, and she

looks at me sympathetically. Her mouth opens to ask, but then closes again quickly. Probably worried the question is too personal for a mere acquaintance. I can tell she wants to be my friend. I am desperate to be hers too. But don't want to seem too keen.

'Is that your husband, the interesting-looking one with the beard I keep seeing dropping the kids off?' she asks.

I smile, pleased. 'Paul. Yes. I can't get him to shave it off.' Then I hand her the first admission. 'He's actually my boyfriend – we're not married.'

'Oh,' Isobel says, surprised. I can see she is wondering about the kids.

'He's a widower – the children are his.'

Isobel nods quickly. 'Right. How sad – the poor children. At least they have you now.' She stands there awkwardly for a moment, before remembering something and digging in her handbag. She pulls out a stack of small square envelopes. She hands me one with Margo's name scrawled on the front. 'Saskia is turning four. We're just having a little party in the back garden. It would be lovely if you could make it. Do bring Jesse too, siblings are welcome.' I open the card to find a tasteful drawing of a bunch of balloons tied and then the date, time and their address.

'We'd love to come,' I say quickly. Hopefully not too quickly.

'Great! Saskia will be so pleased; she talks about Margo all the time. Are you going to The Meadows now? I'm desperate for a coffee – I don't usually in the afternoon, but Joe was snoring all night and I didn't get a wink of sleep.'

The bell rings and children begin to wander out the main entrance. I smile, noticing Margo chatting to Saskia. How nice for her to have a friend. I nod. 'Sure, we can stop for a quick one.'

Margo sees me and waves, running ahead to greet me. I crouch to catch her hug. Jesse comes out next. He is on his own and looks withdrawn. I wave him over to us. 'Fancy a quick trip to see Rocky?' He looks up, excited by the prospect. 'We'll meet you over there,' I call to Isobel, who does a quick thumbs up sign from her position negotiating with Saskia to wear her sunhat.

Just that short conversation with Isobel has filled me up, and I feel more myself. It makes me realise how much I need other people in my life to feel energised. Sitting in that house day after day only pulls me apart and squashes me down.

A quick drive later we're in The Meadows car park. I help them out and they hold hands rushing towards the entrance. 'Wait, wait for me!' I call, locking the car.

I feel a flutter of excitement and nerves, a bit like a first date. A new friend! Someone to talk to! The same man behind the counter waves. 'You again,' he says with a smile. I order two juices and a coffee.

Isobel is already there with Saskia and I point at the counter, but she shakes her head and gestures at her drink. 'All sorted.' Margo joins her friend by the giant dolls' house and Jesse take a position next to Rocky who is lounging back on a bean bag.

Once the drinks are ready I take the seat next to Isobel.

'Margo is such a friendly little girl,' she remarks, watching them play.

'Oh, she's easy.' I glance at Jesse, and say quietly, 'Jesse is trickier to convince.'

Isobel shrugs. 'They're all their own people, aren't they? I often wonder if my input makes any difference at all.' She smiles, watching Jesse as he strokes the cat. 'He seems like a lovely boy too.'

'He . . . has his moments.'

'So, how long have you been with Paul?'

I bite my lip at the question, embarrassed to answer. 'Well, we've known each other for a year. We've been living together for about seven months.'

Isobel's eyebrows raise. 'Wow.' She shrugs. 'When you know, you know,' she says supportively. 'What happened to their mother? Sorry – do you mind talking about this?'

'It's fine, honestly,' I say, shaking my head. I don't usually get a chance. 'She died when they were very small, cancer – it was fast. I think she was gone in a matter of months. Jesse was only two.'

Isobel's forehead creases. 'Oh, that's terribly sad.'

Her eyes linger on the children. And I continue: 'Margo doesn't remember. She was just one.'

'She didn't have much of a break between them, did she?' Isobel comments. I shake my head. I often wonder how Emma did it. She must have been pregnant four months after giving birth to Jesse. 'Irish twins,' Isobel says, nodding to herself. I look at her questioningly, and she pulls a face. 'I don't think that's a very PC thing to say, my mum used to say it.' I shake my head in ignorance. 'It means you have them within a year. Pretty wild.'

'She probably took it in her stride,' I say, thinking of how easy Emma found motherhood.

Isobel laughs. 'Do I note a little competition from beyond the grave?'

I bite my lip and lean in. 'It's awful, isn't it? I'm just getting to grips with motherhood, and all I do is compare myself to her.' I sigh.

She pats my hand. 'Well, if it helps at all, you're doing a great job. As long as they're fed and clothed, the rest is just extra.' Isobel smiles and I look down, grateful for her kindness. 'How have they coped, do you think?'

I take a breath before launching into it. 'Jesse gets muddled. It's harder for him as he was older. I suppose in a lot of ways complete ignorance is easier.' I watch him with the cat, muttering to himself as he strokes him.

'I can't even imagine. And Paul, what does he do?'

'He's a psychotherapist, so he's able to do most of his work from home these days.'

'Oh yes, at the glass house,' she says grandly. 'I didn't meet the last people. But it was more than a few years ago now. Did you say they are friends? All the gossip is probably BS and I try not to get involved with it. The small-town mentality is insidious, though . . .' she jokes with a wicked smile. I wonder how much Isobel really knows because she seems to be off about certain details. They left for the States only six months ago.

I hear a sob and we're distracted. We turn to see the florist comforted by the man who works in the café. He's patting her back and talking to her gently, as she holds a tissue in her shaking hand.

'That's Susie,' Isobel explains in a whisper.

'I met her the other day . . .' I say, trailing off.

'She's a bit odd,' Isobel replies, noting the tone of my voice. 'Ever since they closed the riding school, and everything . . . she's not been herself. Have you seen it? It must be very close to your house?'

I nod, thinking of the discarded equipment and the cold-looking cottage.

Isobel leans in. 'She had a bit of an altercation with the people who own your house. They accused George, her nephew, of something to do with their son,' she whispers, eyebrows raised.

I gasp. I'd been wondering what Susie had alluded to the other day. I'm surprised Paul hasn't mentioned it. Maybe he doesn't know. 'Really?'

Isobel nods. 'They had to close the riding school as it was mostly little kids. The mums didn't want them going any more.'

'Why?'

Isobel looks over to the children playing, and nods suggestively.

Then I realise something. 'But Jack and Gloria . . . they had a little girl,' I say, almost to myself. I am slightly horrified something may have happened – what if the real reason they left was far darker than relocating for a job?

Isobel turns to me. 'Is that what they were called?' Her forehead creases, thinking. 'I don't remember. But as I said, it was a while ago.'

'Less than a year,' I say with a little laugh, thinking it's not that long.

Isobel looks at me, amused. 'No, it must be more like two years now – maybe even three!' Shrugging, she adds, 'Maybe it was the people before? I mean, I never met them, and it's not like they made any effort to get involved with the community,' Isobel says, slightly offended. Then she lowers her tone back down. 'I feel for Susie, I really do. It's sad how it all turned out, and she relied on George so much. She's in bits now, barely holding it together,' she whispers. I glance over at Susie who has composed herself and is clearing away her things. 'She should probably call it quits and have a fresh start somewhere new so everyone can forget all about it and move on.' Susie looks over to us briefly, as if she's aware that we're talking about her. And our eyes quickly dart down to our drinks on the table.

Time has got away from me and the next time I get my phone out my bag I have fifteen missed calls from Paul. 'Fuck,' I whisper, and after texting him that we're on our way, I say goodbye to Isobel and rush to get the kids in the car.

Setting off, I feel anxious. I should have messaged first. I should have let him know the plan. Sweat creeps up my body as I race back to the house. My shoulders hunch up around my ears. Once parked, I stop, and my eyes drag over the cold frontage, the dark grey clouds mirrored in the glass. 'Come on, we should get inside for Daddy,' I whisper, undoing my belt.

'Are you scared?' Jesse asks from the back seat.

'Scared?' A tiny laugh escapes. 'Why would I be scared?'

'Mummy was scared of him,' he says.

'Scared of your daddy?' I turn quickly, teasing. 'Who could be scared of him?' But Jesse doesn't joke back. He just raises his chin slightly. He then undoes his belt and jumps out the car. As he approaches the porch Paul opens the door. He must have heard us coming.

'Hello, gang. I thought something terrible had happened.'

I smile up at him, but his lips stay settled in their place.

'Come on, you two,' he says and Jesse and Margo troop under his arm and inside the house.

'It was a last-minute stop at the café. Another mum invited us, and Jesse wanted to go see the cat. We only had a quick drink,' I whisper nervously to him.

'Sounds fun!' he says, stroking my shoulder. 'Relax, you seem full of tension. As if you've done something wrong.' He turns and walks into the house, and I follow, closing the door behind me. And for the first time I feel completely trapped.

CHAPTER 15

I wake in the night to the sound of soft crying. I lean over and fumble for the switch on my lamp. Turning it on, Paul's weight shifts next to me and I look ahead to see Jesse's small, silhouetted body hovering at the frame of our door. His hand is up near his mouth and his shoulders shake with silent tears. I slip out and walk to him, crouching down. 'Jesse, what is it, darling? What is it?' I whisper. He shakes his head, refusing to talk, and yanks at my hand, pulling me away. His eyes are fixed on the mound of his father.

We creep down the stairs, and he pulls me into his bedroom. Flicking the light, I join him standing over his bed. There, within the creased white sheet, is a damp patch. 'I had a bad dream,' he whispers fearfully.

'It's okay, Jesse. It's okay.' I give him a hug, allowing him a small cry. 'I'll tidy it all up in no time.' I strip off the offending sheets and take the spare from the drawer beneath and quickly remake it. He stands behind me, watching. 'See? All okay now. Nothing to worry about. Accidents happen,' I explain with an easy shrug. I pull back the covers and he scurries inside.

I sit there stroking his forehead until his fingers, which are fastened around the top of his duvet, go limp.

I find it difficult to get back to sleep, and then my head begins to pump with a sickly ache at about three a.m. Before I know it, birds are tweeting, and I'm left wondering if I managed any sleep at all.

'You okay?' Paul whispers, placing a hand on my arm.

'Terrible night,' I croak back.

'You rest,' he says gently, getting out of bed and going to the children. I stare into space. It is as if there is a layer of gauze between myself and reality. Everything is hazy, and it takes a while for my brain to catch up with my movements. Sounds have a tinny delayed quality. Finally, I force myself up and pull on an old fisherman's jumper. My favourite. Is it strange that I just knew when I slipped my thumb through the hole in the cuff that it was? There is a strange pang of nostalgia when I wear it. As if I'm closer to belonging.

I hear the scrape of the bi-folding doors below, and I turn to the window that faces the garden. Paul is holding a package under his arm and stalking through the grass. He checks behind him before crouching and entering the passageway. What's he doing?

Thinking of the children downstairs, alone, I slip on my shearling clogs and join them in the living room. They are lying together huddled between cushions on the sofa watching television. No wonder it's been so quiet. Margo barely lifts a smile when she sees me; Jesse is deeply in the zone. His pupils dart around as the action unfolds. I don't have the energy to tell them it's time to turn it off and deal with the chorus of moaning that will bring.

Coffee. I'll drink my weight in coffee – I've just got to get through the day and then I can collapse tonight. Entering the kitchen, I turn the kettle on. I close my eyes briefly as it boils and wonder if it's possible to sleep standing up.

'Jesse!' Paul's voice booms. My eyes spark open and I turn around. He's furious. I follow his gaze. There is blue pen scrawled all over the wall. Chaos in an otherwise linear space. There is something about it that pleases me. Jesse runs out of the room.

'Why were these left out?' Paul asks, picking up the box of coloured pens and rattling them at me.

'They weren't . . . they were just on the table,' I stutter.

'You should put these up here where they can't get to them,' he says, hotly, putting them on a shelf they can't reach. 'Honestly, you can't leave them alone for a second, okay?'

I turn to look at the stairs where I've just come from. And then to the open doors that Paul has just returned through. 'I've just come down . . .' I try to explain. 'You were with them.'

'Lauren, what are you talking about? You were with them.' An air of bemusement in his voice. He stands next to the wall and touches the pen mark. 'I wonder if there is some spare paint in the garage.' The weight of his disappointment curls around me. I feel dizzy and pull out a chair. He says my name. His face blurs into a round blob with a hole that calls my name over and over in an eerie prick of a voice.

*

I open my eyes and blink. He is slapping my face gently and calling my name, 'Lauren.' His face full of concern. 'Are you okay?' I nod and he helps me onto a chair.

'Water.' He grabs a glass and rushes to the tap. 'I'm going to make you an omelette.' My stomach growls and I realise I'm starving; I can't remember the last time I ate. It must be my head playing up again. 'I should have brought you up some toast earlier. You barely touched your dinner. Why haven't you eaten any breakfast? It's nearly eleven.'

I have no idea how to answer the question. I don't remember getting up this morning. It is as if my short-term memory has completely gone. 'I don't know . . .' I look up and around the room.

The blue squiggles on the wall have disappeared. 'Did you . . . did you paint the wall?'

'What?' he asks, looking at me with incredulity. Maybe I'd dreamt it. The doctor said that this would happen. That I would get things mixed up. 'What, Lauren? The wall? Yeah, a few days ago.' I don't say anything else. I don't want to worry Paul. It will involve more MRI scans, more trips to the hospital. I don't want to be the invalid any more. I want to be the mother – I want to be the one that looks after them.

Paul knocks an egg against the side of a ceramic bowl. The yolk and white slops down and, using a fork, he whisks them together. I gulp the cold water and stuff the bread he's placed in front of me into my mouth.

'What day is it?' I ask, between chews.

'Monday,' he says.

I could have sworn it was Friday. My phone is on the table, and I reach across and take it. The girls have all been chatting away on WhatsApp about the weekend gossip. But I feel so removed from them. I see Claudia has been talking about her birthday, and Audrey bitching about her boyfriend. And I feel so far away. So very far away.

CHAPTER 16

By Friday afternoon I'm determined to claw myself out of this hole. I refuse to go backwards after coming so far. The weather is brighter, and I take my bucket and basket out into the garden to methodically work. After half an hour, I begin to feel light-headed and decide to take a break. *See. Sensible Lauren.* I step up onto the patio and sit on one of the garden chairs. Inserting my earphones, I select one of Paul's meditation recordings. A while ago he downloaded a series of personally voiced visualisations onto my phone. Back at the flat I'd got into the habit of listening to them in the morning. But since I've felt better, my old self-care routines have gone lax. As Paul's gentle, rhythmical voice kicks in I settle back and close my eyes, taking a deep breath through my nose and out through my mouth.

Once done, I look out into the humming garden and realise I do feel a lot better. A parakeet bursts out of the canopy tweeting energetically. It dips down before landing on a branch that hangs out like a lingering hand. I watch as its calls, jumping up and down on the spot, its neck darting around, as if trying to warn me of a danger ahead. I stand and walk towards it – but it flits back into the woods.

Something grips me. An ancient sadness trapped within. Before I know it, I'm crying. My hands are raised to my mouth as I gulp, trying to force it back down. But it won't go – it needs to be released. Tears fall and I try to wipe my cheeks clean, but they just keep coming. *Stop! Why am I crying? I'm happy. I'm happy. This is all I ever wanted. This is what I longed for. A family of my own.*

Composing myself, I wipe my face with the bottom of my T-shirt.

My phone buzzes and I take it out of my pocket and wipe my blurry eyes. Isobel has messaged the nursery group: *Hi everyone, just a reminder about Saskia's birthday party tomorrow. She's very excited to see you all xXx*

A party. My first as a mother. This will make me feel better. More normal. Less . . . less lonely and desolate.

I hear the children, and I wave my hand in front of my hot face, checking my reflection in the phone camera. 'Loz!' Margo runs onto the patio and hugs me tightly. She notices the gardening tools discarded on the lawn and hops down to play with them.

Paul pauses at the doors, leaning against the wall. He must have noticed my red tear-stained cheeks because he presses his lips together and asks coolly, 'Everything okay?'

I nod quickly, and turn to Margo. 'We've got Saskia's party tomorrow, isn't that exciting?'

Her mouth opens in amazement and her eyes widen,

nodding. 'Party, party, party!' She stands and twirls around on the grass.

'What's this party?' Paul calls over to me.

'It's one of Margo's classmates. I thought we could go as a family? The mother, Isobel, is so friendly, we've hung out a few times at The Meadows. I'm sure you'd get on with her husband. I think she said his name was Joe . . .'

I notice Paul's jaw set and I stop. He looks down the lawn in thought. 'I was planning on a big roast. Won't they just binge on cake and chocolate?'

I shrug, exhausted by the thought I may need to fight for this. Despondent, I wipe my brow. Paul watches his daughter spinning on the lawn. 'You should take the kids. I'll catch up on some work, if that's okay?'

'If you'd prefer,' I reply softly. I was hoping I'd get a chance to show him off.

'Next time maybe we should discuss things before you get the children all excited.' He pauses. 'I just want you all to be safe.'

I nod slowly and stammer, 'I know. I know that, Paul.'

He walks inside and I'm left sitting on the patio alone watching his daughter dance.

The next day, just before we leave, I realise I haven't got Saskia a present. Margo is far too excited about choosing an outfit to notice me wrap a book that the children have barely touched. I feel like a terrible parent.

Jesse is determined not to go. He sits in a circle of plastic animal figurines ignoring us as we get ready. I think about leaving him here with Paul, but it will be good for him to get out. Once I mention cake, he sombrely agrees to put on his shoes. Paul stands at the front door watching us leave, his hands in his pockets, and I give a little wave, already agitated I may have upset him. For a moment I think of abandoning the adventure. Maybe we should stay and have the roast like Paul wants. Maybe that way he would be happier with me. But the pull towards Isobel's house is stronger.

They live on the outskirts of the same village where the school is. I can't help but feel jealous of her proximity to other people and amenities as we pass the pretty row of shops and a group of friends congregated outside the local pub.

The more we live in that house in the woods, the more I can't wait for the year to be over, so we can be somewhere less disorientating.

I use the sat nav to take me to their house which is on the other side of the village away from the area I'm familiar with. Once parked outside, I look up longingly. Isobel's house is detached, and sits back from a small gravel drive. The brick is bright limestone, and the door is painted a warm grey-green. Balloons are tied to the knocker and softly rustle in the breeze. Tiny soft yellow roses sit in beds under the ground-floor windows.

Before we have a chance to get out, the front door opens and Isobel pokes her head out, her arm reaching for the collar of a big golden Labrador who's attempting to make a dash for it. Laughing, she waves at me, and I wave back. 'Bloody dog,' she cries.

I grin at her as I help the children out the car. 'Come on, you two.'

Margo, as usual, is eager and runs into the house as soon as she's free. Jesse hangs back, holding my hand.

'So pleased you could make it!' Isobel says, waving us in and shutting the door quickly for the sake of the dog. Then she gives me a big welcome hug and I'm so glad we came.

I look around as Isobel takes us through the hallway. To my left is a cosy television room, with voluminous sofas in soft pastels with large, tartan blankets. We arrive in an open-plan kitchen diner which is full of vibrant colours and a messy cosiness. A huge green chipped aga takes centre stage in the kitchen and an old farmhouse table, covered in children's pen marks, sits under a conservatory on the other side. The kids' drawings cover the walls and shelves are lined with brightly coloured books. The French doors are open to the garden. Fun children's music is playing, and a little machine pumps out bubbles which float across the lawn. There is a big pink bouncy castle in one corner, and a paddling pool full of multi-coloured plastic balls floating on the surface.

I recognise most of the other ten children from Margo's class. There are a few older siblings too and I recognise a boy from Jesse's class. I nudge him. 'Why don't you go and say hello?' I suggest, but he shakes his head and tightens his grip.

'Would you like a cup of tea? Or wine? I have lots of that too,' Isobel says with a wink. 'Tea is great.' I worry that Paul wouldn't like me drinking even one glass while I'm in sole charge of the children. Margo runs outside and swiftly takes off her dress and steps into the paddling pool with an excited shriek. Saskia joins her and soon they are jumping around throwing the balls at each other joyfully.

A man standing by a trellis table full of party food shouts for Isobel. It must be Joe. He's wearing combat shorts with large pockets and a black T-shirt with a band I've not heard of splashed on the front. Isobel rushes out with another platter and shifts a few around to make space. I watch as the pair share a private joke and laugh, eyes gleaming happily.

She returns inside and walks through to the kitchen and then stops suddenly. 'What was I doing? Ah, yes! Tea. Sorry, Lauren.'

I walk over to her. 'Can I help with anything?'

She turns the kettle on. 'No, not at all. I think we're all sorted.' She notices Jesse hovering around my legs. 'Hey, Jesse, do you like Party Rings?' He clings to me but nods. 'Saskia's daddy is handing them out over there, and then he's going to start a game of pass the parcel in a minute. If I were you, I'd get over there quick before they're all gone.'

Jesse looks up at me for reassurance.

'Go on, it'll be fun,' I say. His eyes rest on Joe handing out biscuits and he runs off.

'Thank you.' *What a relief,* I think, as I watch Jesse integrate. The doorbell rings and the dog barks and Isobel runs off again. I lean against the wall and cross my arms, watching the party in full swing. I can't help but stare at Joe, how he is the life and soul, rushing around playing, making the children laugh. I can't imagine Paul hosting a party like this.

A wave of sadness hits me. This is what I'd pictured for our fresh start. I feel cheated when I think of our muted life at the house. All I see is a long stretch of nothing.

Isobel comes back with two women I vaguely recognise from the school gates. Their children whoop and rush into the garden to join the others. 'Lauren, this is Rachel and Lucy.'

I smile at them and awkwardly go to shake their hands. Should I be hugging? Or do I air kiss? It has been such a long time since I've been to a party, I have no idea.

'Hi – little Margo out there is mine.' I claim her, as I always do. 'And Jesse is her brother.' I peer out to find his face but can't pick him out of the madness.

'Isobel says you are living in the glass house on Layton Road. How are you finding it?' Lucy asks, and I feel them all take a step towards me, intrigued. 'I'd love to see what it looks like. I went there once as a little girl.'

Rachel leans in. 'I heard there is a bunker on the grounds left over from the war.'

'No, it isn't a bunker, it's a tunnel,' Lucy corrects.

Isobel laughs. 'You both don't have a clue, they're just rumours. Don't listen to them, Lauren, they'll have you digging holes all over the garden.'

Lucy looks annoyed to have been cut off. 'Well, it is awful what happened with the last lot.'

Rachel nods. 'It's never occupied very long. After . . . you know.' Lucy bites her lip and stops herself from saying something. But then adds, 'Oh, poor Susie.' And they all go quiet.

'She was crying the other day in the shop,' I say, pleased to have my own morsel of information to offer. Then the three women look at each other as if they don't want to be the one to crack.

'Her nephew George. He used to help her a lot,' Lucy begins.

'He was the love of her life, she never had her own kids,' Rachel interjects. 'Susie's sister was killed by George's father while she was pregnant. They managed to save him, just about.'

'They should have just left him in there . . . nothing but trouble,' Rachel says darkly.

'Rachel!' Isobel scorns. 'You can't say that.'

She shrugs. 'I don't care. Good riddance.'

The entertainer arrives, and Isobel is distracted.

'So, it's okay in there?' Lucy asks me. 'I probably shouldn't tell you this, but a lot of people think it's cursed.'

'Oh, for God's sake, Lucy!' Isobel re-joins the conversation. 'What are you saying now? Don't listen to them, Lauren. They're just desperate for gossip.'

'Really? Why do people say that?' I ask Lucy. My heart begins to thud, and there's a light ringing in my ears.

I hear screaming. A chorus of girls crying out. One comes running in and grabs at Lucy's legs. She's wearing a ballerina leotard and has pink ribbons in her hair. Lucy picks her up off the floor. 'Mummy, that boy is saying horrible things.' Her voice wobbles, terrified. I turn quickly. I know they're talking about Jesse. He's standing in the middle of the lawn, his face red, blood falling from a gash in the centre of his forehead. My arms fall and I gasp as I take a few steps towards him. 'He ran into the fence, Mummy. He said he was going to the other side. He said he was dead. Is he dead, Mummy? Is he dead?'

Isobel puts her hand to her mouth. 'Oh my God.'

I run to him, feeling as though I'm sinking. Down, down, down. I hold him to me as I check the cut. 'What is it, what is it, Jesse? Why did you do this?' Joe hands me a clean towel and I press it to the wound. The sun catches my eye, and a piercing pain gnaws at the side of my head.

Jesse sobs against me. Everyone is watching. The party has stopped in time – only the bubbles continue their journey floating majestically across the paused scene.

Jesse whispers in my ear, 'I remembered my name. It's Noah. My name is Noah.' His tears sticking to my cheek.

My heart thunders in my chest as I look around, wondering what I should do. 'We'll go. We'll go home, darling,' I tell him.

I look around and see Margo standing in the pool in her knickers with a thunderous expression on her face.

'I'm so sorry,' I say to Isobel as we stand outside on the front step.

'Oh, don't worry at all! Kids. Poor boy.' She smiles sympathetically, although I can tell she's a bit freaked out.

'Come over to ours for a play date next week?' I ask hopefully.

She begins to fiddle with the pendant of her necklace. 'Oh yes, I'd love that.' But I'm unsure she means it. I manage to get them in the car somehow. Margo was devastated to leave but Isobel expertly handed her a party bag and she's now distracted by the content. The drive back is silent.

On arrival the glass house looks cold and uninviting.

'Are you going to leave us now too?' I hear the pain cracking in his voice.

'No, of course not, Jesse. I told you. I'm not going anywhere,' I reply softly.

'You won't tell Daddy, will you?'

I sigh, unable to promise him that. Besides, anyone can see that something happened to him while we were out.

I mouth the name Noah silently. *Noah.* I must tell Paul this evening. There has to be something he hasn't told me. This doesn't feel right. I swallow as I feel my perfect life shifting further out of reach.

CHAPTER 17

A muted malaise falls like a curtain around us as we re-enter the house. Paul is furious at Jesse's injury, I can tell, even though he's trying to stay calm in front of the kids. This evening, once they've gone to bed, I'm going to tell him what really happened. There was no accident – he hurt himself intentionally. Jesse needs help before it's too late. And Paul needs to come to terms with that.

I do all the actions: the playing, the washing, and the cooking dinner. Everything feels painfully long. I kiss Jesse goodnight and whisper, 'Everything's going to be okay.' Then I sit staring at the unlit wood in the fireplace, nursing an undrunk cup of herbal tea as I listen to Paul reading to them. The soft rumble of his voice ricochets through the dim glowing light of the hallway. They aren't asking a million questions like they usually do, and Margo doesn't beg for another story before he shuts her bedroom door.

He joins me in the living area. I watch as he pours himself a glass of wine. 'Jesse seems fine now,' he says, taking a sip. Kidding himself.

I shake my head. 'No, Paul . . .'

Ignoring me, he walks to the sheet of glass and stares outside. 'Well, it's nice they tried it out. They're just not used to socialising, those two. It's not the best time for parties. He's still finding his feet, remember. At least it's the summer holidays soon, and we can lie low for a bit.'

My voice shakes. 'Don't you want to know what happened?' He wouldn't let me finish the story when we got back.

'You said. Jesse caused a scene and had an accident. I told you we should all stay here for a bit and hunker down. But you wouldn't listen to me. I think that is a case in point, don't you?' He walks over and pulls me from my seat and holds me tightly.

'He's not well, Paul,' I say firmly.

'He's fine,' he replies.

'He ran into that fence on purpose. He's trying to hurt himself. Don't you care?' His arms leave mine and he turns in anger.

'How dare you . . .' he spits.

'Does the name Noah mean anything to you?'

I wish I could see his face. I look into the reflective glass, but can't gauge his reaction from where I'm positioned. 'What?' His voice is hoarse with surprise.

'Jesse said that used to be his name – Noah.'

Paul's shifts around, as if he doesn't know which way to turn. Then he slowly pivots to face me. I can see his expression now. It is dark and haunted. Angry. Our eyes lock and an icy shiver runs through me. He takes a few steps backwards and then buries his face in his hands, making the most horrific noise I've ever heard. Like an animal, dying.

'Paul?' I whisper. 'What is it . . . ?' I swallow. I have unearthed something that was rooted too far down to bury again and I'm scared. 'Paul?' I whisper.

He stalks towards me with his fists clenched, his face red and bloating. He looks ghastly, and I step back. I fight the urge to run as he strides towards me. Then he falls into my arms shaking, and it takes me a moment to realise he's crying. 'Paul?' I wrap my arms around him tightly. 'Paul?' I've never seen him like this. 'Paul, what is it? Please talk to me. Please tell me what's going on.'

Slowly he pulls away. 'Sorry.' He can't look me in the eye. He sniffs and falls back into the sofa, rubbing his face.

'Paul. Please. You're scaring me.'

He croaks, 'Sorry . . . I just haven't heard that name for such a long time.' He clears his throat. 'It's a shock.' My heart hammers in my chest. I never really expected there to be any truth in Jesse's ramblings.

'What?'

He sniffs and wipes a tear away. He looks directly at me. 'Noah . . . he was . . . he was Jesse's twin.'

My lips part. 'Twin?' Of course. What was I expecting?

'He died when he was Margo's age. It was an accident.' He sniffs. 'Emma never recovered from it. She backed into him parking the car.'

I gasp.

'She couldn't process it. She was completely shattered.

And not long after that she was diagnosed, and, well . . . she felt as if she deserved to get cancer. That it was her punishment.' He swallows and lets out a pained yelp before continuing. 'And sometimes . . . is it really bad that I do too?' The words falter in the back of his throat, and he looks at me for reassurance.

I feel as though everything I know has shattered. Perfect, wonderful Emma did this?

I pull his arms around me and comfort him. A rush of love, empathy so huge I can't harness it. 'Oh Paul, I'm so sorry. I'm so, so sorry, Paul. I can't imagine . . .'

'I tried so hard to help her through it, but the despair was ingrained.' He wipes tears from his eyes. 'And then before we knew it, we were dealing with her death too. I couldn't cope with seeing Jesse's pain – losing both in such quick succession. He couldn't hear Noah's name without screaming. So, I simply stopped talking about him.' He swallows. 'How fucked up is that? It goes against everything I believe in. But slowly Jesse got a bit better. Forgetting Noah was his way of coping. And mine too. Over time, his brother just stopped ever existing.' Paul puts his face in his hands again and cries. 'Every person you lose takes a little part of you with them. I let him forget because it was easier for me too. Haven't I done the worst thing? Will you ever forgive me?'

I sit and hold his trembling hands. Paul needs to know the truth, he needs to know why this lie is backfiring on him. 'Jesse is confused, Paul. He's having bad dreams. And he thinks he was here with Emma, and he was Noah. And . . . and bad things happened. Now is the time to tackle this. You can't lie to him forever, you must know that. It's hurting him.'

I allow his head to fall into my shoulder. I stroke his back, thinking about what Jesse said about Emma fearing Paul. Another piece of the puzzle. He must have witnessed Paul and Emma dealing with the aftermath of the accident. Full of pain and resentment and remorse. I can't even imagine how they coped.

Poor Jesse and poor Emma. Poor Paul. And stupid, stupid Lauren.

PART TWO

CHAPTER 18

'He's behind you.' I open my eyes. It takes a moment to realise that was my voice speaking.

'What did you say?' Richard asks.

My head is knocking against the inside of the passenger door. My neck bent unnaturally. Pushing myself up to sitting position, I press my fingertips on the sore part of my neck. 'Nothing,' I murmur, noting the time on the dashboard's digital clock.

'You've been asleep for over an hour,' he says. The bright lights of a petrol station whizz by and I blink and turn to check the seats behind.

Relief settles across my tight chest. There they are. My two little ones. Roxy's car seat faces the other way, but I can see her in the little baby mirror I bought especially for the long journey. Her eyes are closed, and her head is bobbing gently with the motion of the car. Noah is asleep too; his mouth hangs open, and I can hear the low hum of his snore. They are perfect. But I guess every mother thinks that. I blink away unexpected tears. Everyone says it goes so quickly: *Don't take it for granted*, say little old ladies in shops. *They grow up so fast*, they whisper as I wonder how days can drag on and weeks are eaten up so quickly. When I stare at them like this, it is like sand falling through my fingers.

I glance at Richard. He got what he wanted in the end. He always does. I look out the window and linger on my reflection in the darkness. I look exhausted. I tried so hard to stand my ground but there was never going to be another conclusion. *You reach an age, Eliza, when you don't make decisions for yourself any more, you make them for your family.* The memory of the biting words forces me to blink.

'Shit,' Richard says under his breath.

'What?' I look around for the reason he is annoyed. A weary feeling drags over me. I'm too tired to argue tonight.

'I can't find the bloody turning.' He's slowed the car down. 'It should have been back there.'

'You always say you know this area like the back of your hand,' I joke, trying to lighten the mood. He stiffens, I forget it's not a good idea to jibe him when he's on the back foot. 'Just do a U-ey, you probably just missed it. It's so dark, no wonder,' I say, trying to diffuse the situation.

'I'm *trying* to find somewhere to turn around,' he replies tersely and then sighs. 'Sorry. It's been a long day.'

We arrive at a wider part of the road. The car jerks as he takes his infuriation out on the gearstick. We continue in silence. I turn once again to check on the children.

As usual I'm on high alert. I'm expecting Roxy to wake up at any moment crying. Or for Noah to jolt upright and ask for the fiftieth time when we're going home. I try to rest back into my seat and enjoy a moment with nothing to do other than relax until we get there. I didn't want to arrive under the cover of darkness fumbling around tripping on steps and trying to find light switches. But the journey has taken hours longer than expected, what with nappy changes and layby feeds. Another screaming tantrum that needed abating. Richard is right. It has been a long day.

It's been a long two fucking years.

He slows down, trying to predict the turn again. It's there. I don't say anything. It will only wind him up. He glances over at me as if he's expecting me to.

'It's like the turning wasn't there,' he mutters. I can't be bothered.

The car moves slowly along the drive, like an animal hunting in the dead of night. The headlights beam up at the house and the sound of crunching gravel disturbs the silence. Richard turns the engine off, and we sit there for a moment just staring at it. We did it. We left London and bought a house in the countryside. Like swathes of other families who have outgrown cramped city flats unable to afford more square footage, even with a budget that would make anyone else spit out their tea.

I glance at Richard. He is ten years older than me and four years older than when we met. If you'd asked me if he was handsome back then, I would have swooned. But now I have seen all the different sides to him, I'm not sure I can tell. That's the thing about Richard: when you meet him, he seems like the most attractive man on the planet.

He's very striking, but I wouldn't call him conventionally handsome. There is something about him I could never put my finger on. It's a pull, a magnetic urge to be near him. When he walks into a room people take notice. And when he speaks, you can't help but fall under a spell. He has dark hair and aqua green eyes, which Roxy has inherited. Now, he has what people call a midnight shadow. A term I didn't really understand until the babies came along. I mean, I'm in my mid-twenties and on a bad day I swear I look forty-five. Richard is originally from Glasgow. He didn't have a positive experience growing up and has done his best to abandon the thick accent. His father is a failed entrepreneur who lost all his money in quite a cataclysmic way when Richard was a teenager. I think he may have had a gambling problem and conned a lot of friends and family out of their savings. His mother was a dancer. But she was out of the picture by the time Richard was fifteen. I only know this because his great-aunt came over for tea once. Richard hated how much of his history she threw around during the afternoon, and she wasn't invited over again. He doesn't like people knowing the truth about him. He likes for them to have a carefully monitored stream of information he can control.

As soon as Richard left home, he created a persona much like that of an Oxford don. All sweater-vests and gold-rimmed glasses. His father certainly doesn't dress like that. I only know because of my shock when I finally came across the infamous father. He turned up at our flat shouting at Richard about something or other to do with money. Emotions were running high, and I couldn't work out what was going on. But boy, was he a character. All gold teeth and spittle, a greasy pinstripe double-breasted blazer with big gold buttons half falling off and black shoes that had seen better days. NOT an Oxford don.

Richard wears a bow tie sometimes – I know he's feeling particularly vulnerable when he gets that out. The whole charade is expertly executed, and you'd think he went to Cambridge via Harrow. I wish he would have the confidence to be proud of his heritage; it should be an accolade he holds up. I can still hear his Glaswegian accent very slightly, especially when he's cross. Although it hasn't leaked out in a long while.

We've been turning our marriage around. And this fresh start is the best way we can put the past behind us and prove to each other we're committed to the long haul.

And I must love him. I'm sure I do.

When I think of the first time I saw him – well, that person is a stranger. He isn't the same person and nor am I. It's hard to say if we have grown together or apart. It is somewhere in between but also intensely both all at the same time. He is the person I know best; and he knows me better than anyone after everything we've been through.

I would have preferred to stay in the city, and he knows that. But when he saw this house for sale with the incredibly sleek design-led agency – The Minimalist Home – he just had to have it. It isn't just a house. It is *The House*. He stayed here once, some sort of student exchange or something. He couldn't believe it when he found it was up for sale. It's a sign, he kept saying. He became erratic and feverish about it. I can tell this house means more to him than simply somewhere to live. It says, You've arrived. You're good at what you do. People respect you.

Come on, Eliza. Stop it. He's really trying now.

Over these last six months he's reverted to the man I first met, and I'm so relieved. It was a rough patch. But people can change. We were under a lot of pressure back in that tiny flat with two small babies. We've done the best thing for our family coming here. As Richard keeps reminding me.

I think back to that awful period before Roxy was born. He'd been stuck at home after losing his job, and as the days went on, he became more and more wound up. Like a jack-in-the-box, I didn't know when he was going to pop with an angry finger pointing in my face. The last time, before I packed up and nearly left him, was over a parking ticket. I was so preoccupied with Noah I'd accidently left the front wheel hanging on the pavement and some jobsworth gave me a ticket. Richard was so furious he almost punched me in the face; just a tiny moment stopped him, and his hand hit the wall instead. My whole body shook as I moved away, and he apologised repeatedly. My hand protectively held my stomach, with my unborn child, almost at full term.

Then the next day, after he went out I buckled Noah into his buggy and waddled down the cobbled stones to the Tube. I tried messaging my mum, asking her if I could please come to hers. Begging her. But blinking back the tears, I received a reply that made me crumble. *You've made your bed.* She still hadn't forgiven me, and she never will. There was no one else I could run to with a baby in tow, and another almost here. I couldn't think of a relationship strong enough to carry all that weight. I'd severed any ties years ago.

So, I went back to him. And he took Noah out of his buggy and enveloped me in a hug, comforting me as I cried. One last chance, he said. 'Please don't leave me, I promise I'll change. Forgive me one last time, please.' And I did. One more time. And since that day he's been better. And he proved it by really being there for me when I got ill after Roxy was born.

He's not perfect, he's had his moments, but that scary man who stayed with us for a few months seems to have gone away.

Besides, doesn't everyone have a dark side?

As if he can hear my inner babble, his hand covers mine and I glance over at him. 'I shouldn't have snapped,' he says softly, his head bowed in apology, and his eyes peeking up at me mischievously.

'It's okay,' I reply quietly. 'We're both tired.' I fight the urge to remind him he wasn't up every two hours with a baby going through a sleep regression. But now isn't the time for point scoring.

When Richard took me on that first frenzied tour of the house it was a bright September day. Everything was luscious and green. The woods hummed with energy. Squirrels jumped between trees, and birds chirped with impossible brightness. Everything was so heightened and alive. We took a photograph on the porch and laughed as the buzz of the timer kept knocking it out of place. We could never quite get us all in one shot. It was a happy moment – I wait for these and pounce when they happen. I want to put them in a jar and add them to my collection as proof that happy is what we are. Sometimes I wonder if it's my fault. Whether the love I'd felt when we got together was so intense that I still find myself chasing it today.

That day we viewed it, I understood why Richard was so eager for us to jump on the opportunity. We had the cash. He'd bought his maisonette in Kentish Town back in the early noughties for practically nothing, and it was now worth over a million pounds. Yes. Ridiculous. It didn't even have a garden. Just a crappy little roof terrace I was too scared to use once Noah started walking. When Richard saw this place come up with a price tag we could afford, there was no stopping him. We'd even have plenty of money left over to spare. He had to have it. He had to be the one who lived here with his 'perfect family', as he always calls us. His wife, and one of each.

Yes, it is more remote than I'd have liked. Although there is the picturesque thatched-roof pub and lovely little school and a private nursery for the children in the nearest village, it's still miles away. But the space! The space! We walked around repeating that over and over. It had felt exciting that we could inhabit such a place. Once we returned to the flat it felt four times more cramped than it ever had before. And I thought, *I'm crazy, how can I turn that down? For this. Maybe Richard is right, maybe our marriage would be better if we weren't so trapped in the rat race, and he was less stressed. Maybe that's why our marriage has been strained. We just need more space.*

But here, now, on this freezing cold night, the house is so much less enchanting. We sit in silence staring at the sharp angles of the building bathed in moonlight. The only noise the odd mumble from one of the sleeping children and the tapping of the rain on the bonnet. The empty carcass of the house sits with drizzle clinging to the glass like beads of cold sweat during a fever. Not one part of me wants to go inside. I want to be back in the warm chaos of our old home. Near people. Near shops. Near a bus I can jump on and ride endlessly around, almost escaping.

'This is going to be great, Eliza,' Richard says, placing his hand on my leg and forcing our eyes to connect. I feel my jaw tightening. 'I know . . . it hasn't been easy. I'm not proud of how I behaved. But I promise – this is our fresh start.'

I nod in agreement, wanting the moment to pass. It was this or admitting our marriage was over. Admitting what Richard really is. And right now, I'm not sure if I made the right choice.

CHAPTER 19

The sound of Roxy fussing wakes me the next morning. I feel her body next to mine, her hands outstretched searching for me. I lift my T-shirt and pull her into my side, allowing her mouth to find my nipple. Her little hands relax on my skin, and I feel her sense of relief as she begins to suck. Blinking in the darkness, I try to figure out what the seismic change I feel in my throat is. The layers of yesterday dawn on me. The stress of packing, and the long drive. The fraught quick transfer of the kids into the house, and the angry shushing shared between us as we tried to unlock the front door. The silent glass of wine by the open fire, and the kiss he gave me before we went to bed. Holding on to the back of my head as if he knew I would try and pull away.

I really wanted to believe that the external change of scenery would alter the internal battle between us overnight. But all I feel is this sense of panic and confusion. Is it normal to find yourself excusing someone's behaviour all the time? My perception of what's normal is so skewed these days, I often tie myself in knots trying to work it out.

'Morning,' Richard says. The electric blind makes a scratching groan as it protracts, sending daylight flooding into the room and forcing me to rest my forearm over my eyes. Slowly peeking out, I see wet, twisted branches rattling around us.

'Mummy.' Noah is standing up in the travel cot a few metres from the bed. Richard jumps out and takes him. 'Nooo. Want Mummy!' Noah moans and Richard, annoyed, drops him onto the bed and he crawls over.

'Of course you do, Mummy is the best,' Richard says with a hint of annoyance. I kiss Noah's hot, red cheeks and bring him into the fold. It's not Noah's fault, they're both very mummy-ish when they're tired. I wish Richard wouldn't take it personally.

'You're going to finally stop breast feeding tonight? And put them in their own rooms, right?' Richard checks. His voice playful, his eyebrows raised suggestively.

'I said I would,' I reply. Hugging them closer. I've been dreading it.

I love cosy mornings like this. Their little bodies curled around, with fingers grabbing on to my flesh, and bare feet flat against my side, as though we are one being. Richard gets back into bed and nuzzles in with us, placing a hairy hand on my arm, his thumb stroking. I stare at it. It feels like a foreign object compared to the rest.

Richard leans back on the headboard. I get up and pass him Roxy. She sits forward facing her father on his lap. He holds her hands and begins to rock her back and forth, singing, 'Row, row, row your boat.' As her eyes shine with glee, I walk into the en suite desperate to wash off the stench of dried milk and sweat. It takes me a while to work out how to turn the shower on. Finally, the water begins to heat, and I shake my hand dry and turn back into the bedroom. Seeing them together, I lean on the frame of the door, watching. Roxy is one and becoming more comfortable within her body by the day. Her mop of dark hair is long for such a little girl. The doctor said he'd never seen so much on a newborn. It is exactly the same shade as mine.

'How's my little princess?' Richard coos. His voice gentle, caring and full of love. Noah sits next to them quietly looking at his favourite board book. For a second I'm filled with love. I'm so lucky. I must never forget that.

Richard looks up at me. 'Are you okay?' he asks.

Without hesitation I reply, 'Yes, fine.' Then I raise my chin to stare into the stormy skies outside; the wind is blowing forcefully; the rain hasn't let up since last night. I wonder if it will snow – it's cold enough. A shiver runs through me at the thought of being snowed in all the way out here. Miles from anywhere. 'I just didn't realise how isolated I'd feel.'

'Once we've unpacked and the new furniture arrives it will feel different,' he reassures me.

Throwing the duvet off his legs, he stands up, lifting Roxy with him. 'I'll go make us all breakfast while you have a shower.'

I smile gratefully. 'Thanks.' He walks over and my head

knocks back as he kisses my cheek. I feel a burning sensation where his lips left my skin.

As we're sat at the kitchen counter having breakfast, the removal van arrives. There's a flurry of activity which moves the day along at lightning speed. Full of unpacking and cajoling Noah into not doing something which will, no doubt, make a massive mess and turn my attention away from everything there is to do. Roxy is crawling around, following me, coasting along sharp edges calling for me to pick her up. I barely get anything done. I feel Richard's presence everywhere, his irritation at my inefficiency palpable.

Once the removers have gone there isn't even a moment to pause before sorting the children out. They both need my attention all of the time. It's draining.

'Mummy. Go home?' Noah asks again.

I kneel. 'This is our home now, remember?' I brush a tear off his cheek. 'We have a big house with a ginormous garden, aren't we lucky?' I say, pulling him in for a cuddle. His body is rigid with infuriation. Then Roxy yanks herself up onto me and tries to push her brother away. They both begin to wail. I have one of those moments when I just want to be transported away, and close my eyes, trying to breathe through the frustration.

I find the dichotomy of needing them intensely but also wanting to be on my own confusing a lot of the time. It is a funny sort of guilt, and it fills me with shame.

When we fell pregnant with Roxy, Noah was barely four

months old. My body hadn't had time to recover before it started again. To be honest, I wasn't even ready to be intimate like that. 'It's not healthy being in a sexless marriage after kids come along,' Richard said. 'It's the sort of thing that creeps up on you, Eliza. The beginning of the end. Is that what you want?' We only did it a few times, just so I could appease him, really. And I did want to be a good wife.

I was devastated when my period was late.

When I showed him the pregnancy test, he danced around the room and enveloped me in a hug, saying, 'Great! We'll get the baby phase out the way quickly.'

I was in shock, I think. Noah was still feeding through the night, and I was barely sleeping. The thought of throwing a pregnancy into all that was beyond daunting – I had no idea how I'd cope. When we found out it was a girl, he was ecstatic. He said he was finally going to have the perfect family he'd always wanted. I felt proud to give him that, like I had some sort of power over him for a moment. But that feeling always turns into humiliation.

That's the thing about Richard. Even though he spends his time unpicking everyone else's neuroses, muckying his hands with everyone else's shit, *he* needs to be viewed as perfect. No, that's not right – superior. You wouldn't know it the first time you met him. He seems so gracious and self-deprecating and interested in everything you have to say.

Stop it, Eliza. Stop it. He's changed.

Between boxes I stop and stare out onto the sweeping lawn. The silence within jars with the gusty scene outside. I miss the bustle of our old flat. We lived on a bus route and Noah would stand with me, his hands pressed against the window waiting for them to pass. 'Bus, Mummy!' he'd cry, and I'd help him count them as they passed, *one . . . two . . . three . . . four.* He's always feared the outside world, much happier to watch it from the safety of home. But maybe that's my fault. I've always been quite nervous. I didn't have a network of other mothers, or family around to give me that extra confidence I needed, I suppose.

The doorbell rings. I watch Richard jump to his feet. 'Don't worry, I'll get it.' I watch as he opens it to two men in brown overalls. They walk in and chat at the door, pointing to the ceiling and nodding. They bring in their toolboxes, ladders and power tools. Richard walks past me to the kitchen and leaves a box on the countertop.

'Who are they?' I ask, nodding at the men.

'The guys fitting the new security.'

'Security?'

'I told you. Remember?' I mustn't have been listening. It's been a busy few weeks. He shrugs. 'I thought I had. We're quite remote out here, I thought it was important. Especially if I'm not around. I need my perfect family to be safe, don't I?'

I sporadically watch the men go from room to room scoping out the house as I give the children dinner. One of them parts a ladder and steps up it in the central point of the hallway. He then places a half-dome on the ceiling. Drilling a screw in place.

'What's that?' I ask.

The man sniffs. 'A camera. Can go the full three-sixty.' His finger motions around in a circle. 'It's top of the range. Great piece of kit this,' he says, tapping it. I nod as I help Roxy put more puree on her spoon. As she chews, I look up at the menacing reflective surface and the blinking red dot as he tests the device.

CHAPTER 20

We've been at the house a month. I couldn't tell you anything about that time, other than that I've made people food and tried to feed them. I've tidied, falling to my knees picking up half-chewed pieces of toast from the floor. I've washed other people's clothes and hung them up to dry and debated whether a poo stain on a baby vest means it is destined it for the bin, or whether it can live to fight another day. There are an assembly line of meaningless micro-decisions I debate all day long.

All the furniture has arrived now. Richard was very specific about how he wanted the interior to look. He's spent the last few months curating the perfect mid-century pieces to insert into his perfect house, with his perfect family. I've tried telling him much of it's unsuitable for children, but he won't hear it.

Noah is due to start nursery today. I'm nervous for him, but also can't wait to have just a few hours when I'll have a bit more space around me to breathe. No one has ever cared for him outside of us. We didn't have relatives nearby to burden, and Richard is suspicious of outsiders. But now we've made the big move, he agrees it's time. It's so important for his development to socialise. Noah needs this, and so do I.

'Come on!' I shout as I ready the children. Layers need to be wrapped and zipped and small feet must be heaved into wellies. 'We're going to be late,' I huff, and Richard promptly walks out of his new study fiddling with his tie. He pulls on his large padded coat with a fur-rimmed hood and we shut the front door. Smoky breath trails us as we bundle the children into their seats.

I glance over at Richard as he drives. He rushed off earlier to read an email and has been a ball of stress ever since. He's taken a job at a residential psychiatric unit about a forty-five-minute drive away. He starts in a few days. He always says he prefers positions where he's embedded within a full-time setting. He says he can do his best work and help patients 'in a way you just can't when you're seeing them for an hour once a week on a video call.'

I was nervous when he accepted the position, because of what happened last time.

Leaning back on the headrest, I wonder, as I often do, what would have become of me if our paths hadn't crossed. Sometimes I daydream about living in a London house-share and going out every Friday and Saturday night. Maybe I'd have a low-paid starter job and be going on Tinder dates every Wednesday night. Maybe I'd be running around making all the mistakes you're meant to in your twenties. Instead of married with two tiny kids who need me so badly I can't bear it.

But if I'd never met Richard, I wouldn't have Noah or Roxy.

On a long, drawn-out day of childcare I wonder if that would be a bad thing. Having children weaves you into another person forever. Even if you say goodbye, you can never just cut them off.

When things were bad between us, I sometimes wondered if it was his plan all along to get me pregnant again quickly. Because he knew I'd be stuck. I'm hampered with two. I can't easily grab and run. I'm trapped.

One of the absolute caveats of agreeing to this move was that I could start getting my life back now Roxy is one. I'm going to investigate a vocational course or maybe a part-time job. Anything that will get me back out there – living again. It's been so long I wonder if I'll remember how to do it. I can't go on talking to myself all day. Richard is being supportive. I've paid my dues and now the initial baby fog has passed it's time to get back on track.

There was only one place at the private nursery a few villages along, so we nabbed it for Noah and put Roxy on the waiting list. They kindly gave me the numbers of all the local childminders, and we're agreed that we'll go visit them once I've worked out what I want to do. I can't wait to feel like me again. Because at the moment, I'm not entirely sure who I am.

I turn and watch Richard as he drives. I've relied on him for too long. I don't have one little thing that's completely mine. I don't even have my own bank card or one new friend to show for the few years since we've been together. We used to have dinner with his colleagues, but other than that our social life was non-existent. Richard was never keen on my friends; I think he thought they were very immature. I often wonder what they're up to these days. Still living for the weekend, I suppose. I'm the first of that group to have children; like most these days, they probably wouldn't consider it until their thirties. I tried my best to make friends with other mothers in the baby groups in London, but it was as though they looked through me. I think they mistook me for the help the majority of the time.

We hurtle around tight country roads and I see a dead rabbit on the side ahead. All red guts and fur. Our car jolts up and down as we drive over it. 'Sorry,' Richard murmurs.

At nursery, before I hand Noah to the nice-looking woman in a Boden skirt, I crouch next to him. He looks so tiny and lost. He's always been skinny even though I try my best to cook the most nutritional food – he'll nibble away at corners and leave the rest. 'You'll have a great time.' He glances at the others, unsure. 'Look at all the toys they've got,' I whisper and point. His eyes narrow into thin slits, looking at me with pure hatred. His key worker notices his reticence. 'Come on, Noah, all your new friends want to meet you,' she says with a warm smile as his body dives into mine. 'So, you have the settling in timings for the next few weeks? Then he can start at the normal drop-off and pick-times with the other children,' she checks with me, and I nod. She expertly takes his hand and chats away distracting him as she leads him through to the enclosed area. He doesn't even notice the gate shut behind him. I take my chance to move away. Just as I do, he realises he's been tricked, and his face crumbles. He begins to wail and slams himself against the gate, trying to get back to me. Overwhelmed with guilt, I cross my arms and trudge back to the car where Richard and Roxy are waiting for me.

'Well, that was awful,' I say, banging the door shut.

'You wanted to send him,' Richard says with a shrug, staring down at his phone, tapping a message.

'Richard,' I whisper.

He looks at me. 'I just don't think they're ready.'

'It will be good for him, Richard. He can't sit in the house with me any longer. He needs to learn to socialise with other kids.' I swallow. A flash penetrates: the clock and its reverberating tick, and staring listlessly at the children as they fuss, and the mess I need to clear up before he notices.

He promised when we got here it would be different.

Richard puts his phone away and turns the engine back on, shaking his head. 'Well, I hope you're right, Eliza.'

A long pause. I can't win.

'You know I need this,' I say quietly.

After a pause he nods, and puts his hand over mine. 'You're right. I'm sorry. He'll be fine. By the end of the week he'll be begging to come.'

'Thank you,' I whisper. We head off down the road and I manage a smile on my cracked lips. It's happening. It's really happening.

A couple of days later, as I tidy up the breakfast things, I watch Richard get ready for his first day at his new job. He does up his top button and quaffs his hair, neatly pushing his glasses up his nose. I think of the new secretary who'll go crimson as she shakes his hand, and the boss who'll congratulate himself on his new appointment. They will be instantly charmed.

No one else would see it apart from me, but Richard is very nervous. He's redone his tie three times. He still hasn't got over what happened to him at the last unit. One of his patients got obsessed with him and made an accusation. There wasn't any proof, as it was her word against his. Her track record wasn't exactly endearing anyone to her innocence. Besides, Richard is just so attractive and charming, it's far more likely a mentally unstable woman became too attached under his care. Isn't it? The manager had a quiet word and suggested it would be best if he moved on. His confidence has been knocked.

Richard has always had a short fuse. But after that it was as though something was released inside him. The safety catch had come off.

I . . . I was scared of him a lot of the time. But that was a while ago now, and besides, he's changed.

As well as his first day of work, it is day three of operation get-Noah-settled-into-nursery. I sit on the floor clutching his shoes, trying to coax him out from behind the sofa. 'Please, Noah,' I try. 'It will be better today.' Richard walks through and stands at the mirror fiddling with his already much-fiddled-with hair. I call over to him. 'I just need to go to the loo once he's sorted. Can you put Roxy in the car for me?'

I'm excited. I'm planning on exploring the local area once I've dropped Noah at nursery and Richard at work. I can't wait.

I've been so busy with the kids and the house there hasn't really been a chance to get out other than family trips to the big supermarket along the motorway. Richard is quite an introvert and hates doing anything mildly sociable. He always says, who needs anyone else when we've got us? Which I used to think was very romantic.

'It's fine, I'll take Noah on my way in. He's only staying until after lunch, right? That works well. I'm only having a tour and meeting everyone this morning.'

'But Richard. I'll be stuck.'

'Oh, come on, Eliza – don't be difficult. You've got this beautiful house to play with your daughter in all day.' He stands at the entrance to the living room. 'Noah. Come here,' he calls. Noah peers from his hiding spot. 'Come on, Noah,' he says tersely, standing over the sofa. Then he begins to count – 'One . . . two . . . three . . .' and the little boy crawls out, knowing he'll be put on the naughty step if his father reaches five. Richard marches off and Noah runs into my arms.

'It's okay, darling,' I say as his hands grab on to my clothes tightly.

'Mummy take Noah to nursery,' he whines.

'You're going to be late. Come on, Noah.' Richard prises him from me and, ignoring his wails, carries him outside and into the car. I shut the front door hastily and lean my forehead against the panelling. More guilt.

The fraught morning hangs around me like a bad smell as I tidy up the chaos left behind. I don't think I'll ever get used to how quiet it is here. It's as though something is about to jump out and make me scream at any second.

I pick Roxy up off the blanket laid on the floor, and hike her onto my hip. Standing at the large sheet of glass facing the sweeping lawn, I stare listlessly. The grounds are in good condition – the previous owners took care of the property. I smile at the rich pink flowers that cluster at the bottom of the lawn. Behind are tall trees marking the entrance to the woods. 'Shall we go for a walk?' I say out loud. Roxy nods happily, too tiny to realise what a horrible, cold day it is. 'A little rain never hurt anybody.' I pull on her all-weather one-piece and force my crusty boots over thick socks. Then I snap the buckle of the baby carrier, attaching her to my chest.

I moan as I pull back the heavy back door and step onto the patio. 'Right, we need to find ten sticks. Okay, Rox?' She grins, with no idea what I'm talking about. I bend down and pick one up off the grass. She grabs the end and inspects it. 'One!' I say triumphantly. A gust of wet wind blows in our faces which causes her to pull the most hilarious face. 'Oh dear, a bit wet,' I say.

I hope Richard is having a good day at work. Otherwise, he'll come back all stressed and annoyed that someone said something he's taken the wrong way. Over the years I've noticed how thin his skin can be, even though he comes across so cool-headed and unflappable.

I first met Richard at my father's therapy centre in Winchester. I was working there after I'd pulled out of university, just after my second year. I was very lost. My father was desperate for me to go into medicine, and I got onto the course, only just. Everyone was so much brighter than me and I couldn't keep up. I started taking Ritalin and would study through the night. In the end I walked off and ended up in a psychiatric unit – completely burnt out. My father tried to be understanding but all I could see when I looked at him was one huge pile of disappointment. All that money on private education. All that time, wasted. He couldn't get his head around it, even though he tried his best to understand. He used all his special therapy tools to coax me back onto the right path. I really wanted to go travelling, work out for myself what the next right thing was. But he offered me a job doing admin, and, feeling guilty, I took it. I think he thought working for him would give me the confidence I needed to get back to pursuing adulthood. But instead, much to his dismay, it led me somewhere else entirely.

I made tea and coffee and helped with the filing and answered the phone. It was so boring. But I felt like I owed it to him after the mess I'd made out of everything. One day the new psychotherapist turned up – Richard.

It felt like finally someone saw something in me that I didn't even see in myself. He was engaging. Funny. He was my blast of colour after the darkest of days.

The romantic relationship wasn't immediate – we became friends first. He'd always seek me out. My father caught us laughing a few times and, uncomfortable with the situation arising (and controlling as always), he had a word with Richard. Richard reacted by quitting. He told me it was because he didn't think it would be right, and didn't want to upset anyone.

I found his address in the human resources folder and didn't think twice about going over there. He opened the door and we stood there staring and grinning. It was obvious what was going to happen. I moved to London with him after two weeks. My father felt betrayed by Richard. He kept saying I was in a vulnerable position, and he wasn't up for entertaining the idea of this man as my boyfriend. But I didn't care. By that point so much of my life revolved around him – and the highs of our relationship were all-consuming. Before I knew it, I hadn't seen my family for almost a year.

Then, I bumped into an old friend of my parents. He gave me his condolences for my father's death. I'd missed the funeral. Phoning my mother, I was inconsolable, but she insisted that she'd made every attempt to let me know.

She never picked up the phone to me again. Not even when I told her I was pregnant.

Richard tells me there's no point wallowing in it. And that she obviously didn't want me there. I just don't understand how they could hate me so much for falling in love? And the grandchildren – how blistering must her anger be to disregard them too? I wince, remembering the message she sent: *You made your bed*. Grief does strange things to people.

I send her pictures occasionally. Little blue ticks show me she sees them, but they are promptly ignored. My whole childhood was a lie.

I walk with Roxy down the lawn, stroking her back through

the baby carrier. When we get to the bottom, I realise there is a little path between the bushes that heads into the guts of the woods. I stroke a petal between my fingertip and thumb. 'Rhododendron,' I mutter as we slip past, and I peer through the passageway. 'Ooh, I wonder what's down here, Rox?' I say, stepping forward. 'Let's take a look.' A few minutes later we come out into a clearing. To one side is the shed I saw on the estate agent plans. The structure is the same wood and glass as the house. I can't decide if it looks enchanted or haunting. Walking over, I cup my hands and peer in. It's completely empty apart from a sink and a trapdoor. How odd. Stepping back, I look down at the grass I'm standing on. Wondering where the trapdoor could lead.

We'd talked about the possibility of me using this as an office or study space. I'm not sure if I'm keen now. It seems odd so far from the main house. And it's creepy down here. Maybe in the summer it will feel more inviting.

'Time for lunch and a sleep, don't you think?' I whisper to Roxy who nods happily, before resting her head on my chest. I'd better be quick, as I don't want her falling asleep on me before I have a chance to put her down in the cot.

I hear a screech and look up to see a large hunting bird circling. Then I glance into the woods hearing a snap. A bolt of electric blue in a sea of green and brown.

And a face.

I scream.

CHAPTER 21

Roxy wails, terrified by my shriek, which rang like a bell around the enclosed space. My heart jabbers in my chest and I pant as the person runs off between the trees.

'It's okay, it's okay, baby.' I jiggle her up and down, patting her back. 'Mummy's sorry.' I kiss her cheek. 'Mummy's so sorry.'

I turn on the spot. Confused. Did that just happen? The patter of rain hastens my steps and I jog back through the passageway and up towards the house feeling vulnerable. My eyes dart around, and I turn to check no one's following me.

There was a face in the woods – I did see that, didn't I?

I still don't trust myself. After Roxy was born, I wasn't well, and I'm all too aware I could go backwards any time. The extreme sleep deprivation got to me. I'd put something down and come back an hour later and it would be gone. The bath overflowed, and I left the gas on once. I started seeing things that weren't there. 'What if she hurts the babies?' I heard Richard whisper down the phone once.

In the end I was sent to a specialist mother and baby unit

to recover. I was allowed to take Roxy and Noah with me as they were both so small, which was a relief. I was discharged quickly. A few weeks of sleep and support really did the trick. And they knew I had a trained professional at home to care for me.

My shoes slap on the patio and I rush back through the doors into the house, dragging the glass panels across and locking us in. Safe. I consider calling Richard, but don't want to stress him out while he's at work. I begin the routine of putting Roxy down for her nap. She grins up at me happily as I press her nose lightly. 'Beep,' I say, and she giggles.

Leaving her, I walk into the living area gingerly, unable to shake the unsettled feeling I picked up in the woods. I look up at the little red dot of the security camera. I don't like the way it keeps tabs on me as I wander around the house. Wrapping my arms around myself, I look out at the deluge of rain.

I think of Noah at nursery. I hope he's making friends and laughing with the girls who work there – slowly carving out his independence. Is it strange that I miss him when all I've wanted is a little time for myself?

Never happy, Richard's voice reminds me. I blink.

Getting out my phone, I click over to my messages and scroll through the latest photos I sent my mum. A knot forms in my stomach when I see the two little blue ticks. One of the photos is of Noah cuddling Roxy. They look impossibly cute. How could she ignore that? An angry burst. How could she?

Richard and I don't do social media. When we first started

dating, we dared each other to delete our accounts to see if we could live totally free from the chains of all that. We even check each other's phones every week to ensure we've complied. Richard is proud of the fact he only has one page of apps on his screen. He won't use Amazon – he believes it's all a sickness, and doesn't want the kids to think everything can be delivered the next day at the click of a button. Convenience and choice are a curse, he always says.

When Roxy finally wakes I've been sitting waiting for her company by her closed door for twenty minutes. I wonder how I'll cope when she's in childcare too. They're all I've known for such a long time. And before that I never had the chance to establish myself properly. What if I try to do something but I fail? What if Richard is right, and I should keep things simple, especially since I so easily crumble?

Richard returns with Noah just after three. As soon as I hear the key in the door, I rush towards it.

'Mummy!' Noah shouts, thrilled to see me. And I pick him up and hold him tightly.

The red blinking light of the camera catches my eye.

'Richard?' I call.

He wanders back through to the hallway from his study, which he'd dived into. 'That camera, is it on all the time? I keep noticing the light.' I nod at it.

He shrugs. 'It's on a motion sensor. I thought it best just to leave it running. We're so isolated here. You never know.'

I think about its trajectory. The transparency of the glass

enables it to rotate around much of the living space, and even the garden. He walks over and puts his hand on my back.

'I just want to make sure you're all safe when I'm not around.'

'I don't like the feeling I'm being watched.'

He laughs. 'It's only me.' He pulls a strand of my hair behind my ear, and I let him kiss me. It is sweet, tender. A flash: *You think you are so fucking clever, don't you?* His eyes bulging at me as he threw a glass.

I think of the person in the woods, and debate telling Richard. Did I imagine it? I was so sure I saw someone. I don't want him to panic – or worse, accuse me of seeing things. I sigh, wishing we were back in London. With the friendly neighbours who knew my name. Nobody who cares about me knows that I am here. But then again, I suppose Richard is the only person who does truly care.

'How did your first day go?' I ask. Watching as he boils the kettle.

'There are a lot of people in a bad way. It's completely underfunded.' Sighing, he adds, 'I've got my work cut out.' Revelling in his hero status.

'They're lucky to have you,' I stammer.

He smiles, pleased. 'Thank you. But enough about me, how was your day?'

'Oh, I didn't do much really. I had a little explore in the garden. I found that shed we saw on the plans. It's weird that it's so far from the house. Why do you think they put it there?'

He shrugs. 'People like to be out in nature, don't they? It's a luxury these days. They pay thousands to go on tech-free weeks in the middle of nowhere. That's an idea.' He laughs. 'Let's Airbnb it, I bet we'd make a fortune.'

'I don't think I'll use it. Sort of freaked me out a little,' I say, and he shrugs again. I step forward. 'Can I borrow your laptop? You said I could this afternoon. I've got so much to organise, along with ordering my own computer.' I remind him of his promises. His face drops. He dips his teabag a few times, thinking. 'Richard?' The pedal bin makes a clanging noise as he opens it with his foot, dropping the bag in before stalking across the living room.

'Richard? Where are you going?' I ask, surprised.

He stops and turns to me. 'To get a piece of paper to write a list of everything you want.' The comment laced with sarcasm.

'It's not a list . . .'

'It's fine.' His jaw sets as he glances back at me with a glare.

'It's just everything we talked about . . .' I stammer.

'I just think you live in a bit of a dream world sometimes, Eliza. Coming to me asking for anything you want while you live in your beautiful detached palace all paid for by someone else,' he spits, leaving the room.

My lips part in shock, and I blink back tears. He's not spoken to me like that in a while. Another flash: in the flat, with Noah as baby. I was in his room trying to find the Calpol, as he was screaming and boiling hot. Suddenly I heard Richard shouting obscenities. He came stalking in, spitting in my face, furious that he'd stepped on a soiled nappy that I was just about to come back for. I'd forgotten a bag and needed to retrieve one midway through.

The memory fades and I try my best to shake it off. I hold Noah tightly and take him over to Roxy, who claps at the sight of her brother. I fight the big fat glob of tears in my throat. 'I'm going to make your favourite dinner. Roxy has been waiting for you to come back all day . . .' I keep talking and talking. Wanting to get as far as I can away from the exchange.

It's fine, I tell myself. *The old Richard isn't coming back, he's just had a long day. It's a blip. He's allowed a blip.*

Later that night we're having our customary glass of wine before bed. Richard lights the wood burning fire which hangs at one end of the huge living space. 'Are you okay?' I ask softly. He doesn't reply. He has a glazed look, and I'm not sure he's even listening. He's been quiet since we spoke earlier. Usually, he would have found me to apologise. I gingerly take a sip, feeling nervous to say anything. In case it's the wrong thing. The reflection of the fire licks his face, mirrored in his eyes. The silence builds and I feel tense.

'Richard,' I whisper, breaking it. 'Are you going to say anything about earlier?'

His head turns. 'What, darling?' He smiles at me.

I can talk to him, it's Richard. He's very composed these days. I clear my throat. 'I thought maybe we could talk. I'm feeling a bit upset about how you spoke to me earlier.' His smile falters but he leans over and strokes my hand tenderly, and I continue, my voice picking up strength. 'You know . . .

when I agreed to come out here, we made some promises to each other. To be kind, to listen. To *really* listen, you know?'

He moves closer to me on the couch, nodding. 'I'll try harder.' Emotion cracks in his voice.

'Because you know . . . you know we both have to try to make this work. It's a marriage. An equal partnership.'

He is nodding, agreeing with me. 'Yes, of course. Equal.' And he leans forward and pecks my cheek, his finger curling a tendril of my hair, deep in thought. 'My perfect family,' he whispers.

CHAPTER 22

A few weeks later I wake to hear Roxy crying and I push myself out of bed. Creeping downstairs, I hope to catch her before she wakes Noah too. When I click on the light, she's standing up in her cot, her face red and wet. I pull her into my arms. She catches her breath, and sighs with relief as her head falls into the seat of my neck. I rock her gently. Hearing Noah's soft voice calling, I turn.

We huddle in the kitchen. As I make breakfast Noah sings to Roxy, and we all laugh. The sun comes up slowly, sliding easily up through the glass. Big squares of light hang sharply against the furniture and muted paint. Bringing with it the hope of a new day. Although I know from experience, it is all downhill from here. Boredom looms. Days on my own with them are broken up into chunks of time that I tick off mentally as the hours progress. Pre-morning, breakfast, mid-morning snack, lunch, Roxy's nap . . . Then the monstrously long afternoon, which takes us down the other side of the hill and into bedtime.

Sometimes, if I'm lucky, Richard will help me in the

evenings. But then he'll make a big show of how magical every moment with the children is. How lucky I am to have this special time with my children when so many mothers must leave theirs to work.

I've not got very far with that, either. I thought once we got here, I'd get this whole new lease of life and be ready to tackle the next chapter head on. I imagined myself filling out online applications and marching confidently into job interviews. But instead, I feel bogged down by self-doubt. The few times I've managed to borrow Richard's computer I've scrolled through job vacancies and courses at local colleges, but every time I've put myself into the shoes of each version of Eliza leaving the house, I've seen myself failing miserably. Richard has walked in to check on my progress and reminded me of the reasons I wouldn't be suited. Or he's checked through a job application and given me sympathetic looks as he's scrolled through, pointing out my grammatical mistakes and deleting most of it. A sales position at a local company. 'Come on, Eliza, you'll fall to bits the second someone's rude to you. You need thick skin for sales.' Or a course in nutrition I've been looking at. 'Don't you need some sort of background – I'm not sure you'll meet the criteria for this.'

I look out at the rain tapping on leaves outside, feeling dismal. The momentary joy of the last few minutes with the children goes missing. Richard walks into the room and I stiffen. We stop singing; the words leave my mouth in a drizzle and trail off. He's wearing a knit vest over a shirt and tie. He fastens his watch and then pushes his glasses up his nose.

'Dada!' Roxy squeals. He smiles at her, messing up Noah's hair as he walks past. I know Noah hates that. I sit upright in my chair. 'I was thinking we could go to that café today? The one that we passed on the way back from nursery that time? The Meadows?' I need to get out of here. I need to see other people, make small talk, and eat something I haven't cooked. There is an urgency I've not felt before.

He kisses the top of my head. 'Why don't you go on your own, have a little break from us? You deserve it.'

I look across at him in amazement. 'Really?' I whisper. Unable to remember the last time I've been out without having a child to negotiate with. 'Okay.' I nod quickly, before he changes his mind. An excited buzz runs through me. A few hours of freedom outside, all on my own.

I shut the car door and start the engine. I have that just-passed-my-driving-test feeling of liberation as I make my way down the drive. Leaning forward, I fiddle with the radio, flicking through to something fun. A song we used to listen to on repeat at school begins to play, and I mouth the lyrics, getting lost in a rush of nostalgia: on a dance floor at uni, arms raised to the ceiling, eyes closed.

Free.

I turn onto the country lane at the end of our drive. For a second, I daydream of going straight to my mum's house. Maybe if I went there and she saw my face, I could explain, and she'd let me in. I think of the crumpled five-pound note in my pocket. That won't get me very far.

A fresh start is all we need to put the past behind us, Richard kept saying. Over and over. A better 'work–life' balance will make everything improve. But now we're here, I've realised I'm still alone. He hasn't really let me go. Everything still has limits.

Back in London there was a 'stay and play' at the local church on a Monday morning. I used to go to see other mums while the kids all played with toys in the middle of our giant circle. I think of Mia and Grace, two women who I became friends with. Well, they probably wouldn't call me a friend – they probably don't even remember my name. I used to really enjoy those mornings. Drinking tea and watching all the children bumble around. It felt normal. I'd tell them about my life, omitting all the crap bits. They would always be so impressed by my husband and his work. I enjoyed the look they gave when I talked about him. I soon found myself embellishing my life to get those looks. To think that I could be someone with an enviable life. I found that quite amazing. Then I'd get home and feel awful that I'd done such a thing. He is right. I can be very bad.

About five minutes into the drive, I notice a flashing light on the dashboard, and slow to a stop. I open the glove compartment and flip through the manual to find out what the alert means. Low tyre pressure – a puncture? I get out to check the wheels. The front tyre is completely level to the floor. I tut and stare in the direction I was going. The image of sitting in the café and chatting to another woman about our kids as I sip on a coffee, laughing, slowly disintegrates. Replaced instead with a recovery truck, and an angry Richard.

Hearing a vehicle pull in behind, I turn to see a young man hop down from a small white van. 'Are you okay?' he asks.

I pad my pockets, looking for my phone, but I don't have it on me. 'Yes . . . well, no. I have a flat. It's fine, I just need to make a call.' I open the car door and dig around inside pockets and under seat wells. I get that sinking feeling. I can't have left it in the house, can I?

'Are you staying around here or just passing through?' he asks.

'I live at the house down Layton Road,' I explain, still rummaging around for my phone. I have that familiar curling and tightening of my chest. How will Richard react to this? I chew my thumbnail.

'Oh man, the glass house in the woods?' I look over at him properly then. He blinks. And shifts on the spot. A frown forms and he scratches the back of his head and looks at the floor. I glance at his van. There, straddled on the back of the driver's seat, is an electric blue sweater. Fear washes through me and without too much thought I open the car door and sit down, swiftly banging the door shut and bashing my hand down on the lock. He comes over and stands right up close against the door.

'Hey, I can explain.' His breath rushes against the glass as he speaks.

'Just leave me alone.' I lean forward and start the engine.

'You really shouldn't drive on that wheel. You'll damage it. Please, let me explain.'

My heart pounds. I feel defenceless in this broken car

without my phone. 'Please leave me alone. I'm fine, I don't need any help.'

He gesticulates around, frustrated, and then pats his chest. 'I'm George. I'm a neighbour. I live in the cottage at the end of your land.' He's pointing back the way we came. He takes my side glance as an invitation to continue. 'I was in the woods walking. I hadn't realised the house was occupied; it's been vacant for ages. It's been looked after by some faceless rental company, right?' he says, as if to prove he's in the know. 'I sometimes cross over the fence and have a potter around. Honestly, I'm just nosy.' I stare at my hands as he talks. Should I believe him? 'Honestly, I got the shock of my life when I saw you. I should have just stayed and said hello. But then you screamed and I just legged it.' He pauses and sighs, and then says sincerely, 'I'm really sorry if I scared you.'

My hands fall from the wheel. 'How do I know you're not some sort of psycho axe murderer?'

He lets out an easy laugh. 'Do I look like one of those?'

For the first time I look at him. Not just a glance, a proper, good look. And no, he doesn't look like a psycho axe murder. He's very handsome. A wide smile, pale blue eyes. Dirty blond hair in nineties curtains. He could do with a shave, and he has some sort of black grease wiped on the leg of his jeans. But, I quite like the fact he isn't trying to be perfect. I look at my hands again. I should know better than to take something at face value. I've made that mistake before.

'I take the horses trekking in the woods by the house a lot as well.' He notices my eyes lingering on the dirt on his trousers and he smacks it away. 'I was helping Susie move some old furniture,' he mutters self-consciously.

'Horses?' I repeat.

'Yeah – the riding school. My aunt Susie's. She's a waifs and strays kind of lady.' He laughs, brushing his hair back out of his face. 'Want me to help you with the jack?'

I decide I don't have much choice, and I could do with a hand. Besides, I really do want to believe him and feel at ease with him despite my initial misgivings. Finally, I relent, and I open the door. 'Yes, that would be great – thank you.' As I climb out of the car a cold rush of air hits me in the face and I shiver, pulling my coat around myself for warmth.

'Least I can do.' He kneels next to the tyre to look at the damage. I watch as his fingers find a ridge in it. He seems to know what he's doing, and I can't help admiring how capable he seems. 'Looks like you either hit something sharp or someone did this on purpose. With a blade.'

I laugh lightly. 'On purpose?' I shake my head. 'We're all the way down there, I don't think . . .'

He walks around the back, and I follow him to the boot. He pulls up the lining but there is an empty space instead of a spare. 'Sorry, doesn't look like it's a roadside repair job.'

My heart sinks. Richard's going to be so cross.

'You want a lift back?' he asks, pointing to his van. 'It's freezing out here, you don't want to be hanging around for the recovery guys. They could be hours.'

I bite my lip. 'If you don't mind? I seem to have misplaced my phone.'

'Sure, of course.' I climb up onto the passenger seat of his van and pull the belt across. 'All good?' he asks and I nod as he revs the engine.

'How come you know so much about cars? Are you a mechanic or something?' I ask.

He checks his mirrors before turning the van around. 'Just dabbled a bit. Like I do with the horses. Susie says I can't keep my hands to myself for a second.' He laughs. 'Do you ride?'

I wince. I don't feel like talking about things I used to do. He glances over at me and then back at the road. 'It's full of insufferable riding kids but they're mostly a laugh.' He looks over at me again. I sense that he's trying to work me out. 'I wouldn't worry, your boss will understand about the tyre, it's not your fault.'

Roxy was with me in the woods, he must think I'm the nanny.

'Oh. I don't work there. I'm with my husband and children,' I say quietly.

His eyebrows shoot up when I say that. 'No way. You just look so young.'

I look out the window, and watch the hedgerows clip the wing mirror as we pass.

'Are you okay?' he asks.

It has been such a long time since someone's asked me how I am that I choke up. Swallowing thickly, I shake my head. 'Yes, fine. Sorry. I'm just upset about the car.' I notice the sign coming up for our drive. 'Is it okay if you drop me here?'

He slows down. 'I can take you up to the house if you want? It looks like it's going to rain.'

'It's fine. I fancy a bit of a walk. Thank you so much.' He looks sceptical but slows, and I unclip my belt and turn to open the door.

'Hey.' He touches my shoulder. I turn my head and stare at his hand before he quickly removes it. I blink. 'Come over for a ride? I'm sure we could chuck in a freebie seeing as we're neighbours,' he offers.

'Thank you. I'll think about it,' I reply, turning my back to him and slipping out of the door. As the van crawls away, I think of the scene that would play out if I asked Richard. I know from experience that he'd flap around with a thousand excuses. I'd try to be firm but would quickly get shot down. A tear races down my cheek as I begin the walk. Finally admitting to myself how stuck I really feel. And that all the high hopes I had for this place really aren't coming to fruition.

CHAPTER 23

I wrap my coat tightly and hug myself as the freezing wind rattles through my hair. I dip my face into the collar for warmth, and turn the corner. As the house comes into view, I trip. Pain crashes through me. And I groan, turning onto my back. I lie there for a moment watching the ice white clouds pass above my head. A few drops of cold rain fall numbly onto my face.

I muster the energy to push myself up to sitting position, and I look down at my hurt knee. Blood has begun to collect on the fabric of my jeans. It is quite nice to see it. A strange release of something. I touch the area but then jolt my finger away.

I think of my mum back at home. She used to wash the pans at the sink staring out onto rolling hills listening to the radio. I wonder if she ever thinks about me. Or if she's completely scratched me out from her mind so she can pretend to herself that I never existed. I wish I was there with her. I would stand next to her and place my cheek on her shoulder and wrap my arms around her waist. If she saw the children in person, the anger she feels would melt away and she'd hold me back. Her stoic face crumbling. I'm sure of it.

I think back to those first few months when I met Richard. The secret kisses. *He's not who you think he is!* I hadn't once considered the predatory nature of it. Fresh from a mental health crisis, and straight into his arms. Everything was so dark at that time – he seemed like my only crack of light. I wanted to believe in it. 'You can understand that, can't you?' I whisper, surprised to have spoken out loud.

I look over at the building, still some distance away, and yank myself to standing position. Taking a few tentative steps forward, my slight limp straightens out as I get used to the pain. I'm suddenly desperate to see the children. Roxy's morning giggles and Noah's funny mispronunciation as he sings. The way he's started to whisper, 'Mummy, love you,' into my ear. Those tiny moments of life as a mother that really are my only reason to be here.

A loud banging noise resonates as I get closer. Richard is standing with an axe high above his head underneath the raised garage door. He's wearing a red checked shirt and a black padded gilet. His arms fall, and a crack tears through the log in front of him. He pauses, pleased, as he admires his handiwork. I feel a thin line of blood trickle down my leg.

He notices me standing in the rain. 'You're back,' he says, resting the axe against the wall. 'Come on. You're all wet.' He gestures with his hand for me to come beneath the retractable door.

I sniff. 'I got a flat.'

'Come inside. Let's get you all warm.'

I nod, following him. It isn't until I'm getting changed upstairs, my teeth still chattering, that I realise he didn't seem at all surprised.

We eat dinner together after the children are in bed. The lights inside are dimmed and if I look up at the ceiling, I can see a litter of tiny stars shining down from the dark navy-blue sky. Jazz is playing through the Sonos, loudly. Too loudly. Richard hums occasionally and drums his fingers on the table in time with the ramshackle beat. I try to eat. But I'm not hungry. I push the food around my plate with my fork.

I've cooked his favourite, steak. The plate scratches loudly as he knifes at his food. His jaw clicks as he chews. Ramming the chunks of meat into his mouth, his fat tongue licking his lips as he swallows. He's in a very good mood. Giddy, in fact. I glance up at the security camera. The little red light is on. Richard's phone is next to his placemat. It never leaves his side.

I clear my throat. 'The tyre . . . I don't know what happened.'

I watch his reaction carefully. He waves his knife in the air.

'Don't worry about it, Eliza,' he says between munches. 'It's been collected and it'll be back with us by the morning. We're insured.'

'I don't really understand what happened,' I say, thinking about George's comment about how the damage was caused.

'Eliza, it's fine if you bashed it,' he says swiftly. 'You're not the best driver, as we know from experience . . .' He hoots, as if telling an 'in joke' – but nobody else laughs.

I blink. 'Sorry.' The word slips out before I can catch it. Conspiring against the urge to plead my innocence. 'Have you seen my phone?' I ask. His hands pause mid-cut. Then he looks up at me with his brows raised. I shrivel up slightly.

'Have you lost that too?' His chewing tempers as he stares. 'Oh dear, Eliza. Not this again.'

I shake my head. 'No – it must be around here somewhere. I saw it this morning.'

He stands up and throws his napkin down and strides over to me, the energy forcing me to sit back in my chair and brace myself. To my surprise he merely bends down and kisses my lips. 'That was delicious. Thank you.' He moves a hair from my face. 'Maybe one of the children hid it, you know how Noah does that sometimes.' His eyes run over my features. 'You're looking very pale, Eliza. The move has taken it out of you a bit.' He begins to walk from the room. 'You should have a bath. Relax. A bit of self-care would do you the world of good.'

I stare at my untouched plate before standing up and knifing the contents into the bin. After tidying up, I turn off the lights in the living room, and quietly walk through the hallway to Noah's room. The back of his head is cocooned within his dinosaur duvet. We've just moved him out of his cot to make way for Roxy and he's now in a toddler bed. I can just about squeeze in between him and the safety rail. I spoon myself against him, my feet popping out the bottom of the short covers.

I clutch his body and we breathe in unison. Then I hear

him whisper, 'Mummy. Love you.' And he turns around, so we face each other.

'Love you too,' I reply.

I hear the door open, and a pool of light floods the wall. Richard's shadow looms against it. I hug Noah tightly as he slowly shuts the door.

CHAPTER 24

Later that week I'm rushing to get Noah ready for nursery. My anxiety has been building for a while. I've remained quiet about it, and tried focusing on breathing exercises Richard has taught me. The truth is, I feel like Richard is spiralling. He's unnervingly distant. He won't make eye contact. It's as if he's thinking bad thoughts about me, and if he looks, he might say them out loud. The happy, relaxed demeanour he adopted to get me here has long gone.

When I hear banging from the kitchen I swallow.

'Big bang,' Noah says and I nod.

'Probably Daddy fixing something,' I whisper.

I try to comb his hair down with my hand; it's got all tufty from the night's sleep. His nose is full of snot that just won't shift in this freezing weather. His cheeks are permanently red too. I grab a pot of cream and try to apply it. But he twists and turns. 'Me do it. Me do it, Mummy.' He dives at the tub and is suddenly covered. I sigh.

Another crash.

'Richard?' I call, whipping Noah's jumper off, and replacing it with a clean one, tossing the other towards the wash basket. Then I pick him up and walk down the hallway into the living area which is bathed in buttery morning light.

I stop. He's standing on top of the kitchen counter with most of the contents of the cupboards and shelves out. 'Richard. What . . . what are you doing?'

He shakes his head in frustration. 'Where you put everything. It doesn't make sense. The cups and glasses should go here opposite the dishwasher, and the mugs next to them there by the tea and coffee and, of course, the kettle.' He scratches his face irritably, and his eyes dart around in that way they do when he's stressed. 'It's madness, Eliza, I don't know what you were thinking. These pots and pans . . .' He picks the items up and thrusts them in the air. 'You have to cross the entire kitchen to get them from the oven, and for fuck's sake, why aren't the knives and forks over here . . . ?' He juts open a drawer. 'It's been driving me mad.'

Noah squirms in my arms as I follow his movements around the room. 'Okay,' I stammer. 'Don't worry, I'll put everything away in a better place.' I step towards him. He is sweating. As if in a frenzy.

'It's just not on, Eliza. I mean . . . what were you thinking?' He looks at me, incredulous.

I blink. I think back to the day I unpacked the kitchen. There was so much going on. The kids were both hanging off me, and I didn't have a chance to think it through. 'It's fine, Richard – I'll fix it this afternoon while Roxy's napping.' I put Noah down and he trots to the toy kitchen we got him last

Christmas. 'Come on, darling, we're going to be late,' I say, but he ignores me. I turn to Richard. 'I'll drive you both in, and then do some shopping. I've barely left the house all week . . .'

'It's just madness, Eliza,' he says, ignoring my words. 'I mean . . . how could you be so stupid?' He spits out the last word and I blink.

Stung and breathless, I stammer, trying to get a footing in something I feel could get out of hand. 'I'm sorry. I'll sort it as soon as I'm back.' He shakes his head, taking in the mess, and then looks up at me – as though I created it.

'I'll sort it today,' I say again, quietly. I turn to Noah. 'Come on, darling, time for nursery. I'm driving you and Daddy today.'

He shakes his head and tearfully says, 'Mummy. Want to stay.' I walk over to him and brush his hair down again. 'Mummy. Stay with you,' he whines, putting his arms around my neck.

Guilt yanks at me. I swallow before forcing a laugh. 'Why, darling? It's boring here with me and silly-pants.' I glance at Roxy who is sitting in her high chair, her legs dangling down. I pull Noah closer and kiss his cheek. 'Today will be better. And then tomorrow will be better than that. That's how it works.' Tough love will get him out of here. Tough love will send him on his way.

Richard jumps down from his spot on the counter, and walks towards us. He stops, considering something. 'I think maybe we overshot this idea of nursery.'

I blink. 'What?' I ask, breathless.

'He should stay home with you. He obviously isn't ready.

We've tried it for a few weeks and he's miserable.' Panic clutches at my neck. 'But we need childcare – I won't be here to look after them, remember . . .' I muster.

He shrugs, looking out the wet, mottled glass. 'The kids' welfare is more important, isn't it? It's been a big move. We don't want to scar them for life, do we?' His eyes bore into mine – to make me aware the question really is: do you? 'Let's give it six months and reassess. Nursery will have another place for Roxy by then. And maybe you'll have worked out what you actually want to do,' he adds pointedly.

'But . . . Richard.' I step towards him, ignoring Noah's smug toothy grin. My eyes rush around the living area. The thought of day in, day out stuck here. No car. Two kids. No way out. Just the clock reverberating. Shaking his head sadly, he comes towards me and puts his hands either side of my shoulders. His neck scooped down slightly, ready to belittle. 'You know it's the right thing to do, Eliza. You weren't serious about this job thing anyway. It's not as though you actually followed through on anything.' Before I can reply he lets go. He smacks a kiss on Noah's delighted face and marches towards the door, grabbing his coat. 'I'll see you later. Have fun.' With that he disappears. The slam makes me jump.

Noah's voice chants, 'No nursery. Stay home with Mummy.'

The bright light of expectation within fades.

Then it occurs to me.

What if all this time he hasn't really been 'trying'?

He's been prepping.

CHAPTER 25

Weeks pass. I feel myself disappearing. I'm not sure what day it is, all I know is it must be a weekday because Richard is at work. The sounds of the children are my only constant – laughter, whines, cries. The perpetual, 'Mummy. Mummy. Mummy.'

My other obsession is the camera. I hear it whir deftly inside the glass dome all day. My every movement is sent directly to my husband's phone. He said it's only for emergencies. But I don't believe him for a second. I try to remember what it's like living unhampered by someone else's mood. But I can't. I'd let myself believe we'd got over the bump in the road, but now I think I just desperately wanted to believe that we were a normal family.

After Roxy's nap there is some respite from the rain, and determined not to be stuck inside all day, I get them dressed in outdoor gear. I must get out. I crave fresh air. We leave out the back doors. Holding Noah's hand, I help him onto the patio. He moans as soon as I close it behind us. 'Mummy. Cold.' I've put Roxy in her baby carrier, as it's easier to help Noah if I've got my hands free, and I'm hoping we'll be out for more than five minutes. Her head tilts back and her long lashes blink up at the tops of trees.

We walk to the end of the garden. The cold air bites, and Noah moans, 'I want go back. Watch telly.' But soon he's distracted by rocks and snail shells and begins to enjoy himself.

At the entrance to the path I hold one of the bright rhododendron flowers in my hand. Noah pulls at one and crushes it in his fist. 'Pretty flowers,' he says. I nod, agreeing; they are jewel-like against the twisty branches and evergreens. The children are both excited at the prospect of walking through a tunnel, and squeal as we pad through the passageway. A puddle appears ahead, and Noah runs to it, before stomping in it in his bright wellington boots. 'Splash, splash!' he cries, wiggling on the spot.

Once out the other side we come to the clearing. I look longingly over to the spot where I saw George a few weeks ago. Each time we've come I've lingered, hoping. Noah wanders up to the shed, and his wellie makes a thwacking noise as he kicks the side of it. I step up to the door, and I press down on the handle. To my surprise it opens. I wonder how it was even locked before, as there isn't a hole for a key – like many things around here, the mechanism is hidden.

'Monsters, Mummy?' Noah whispers, his voice quivering.

I close my hand around his. 'No. Mummy checked and there aren't any monsters around here.' I read somewhere that you shouldn't dismiss monsters as silly, imaginary things. Because in life, monsters do exist. They're just not purple and fanged with red eyes and knobbly knees. They look like you and me. And I need to make sure if he encounters one, he'll trust I won't dismiss it as fantasy.

Noah follows me inside the bare shed. There is a thud behind us. The wind has shut us in. There is a sink at one end, and I wander over to it. Water spits erratically when I turn it on and quickly off. The hard concrete floor is solid, and I walk to the wooden hatch and look down at it. Noah copies me. There is a metal loop intended for a padlock. With a straight back I lower myself to the floor, one knee bent. It is tricky with Roxy on my chest and I almost keel over. 'Mummy, we go?' Noah says, looking around anxiously, pulling at the hem of my coat just as I stop myself from falling. 'Don't like it, Mummy,' he cries, voice wobbling.

I sigh and get to my feet. 'Yes, come on.'

He's right. It's creepy. I take his hand again and squeeze it and together we walk to the closed door.

I push down on the handle. But it's stiff, like it was the first time. Trying not to panic, I repeat the movement. But again. It stays stuck in place. A drop of terror diffuses in my chest. We're trapped. I don't have a phone. Richard is at work and has no idea where we are.

I let go of Noah's hand and try it again with both of mine. But it's rock solid. My attempts are futile. I look down at Noah staring up at me and try not to let the rising panic become visible on my face.

My pupils dart as I project outcomes internally. How would Richard ever find us? More likely he'd assume we left. Would he even think to check down here? How long until they'd come looking? Days? No nappies, no food, or blankets for the freezing nights. Would we starve to death?

'Mummy?' Noah asks, looking up at me.

Removing my hand, I look back and scan the four bare walls, then I turn to the handle again. It's chunky and there is something oddly robotic about it. 'It's okay.' I stammer, unsure if it is. Staring at it, I whisper, 'Open, please open. Please fucking open.'

Hearing a click, I push down and to my disbelief it slides open easily. I gasp for a breath I had no idea I'd been holding out on. Not daring to let it go again, I step outside. 'Come on, quick.' I help Noah down and we leave the shed, and I bang the door firmly behind us. There is no way I'm ever going inside that horrible, dank box again.

Back in the clearing, I look the way we came, and then the other way – the way we've not gone before. The weather's been so hideous we've either been scuppered by rain or one of the kids has whinged too intensely and we've gone back. I remember what George said about his cottage, and I wonder if it's visible at the bottom of our plot.

'Come on, Noah, let's go down this tunnel too.' He looks unsure for a moment. 'We might even see some horses!' This piques his interest, and we continue on. Twigs snap and skeleton leaves stick to our shoes. About halfway down Noah begins to flag.

'Mummy, I'm bored.'

'Oh Noah, only boring people get bored,' I sing, repeating the saying as I do often. It is something my father used to say to me. The thought of him makes me feel weighted down in sadness and regret and I do my best to push the sorrow away.

Finally, we find ourselves in a field full of grass so long Noah's head only just pops above it. Ahead I see a wooden fence enclosing a paddock. And inside are horses. Horses! My heart leaps and I break into the largest smile my face has managed for a long time.

'Come on!' I shout, exhilarated. I take Noah's hand, and we run to the fence. Placing him on the bottom rung, I stare ahead, taking in George's cottage all cosy with a thatched roof and smoke bellowing from the chimney.

Nostalgia hits me as I stare at the striped vertical jump in the paddock. I'm transported back. The feeling of flying, and the adrenalin hitting as the horse makes that first leap. Being air-bound for seconds, soaring through the sky. Holding my breath as we made it over the obstacle and landing on the hard ground without the slightest stumble. I bat a tear away as I think of how long it's been since I've ridden. How free I was back then.

'Mummy?' Noah asks. 'Why sad?'

I sniff and brush another tear away, leaning on the fence next to him. 'I'm not sad, baby.' I watch the smoke as it dances from the chimney, gently moving off into the sky. Then someone walks out of the stable block the other side of the paddock, holding a saddle on their forearms. George. My heart stops for a second. He notices us and smiles and waves. I raise my hand and wave back.

'Come on.' I sniff. 'Let's go back.' And I lift Noah off.

'Mummy, read farm book?' he says as we slowly make it through the long grass.

Before we enter the tunnel, I turn back, just once, to see George walking into the paddock and patting one of the horses. I wish we'd stayed to say hello.

'Yes, good choice,' I mutter to Noah.

It's going to take us a while to walk back. His little legs have done well to get this far. But I'm expecting to have to carry him most of the way. One in the baby carrier and one cemented to my side. I never knew how strong I was until I had kids. I look down at Roxy who's still happily snuggled.

We make it up the first passageway. As we pass the shed, I give it a wary look and shiver at the memory of being trapped inside.

Breaking free at the bottom of the lawn, I concede to Noah's moans and pick him up. Looking up to the house, I wince at the shadowy figure behind the glass. Richard is back earlier than usual. He pulls the doors back and stands in the gap with his arms crossed. I swallow. Once we arrive at the lip of the patio, I put Noah down on the slabs and he toddles towards the warmth of the house and his father. 'Noah, wait. Wellies muddy, remember,' I say and he stops. Richard watches us. Not making one movement to help. Once inside I take Roxy off my chest and go to help Noah. 'How come you're back?' I say, looking up at Richard from my position on the floor. He stares down. 'We went to get some fresh air,' I explain.

'I saw. What am I going to do with you?' he asks.

Pricks of moisture come to my eyes. 'Richard . . . we need to work something out.' My voice cracks. 'I . . . I can't live like this.' I feel weak and so very compromised.

He shakes his head. 'Like what? What more could you want?' he says. 'This is our fresh start.'

The meaning of the sentence has twisted, and I feel sick.

This is my life now. Just tiny moments of surrender.

CHAPTER 26

A few days later, and it's the weekend. Richard has fallen asleep on the sofa with Roxy in his arms. I stand over them. He looks so peaceful lying there cuddling his snoozing daughter. Her teeny hands resting on his face. If I were anyone else, I'd take out my phone and snap a photograph to post on Instagram with a few hashtags and then feel a bit guilty for touting such an intimate moment around. But I don't have an Instagram. Or friends and family that might comment underneath #adorable. Or even a phone. Richard says I can't have another one, it must be somewhere in the house, and it will pop up when I least expect it. The sadness that I've got no one to share this phase of motherhood with is with me all the time. The loneliness is so embedded I feel like I'm drowning in it.

I look up. There is a rainbow just visible above the trees. The sky is now a stark blue. I walk to the glass and close my eyes as the intense light falls on my drained face. It has been so long since I've seen anything so cheery. Why do rainbows feel so hopeful? Is it because they are so fantastical – it seems unreal they should even exist?

I tiptoe through to the hallway and open Noah's door. He's asleep too. It's not often I manage to get them to nap at the same time. Pleased, I sneak to the front door and lift my coat off the rack and pick up my boots. I almost open the front door, but worried the notification from the doorbell to his phone will wake Richard up, I creep instead to the back doors. Holding my breath, I pull them back. He doesn't stir and I thrust my feet into my boots and step outside, pushing the door back across the other way.

A breeze whips my hair around my face and I feel a whisper in the rustle of leaves: *run*. But I have nowhere. I am stuck. For I cannot live without my babies. And he would never let me have them. Even to share. People better natured than Richard do terrible things to keep control of their kids. I know that.

Richard has never physically hurt me – not in a reportable way. He once pushed me and I fell, hitting my head. But he drummed it into me that I lost my footing – I even started to believe it myself. In some ways what he does is worse than relentless violence because it is so hard to articulate to someone else. It is subtle, insidious; it has steadily eroded away the woman I used to be.

I tramp down the passageway. I want to have another look at the cottage across the field. I mutter to myself as I walk. Practising what I would say if I attempted to talk to someone about my predicament. I bite my nail as I think of Richard laughing in the face of an accusation. Belittling me. He'd hold up his certificates and explain he's been stuck caring for his sick wife. When I think of his face when he deposited us at the post-partum unit, I remember noticing the little smile of triumph on it. I must have imagined it, I'd thought. I kept imagining a lot of things.

One of the incidents that tipped him over the edge, when he decided I needed more help than he could offer, was when Roxy was a few months old. I'd managed to get them both asleep and took the chance to have a nap myself. As soon as I stirred, I jumped up to check on her as I usually did. But she wasn't in the cot by our bed. I held my breath as I ran from room to room, but my darkest worries were confirmed. She was gone. I held Noah's squirming body to my chest and, panicking, I called the police and jabbered down the phone hysterically. I couldn't get hold of Richard. There was quite a scene. Blue lights flashing, men in caps trying to calm me down as I rambled on in a frenzy.

Then Richard arrived home with Roxy asleep in the buggy. I couldn't believe it. He said he'd taken her for a walk to get her to sleep, and so I could also get some much-needed shut-eye as well. 'The motion sends her off, you see, Officer.' Then he apologised on my behalf. He was a therapist and he was worried about me. I kept forgetting things. He was in denial about my mental state. But my postnatal depression had obviously taken a nasty turn and it couldn't be ignored any longer. He looked tired and worried, and the officers were extremely sympathetic towards him.

I was left standing there, confused. I was so sure I'd put Roxy down in the cot. I remember because for the first time she didn't stir. She'd closed her eyes and settled and went off to sleep. But I must have got it wrong. Richard was right, I must have imagined it.

He has all my files. Not to mention all his recordings. Everything he needs to prove I am an unfit mother. He would win. My choice is to leave, alone. Or stay with him.

My fingers brush the delicate pink petals as I rush down the passageway, checking behind me, in case he's woken up. My feet squelch as I pass our earlier footprints. The silence of this journey jars against the constant noise of being with two small children. I arrive at the shed in the clearing. I don't linger. I speed through the next passageway and run as fast as I can through the long grass to the fence.

The cottage still has smoke billowing from the chimney. It takes all my effort not to lob myself over the fence and run to their front door. But I fast-forward the tape in my head. My garbled explanation that would sound barmy. The police showing up. And then how they would arrive at our perfect house in the woods and meet my exceptional husband.

Once again, I look back the way I came to check no one is behind me.

And when I turn back towards the paddock, I see George opening the gate at the other end. He's holding the reins of a large brown mare; its dark long mane sweeps as it walks. George sees me and stops, surprised.

I turn to check behind me again.

We stare at each other for a moment before he leads the horse across the paddock to where I'm standing. 'Hey,' he says. He's wearing a navy beanie and an oversized grey marl hoodie with a scarf tucked into the neckline. He's even more handsome than I remember. 'You came back.'

'I was just walking,' I reply sharply, with a shrug.

He nods. I feel bad for being unfriendly. Reaching forward, I hold out my hand and the horse steps towards it. I place my palm on her forehead and smooth it down the length of her nose. Hooves inch further towards me. 'How old is she? About nine?'

'She's nearly twelve.' George runs his hand across the horse's wide protruding belly. 'Power. That's her name.' She snorts, her head bobbing up and down as she enjoys the attention. George raises an eyebrow. 'She doesn't like many people. Only person she'll let on the saddle is me.'

I continue weaving my hand up and down her nose. Steam floats from her nostrils. 'Here, girl,' I mutter. 'Here, girl.'

I glance at George who is watching me from under his hair. 'You've got a way with her.'

'I used to have a horse that looked just like her.' I drop my hand, remembering. What I would give to start again. Turning, I look behind me. George frowns, and looks up towards the house too. 'Want to come in and meet Susie? Have a cup of tea?'

'I should go.' I need to get back before Richard comes looking.

'She'd love to meet you,' he says, trying again.

I shake my head, and take some steps back and begin to turn.

'Wait!' he calls as I stuff my hands in my pockets. 'What's your name? You never said.'

I twirl on the spot to face him again briefly. 'Eliza. My name's Eliza.'

And I rush back through the long grass to the first passageway, feeling breathless.

A branch swings into my face and I push it away as I walk through the undergrowth. I think of how weary and bogged down I feel compared to George. A swirl of anger collates inside. George is so carefree with an aura of absolute ease. I want that. What a gift not to be constantly tired and full of anxiety.

The sound of Roxy howling quickens my step. And as I approach the end of the first passageway, I hear them congregated in the clearing. I stop. Scared. I want to turn and run the other way. But the agony in Roxy's voice pulls me forward.

In the clearing, by the shed, stands Richard and the two children. Roxy is pushing against his chest with her little balled-up fists, beside herself with rage. I rush over and remove her from his arms. He lets me take her. 'Shhh . . . shhh, darling,' I whisper, trying to soothe her.

'We woke up and you weren't there. We almost thought you'd disappeared,' Richard says, his voice flat.

'Just walking . . .'

'Oh, yes. We all know how much you love that.' His words are laced with a snide quality that makes my heart sink.

'I can't sit in that house all the time. It's not healthy, you know that.'

'Yes, you need to get away from us, apparently. Get that

space you so desperately want,' he says through gritted teeth. He puts a hand in his pocket. The door to the shed makes the same clicking noise I heard earlier and swings open. I rock Roxy in my arms, shushing her. Noah, whose hand is being held by Richard, looks horrified at the open door.

'And then I remembered you saying you wish you had a bit of time to sort out the shed. Because you wanted to use it for something? Maybe now's a good time.' He looks up at the sky. 'The sun's finally come out.'

'What?' I whisper, clinging to my daughter. I dare a glance at the open door and the cold concrete floor. He puts his hands on Roxy, and she cries out as he tries to remove her. 'No,' I whisper, trying to stand firm. Then my eyes settle on Noah's confused face as Roxy's wail hits the back of my eardrum and I let her go. Richard holds her tightly and clutches my arm, guiding me backwards. The heel of my boot hits the back of the ledge as I cross the threshold. He grips me, stopping me from falling. Noah's tiny features are furrowed; my heart aches for him.

Richard brought the children out here for a reason. So that I will submit with a smile on my face. He knows I won't cause a scene and scare them. I whisper, 'How long?' He shakes his head. He wouldn't tell me that. I realise, it's part of the fun. 'Daddy's right,' I say, clearing my throat. 'It needs a good clean.' I look at the sparse interior as I say the words. 'I'll come back to make you dinner.' Hoping that might fix a time. 'Okay?' I nod to reassure Noah, who is desperate to believe everything is okay.

Richard shuts the door and puts his hand in his pocket again. The painful clicking noise repeats. My hand falls on the handle – it's rock solid. The lock must be activated from his phone like the camera inside the house. I watch them march away. Roxy's cry has subsided slightly and Noah's head strains to watch as he is pulled back towards the path by his father. I smile at him as he disappears. A big plastered-on smile that I hope hides my terror. The instant he disappears out of sight the corners of my mouth drop, and a tear rolls down my cold cheek.

CHAPTER 27

I wipe the tear with the back of my hand. I am alone. Every shift and sound I make resonates against the looming silence. I move my gaze from the passageway to the trees where I first saw George. I remember the quiet smile on the face watching me and Roxy, just before I screamed. I put my forehead on the glass and wish he would appear at that same spot right now.

Pulling myself together, I look around. I tap the wooden panelled walls, and the sound that comes back is thick, low and full of bass. I'm within something impenetrable. Slumping against the wall, I let myself slide to the ground. My head tells me to panic, but I can't bring myself to waste the energy.

There was an incident in London. Not far from our intense honeymoon period. Just before Richard began to change. It was a constant stream of meals out, big romantic gestures, and lazy mornings in bed. A time of enhanced reality. I thought it would be like that forever. I grinned from ear to ear thinking I'd finally found the key to being happy within my skin. And it was him.

One day he had to travel for a conference. I was staying behind and although I was going to miss him terribly, I was excited. A chance to see my friends – and show off my new relationship with my older, sophisticated man. Richard and I had been so stuck within our bubble; it was selfish but, for that period, no one else mattered. I was addicted to the feelings he gave me. And how good I finally felt about myself.

My friends were all impressed, if a little peeved that I'd basically ignored them for six months. But they let it slide. We all dropped off the radar for a bit when new relationships began.

The door handle to the bathroom at the top of his maisonette was a bit broken, and sometimes if you shut the door from the outside, the whole mechanism collapsed, and it fell off in your hand. Richard kept meaning to get it fixed. But it wasn't a priority, and he was busy. Besides, if you were using the bathroom, you usually closed it from the inside. I'd sat on the bed chatting and joking with him as he packed. We'd kissed passionately at the front door as we said our goodbyes. I trudged back up the stairs and went into the bathroom to pluck my eyebrows, leaving the door ajar. He later told me he'd come back up to grab his scarf and must have knocked the door shut. I turned and ran at it. My hand jutting at the knob, banging, shouting for him to come back. But it was too late. Blood drained from my face as I heard the front door bang. I'd never felt panic like it. A box room without a window and my phone was in the kitchen.

He was gone for fourteen hours. I didn't know what to do with myself. I cleaned the entire room until it sparkled. I drank out of the tap. I cried. I tried shouting for help but knew the little deaf old lady next door would never hear me.

I knew he'd come back. He would realise when he couldn't get hold of me, surely. I didn't know the time, and couldn't even tell if it was day or night. Scary thoughts burst in when you're in a situation like that. How long could I survive in here? He was devastated when he returned, early – he said he'd nearly called the police because I wasn't picking up my phone. I fell into his open arms, relieved.

I think about that now. And wonder, did he do it on purpose? Was it a taster – to see what kind of thrill he'd get? I look at the door. It's programmed to lock via his phone. Did he set this up on purpose? Was he preparing this the whole time as we arranged our move? When he kissed me, when he held me, when he whispered that he'd changed for good?

I wonder what he's planning to do with me next. The thought makes me stand up. I need to move around as my knee is aching, so I limp over to the sink to check it's still working. Freezing water cascades out, and my hand shakes as I cup liquid into my palm and drink. Maybe if I had something hard to bash against the glass, it would break? Possibly. But the room is completely empty. Besides, even if I got out, where would I go?

I begin to circle around the trapdoor to keep myself warm. I want to see what's below, but I'm too scared. The thought there could be a worse level than the one I'm on lingers. What if this is just the waiting area for something far worse and more permanent? I crouch down and flick the metal flap and lift the hatch. I hold my breath as the door rises, expecting darkness. My shoulders fall. All I see is another closed element – this time with a lock. Part of me is relieved, the part that doesn't want to know what's coming next.

I wish I could transport my children somewhere safe. I bite my lip and let out a sob as I think of my mother at home. I imagine Noah and Roxy in a few years, carefree in the garden helping her weed. Or sitting at her green-painted wrought-iron table, the one she's had forever that belonged to her parents. At Easter we'd paint boiled eggs – she loved doing that with me. And she'd cook her favourite chocolate roulade at Christmas – Noah would ask for a double helping. Half of it would end up all over his face. I try to hold all those joyful imagined memories in, but they fall from my eyes as tears.

A thought springs then. I promised Noah I'd give him dinner, and Richard will have to explain why I'm not back. He will ask for me. He always does. I get a tight feeling in my chest, scared for their confusion. But Richard is so smooth – I'm sure he'll be able to find the right words to explain me away.

A cold dagger or fear plunges into me as I think of other reasons he may have to explain my absence in the future. How far will he take this?

It has begun to snow. I place my forehead back against the glass. My fingers splayed on the surface. Freedom is just there on the other side. But it may as well be on Mars. My breath fogs up the view as I watch the tiny pinpricks of ice turn to big fat fluffy feathers landing on the grass. Mesmerised, I just stand there watching. Trance-like, I blank out all the darkness and close my eyes, remembering the moment my babies were first given to me, and the love and fear I was handed then.

Sometime later I'm sitting on the floor. My knees up and my arms slouched over on them. Head bowed between my legs. Hearing a clicking sound, I look at the door. Too scared to move a muscle. Did I imagine it? Finally, I push myself up. The cold has infected my limbs, causing them to ache painfully from sitting in the same position for too long. I move towards the handle and reach for it. Curling my fingers around the metal, my head buzzes. 'Please open, please open,' I whisper to myself, my lips barely moving. A gust of biting wind bellows in my face and I allow the fleeting relief to wash over me.

My boots land on the untouched layer of snow as I step tentatively down from the structure. I raise my face up into the sky and enjoy the icy dots melting on my skin. Turning, I walk to the house. 'I'm coming,' I whisper.

Once through the passageway I look towards the balmy light flooding the lawn above. I note, on face value, how lovely the scene within appears. My family sits around the dining table. The commanding head of the household, and the little boy and girl sat listening as he talks at them. Noah's legs rock back and forth in his infant chair. I can hear the loud and dramatic music even before I open the door, which thuds against the glass, vibrating. I pull it back and the heat within wraps around me like a blanket, and I feel as though I could collapse. Richard grins at me. 'Ah! You're back! We were just wondering how long you were going to be.' The dimmed lights, the soft muted colours. It all looks so civilised.

'Roxy, here you go, zoom zoom.' He loudly flies a spoonful of food into her mouth. 'Yummy. Yeah. See? Isn't it yummy?' He looks frantic – I wonder if he's been taking drugs again. He's been known to dabble.

Noah looks at me. 'Mummy!' he cries and I draw back the chair next to him and pull him onto my lap. They're up far too late, usually they'd have been asleep for hours by now. Roxy has that crazed hyper look on her face, the one she gets when she's been overstimulated.

'All done?' Richard asks, his voice bellowing to reach above the noise. His eyes are shining. I shake my head, too angry to speak directly to him. There is a crash of cymbals – the music reaches a crescendo; it's too much after the silence of the last few hours. I pick Noah up and hike him onto my hip as I walk over to the amp and turn the music down. I stand there a moment. Trying to compose myself.

'Mummy!' Noah says again as he begins to fiddle with the chain around my neck. 'Mummy done? All clean?'

'What?' I whisper, planting a kiss on his cheek. Then remembering. 'Yes, very clean,' I say, trying not to cry.

'Snow, Mummy,' he says, pointing outside at the coating humped over everything in the darkness. And I nod, moving his arms and legs so they wrap around me. 'Mummy cold?' he asks, looking at me with concern and putting his tiny hands on my bitter cheeks.

I swallow back the tears and shake my head. 'Me? No

darling. Not cold at all. Mummy likes the cold,' I say, kissing the tip of his nose and giving him a carefree smile in the hope that it will dispel any concern.

The constant low-level anxiety eases a little as soon as Richard leaves for work the next day. The kids are all over me. They can tell there is an imbalance, and something isn't right. I force myself to do productive things to keep them occupied. I get the art box out and tear some pages from a drawing book for Noah to colour. Roxy enjoys watching him from her position on the high chair. Occasionally holding a pencil so she can feel as though she's joining in. Noah's concentration span is limited. But he loves drawing. I stroke his back as he works. Roxy waves a green felt tip in the air and I grab it before she covers her face in ink.

'What's that?' I point at a flume of colour on Noah's page.

'My mummy – blue,' he says.

'Beautiful.' Then I point at the angry scrawl of red on the other side.

'Daddy,' he says, nodding to himself.

I bite my lip, wanting to unwrap this for him. It's my job to make him feel secure. Even if I'm not. That's the role of a mother. To make a child's reality as perfect as possible, no matter the situation you're truly in.

The next afternoon I'm in the kitchen tidying up after lunch when the doorbell rings. *Ta-da!* I freeze. Noah looks up at me excited. 'It's probably just a delivery,' I say. They must have got the wrong slot; Richard likes to be around when anyone comes to the house. I peer into the peephole and gasp when I see George's van. He's standing to one side cradling a bunch of flowers. I pause and bite my nail, hoping he'll go away. Richard could be watching this in real time on his phone. Why did I go down to the paddock? Why did I stir this all up?

'Mummy, door!' Noah calls over, wanting me to get it.

'Hello?' George shouts, hearing us inside.

'Coming,' I say, opening it, not the whole way, but enough.

He smiles when he sees me. 'Hey – sorry to turn up unannounced. I'm off to make a delivery at the farm and Susie asked me to drop over a bunch of her flowers. A welcoming thing.' He hands them to me awkwardly. They're pretty. White roses and big snowdrops smothered in delicate foliage.

'These are beautiful.' I close the door slightly, hoping he'll get the hint. 'Will you tell her I said thank you?'

'I never see you in the village or at The Meadows.' He looks onto the drive. 'Did you get your car fixed?'

'Yeah, just a stupid accident. I must have bashed it.' I cough. 'My husband takes it to work,' I say, explaining its absence.

He nods. 'Man, it's weird seeing it from the front like this. It's nuts.' He takes a few steps back and admires the building. 'Pretty isolated to be here like this on your own?' he questions, looking around.

I shrug. 'I like it,' I whisper unconvincingly.

'Mummy! Roxy naughty!' Noah shouts and the distinctive sound of Roxy crying begins to blast behind us. It's a relief to have an excuse to get away. Noah toddles up behind me and hangs off my legs, checking out our visitor.

'Hey, little man.' George crouches down to him.

'My mummy,' Noah says, patting my leg.

George looks at me and grins. 'Yeah. She sure is. You're a lucky guy.' He tries to peer inside, to get a look. 'Walk down to the stables later if you're bored. We've got a miniature one – maybe he would like to try. Do you like horses, mate?' he asks Noah, and looks up at me. 'I could hold him on. It would be safe—'

I cut him off, noting the crushing look of hope in Noah's eyes. 'He's a bit too young, maybe in a few years.'

George nods to himself. I can tell he's thinking that he won't bother trying to be friendly again, and mentally puts me in the rude-out-of-towner box.

I step back, closing the door further. 'Sorry, they need me. Thank your aunt for the flowers, will you? It's very kind of her.'

George backs away. 'If you need anything, let me know.' He looks deflated as I shut the door. I'd love to have the type of life where moving to a new area means making friends, and getting involved in the community. Taking the kids to the stables and having a cup of tea with Susie. Maybe I could even have volunteered there. God knows I'm capable. But no. None of that's for me.

Nothing is for me.

I peer back through the peephole to watch him leave. He's standing in front of the door with a bewildered look etched onto his face. His hands on his hips looking up. His eyes then fall to the ground before kicking the gravel with his trainer and turning back to his van. He performs a three-point turn, and I watch the vehicle trundle back down the drive. I'm relieved he's gone, but I feel wretched having been so dismissive and rude.

For the rest of the day, I try not to think of Richard, and what he'll do when he gets back. I help Noah prepare his pictures to show off his fun day at home, and I cook a delicious dinner. Maybe he'll be so blinded by the scene that greets him, he'll have forgotten the incident with the flowers.

But Richard doesn't let things slide. I know that.

He arrives back, and I brace myself. He helps me put the kids to bed, and we eat dinner around the table while his music plays. He uses his knife as a mini conducting baton as he enjoys his meal. I keep waiting for him to drop it – to take the information and smash it against the wall. He looks at me a few times as he chews, as though he is about to speak. But he never does.

There's something terrible about these silences. The emptiness is filled with every awful possibility. All I can think about is the flowers I laid to rest in the bin. And what he's going to do when he finally acknowledges them.

CHAPTER 28

A week passes. There has been no word from Richard about the young man who showed up at the house holding flowers. I've started to let myself think that maybe he wasn't watching, and it simply passed him by. Maybe the whole incident that pitched up a tent in my mind simply doesn't exist for him. He kisses my cheek before he leaves. I look up at the camera mournfully. There is something about knowing where I am all of the time that he likes. That tight grip completely passed me by at the beginning. It was like being indoctrinated. The process of being taken, before I was completely took.

Between blasts of anxiety, I'm transported somewhere else, to those short moments I found myself with George. They're laced with honeysuckle light. The way he looks at me cautiously from under his hair. His white teeth that catch on his big wide smile. The way his T-shirt lifts, showing off his stomach as he scratches the back of his head. These brief flashes distract me from my predicament. And I raise my hand to my mouth, touching my lonely lips as I think of him.

*

I wake up to Noah softly calling, 'Maaar-meee, Maaar-meee,' the volume rising with each utterance. Richard huffs next to me, and I get up before he gets too annoyed. I stumble down the stairs. White blinding light pours through the glass and I wince. Groundhog Day. When Richard leaves at nine a.m. I've already entertained the children for three hours.

I take my time readying them for our daily burst of fresh air. I never rush these days. I want to crunch through time in large, lazy mouthfuls. I pull my hat down over my ears and put Roxy in the baby carrier. I take one last look behind me at the red stalking light before holding Noah's hand and stepping onto the patio.

We've been here for over three months now. It could be a year. It could be multiple years. We walk down the lawn and through the first passageway. My heart hammering in my chest. Will he be there? Will I meet Susie? We march past the shed and I refuse to even look at it. As we come out of the second passageway and into the long grass I see Power ahead.

Her neck is gracefully dipped down into a metal trough, and she's munching. Her ears flick and twitch when she hears Noah's excited cries, and she looks up. Gathering at the fence, I place Noah on the bottom rung and he puffs out his chest and neighs loudly. Roxy holds her hand out, attempting a wave from her outward position in the carrier.

Power strides over, and Noah squeals as she approaches. 'It's okay, she's just coming to say hello,' I laugh, patting his back, enjoying his exuberance. He has a natural fascination with anything animal related, and I'm sure he'd love to ride.

Richard would never go for it. He'd worry about all the people we'd meet.

Power swings her head over the top of the fence and I show Noah how to stroke her. He's awestruck. The horse looks at me, her glassy eye going deep. She moves her head onto my shoulder and sighs. I lean my cheek on hers and do the same. It is as if she knows exactly how I'm feeling.

'Mummy?' Noah whispers.

The sound of a gate opening causes me to shift. Another horse, this one fully tacked up with dappled grey spots, is being led through the other end of the paddock by George. My heart leaps. He sees us, grins and waves.

'Hello,' George says simply, stopping in front of us. Roxy giggles at him.

'Him,' Noah says, pointing, recognising George from the other day.

'Hi,' I say coyly, as I stroke the back of Roxy's hair.

'That's Greta.' He nods at the other horse. 'You know Power.'

I start stroking her again. 'She's beautiful.'

'Want a ride?' George asks. 'I think she'd like you to.' He begins to take the saddle off Greta, and swaps the equipment over to Power.

My hand makes an unvoluntary movement – squeezing into a fist, remembering the blisters I got when riding was the most important thing in the world to me.

'She was in a bad way when Susie found her. They were talking about putting her out of her misery. She was half the size in some rat-infested stables. The owner had died of dementia and poor Power was left tied up in a stable to rot.' I stare into her eyes as I listen to the story. 'She still won't sleep inside. Even in this freezing weather she'll only stay out here. I have to put on a thick coat to keep her warm at night.' He stops talking, admiring the way the horse has taken to me. 'She'd love you to have a ride, I think,' he says softly. He finishes tugging and fastening the tackle around her and walks over to me, lifting a riding hat from the top of one of the fence posts.

I motion to Roxy attached to my chest. 'Pretty tricky to ride with this one.'

'I can take her,' he says as if it's nothing. 'I look after kids for a living really at the school. I'm very trustworthy. DBS checked and everything,' he jokes.

'She's not really used to other people . . .' I begin.

George reaches across the fence and touches Roxy's cheek. She giggles and holds his finger, shaking it about. 'We could give it a go. If they get upset, you can just jump back down,' he shrugs. 'No big deal.' He smiles sympathetically. 'Must be hard work up at the house all on your own with these two all the time.'

'I couldn't . . .' I look behind me. Richard isn't due back for hours.

'She needs some exercise.' George thrusts the riding hat into my hands, and I hesitate.

'The kids . . .'

Then George skilfully jumps over the fence. 'They'll be okay. It's only for a few minutes.'

'Horse. Mummy ride horse!' Noah says, excited by the prospect.

I nod and unclip the baby carrier and hand Roxy to him. Any anxiety is quelled when I see her reaction to him. 'Hello, little lady.' He grins at her. She's fine. I'm only going to be a few minutes. Noah holds up his hand to George, wanting him to hold it, and George obliges.

I step up onto the fence, hop over and jump down into the paddock. 'I'll just go around once,' I say, turning back. I'm enjoying the children's look of wonder at this scene unfolding. They've never seen me do anything like this before. I approach Power. She gnaws at the floor with her hooves. I hold the reins to steady her before putting a foot into a stirrup and pulling myself up and onto the saddle in one clean motion.

'Mummy!' Noah squeals. 'Cowboy!' He points at me, and I laugh. Just sitting up here, I feel like I can breathe. I close my eyes and let her walk. The up and down motion flows through into me. A flutter of air rushes into my face and I let out a huge sigh. Then I very softly tap my heels.

The motion propels Power forward. With my eyes closed I can almost pretend my mother is cheering me on from the sidelines. We move faster and faster. My walk becomes a trot, and then my canter becomes a raging gallop. It is as if Power knows I need to run something out of me. My body is lifted up and down by the shuddering crusade. My soul is dancing. We go around, and around again. I never want to stop. I feel, for the first time in a such long time, like me. My body has belonged to others for so long. Pregnancies, breastfeeding. Richard. And now instead of being trapped by others – I'm flying.

I slow Power, and, leaning forward, I pat her neck. I glance to where the children and George are standing clapping and cheering me on.

Then, I move my feet out the stirrups, and balance forward. Holding the front of the saddle, I hop up, so I'm crouched with my feet on top of the shiny leather saddle. I glance over to them. George is staring with a quizzical expression.

I'm showing off now.

Then, as Power walks forward I carefully rise so I am standing. My arms are out either side for balance. Noah's excited screams echo around the field and George claps and whoops loudly. I notice him pull out his phone to take a photo, and I grin from ear to ear for the shot. Enjoying the gracious applause from my audience.

Beginning to wobble, I jump back onto the saddle and come to a stop in front of them. Feeling more capable, powerful, and more like me than I have in forever. I hop off.

'So . . . you do ride then?' George says, a cheeky sparkle in his eye.

I grin. 'Just a little.'

'Very impressive. Where did you learn to do that?'

'I guess I was one of those insufferable riding kids,' I joke, stroking Power. 'I've really missed it.'

'You should help me out at the stables if you're bored. Susie would let you ride for free for a few hours' work. I know it's tough with small kids, but maybe on a weekend when your husband can lend a hand or something?'

'Yeah, maybe,' I say, reattaching Roxy to my chest.

'Come whenever you want.'

I smile, knowing I probably won't do that again. 'Thank you, George.' My eyes glistening. 'Thank you.'

I take Noah's hand and we turn back towards the house. Noah sings, 'Bye, George!' I swallow. The enormity of what I've done rushes through me. Half exhilarated by the experience, and full of dread for the consequences they may bring. Have I broken some sort of seal that I won't be able to close up again? How will I live so near the stables and never come back?

'Mummy a cowboy!' Noah whispers excitedly. Halfway back to the house I stop and kneel to his level. I begin to ask him to lie for me, but he's too small. And it's not fair. Standing up, we trudge back past the shed and up through the passageway.

At least I got to ride one more time.

CHAPTER 29

That evening, Richard arrives home later than usual. Noah's in the hallway lining up his plastic figurines while I put Roxy to bed. I chat softly as I lay her down. She's tired, and her lids struggle to stay open. I hear the front door open and close and Richard's voice as he chats to Noah. 'Goodnight,' I whisper to Roxy. Snapping the light off, I quietly shut the door.

I stand watching Richard with his son. 'I'll put him to bed,' Richard offers, picking the boy up and walking to his room.

'Night, night, Mummy,' Noah sings, and I kiss his cheek as they pass.

I walk back through to the kitchen and stand at the fridge wondering what to cook. A few minutes later, I've decided on soup, and Richard is back.

'He was tired,' he says. 'Busy day, was it?'

I shrug. 'Yes. You know, the usual.' He strides into the kitchen behind me. I look down at the knife in my hand. 'Noah said you rode a horse.' He laughs.

'Rode a horse? What an imagination,' I scoff. 'We saw a horse in the woods. He must have got mixed up. You know what he's like. You can't take his mindless babble as anything other than that.'

'Right,' he says, thinking as he stares at me intensely. I move a strand of hair behind my ear and turn to focus on my task, and block him out. I shudder as I hear the slash of a blade removed from the knife block behind me. He places a chopping board next to mine with a clatter and grabs a few tomatoes from the punnet.

'He kept saying the name George. He said he held his hand.'

'Oh, how funny,' I pause, trying to stay calm. 'There was a boy riding.' I allow myself a glance at his face as he processes the information.

'I don't want you going down there again,' he says firmly. 'You are to stay on the lawn next time you go out.'

'We were just walking, Richard,' I try to reason. 'We need to get out of these four walls, this small patch of land . . .' I have to stop myself from launching into a full-on frustrated rant. I sigh, thinking of Power. 'It was a beautiful animal. It reminded me . . .' My sentence trails off. I think of how perfect my life was back in my early teens. Horse meets, French-plaiting manes, rosettes and mucking out stables with friends. We were always laughing.

I can feel his eyes on me. 'You look tired.' He grabs a bottle of wine off the counter and pours some. 'I think we need to do some work, Eliza. You seem to be slipping.'

I shake my head. 'No I'm not – I'm just tired.'

'Would you like some?' he asks, nodding at the bottle.

'Yes please.' If I drink some, it will mean he'll have less. He doesn't drink often. But when he does, things can get very bad indeed. 'How was your day?' I ask, changing the subject, as he hands me the drink.

'My day . . . mmm.' He takes a sip. 'Stressful, Eliza.' He places the glass down with a clink. 'It's stressful when so many people rely on you.' Then he places both hands on the counter staring down at the shiny surface collecting his thoughts. In a flash he turns, and is right up to me. He begins to stroke the back of my hair. Every inch of me tingles with fear and apprehension. 'When you have other people's well-being in your hands, the pressure is unbearable. They sit there pouring out their crap into me, expecting me to just take it. And you know what the worst thing is? Do you, Eliza?'

His face is right up to mine and I shake my head, too scared to breathe. The delicate and punishing feeling of his fingers running through the strands of my hair is unbearable.

He darts a finger into his own chest. 'No one is thinking about me,' he roars. 'I can feel it choking me. Do you know what that's like, to constantly feel as though you have a vice of other people's crap around your neck, tugging and tugging . . . ?' His finger traces along my jaw, then he places his whole hand around my neck. The knife I'm holding clatters to the floor as he shoves me away from the counter. A pip of a tear slides from my eye as the blur of the ceiling shuttles past.

'That pressure of everyone else's pain being stuffed down my throat as if I can just magically make it disappear if they unload it onto me.' I gulp some air but nothing comes in, his hand is so tightly welded.

'You have the easiest life in the world, Eliza. Bumbling along. Everything done for you, provided for you. You have no idea. You were a state when I met you. Do you know where you'd be? You'd be dead,' he spits, and for the millionth time I wonder where I'd be if I'd never met Richard.

I grab my throat as he lets go and I swallow down the soreness he left there. 'I'll have the food in my study,' he calls behind as he stalks off into the hallway.

Silently crying, I finish cooking and tidy up. Shaking, I make him up a bowl and put the rest in a Tupperware. I feel too nauseous to eat tonight. Drying my tears and patting my red cheeks, I walk down the hallway and poke my head around his study door. 'Goodnight,' I say, placing the tray on the corner of his desk and quickly leaving.

He swings around. 'Are you going to bed?' I nod. 'Good. You're tired. You need your rest. We have a big day tomorrow. A fun surprise.'

My lips part, about to ask what. But I decide against continuing the conversation. He wants me to ask so he can sing, '*It's a surprise.*' In a menacing voice. And I don't need to hear it.

'Goodnight,' I whisper as I pull the door shut.

I keep my leggings and jumper on and slide into Noah's bed. Hoping I'll be able to sleep. Even just for a couple of hours. So I can deal with whatever he has in store for me tomorrow.

CHAPTER 30

I had strange dreams of being inside the shed. I was there so long I didn't want to leave. I became part of the walls and the floor. The trapdoor opened, creaking in a slow, menacing manner, and I slid down, down, down, until I was buried in the centre of the earth. My skin falling away and dissolving into the thick mud.

I wake with a start. Noah is playing with some bricks on the floor. Everything is quiet and still. Eerie. I hear Richard call my name and remember today is different somehow. The 'surprise' – my stomach plunges. What has he got in store? I've been in this long enough to know that if something sounds good, it doesn't always turn out very nice.

I shower, scrubbing my skin until it's raw. I look down at my knee, relieved it is healing. I'm not sure he'd let me go to a doctor. Thoughts of the shed are in me, and I layer up, just in case. Trying not to overthink, I walk down the stairs and into the living area. They are playing on the rug between the sofas. 'We're leaving in ten,' Richard calls. 'Can you get the kids' stuff ready? I've done their nappies. They might need another layer.'

When I go back into the kitchen holding their things, I find Richard making toast and humming a nursery rhyme. Noah is softly singing too. Roxy is moving her head around to the tune. They're slightly out of time with one another. Richard's low voice tremors slightly – and Noah's is high and innocent. The whole effect is haunting and poignant.

I stop for a second and stand there watching.

I wonder what would happen if I was no longer here. Would Richard talk about me? Would he make sure they remembered? Or would his last act of vengeance be to make my children forget? He would replace me quickly, I am sure of that, with someone just as vulnerable probably. He only likes people he can trick and control.

'Where are we going?' I dare to ask. For a second, I imagine we are a normal family off to an amusement park or a zoo or even a sparkling shopping centre with lots of people milling about. I daydream of picking up the children and getting lost in a crowd.

'We're going for a family walk in the woods!'

'Oh.' I try not to sound disappointed. Anything apart from the same old dreary walk.

'Great.' I smile. I don't want him to know any hopes have been dashed.

Noah doesn't want to wear his wellies. I stand there watching his little frustrated body heaped on the floor sobbing. I wait a few minutes and then sit next to him and offer a hug. Crying, he flings himself into my arms and I console him.

'You let him get away with that sort of behaviour. You need to be firmer,' Richard accuses.

'He's a toddler, Richard,' I say, looking up.

Once Noah has calmed, we finish getting ready. I look on as Richard takes the baby carrier off the coat hook and slots his daughter onto his chest. I open the front door and hold Noah's hand as we troop around the front of the house. 'Wait!' Richard calls. I stop and turn. 'I forgot something,' he mutters, opening the automatic garage door and nipping inside.

'Mummy. Cold,' Noah whines at me.

'It'll be fun.' I squeeze his hand. Richard returns and the breath is winded out of me when I see what he's holding.

A rifle. My knees go weak.

'It's a BB gun.' He laughs at the shock on my face. 'Thought we could find some rabbits in the woods,' he whispers. 'What? Did you think it was a real gun?' he teases.

'Richard . . . I don't think . . .' I look down at our tiny son.

'Come on, it will be good for him,' he concludes.

The panic kicks in, a drumming in my ears – *boom, boom, boom* as we walk down the lawn towards the dark entrance of the passageway. We pass the bright rhododendrons and bow our heads as we enter the innards of the undergrowth.

Boom, boom – we march in a procession. Roxy's wholesome chatter and the squelching of mud the only sound. We enter the clearing and pass the shed and I hold my breath but Richard continues without stopping. As we proceed through the second passageway, I begin to worry that George will be in the paddock. But thankfully, when we step onto the long grass, I see it is deserted.

Richard marches us to the left, where there is a stile to cross into the deeper parts of the forest. He seems to know where we are going, as if he has a predetermined route. I try to stay calm. We have the kids, what could he be planning really? My eyes shift over the rifle and to Roxy harnessed on his chest. All I can do is help Noah over the stile, and follow.

Crows caw and half-dead leaves twist on the floor below. It is deserted, as if we are the only people in the whole world. Like you could scream and scream, and no one could ever hear you. Richard looks back at me and grins. Roxy is holding the muzzle of the rifle, a cheery expression plastered on her face. A shooting pain in my chest. 'Richard, don't you think they're a bit young . . . ?' I whisper.

Richard's laugh booms around the inner sanctum of the woods. Then I follow his finger to where it is pointing. Ahead is a felled tree with a line of old tin cans. 'I came earlier,' he says and adds with a whisper, 'Do you really think I'd pop off Peter Rabbit in the woods in front of a two-year-old?' He shakes his head. 'Really, Eliza – who do you think I am?'

'Oh, right.' Relief. 'No, no . . . of course not.' I've been worrying over nothing. This really is just a stupid game. He reaches behind him and unclips the carrier and I take Roxy from him, pleased to have her back. Then he crouches to the ground and leans forward, peering through the spyhole, one eye shut. I sit down and put Roxy between my legs, and she begins picking up leaves and scrunching them. Noah toddles over and sits with us, watching his father with interest.

CRACK. Richard pulls the trigger, and a can pops in the air. Noah jumps, his eyes bulging. 'Shot!' Richard shouts. Jumping up and walking over to inspect it on the floor. Noah hugs into my side.

'It's okay.' I kiss his head. 'It's only a game.'

'It's so beautiful out here,' Richard says, breathing the air in with exaggeration. Turning on the spot. 'We're so lucky to live in the countryside away from all those yucky, yucky cars,' he says to the kids.

Noah scrunches up his nose and agrees. 'Smelly.'

Richard gets back in position and takes aim, popping another can. CRACK. 'Yes,' he spits, punching his fist in the air, congratulating himself. He glances over at me looking for praise.

'Well done,' I murmur.

I'm relieved this is all the surprise turned out to be. A morning of congratulating my husband on his stupid new hobby. CRACK. I wince. I'll be happy once this is over and we're back at the house eating lunch. CRACK. He misses. 'Fuck,' he shouts, swearing in front of the kids. He tries again. CRACK. But misses. He looks down at the gun and shakes it. 'Stupid piece of crap.' Frustrated, he stands up and looks around. 'I think it needs a clean,' he huffs, beginning to fiddle with the rifle. I lean back on the tree behind me.

After a while, Richard trudges over to the cans, muttering to himself, and begins to replace them on the trunk. I close my eyes briefly, wondering how much longer this is going to take.

'Look, Mummy!' Noah whispers and I follow his gaze. A pheasant about ten metres away. Its colour iridescent as it picks at something on the floor. I glance at Richard, hoping he didn't hear, but it's too late. He's stalking towards it, the rifle in his hand, lowering his centre of gravity as he gets closer. Desperate to regain some of his lost pride. 'Shhh!' His finger raised to his mouth. To my horror he kneels on the floor between us and the bird. Noah looks at me questioning what's going on. I get up and lift him and turn him the other way, so he can't see.

'Daddy?' Noah whimpers. The snap of a twig alerts the bird, and it jumps away into the foliage before Richard can take a shot.

'Eliza!' He turns, furious.

'Sorry, I didn't . . .'

Anger is etched onto his face. Noah's chin digs into my shoulder. Richard walks past us in a rage and picks up Roxy with a huff and walks back the way we came. I hike Noah up onto my hip and follow.

As we clamber over the stile Noah shouts, 'Horsey! Power!' And I look over to the paddock. To my dismay the horse is there, and so is George.

'Eliza!' He waves at us.

Richard looks at me. A delighted glint in his eye as he checks my reaction carefully. I can feel a blush rising up my neck. He strides through the long grass over to George.

'All right, *mate*,' he says, holding out a hand assertively as he approaches the fence.

George takes Richard's hand; I see him wince slightly at the force of the shake. 'Nice to meet you. I'm your neighbour, George.'

'I'm Richard. You seem to know my wife.' He turns to me.

George looks between us; he must be able to sense the tension. 'Just helped her out a few times, gave her a lift when you got that flat, is all.' He shrugs, his eyes not leaving me as he speaks. I wonder what he's thinking. Is he intimidated too? Or impressed? He doesn't seem to be.

'A veritable knight in shining armour,' Richard coughs, the tone of his voice nasty and sardonic. I look at the floor, kicking the post with my toe. I hug Roxy and wish Richard would be nicer.

'Yeah, well . . . it's nice to have the house occupied. Susie got all antsy about squatters.'

'We should get back,' I say, my words so quiet they can hardly be heard. 'The kids need lunch.' I want to get George away from my husband.

'My wife – always thinking of others.' Richard pulls me to his side and hugs me and I feel ashamed.

George shrugs awkwardly. 'Cool – well, see you next time. Come for another ride, Eliza. You know you're always welcome.'

My stomach plunges and Richard presses me into his side harder.

'Thank you,' I manage weakly.

We walk back up to the house in silence. I half expect him to push me into the shed as we pass it. But he doesn't. The day continues as normal, although I'm shaky and tearful. Eventually we get into bed together, and he pulls out his book. Before reading he pauses and turns to me. 'You think I'm stupid, don't you?'

'No,' I whisper back, expecting him to elaborate. But he doesn't – he looks down at his book and begins to read. Slowly turning each page.

CHAPTER 31

Richard's voice pierces into my dream. 'Eliza . . . Eliza . . .'

My lids are so heavy I'm unsure if they'll open. Then a hand on my shoulder and a hard shake. 'What? What is it?' I open my eyes. It isn't the morning. Usually light gleams through the edging of the blinds, but here, now, there is just darkness. His belt rattles as he pulls his trousers up.

'What's happening?' I whisper.

'Get dressed.' He clicks on my bedside lamp and throws a jumper at me.

'What time is it?' I croak, coming to my senses.

'Come on, get up.'

'Where are we going?' I ask softly, trying to catch his eye. But his gaze is wild and impossible to pin down.

'Get dressed,' he repeats, and I pull the jumper over my head.

'The children . . .' I begin but he shakes his head.

'Fast asleep. They'll be fine. We're not going far.'

He's hatched a plan and there is no way to derail him. 'Get dressed,' he repeats before walking out of the room. When

I arrive downstairs, he's by the back door. In one hand my muddy boots and coat, in the other the air rifle.

'Please, Richard. It's freezing. Why don't we just stay here, have a cosy glass of wine by the fire?' I use my most suggestive voice. He shakes his head and beckons me over. Once by the door he forcefully puts a foot in each boot. 'Are you cross because I rode the horse? I'm sorry. It wasn't for long. I promise the children were safe, they were never out of my eyeline. I won't do it again. I won't . . . I promise.'

He pulls back the door and as the outside air catches my face, I realise how cold it is tonight. I try so very hard not to be scared. He pulls my hand and forces me down the lawn. I look back to see the warm glowing light of the house, where my children are sleeping.

How much damage can an air rifle actually do? Close range it could cause some real damage, I should imagine. Panic rises up my insides and curls around my ears. I don't want to leave my children. I don't want to never see them again. I want to help Roxy when she gets her heart broken for the first time. I want to catch Noah's eye as he stands at the end of the aisle watching as his partner walks towards him. I want to be part of their lives. I want to be there for them.

I don't want to die tonight.

I am rushed down the lawn, and trip a few times as I'm shoved along the passageway. We pass the shed and I expect him to stop and force me inside. My heart hammers and my mind races. Should I make a run for it?

The light from Richard's phone shines behind as we walk

down the bottom passageway. I stumble and my knees hit the floor as we enter the long grass of the lower field, and he drags me up by the arm. I glance over to the woods. A shallow grave under the canopy, is that to be my destiny? But he yanks me down towards the paddock.

'Richard?' I whisper. Power is lying on a mound of straw in one corner, wearing a padded under-rug.

'There it is,' Richard says, and we stop at the fence. I look at the gun and then at Richard. He is grinding his teeth and sniffing. 'I was hoping it would be here. What sort of idiot leaves a horse out at night like this? It's basically neglect.'

'She won't go in the stables . . .' I mutter.

'What?'

'Why are we here, Richard?' I stammer.

'Because you need to be taught a lesson.' He stares at Power with a faraway look. 'There is this old Gaelic tale my grandfather used to tell me. About a demon horse that used to sweep the countryside with epidemics and rotting fields.' He sounds insane, twitching, and he looks at me. 'The moment you set eyes on it, you were gone. Like a disease, it infected you. You think I couldn't see how you looked at it? How your cheeks heated up.' And I realise he isn't talking about the horse at all. 'You couldn't bear to even look at him in my presence?'

I plead up at him. 'Please, Richard, can't we go back to the house? Noah . . . Roxy . . .'

He continues. 'Some bloke bringing *my* wife flowers, saving her when her car breaks down. Who does he think he is?'

I shake my head, my hand grabbing at his jacket, trying to

pull him out of this. 'Richard, please. He's just some harmless boy. This is ridiculous. Let's go back up to the house, yeah?' I take his face in my hands and try to force him to look at me, but he won't.

Instead, he pushes me away and leans the barrel on the fence. I shove it off but he thrusts me so hard I fall to the ground. Raising the gun, he points it at Power. 'Please don't,' I beg. I get up and yank on his sleeve. 'Please.' But he pushes me again. I back away as he raises it to his eye. His finger curls around the trigger. Power is standing now – she has noticed the commotion and has begun to wander towards us.

'No!' I call, trying to make her stop. I try to prise the gun out of Richard's hands but he's too strong for me. He flings me off and I watch in horror as he takes aim. CRACK. Power makes a horrific crying noise and tumbles to the floor. I am knocked as Richard runs past me back up through the long grass. Lights ping on in the cottage windows, and I stand swaying, before turning and following Richard back up to the house.

I find Richard sitting by the shed laughing. 'Well done for being such a good sport, darling. I hope your ride was worth it.' I stare at him in shock. 'I hope your special horse is okay. I wouldn't want you to have anything on your conscience.'

CHAPTER 32

I don't sleep. I listen to him breathing next to me and repeat the scene over in my head. Richard taking aim and Power falling to the floor. My scream and her look of recognition as she saw my face. All night I stare into the darkness lost in shock. In the end I go and sit on the bottom step in the hallway waiting for the children to wake. As soon as Roxy begins to cry out, I go to her and take her to Noah's room and we all lie there holding each other. I wish I could bind them to me with reams of impenetrable fabric that he could never break.

I hear Richard coming down the stairs. He pushes Noah's door. 'Come on, you lot. You can't stay in your pyjamas all day, you look feral. Come on, Eliza, we're better than that. Get up for the day properly. That's the best way of shifting the dark clouds.'

He is in a very good mood today. He hums as he potters around the house. He reads the paper. He makes a call to a client. He watches football in the afternoon. There is an air of smug satisfaction to everything he does. Because he knows I've been firmly placed back in my box.

*

At about two in the afternoon the doorbell rings: *Ta-da!* I glance at Richard who is relaxing on the sofa, the broadsheets spread open around him. His eyebrows rise and he calmly gets up. 'Another friend popping over, Eliza?' he asks, and I shake my head. Praying it isn't George again. He walks to the door and leans with one eye closed as he checks the spyhole. He stands up straight in surprise. 'You'd better put the kettle on,' he says grimly, and I wonder who it could be that he's planning to invite inside.

He swings open the door. 'Officers, hello.'

'Sorry to intrude, sir.' Two men are standing on the doormat. They're wearing white shirts and black padded vests and caps on their heads. The tea towel I'm holding falls to the floor.

'No problem at all. Can we help with something?' Richard says, concern etched on his authoritative features. Here he is, the perfect guy. Looking sharp in his perfect house with his perfect wife and two perfect children playing happily on the floor. I notice the younger officer look around the imposing space with fascination.

The older one speaks. 'We've had reports of someone using an air rifle in the area and we're going door to door to see if anyone knows anything. They shot a horse at the riding school down the road.'

'You're joking?' Richard says, stunned. 'Who would do a thing like that?' He shakes his head in disgust and looks over at me. 'Did you hear, darling? How awful.'

'We don't want you to panic – it's probably just some kids.'

'We haven't heard anything. But with these two loons we're a bit distracted, you see.' He points cheerfully at the kids.

The younger officer nods. 'I've got two myself, sir. Complete chaos over at ours.' He smiles at the thought of his own children. 'Well, sorry to disturb you. If you see anything, give us a call.'

'Of course,' Richard drawls. 'Do you have a card or something I can take?' And they continue with their small talk.

I take a step closer. My mouth opens and closes as I watch the officers laughing and nodding as they chat. Then I watch as the door begins to close and they say their goodbyes. I will myself to cry out. Imagining a moment in which I would say that very small word which might change everything: *help*. I step forward again. One of the officers notices me and turns his head to say, yes? My mouth opens. Then my eyes drift over to Richard, a dark glare in his eye. I glance at my children happily playing and our beautiful home, and I think of the last time the police came around and how they fell for Richard. Hook, line and sinker.

And the special look of pity they reserved just for me.

'Something you want to say, ma'am?' the officer asks.

Richard's smile is frozen in place, a flicker of anger emerging.

'Is . . . is the horse okay?' I stammer.

The officer smiles. 'We think it'll be okay, but it will have had a nasty shock.' I nod, grateful that she isn't hurt. Feeling terrible that I didn't go to her. They say their goodbyes and Richard promises to be in touch if we hear anything. And they are gone.

Richard stands there. His shoulders relax, and he turns to me. 'I'll make you a bath. You need a night off from the kids.' And he stalks down the hallway and up the stairs. 'You deserve it.'

I lie back in the bubble bath he filled and sip the glass of red wine he left on the side for me. I watch as the orange light of the candle flickers around me. A tear slides down my cheek.

The shame pours over me.

As I enjoy my reward.

CHAPTER 33

I dream about the shed again. Falling through the hatch door in the floor. Down, down I go. My body covered in warm gritty mud. I breathe in the dirt, and roots twist around my limbs pulling me further and further down until I reach my final resting place. No one will ever find me here. I'm too well hidden. I shout, scream and bang. But no one ever comes to help.

The noise of the electronic blinds groaning wakes me and I turn to stare at the trembling trees. Another cold, rainy day in the woods. More of the same. Mundanity punctuated by moments of sheer terror. I wonder if the changing seasons will be all I have to look forward to now. I don't take the children outside this morning – I can't muster the energy. I'm too scared I'll get carried away and end up by the paddock, to see George and check on Power. Nothing good can come of it. And the last thing I want to do is drag George into all this. Richard can hold a grudge. I wonder briefly what would happen if I disappeared. If no one is looking for you, how do you ever get found?

*

That night he locks me in the shed again. I try fighting against it at first, but he threatens to get Noah and bring him in with me, and not wanting to test the threat, I step inside willingly.

Lying on the hard floor, I stare up at a corner of the ceiling. My pupils track a huge spider as it builds a web. The detail in its effort to assemble his net is spellbinding. It makes me think of Richard, and how methodically he built his own trap. All the little red flags in those heady early days. I was too young, too foolish, too desperate for something good in my life.

I remember once we were holding hands on the promenade in Brighton. An ice cream in my other hand, laughing as I swooped to catch a dribble on my thumb with my tongue. It was a beautiful calm day, and I was in love for the first time with a wonderful man who loved me back. A shiver ran through me as we walked; it was as though I could feel her eyes on me. Glancing back, I saw her on the other side of the road. Slightly older with long brown hair. A thick fringe, and a slightly deranged look in her eye. The sight of her destroyed my cheerful smile. I didn't say anything and forgot about her quickly. We pottered around a large antique shop in The Lanes. There were pretty hand-painted plates, and I began to make a neat pile of the ones I planned to buy.

'Leave him.' The sound so close I felt her breath on my cheek. A hand clutched the top of my shoulder, her fingers dug into me. And I took three steps back in shock, shaking her off.

'What?' I whispered, looking around for help.

'He's dangerous . . .'

I laughed at the comment – Richard? Dangerous?

'Just go. Just leave right now . . . go home . . .'

'Excuse me . . .' Richard's voice called as he darted over to us. She let go and ran away, towards the entrance doors. 'Hey!' Richard shouted as she slipped out. The whole thing was over in a matter of moments.

'Are you okay?' he asked, wrapping his arms around me.

My heart was thudding, and my breath scant. 'Yes. Do you know her?'

He looked sad and nodded. 'She's a former patient. She's been through a lot, poor thing.' His eyes brimmed with empathy.

I thought, *What a good man.* It must be emotionally draining to put so much into helping others when it's impossible to save everyone. 'Oh dear. How awful,' I muttered, staring at the door. 'What happened to her?'

He shrugged, looking self-conscious. 'She got a bit, er . . . obsessed. And was moved into someone else's care. It was . . . stressful.' *Poor Richard*, I thought.

Now, I think of her often. How I wish I'd taken her advice and run wherever she was going. I now understand her frustration at not being believed. I'd put Richard on a pedestal and disregarded everyone else's advice. He is right – I'm stupid, and worthless. And I got myself into this.

The branches of trees scratch against the roof of the shed like nails against the closed lid of a coffin. *Get out.* My eyes graze over the flickering shadows. I can't die here or live like this.

I can't let the children grow up here. *You've got to get out*, I mouth in the dark.

The door unlocks as the birds begin to tweet. He makes me a cup of hot chocolate and lets me lie in bed for a few hours. A reward for all my hard work last night. I turn and gently place my cheek down onto the pillow and blink out a tear. The sound of the children downstairs is painful. Roxy is crying – I wonder how she slept last night. Noah threatens a tantrum. I force myself to sit up. Everything aches from cold nights on the hard concrete floor. The mirror on the wardrobe door catches me and I stare. My long hair is wispy and dry – I can't remember the last time I went to a hairdresser's. I'm thin, way too thin from weeks of barely being able to eat. I fold my arms around myself in a hug.

'Eliza!' I hear him call from downstairs.

Gingerly, I get up and wander over to the window and stare at the trees shaking in the cold morning mist.

I'm going to have to kill him before he kills me. The thought is so stark and brave I feel as though I've finally woken up.

PART THREE

CHAPTER 34

Lauren

Are you scared? My eyes flick open at the memory of Jesse's quivering voice. My pupils dart and my chest heaves with fear as I recall the nightmare I've woken from. I was a statue on the carousel, frozen in time, a pole skewered through the centre of me, holding me in place. Going around and around for eternity. Red lipstick smeared around my lips like a deranged clown.

The dream hangs around me, and I turn to find Paul lying next to me. The light has begun to take over the darkness outside, and I can just about make out his features. I gently run my fingers over his cheek. What he's had to go through in the last few years – how utterly horrific. Who knows how anyone would have reacted in his position? How strong must a person be to live through something like that? All that grief, I can't imagine. I lean down and kiss his forehead. He stirs and I move away, not wanting to disturb his much-needed sleep.

Asking Paul about life before me has always been tricky.

It's felt as though I'm prying, and Paul gets visibly upset. A dead wife and son, and two motherless children. A future that will never be complete. And then all my feelings around it, of not being good enough, of being a replacement. And my guilt for adding another burden with all my incapacities. I'm not exactly mum material. Sometimes I catch him watching me play with Jesse and Margo with a worried expression, as if he's nervous I'm overexerting myself and I can't cope.

An aggressive beeping distracts my thoughts and Paul reaches over and turns the alarm off and releases the cranking blinds. He sits up and stretches, yawning loudly. 'You slept well,' I say, smiling.

'I was shattered. Last night took it out of me.' He reaches across and cups my face. Stroking my cheek with his thumb. 'Do you hate me now?'

I shake my head firmly. 'Oh Paul.' I stare into his apprehensive eyes. 'Paul, I could never hate you. I love you.' I move over to him and put my head on his chest. He lays a hand on me. 'You took me into your family. You've shown me what being loved truly means. I know there is history and baggage but . . . I'm here for that. Just like how you were there for mine. I'm ready and willing to do whatever I can to help,' I say.

He strokes my shoulder and clears his throat. 'Lauren, you are the best thing that has ever happened to us. You're giving me the perfect family I thought I'd never get back.' He leans over and kisses my shoulder. I raise my chin and we kiss on the mouth, and then his hand grazes down over my hip bone and under.

*

Afterwards, he throws the duvet off his legs and gets up. I prop myself up with my head on my hand, lying on my side. He picks up his phone and has a quick scroll before chucking it back down and walking through to the en suite. I watch his naked bum cross the room with a lazy half-smile.

When the door closes behind him, I sit up and stretch, looking out into the dreamy blue morning. What bliss. Then I turn to his nightstand. He hasn't locked the phone like he usually does. Hesitating briefly, I whip it up, and touch the screen to keep it alive. I can see his outline in the shower through the opaque glass panel in the door.

I've always wanted to see a photo of Emma. In my mind she was a great beauty. I open his photos and scroll back. The images flick past through our last six months. And then of the children on his own with them in the flat. I try to stop myself pausing on these, even though I am intrigued. The photographs stop abruptly a year ago. I sigh, disappointed. This doesn't overly surprise me – Paul is particular about systems and organisation; he probably keeps everything backed up on a hard drive, so he always has optimum space on his phone. Or maybe he doesn't like a daily reminder of his past, so easy to access.

I click on a photo at the very top. A family picture, but the framing is off. It's as if it was on a timer and the phone knocked out of place. A man and woman – but their faces cut off just above the chin. It must be them. I recognise the children immediately, even though they are around two years younger – possibly more. Margo is a chubby baby with a fat mop of dark hair. And a miniature Jesse holds the woman's other hand. He looks about two and is smiling with a frown. His side is inched into the woman's skirt. He does that with me sometimes. I can't see Paul's face. But it must be him. He has a shirt like that.

The phone falls out of my hand when I realise their location. The black-stained wood and glass behind them. And that unique front door.

The shower turns off and I scrabble to replace the phone on the nightstand. Holding my breath, my mind rushes through what this means.

Jesse wasn't lying after all. He was here with his old mummy.

Paul re-enters the room drying his hair with a towel. Grinning, he sits on the side of the bed next to me. Kissing me gently, he whispers, 'That was amazing. Thank God I found you.'

If he was lying about that, what else hasn't he been honest about?

CHAPTER 35

Eliza

Over the next week all I can think of is how I will do it. The knives in the kitchen, the BB gun in the garage. The steep steps that cascade from our bedroom onto the hard concrete floor. Or poison. What's the deal with that? And then I'm flooded with the consequences. What if they don't believe me? What if they decide I'm a crazed woman who killed her kind, wonderful husband? And actually, I'm in need of an extended stretch in a mental institute. What will they do with my children then? That is not the future I want, either. There must be another way.

Another night in the shed. The birds begin their morning song. Chirping joyously about the dawn of a new day. Whoop-de-doo. I'm holding a little rock in my hand, rolling it between my finger and thumb. I picked it up off the floor last night and I haven't been able to let it go. I'm strangely connected to it.

As the darkness becomes silvery, I hold it up and press the

sharp edge of one side into the dank wooden wall. It makes a satisfying mark. Standing, I dust myself down and walk to the back and crouch and begin to stab at the surface.

E was here

I smile with satisfaction at the indentation. Gaining pleasure from the act of defiance. Maybe one day when I'm long gone, however this story ends, someone will see that scratch in the wall and know there was a person here once.

I sit next to it with my knees up to my chest and stare ahead, trying to find the thing I need to carry this off – where is my courage? I need it all.

I begin to wonder if he will unlock the door today. The sun that rose with so much hope has begun to fade. I'm trying to come to terms with another freezing night locked in here. I'm starving, and can feel the concave of my cheeks as I swallow. The terror of this predicament feels beaten from me. I wonder where my final resting place will be. The woods most probably, and in this moment of feverish delirium I decide it would be a fitting place, with horses riding over me. The pelting of their hooves drumming down as I melt away.

'Stop it,' I whisper to myself. I cannot do this – I can't give up. I must be strong for Noah and Roxy.

Then I hear the lock click. Wobbling, I stand, and walk to the door and press the handle down.

I see his silhouette in the glass waiting for me with his arms crossed. I stop and stare. Wondering how I could have been so stupid not to have seen through him. All the red flags I simply ignored because I so wanted the version presented to me to be true. All the fairy tales tell you that being swept off your feet is how it's meant to begin. They shouldn't teach little girls love like that. They should teach them to fall slowly, carefully. And above all else, never to lose yourself in the whirlwind.

He pulls back the door for me. My eyes search the living room for my babies. But it must be later than I thought. Before I can rush through to their bedrooms, he grips my arm. 'Where are they?' I whisper.

'Sleeping.'

I try to move, but his grip only fastens.

'Let me see them, please?' I plead.

He sighs. 'They're perfectly safe, Eliza.' He pulls me to him and stares intently. 'I feel sad it has come to this. I was going to give you the benefit of the doubt, thinking maybe we'd build a new life here and that you'd finally left those silly ideas of taking away my children behind.'

I shake my head. 'You're lying. You planned this for months.' A tear rolls down my cheek. 'You set this ball in motion when I tried to leave you and go to my mother's.' I swallow as the words wobble out. 'What are you going to do, Richard? You must know you can't do this forever. The children will get older, and they'll notice. Can't you see that? Noah isn't a baby any more.' My voice cracks under the pressure. 'He sees more than you realise. Please, let's work this out amicably. There is another way.'

He shakes his head, hardly listening, and pulls me through

the room. 'Eliza, we both know you can't take care of the children on your own. Look what happened last time.'

I shake my head, unwilling to fall for this again. I can see what I was in denial about before. He was slowly plotting my history, knowing what he needed on record to rewrite who I am. Having me committed was perfect. It is written in stone for anyone pushing paper to see. He hid things, he turned the hob and hot tap back on. He told me things and then denied them later.

He slowly broke me down.

As he pulls me through the hallway, I look longingly at Noah and Roxy's bedroom doors. He pushes the study door open and gestures to the chaise longue. 'I want to be able to trust you, Eliza. And if you prove that I can, things will get a lot more comfortable for you around here.'

The urge to resist is strong. To scratch and bite and hit. But I need to buy time for the sake of my kids. I can't knee-jerk this. He has proved to be a meticulous planner. But I can plan too.

I lie back on the sofa. It feels impossibly soft after the hard nights on the floor. I'm worried I will simply drift off to sleep.

'Eliza,' he says sternly, and my eyes ping open. 'Have some water.' He hands me a glass; I sit up and take a sip with shaking hands. I know it will slosh about uncomfortably inside my empty stomach. 'Eliza.' His voice is different. The emphasis on syllables have changed. The rhymical ups and downs are hypnotic and pull me into a trance. 'E-li-za,' he sings, as though my name is three miles long.

'Why are you doing this to me?' My voice cracks.

'I'm helping you, Eliza. I love you,' he says softly. 'You know that.' I catch a sob in my hand. He squeezes my shoulder. 'Come on. This will make you feel better. I promise.' The kindness in his voice grates on me and I fight the urge to stand up and scream.

'What . . . what do you want me to say?' I ask, wiping the sleeve of my top under my nose. I know the drill – I know what he wants. He brings out his phone and places it between us. 'Confess. Relieve yourself. You'll feel so much better.' He presses the screen. I am not quite ready to give in yet.

'I'm a good mother,' I whisper. He grimaces and shakes his head. 'I'm a good mother,' I say with force. I know he will delete this, but I want to say it out loud. I want the universe to hear it. 'I love my children and care for them deeply. I want them to be happy and loved and be free to do what they want with their lives. I want them to have healthy relationships and I want them to be kind.' I turn my head and look directly into his cold eyes. 'And what I want most is for them to be nothing like you.'

Richard sighs and stops the recording. 'Eliza, how can I trust you if you don't prove it? I need some collateral, Eliza. I need to know I can trust you. That you won't get any silly ideas. Prove it to me and I promise things will get better.'

I can taste something rank in the back of my throat, and I try to swallow it down. I look out the glass. From this position you can see directly into the woods to one side of the house. It's pouring. I can see drops smattering into a muddy puddle.

'It doesn't look very nice out there,' he murmurs. The

thought of going back into the shed without a meal makes me feel undone. Hatred twists in my stomach. 'Give me what I need to help you.' I know what he wants from me. I weigh up my options. Dragged into the cold to starve. Or do as he says and live to fight another day. He presses the record button.

I stammer, 'My name is Eliza Bloom. I'm documenting this in case I do something bad when I am not in my right mind. When I had my daughter a year ago things began to unravel. I couldn't sleep. I . . . I began hallucinating. I'd do things which scared me.' His eyes bore into mine and he nods for me to continue. 'Throughout my life I've had moments where I've stumbled, and have had to lean on others for help. It happened in my early twenties, and again after having children. The truth is, I don't trust myself with them at all. I . . . I feel myself falling again.'

I think of all these horrible soundbites being beamed up into the cloud ready to be sent over to a lawyer or the police or anyone else he needs to get on side. He pauses the recording and asks me again, 'Do you want to go back out there?'

I sniff, looking at the storm raging. He leans forward and turns it back on.

'I'm lucky my children have such a wonderful father. I know I'm a danger to the children without that stability. I would never be able to look after them on my own, I don't know what I am capable of.' He nods for me to continue, and I say the last bit so quietly, it is almost inaudible. 'I'm a danger to my children.' And he sits back in his chair, pleased.

The look of glee on his face is unbearable.

CHAPTER 36

Lauren

I wake the next morning with the image in the photograph lingering. I turn onto my back, and stare at the ceiling, as I continue mulling it over. Maybe he came here with the kids after Noah died to visit their friends? Maybe he didn't tell me about it because he was afraid to tarnish our fresh start with his previous relationship. Yes . . . that must be it.

I stand at the window watching the morning haze melt into the brightening sky. I can understand why his relationship with Jesse is strained now: having a carbon copy of someone you miss, and all the horrific memories attached to their loss, must be a deafening double-edged sword. Paul has handled it terribly. You can't lie to a child about something like that, no matter how difficult. As someone who helps people living with the consequences of childhood trauma daily, he must know that foggy, misunderstood memories always surface in the most dark and disturbing ways.

Yes, he did it out of love. And it must have all been such a blur, losing the two of them in such quick succession. Much easier to block it out and allow Jesse to believe his brother never even existed. That way Paul didn't have to deal with his son's grief when he couldn't even handle his own. My job is clear. I'm going to help Paul to tackle this head on. In the long run it will make our family stronger.

When I go downstairs Paul peeks at me from behind the kitchen island. I go to him and put my arms around the man I love.

'You okay?' I ask.

He nods, pecking my lips. 'Yes. I think so. I'm feeling quite wobbly, to be honest.' He clears his throat. 'I'm going to put some feelers out to find the best child therapist money can buy. And . . . well . . . I think I could do with talking to someone as well. It's been a while.' He swallows and averts his eyes. 'I don't think I realised until we spoke how broken I am.'

I stroke his cheek. I've never seen him so vulnerable. 'It's okay, we'll work it out. I'm here,' I whisper.

He nuzzles my neck and continues. 'I've been holding everything together – and I fucked it. I should never have allowed Jesse to get confused like that.'

Paul isn't perfect. In a way it's a relief. 'It's okay. What you went through . . . no human should . . .' I pull my arms around him tightly and murmur, 'All this time I've been so obsessed with how I fit in here, I've totally forgotten to look after my man too.'

'You fit in perfectly, my love.'

We stare intently into one another's eyes and all the worry I felt melts away. We kiss. Then the sound of nervous giggling and we turn to see the children enter the room. Their eyes shining, thrilled at the sight of us together.

It is the last week of term. Aware our child-free time is about to evaporate, we're hell-bent on making the most of the few days we have left. Paul goes out for a run in the afternoon. I make myself a mug of chamomile tea with the intention of sitting in the children's rooms organising toys and clothes ahead of the carnage.

But instead, I find myself outside Paul's study. I push the door open with one finger; it creaks as it turns into the room. There is a red oriental rug on the floor, and a white sheepskin thrown over the back of his desk chair. I run my fingers over the chaise longue which was here when we arrived. I slip myself onto it and slide back against the black leather, staring at the ceiling for a moment. Then I turn to look at Paul's sparse shelves: a pot of devil's ivy hangs down as well as a few framed photos of the kids when they were small.

Standing, I cross my arms and wander around the space. To one side of his desk is a plastic storage box. I kick it and then crouch, flipping the lid off. Inside is a pile of beige medical files. Removing a chunk, I realise they are his patients. I sit back on the floor and wonder if my file is here.

They are in order, of course. I mouth the alphabet as I get to my own. *LAUREN JONES*. I open it. *Traumatic Brain Injury (TBI). Cause – blunt force head injury. Attacked during a mugging.* I wince at the sight of the photographs of my mangled body. I look half dead. Not attractive. Another one. Half my head was shaved for surgery. My hand instinctively goes to where it stops just below my ears in a bob. Turning the pages, my eyes track over our conversations which he has transcribed. There isn't anything I don't already know. I put it down.

Next, I look for an Amanda's file. It takes a little longer as I don't know her last name. *AMANDA GROSSMAN. Anorexia nervosa, acute OCD.* My eyes flick up to her photograph. Long dark hair. About my age. Pretty. 'Wow, jealous much?' I whisper to myself. I bite my nail, flicking through their reams of conversation. Hours of talking. Irritated, I put it down and take another file. *GRACE FREEMAN. PTSD brought on by violent and coercive relationship.* Long brown hair, big full lips. Very attractive. My age. I flip the file shut, feeling sick. I take another. And another.

In a moment of haste, I pull them all out feverishly, splaying them on the floor in front of me. Studying the pictures. Most of them are female. A lot of them have long dark hair. I put them in a line.

A collection of women . . . who look very similar to me.

Was I special? Or am I just the only one who reciprocated his advances?

I feel nauseous. He's always on the phone to them.

Is Paul just a predator hidden in plain sight?

Realising how much time has passed, I quickly tidy up the files and put them back in the box. Thoughts chip away at me. I've been so set on Paul being the good guy. But what if I'm wrong? As soon as I leave the study Paul returns, wiping his feet on the mat inside the front door.

'What you up to?' he asks. I shrug.

'Nothing, just going to have a bit of a sort-out,' I reply, slipping into Jesse's room and gently closing the door behind me.

Once the kids are back, I give them dinner and start the process of getting them into bed. As I bathe them, I sit on the mat on the floor and blow bubbles through my fist which float out and pop, as their wet faces gleam, laughing. I pat them dry and help them into their pyjama sets and we cuddle on Jesse's bed and read a book until Margo falls asleep. I carry her into bed and place her down, gently kissing her forehead.

Just as I'm leaving the room she whispers, 'I love you, Loz.'

I get a slight pain in my chest. 'I love you too, darling girl.' And I snap the light off.

I pad through into the living room. He is sitting on the sofa, a glass of wine in hand. 'They're asleep?' he asks.

I nod. 'They were exhausted.'

He pats the cushion next to him and I hesitate before walking over. I sit down and he puts a hand on my thigh and sighs. 'What a long day. At least the kids finish school soon and then we can really hibernate for a bit. Just us. Without all this rushing about.' I think of the long stretch we have in front of us, without the kids at school.

'Lauren, you left the hob on. No biggie, just thought I'd let you know,' he says, smiling softly at me.

I look up into the kitchen in surprise. 'Really?'

'Don't worry – I just thought I'd let you know so you double-check things like that in the future.'

I nod, surprised. 'Of course. Sorry.'

He shrugs.

'Paul, how did you meet Emma?' The question has been bothering me since I looked through the files.

'Why do you ask?' He takes his hand off my leg and sips his wine.

'I'm just interested.' I try to keep my tone light.

'We worked together. It was an office romance, I suppose.'

'Oh, right.' The panic which had been churning subsides slightly. 'So, she wasn't . . .'

He looks at me. 'What, Lauren?'

'It doesn't matter.' I shake my head, deciding against it. I'm being silly. Neurotic. Overthinking things again.

'You can say it, Lauren. What is it?'

'It's just that . . . how we met – I was wondering if she'd been a patient.'

He stands quickly, and I'm taken aback. 'I can't believe we are back on this again.' The calm state he was in has flipped and he stalks around. 'Look, I know how we met was unorthodox, but we both wanted to be there.' A twisted look appears on his face. 'Is this what will finally tear us apart, Lauren? Because I have put a lot on the line for this. For you.'

Why do I feel the need to pick at something until scabs begin to bleed? 'I'm sorry,' I stammer.

He turns to face me, incredulous. 'You're always *sorry*.' He mimics my voice, making me sound childish. Then he stalks away, thundering past. 'I need to lie down.' He turns to me. 'If you don't want us, just tell me.' He leaves, his feet stomping up the stairs to our room. I'm left sat there in shock.

All I can think of is Margo. The image of her all cocooned in her white towel after the bath. I see one of her cardigans discarded on the floor and stand up to retrieve it, bringing it to my nose and hugging it to my chest. The thought of a future different from the one mapped out, one without them, is horrendous.

I don't feel like joining him upstairs and try to distract myself by watching a bit of television. I stare at the box, but after a while my head hurts. I lie back on the sofa and listen with my eyes closed.

A vibration in my pocket rouses me, and I pull out my phone and hold it above my head to see a lone message from Claudia.

Hey, just checking in. How's it all going on cloud 9? Xx

I stare. I want to lie. I want to say I'm living out the rural dream with my perfect new family.

Hey. I'm okay. Just feeling quite isolated here. I'm sure it will get better once we're more settled.

I wonder how long that will take. Will I ever feel settled here? Or am I just kidding myself.

Mmm . . . Hope so, babe. How's Paul?

He's good, busy with work. Deciding not to lie, I delete the message, and then write: *He told me some things about the past that I'm finding difficult to digest.* Send.

Yeah? Like what? That doesn't sound good, Lozza

About his ex and his kids. I don't know. It's just unnerved me. It feels good to open up about how I'm really doing. *If I were to come back (not saying I will or anything), could I maybe stay with you? Just until I get back on my feet x*

I watch her type a reply a few times and then give up. She's probably trying very hard not to say, 'I told you so.' Finally, she gets back to me:

Of course. I'll always be here for you x

I'm floored with relief.

CHAPTER 37

Eliza

The next morning Richard hums as he gets ready for work. Leisurely he irons his shirt and carefully positions his bow tie. He cleans his glasses thoroughly with a silky slither of fabric. He looks at his reflection, pleased. I think of him going to work in a hospital full of people at their most vulnerable. It makes me shudder to think of the keys to doors he can open.

I think of myself back when we met. Freshly out of crisis, caught between the living and the dead, and learning how to be again. Totally bewildered and clueless. Taking it a day at a time. Holding my breath. He must have earmarked me when he'd heard the office gossip. I thought he was my right person. But actually he was just somebody who knew the right things to say. At just the right time.

It is utterly revolting how he built me back up after my so-called postnatal depression, purely to get me here and control my downfall. I see it clearly now. He used his expertise to control me. And now he has these tapes, how will I ever get my children out of here?

I don't feel strong enough to go out today. I have lost all motivation to even try to be a good mother. They are on the carpet in front of the television. Noah is staring up at the bright colours as the energetic noises reverberate around the cavernous room. Roxy is busying herself fiddling with some magnetic bricks. I lie there motionless. I'd usually force myself to keep the telly off until after four. But I just can't muster it today. Part of me has given up.

'Mummy, I bored,' Noah says, pushing me as I lie there.

'Only boring people get bored,' I mutter without a lick of enthusiasm.

Come on, Eliza, I tell myself. *We must get out.* I look up at the red blinking light of the camera. *You cannot let him win.* It whirs as I layer Noah up. I strap Roxy in her jumpy jungle gym and face her towards the garden so she can watch us as we kick a ball on the lawn from behind the glass.

Noah jumps up and down like an excited puppy as I heave the door, and he rushes forward as soon as the gap is big enough. I kick the ball onto the grass, and he charges after it, shouting with abandon as he makes contact, looking chuffed as the ball rolls away.

I clap and cheer and rush to pick it up. My voice evaporates as something catches my eye in the bush below. A movement. A person. I look back up at Roxy in the living room – and then back again. I see George's face jolt between branches and leaves. He makes a move towards us, but my hand shoots out in front of me. My palm flat. *Stop.* I shake my head and he nods, understanding, and stays where he is. I look back towards the house where the camera is and move my body in front, to obstruct it. I pick up the ball and kick it in the direction of the bush. 'Oops! I'll get it,' I shout at Noah. But he is distracted, crouching next to one of the beds, poking a stick at an insect. I don't have long. I move quickly.

We stare at each other. As if we have a million things we want to say.

He stammers, 'I was worried – I never see you.' His eyes rush up and down my features. 'You look different,' he says, frowning. My hand wipes under my eyes and I look at the floor, self-consciously. 'Sorry – I didn't mean to . . . I just mean you don't look very well.' He steps closer. He smells of tobacco and hay. 'Your husband . . . he . . . doesn't seem very nice,' he whispers. 'And you . . .' He scratches the back of his head. Choked with emotion. 'My mum died before I was born. My dad killed her. I should be dead too, but they cut me out.' His curtains hang over his face as he rushes the words out. 'My aunt told me he stopped her from seeing her family and isolated her before . . . before it happened.' He peaks over as I digest the information. 'I . . . I can't stop thinking about you.'

I look out at Noah who has begun to wander the lawn looking for me. Roxy is jumping up and down wildly, frowning. I step into George and put my head on his chest and close my eyes. I don't move. His voice wobbles as he speaks. 'Is he . . . is he hurting you?'

I shake my head. Roxy has begun to wail, and I can hear Noah calling for me. 'I'm fine,' I say. I look up. Blood pumps around my body. I want to stay here forever. I look up and our lips connect. I want to melt into the moment and for it to never end.

The children crying pulls me out of it and I open my eyes and falter back, my hand on my lips. 'Sorry,' I muster.

He shakes his head, looking at me in wonder. 'Wait!' he shouts as I run back onto the lawn.

I collect Noah up. 'Sorry, darling, I think I lost your ball.' We go back into the house, and I shut and lock the door without looking back.

Richard comes home from work in a mood. Something must have happened. He never goes into detail about his day, other than to moan about his boss. My husband doesn't like authority. He doesn't like being told what to do.

'What were you doing in the garden?' he asks, opening a bottle of wine once the children are in bed.

'Nothing. Just kicking a ball around. Noah was going insane,' I answer casually.

He looks at me pleased, and I wonder if he knows he's caught me in a lie. Could the camera see that far into the garden? Staring into the flames of the open fire, he sips his wine and pats the empty cushion next to him on the sofa.

'Come sit.' I do as I'm told, and he places a hand on my thigh. 'Don't worry, Eliza, I will get you better. You'll see.'

As I sit there frozen, I close my eyes and transport myself back to that kiss. I will hold on to it until my last breath.

CHAPTER 38

Lauren

It has been several days since our argument about how he met Emma, and Paul's brooding. All monosyllabic and detached. It's painful. There was a time I loved nothing more than hibernating with my three new loves, but now I just feel trapped beneath the weight of them. I must get away for a few hours and gain some perspective on the situation. I've had enough of the emotional rollercoaster our relationship has become, and need some space. I should be able to have some semblance of my own life without having to ask permission. Shouldn't I? That's right. Isn't it? I hate that I'm constantly questioning myself.

I don't tell Paul I'm leaving; I just take the keys and go. Jesse went to play in his room after breakfast, and Margo followed Paul into his study as I cleaned up. I slip on my sandals and quietly shut the front door. The car opens with an oinking sound, and I pull the door and slope into the driver's seat.

I look up at the house before turning the engine on. Jesse

is staring down at me from the master suite. A solemn ridge lining his brow. He places a palm on the glass. I wave at him and smile, but he stays motionless, and I feel a yanking in my heart. I've promised these two tiny people so much. And for the first time I wonder what happens if I can't follow through.

The image of Jesse stays with me as I trundle down the road. 'Get a grip,' I whisper to myself. I'm not leaving Paul. I'm catastrophising again. He's right: so much information is lost to me, I can find it comforting to find problems to replace it with.

I think of the box of patient files. How can I explain that away? Well, he has an area of expertise. And it happens to be women dealing with trauma. Okay. That makes sense.

I breathe in deeply, like he's taught me, and roll my shoulders back trying to ignore my phone vibrating in my bag. I lean forward and put the radio on to drown out the noise. He'll be wondering where I dashed off to. *Good. Feel some of the anxiety I've been carrying.* Maybe it will make him reassess his own behaviour. We need a re-balance. This is me taking back control.

And it feels good.

Once I pull into the car park at The Meadows, I take out my phone. Biting my lip, I note the fifteen missed calls. I scroll to Claudia's number; my thumb shakes as it hovers above the call button. But then I stuff my phone back in my bag, imagining her patronising tone as I admit defeat.

I'm not ready for that, yet.

It's busy inside. Families are having coffee and croissants. Lone fathers stand in tracksuit bottoms buying the weekend paper and fresh bread. Others chat by the counter, laughing. It all feels so normal, but also alien. Paul just hasn't wanted to get involved with life here. It's frustrating. I didn't move to the sticks to sit in a house in the woods. I want to live my life. I crane my neck hoping to see Isobel. I haven't heard from her since the party, and now school has broken up for the summer, I wonder if I will before term starts in September.

I order a coffee and sit on a stool at the window. It is sunny today, not as hot as it's been but the meadow ahead is luminous and yellow. Fumbling around in my bag, I remove the scrapbook I began during my counselling sessions with Paul. He said it might help if we arranged photographs in chronological order and I could write little messages with anything I could remember underneath. Thoughts, feelings, even little sparks of memories which were few and far between. Especially at the beginning when I couldn't even remember that my friends had come to visit. I look at my tiny concentrated scrawl. This had been a lifeline. A glimmer of hope when I'd given up on any future. Because if I couldn't remember my context, how was I ever going to have a fulfilling next chapter?

I flick to the first page. There's a photograph of me as a child with my parents. I have a string of amber beads around my neck and my hair is bunched in messy pigtails. My mother's face is all tanned and freckly. Wind has blown her curly hair up, and she's laughing. My eyes are tilted upwards, squinting as I watch her with adoration. My father stands above us, with his white linen shirt open, and his hairy chest on display. He's wearing shades and a big grin. I wish I could speak to them just once. I have so many questions.

They died on a family holiday on the Greek island of Lesbos. Our car crashed after swerving to miss a truck full of sheep on a steep mountain road. I was the only survivor. You would have thought after that I'd used up all my bad luck. But it doesn't work like that, does it? Once the foundations are pulled away, you are shaky for the rest of the build.

I was only four. The same age as Jesse. I flip through the pages. My old flat. Me with a boy when I must have been about seventeen. Another on a night out with my group of friends. I have written their names in biro and drawn little arrows. Audrey, Claudia, Alex and Flo. Blurred Christmas lights swing behind as we stand in a line, arms lounged around one another, mid-laugh. A passer-by must have taken it. I blink – I feel like there is some sort of recognition there. A moment in time I can feel the ends of with my fingertips. Cold air and shouting as we fell out of a taxi, cash changing hands as we worked out the fare. I gasp. Could I really have had a memory?

'They look like a good-time bunch.' I turn sharply to see Susie next to me, peering over my shoulder. I take my thumb out of my mouth, realising I've been chewing the nail. 'People don't print photos any more. It's such a shame,' she mutters.

'My friends,' I offer. 'Yes, digital photos seem so throwaway.' I think of the trillion pictures of the kids I have on my phone.

She nods. 'People snap, snap, snap trying to hold on to

memories. But it doesn't work like that. You forget to engage the part of your brain that creates them, and all you are left with is a photograph.' My lips part, surprised, and she adds, 'I read an article about it.'

'I haven't thought about it like that,' I reply, glancing down at my scrapbook.

'How are you getting on at the house?' she asks.

I think about the gossip at Saskia's party and am careful as I pick my words. 'Well, it's quite overwhelming being in such a large space after our cramped flat. And we're so isolated there – I'm not sure I'm built for it, to be honest. But we're not staying long. It's just a stopgap.'

I expect her to say a few pleasantries and leave, but instead she pulls out the stool next to mine and sits down. She's very short, and her feet hang inches from the floor as she balances, like a child. 'There used to be a beautiful old country house on that plot. Was ripped down to build that monstrosity.' She tuts. 'I'm surprised you're not scared living there after what happened.'

'What happened?'

'There was a young doctor and his family who lived there. They were such a lovely family. The poor wife got very ill. They found her naked in the woods one night chanting God knows what. And then they decided to move somewhere a bit less isolated. It was terrible. They were a lovely family.'

My hand rises to my mouth. I had no idea. 'Really? When was this?'

'Oh, yonks ago. At least fifteen years. It was sold quickly to a property developer who modernised it and was rented until a few years ago when it was bought again.' She shakes her head. 'If it were up to me, I'd tear it down. All it's brought is misery around here.' She looks out the window and presses her lips together as if wondering whether to vocalise a thought. 'My nephew. I'm sure you've heard all the gossip about what he was accused of . . . he would never . . . he was a good boy. He loved kids . . .' she stammers, shaking her head. 'They should pay for what they did.' She sniffs and looks directly at me. 'That woman accused my lovely George of doing something evil.'

'Gloria?' I'm surprised.

'Her name was Eliza,' she says simply. 'Richard and Eliza.'

'Oh.' I shake my head at this information. 'They must have lived there before Jack and Gloria then,' I say, relieved we don't have any connection to this dark story after all. It's nothing to do with Paul's friends.

'I've never heard those names. These two had a baby and a toddler.' Then she looks over at me. 'Something bad happened there. I just know it. They threw around all these accusations and then disappeared.' She shuffles her stool forward which makes a grating noise. I sit back in my own chair wanting some distance from her wild eyes. 'It's not fair. They got away with it. My George, he was a good boy. He was.' Her eyes fill with tears and she stares out at the meadow with a faraway look. 'I couldn't get Power, his horse, to leave. She wouldn't get in the trailer. And I left feeling like I abandoned her too.' And then she pauses. 'Sorry . . . It's all just been very upsetting.'

With that, she stands abruptly and walks away, stumbling through the tables. Ditching her flower station and leaving out the main doors. The man behind the counter watches and shakes his head with a concerned look, before taking another order.

CHAPTER 39

Eliza

The next few weeks are full of nothing but passing time. We all teeter on the precipice of Richard's moods. Noah is suffering from the erratic nature of his father's outbursts, and I can't bear it. Roxy is the only one who smiles. She has the gift of ignorance. Even the sight of her gradually learning to walk as she pushes her little trolley around can't spur me on to lift an encouraging cheer.

Richard barely talks to me. I am someone who deals with the practicalities of looking after our children and keeping up with household chores. He doesn't engage with me outside of that. I feel him disassociating, and it scares me to think what he has planned that he must equip himself with that mindset.

Richard is planning something. He keeps muttering about George – 'the stable boy,' he spits as he mumbles to himself. Richard can't just let something drop. Especially when his pride has been bruised.

Why didn't you just leave? The question echoes, shaming me to the core. I must get the children out of here, or they will either become him, or become his next victims.

The days roll on and I begin to wonder if I'll ever find the strength to fight this. Then one morning my eyes spark open, as if something spiritual has flung a bolt of lightning in my face. I'm going to get George to get us help. He understands what is going on here. He will tell the police what he suspects before they have a chance to meet Richard and are swept away with his charm and pretence. Finally, they'll listen without assuming the worst of me. I'll explain the recordings, and how he tricked me into coming here. And how he locks me up to keep me compliant.

I imagine a detective picking up the case. Finally, someone threading all his misdemeanours onto one long string and working out the truth. They'll find that woman who approached me on the promenade and she'll back me up with her own experiences. They'll see who he truly is and the children won't be removed from my care. We'll be safe, at last.

I'm barely there as I tend to the children, ruminating. Running through it all, working out the ins and outs. Weighing up the risks. Not daring to contemplate the consequences.

My only issue is getting down to the bottom of the garden. Richard forbade me to go further than the lawn and his interest will be piqued as soon as we leave the house, and my every movement will be studied. My lids twitch as I run through it. Rewinding the tape and playing it back again on repeat.

*

As soon as Richard leaves the house for work, I launch into action. I scrawl a note, just in case George isn't there. You're right. Please tell them we need help. SOS. I don't want to address it to him or leave my name in case this all goes horribly wrong. The possibility of Richard finding it fills me with dread. I stuff it into my pocket and look up at the sky through the clear ceiling.

Grey clouds have threatened rain all afternoon. I'm in two minds about whether to abandon the plan for another day, or risk it. I've got myself all pepped up to go through with it, and the thought of waiting another minute feels like a new kind of torture. Just as I'm about to give in, the clouds unexpectedly part and the sun magically appears. A sign.

I pack Noah into outdoor gear and heave the doors open. We both wave at Roxy buckled into her jungle gym and pull funny faces through the glass, as she giggles.

I run through it one more time. I'll get Noah to run into the bushes and then I'm going to grab him and run down to the paddock. Later, if Richard asks where we went, I'll say he fell over and hurt himself, and it took me a while to sort it out, as he was so upset. His tantrums can be impossible to manage. Richard knows that, even though he berates me for them. I'll have to leave Roxy, but she can't get out of the gym, and although she might get upset, she'll be perfectly safe.

We step onto the grass, and I pull back the cover of the sandpit. 'Ewww, Mummy!' Noah shouts, pointing at a dead slug inside. It's moist and pus falls from its centre. Using a stick, I ping it over into one of the beds. I study Noah's face. I hate lying to him.

'You know in the bushes over there? I heard that's where the little people from Locky-Zocky Land live.'

He turns to me, his eyes wide. 'Really?' It's his favourite show about little enchanted stop-motion characters who live in the woods.

'Shall we go have a look?' He doesn't need much encouragement and toddles off towards the rhododendrons.

I stand there a moment watching his excited trotter down the beautiful garden and I'm momentarily struck by sadness at the thought of the life I was promised when we arrived.

Raising my hands, I cup my mouth and call his name. He shakes his head stubbornly.

'Noah!' I shout again.

I follow him down to the bottom of the lawn which scoops into the bushes. He disappears behind the leaves. I check on Roxy one last time before following him.

As soon as we're hidden, I grab him. He struggles to get me off. 'Locky!' he shouts, but my grip only tightens. I run and run. Cold air floods my chest as I heave with exertion.

I run past the shed and down the next passageway and out to the long grass. Panting, I reach the fence. I'm overwhelmed with crushing disappointment that George isn't there. The site is deserted. His white van isn't outside the cottage and the chimney isn't bellowing smoke. 'Mummy,' Noah moans and I try not to burst into tears. I swear under my breath and pull out my scrunched-up note. The weight of responsibility this little piece of paper has is enormous.

'Mummy, Locky,' Noah whines as I look for somewhere to

leave it. Nowhere obvious jumps out. Anxiety sits in my chest as I think of Roxy utterly bewildered at our disappearance. Urgently, I pat down the wood and try to slip it between two pieces of the fence. But it's too thin and it floats towards the floor. I grab my precious note before it flits away.

Quick, I must be quick, or the moment is lost, and this has all been wasted. Patting around, my hand is suddenly pinched by something sharp on the paddock side of the fence. I look around it. There is an old rusty nail sticking out, curved at the end. I quickly stab the paper with it and turn back. Running with Noah who moans as our bodies knock together. A big grin spreads across my face. I did it, I did it, I did it. The words run through my head in time with my footsteps splashing into the muddy floor.

Finally, I make it to the rhododendron bush and compose myself before breaking free onto the lawn. I put Noah down and crouch, wagging my finger as though I am telling him off – for the benefit of the camera. I then hug him to me and whisper, 'You are my best boy. My best, best boy.'

The thrill of knowing my bright white little note is there, stuck on the nail, brazenly flapping for all to see. There is no way George could miss it. Like a white flag waving – I just know it will save us. It must. I've done it now, and I can't take it back. Even tonight when Richard comes home and I'm feeling less brave.

It is done.

CHAPTER 40

Lauren

I'm shellshocked from my conversation with Susie. The man behind the counter keeps looking over suspiciously – as if I've done something to upset her. I feel as though everyone is watching me. My chair scratches loudly as I push it back and I mutter, 'Sorry,' as I gather my things. Composing myself in the car, I feel shaky, upset my excursion has ended this way. I feel even more like an outsider now. Susie's faraway look reminded me of Jesse banging on the glass trying to get to his lost mother. The handle creaking.

Both are stuck in an in-between place. Longing for a lost loved one.

Ghosts.

I realise my hands are gripped together and my shoulders are hunched. I try to roll them back and I hold up my hands to watch them tremor. Shaking them out, I squeeze them, hoping the hideous tingling feeling will subside.

I start the car and begin the journey back to the house.

There is something about that place I've grown to deeply dislike. For all its mod-cons and palatial layout, its linear lines and elegant finish, it feels clinical and cold. I believe Susie when she says: *Something bad happened there.* It feels cursed. And the story about the doctor's wife all those years ago. It must be true. I can feel it. The air echoes with pain. The outer walls, although they are transparent, are as confining as a thousand thick layers of titanium.

I'll be pleased when this year is over, and we leave. I think of Isobel's home which sits on the edge of the village. Inviting with bright colours and relaxed soft furnishings with a big dog bounding around. That is somewhere I could feel at home. Once we are somewhere like that everything will click into place. I'm sure of it. I should talk to Paul about making the move earlier. I know we have been incredibly fortunate to stay in his friend's house, rent-free. But we've tried it for a few months, and it's just making us all miserable. I'm sure he'd understand that, wouldn't he? He always says my happiness is paramount.

The car rocks back and forth as I hurry to get back. I am gripped by that sudden urge to hold the children. When I was told I couldn't have kids after what happened to me, I wasn't devastated. It was almost as if I knew that hole would be filled. And then when I met Margo and Jesse I understood.

I was meant to look after *these* children.

I think again about the photograph of Emma and Paul. It must have been quite soon after Noah's accident, as he wasn't there. Odd to pose for a relaxed family photo so soon after such a horrendous accident like that. Something occurs to me – the timings don't work. The age of the kids – it must have been about two years ago. Before Jack and Gloria lived at the house. When this other pair lived there: Eliza and Richard.

I don't understand.

Did Paul know this couple too perhaps?

Just as I speed past a turning, I notice a figure by the side of the road up ahead. The strange sight compels me to press gently on the break. As I get closer, I realise it's Susie. She is clutching a bouquet of flowers, staring at a large oak tree. She turns her head towards me as if in a trance. Continuing past, I glance at my rear-view. And she turns back. A shudder runs through me.

CHAPTER 41

Eliza

The image of the note stuck on the fence is burnt into my mind. I think of it all afternoon. It's been so long since I've had hope, I'd forgotten how it changes everything around you. It pares back the greyness of a life unlived and amplifies dulled senses. Someone is going to come and help me! Any minute now blue flashing lights will fling around the insides of this depressed house. Sirens will blare. George will come pointing his finger and telling them to listen to me. They will restrain Richard with cuffs, holding his arms behind his back. The children and I will be cloaked in foil blankets and given sugary drinks to help with the shock. Then they'll take me home. And my mother will understand. And we will be safe. At last.

I tell myself only this story, for the alternative is not worth thinking about. Besides, is there anything worse than this? If nothing changes, nothing changes.

I play with the children on the floor. I admire how well I've managed to keep them through this. I'm malnourished and dark-eyed. Little more than a shell at this point. But my one success is that I've kept the children eating well, clothed and clean through these dark months.

I swallow down the feeling that I don't know how long I have left with them. Or what he'll do if he finds out before safety can be reached. All I know is I'm ready to fight. At least there will be an ending of some sort to this. Because if that little note just floats off lost forever – that seems worse in so many ways.

I've moved Noah's mattress into Roxy's room. I want them together tonight. I want my most precious possessions in one place. I don't ever want to ever stand in the hallway and be forced to decide which door to rush in to.

I sing them to sleep. Their breathing slows as they drift off. I sit there for a while just watching. Then, I put on some proper clothes for once, so I'm ready. I creep through to the living room and find Richard staring into the fire, drinking a glass of red wine. He looks up at me. 'Hello,' he says curtly, with a relaxed smile. He's in a good mood. This puts me on edge. Good moods are so much worse than bad ones in many ways.

I wonder how he'll react; he'll fight. He'll play the part he knows so well. He'll shake his head sadly and explain my history. I'm a mess. I'm hallucinating again. He'll pull them over to one side of the room so I can't hear and whisper about how sick I am. How he's forfeited so much of his life to care for me. He's tried his best but it's just not good enough, he'll say. He's worried about the children's safety after finding some strange recordings I made. He'll suggest they use their special on-the-spot sectioning powers to take me in before anyone is hurt. He'll look full of sadness and regret, because all he's ever wanted is for me to get better.

I must be careful not to fade into the background. I must stand up for myself.

'I'm going to cook us dinner. You need to eat, Eliza – you look terrible.' He goes to the kitchen and begins to hum. 'How was your day?' he asks. I'm confused. He's barely spoken to me for weeks.

'Okay,' I stammer.

'You look like you had fun in the garden with the kids. That's nice,' he says, taking various groceries out of the fridge. A knife is pulled out with a swish.

'Yes, it was a lovely day – sunny in the end, not too cold.'

'That's good,' he murmurs as he takes a cucumber over to the sink and runs it under the tap. 'I had a brilliant day . . . thanks for asking.'

'Oh . . . sorry. Did you? That's good.' I wonder what this is all about.

'I got something sorted out that has been playing on my mind. Keeping me up at night really,' he says, shaking his head.

'Oh?'

'Yes – you know when something is *really* grating on you.' He exaggerates the word and begins to slice.

'Something at work?' I ask.

He shrugs and shakes his head. 'No. Something else.' I feel a thudding sensation then. And a low-level ringing in my ears. 'But it's fine. You'll be pleased to know I've sorted it. That's what I do after all, isn't it?' He looks at me, a small smile, barely there at all. 'Can't leave any loose ends hanging, can we?' I shake my head, wondering what he's talking about.

The doorbell rings. *Ta-da!* I turn to it. Relief swells in my chest. Whatever he's going on about doesn't matter because they're here, and they're going to save me. No sirens or flashing lights, but that's because they're biding their time, and worried he'll make a run for it. I imagine George outside grabbing the arm of an officer, pushing them on, trying to get us out as quickly as possible.

I balance on the counter, the moment so rich in opportunity I cannot stand straight. I'm never going to spend another night in that shed. I'm leaving. My children are safe.

Richard wipes his hands with the tea towel. 'I wonder who it could be!' he says cheerfully. My heart thuds as I watch him walk to the door. He pauses and turns back to me, giving another delighted smile before opening it.

Everything will unravel now. I'm merely a passenger on the journey through this transition. Soon I will be able to breathe again.

He opens the door. It's the same two police officers from the other night. I walk forward a few steps, expecting them to beckon me away. To safety. I think of the children's things. I'll have to explain I can't leave until I have them. Roxy's favourite cat and one of Noah's dinosaurs at least. I'll need the nappy bag, of course. I wonder where they'll take me. I wait for them to approach me and ask the question I'm waiting to confirm: *Is he hurting you?* I'm ready – I'm going to say, *yes.*

'Mr Bloom,' the older officer says, wiping his black boots on the mat.

My lips part, waiting for the next sentence. Waiting to tell them the truth. I peer over their shoulders into the night, expecting George to be on their heels. But he's not there.

'You called us about a very delicate situation, sir?'

And I realise they're not there for me at all.

CHAPTER 42

Lauren

Instead of driving off, I slow down and stop. A car speeds past and I open my door and get out. 'Susie?' I call softly as I approach her. She notices me and wipes a tear off her cheek. 'Susie,' I say gently. 'Are you okay? Can I give you a lift somewhere?' She shakes her head and turns back to the tree. The flowers that were in her arms now reside at the bottom of the trunk.

'It isn't fair. That wonderful, cheerful little boy I raised is gone and replaced with a version of him that was never true. I know they all gossip about him behind my back.' She sighs. 'I think that's worse than death, isn't it? Someone taking away who you were.' She looks over, her wet eyes daring to dart to mine. I gently nod, unsure what to say. I shuffle on the spot. 'I'm embarrassing you.' She sighs. 'That's all I am these days. An embarrassment. I think Peter is going to make me give up my flower stall at The Meadows. I can't seem to get anything right these days.' She takes out a tissue and blows her nose.

I stare ahead at the tree and stuff my hands in my pockets. The pink lilies droop in the direct sunlight. 'It's unfair that other people get to turn him into some sort of monster that is the direct opposite of who he was. It breaks my heart.'

'I'm so sorry, Susie,' I say, unsure what else to offer. I have no idea what really happened. The mothers at the party offered a very different version of George.

'I behaved badly too,' Susie mutters with a frustrated tut. 'I was so furious. I couldn't see past it at all.' Then she takes something out of her pocket. A little crumble of paper. 'I found this in the paddock the day they came for George. They were there when I came back into the house after finding it. And before I knew what was happening, they took him to the station. Saying that woman had accused him of trying to make off with their son.' She hands me the piece of paper with a shaking hand. Inside in mottled ink it says, *You're right. Please tell them we need help. SOS.* My forehead creases as I stare at it. 'I was so angry with her. I never showed it to anyone until it was too late,' she whispers. 'I've carried it around with me ever since.' She sniffs again and looks around sadly. 'Will you take it? I need to let it go. I need to let them both go.' I nod at her, and then stare at the hopeful looping handwriting. Susie whispers, 'What if my anger stopped her from getting help? What if he was hurting her and I was so blinded by my poor boy?' She dries her tears, but they fall freely. 'I couldn't save my sister, I couldn't save George, and I didn't save her,' she says quietly.

She walks slowly to her car, wavering. I look up and wince, wondering what else I can say. But she drives off before I find the right words and am left standing there holding the little white note.

CHAPTER 43

Eliza

Richard opens the door and gestures for the officers to come inside. 'Yes. Thank you for coming all the way out here.' His straight mouth twitches with anger. I watch, dumbfounded, as they crane their necks around the interior with the same captivated expressions as last time. My head is swirling, trying to work out what's going on. They haven't come here to take Richard away. They were invited by him? So . . . George didn't get the note?

I think of my sad little piece of paper being tugged away by the wind.

'Please, have a seat,' Richard says, gesturing to the sofa. They remove their caps and sit in unison. Like carbon copies, twenty years between. Their backs upright and their black boots firmly on the ground, poised. 'Would you like a tea, or coffee? Anything?'

'Best get to it,' the older one replies. Richard's demeanour is sombre, but friendly. In control. He's masterful at this.

Turning to me, he says, 'I think Eliza should tell you what happened. She was there.' I look at him in shock. My mouth gapes open and I shake my head. Richard speaks quickly. 'It's hard for her, you see. Nothing like this has ever happened. We moved from the city to get away from undesirables – sod's law,' he says with a sad sniff. 'You were in the woods, weren't you, Eliza? Why don't you start at the beginning?' He moves over to me and puts an arm around my shoulders, gently guiding me to a chair. He moves onto a seat next to mine and holds my hand with both of his. 'She's still in shock. It took me ages to get it out of her. I can tell you what she told me if that works?'

The older officer nods firmly. 'That's a start. Sorry this is so tough for you, Mrs Bloom. We just want to get to the bottom of what happened and see if we can help.'

Richard squeezes his fingers around my hand painfully. I open my mouth to speak, but he gets there first. 'She was walking in the woods behind our house. The bottom of our land joins the riding school where he works.' He points in the direction as he explains. His voice building with anger. 'Eliza only turned around for a moment, and that stable boy grabbed our son, he was going to run off with him. It was only when he stumbled and fell, running off. Is his name George? We think that's right.' I look at Richard flabbergasted, my eyes widening as I take in his lie. 'I mean, what if he hadn't fallen? What if he tries it again? Our son is barely two years old, Officer.' Richards stands and turns in a frustrated rage. 'I'm minded to go round there and bloody castrate him.'

'George?' The word falls from my mouth in confusion.

Richard is pacing angrily. The officers' faces are frozen with a look of deep sympathy etched on them. 'Tell them, Eliza – for God's sake, tell them what happened,' he spits. They turn to face me.

The younger one has a notebook and pen suspended, waiting.

I lick my lips. 'I . . .' I pause. *Help me.* I try to say the words. Would they believe me? The way they've allowed Richard to control the whole meeting, how they looked around this house in such admiration. How they seem just slightly intimidated by my husband. They've already fallen for his charm. 'I . . . can't . . .' I say, my words so weak they drift into the air and dissipate.

'Sorry. My wife – she had a terrible bout of postnatal depression after our daughter was born. We thought a move out here was just what she needed. The fresh air and the calmer surroundings.' He pulls me into him. 'And now this,' he says, laden with sadness.

I watch as if I'm out of my body as he tells all the lies for me. They jot it down and offer victim support and look at us with pity as they explain the next steps.

An hour later Richard waves them off as I cower in the living room. As soon as he shuts the door I run to the bathroom and throw up. As I lift my head out the bowl, I hear him whistling. My fantasy of Richard being carted off has now been replaced with George's image. Handcuffed and head down in the back of a police car. There is no way he'd want to help me now. I feel sick. I have a shower and try to scrub the shame off. But it is fixed. There is no way I can rid myself of this.

My note is lost and with it all my hope.

The next morning, I watch as he flips his tie and tucks it through the knot. Roxy cries out, and I realise with a jolt she's been calling for me to pick up her spoon. I lean over and retrieve it from the floor. Richard walks over and tosses Noah's hair. The boy looks up at his father nervously. Next, Richard pulls a funny face at Roxy, and she giggles. Her reaction sickens me. The fear that some of him may rub off on them is too horrific to bear. I don't want Noah to be a man like that. I want him to be a partner, an ally. I want him to meet a girl and fall in love and treat her with respect.

Richard doesn't like talking about his own father. His mother he could discuss wistfully for days. She disappeared, and he was left with his dad at the impressionable age of fifteen. The framed photograph of her hanging in the study is his prize possession. In it, she is a young woman. Her dark brown hair is cut in a bob, and she wears a white shirt with a peter pan collar, and a thin black ribbon tied in a bow at the centre. While it has all the markings of a formal photograph, with her hands cupped in her lap, her expression gives her away. She smiles fully with her teeth on show, and her eyes squint ever so slightly, lost in a moment of joy. She was a dancer and apparently got into the Royal Ballet School, but I believe she turned the offer down once she met Richard's father.

I often stare at her picture, trying to work it out. What

happened to Richard after she disappeared for him to walk into the darkness, when it's so obvious she danced in the light?

I watch as he sips the last of his morning coffee and ties his brown brogues, adjusting the hem of his trousers over his colourful pink socks. *That Dr Bloom has a fun flair*, they must think, with a bemused smile.

'I'm not expecting them to come again, but if they do, remember what we discussed. I'll be watching.' He glances at the camera. 'You lied to them. Police don't like liars. But if you're good, I might think about calling them and saying you had a funny turn and imagined the whole thing.' He smiles and kisses Roxy's cheek. 'Besides, the damage has been done. Mud sticks in small villages like this.' I think of George and my whole body shudders in anguish. What must he be going through?

Richard leaves the house. I stare into space. Noah reaches over to me, and I pull him off his toddler chair and onto my lap, cuddling him.

'Mummy, we go home?' Noah asks hopefully.

I bring him close to me again and get a surge of something I didn't know I had left.

'Yes. Yes. We can go home,' I promise.

CHAPTER 44

Lauren

I walk up to the front door. I'm shaken from the conversation with Susie by the tree. I stand there for a moment before searching for my house keys. Rummaging, I realise I don't have them. In my hurry to leave, I must have forgotten them. I think of the hob I left on the other evening. I'm so forgetful these days. A dot of rain lands on my face and I look up to see a dark grey cloud has infiltrated the wash of blue above. It feels like a winter's early evening rather than a summer's afternoon. I feel tired. Heavy and so very confused.

Not one person I've met has heard of Paul's friends. But this other couple, was it Eliza . . . and Richard? Paul must know them too – because of the photograph. Maybe it all connects to Noah somehow? I rub the side of my head. I feel a migraine coming on. The twists and turns have agitated it. I think I could sleep for a very long time. I press the doorbell. *Ta-da!* it sings at me.

I wish I was coming home to another house. This place has

infected my blood, my bones and my bile. 'Where have you been?' he asks, holding the door open tightly, as if there is a chance he may not let me in.

'I just needed a couple of hours to myself,' I say quietly, thinking of all his missed calls. Then to my surprise he envelops me in an embrace that makes me doubt myself again. 'And did it work?' He sways me gently and I feel as though I'm falling into a trance.

'What?' I whisper.

'The time to yourself? Do you feel better?'

'I feel . . . I feel . . .' My words falter. How can I explain this to him? I gain a caustic taste as I think of the note in my pocket. 'Did Gloria and Jack ever mention an Eliza, or Richard?' I ask.

He stops swaying me for a moment. Then he coughs and lets me go, turning his back. 'I think they may have owned the house before. I recognise the name from some paperwork I found clearing Jack's stuff out of the study. Why?'

'I just keep hearing rumours about them. They just sort of disappeared.'

Paul shrugs. 'I have no idea. Sorry.' He walks towards the study. 'Go and have a bath and relax. You can't pour from an empty cup, Lauren. You don't look great.' I raise my hand to my face and stare into the mirror on the wall. He's right. I don't.

I lie back in the hot water. Trying to straighten out my thoughts. My head aches with information I can't seem to process. If he didn't know this pair, then what about the photograph? I can't ask him about it without admitting I went through his phone. The door opens a creak, and Margo comes in holding her stuffed cat. She drops it as she walks to the rim of the bath, reaching over, trying to scoop up some of the bubbles with her hand. She looks impossibly cute. I smile at her and then lift my hand to move an eyelash that has fallen onto her cheek. I press my finger onto it and hold the tiny hair over my lips. 'Want to make a wish?' I ask and she nods excitedly. 'What is it?' I ask. She grins with embarrassment and shakes her head. 'Go on, tell me,' I say, smiling with her.

'Lauren marry Daddy,' she lisps. 'Like in my book,' she adds.

I think of her colouring book with all the wedding dresses. My smile falters but I save it before it tumbles into a frown. 'We'll see, sweetie.' She nods.

'Lauren?'

'Yes, darling?' I whisper.

'Are you sickie?'

'What?' I laugh. 'No.'

'You sleep a lot,' she says with a worried expression. I frown. They watched their mother waste away; I hope they aren't reading into all my naps and headaches thinking history is repeating itself. 'Daddy says you're sickie.' Margo leans over and feels my head as if checking for a temperature.

'I'm fine,' I whisper. 'Don't you worry about me, okay?'

And she nods. 'Okay, Loz.' Then she turns and picks up her soft toy and wanders out the gap in the door.

I close my eyes. The mist rising from the heat of the bath

almost causes me to drift off. Maybe Margo is right. I'm sick. I do seem to lose hours and days merge into one another.

'Lauren.' Blinking, I see Paul leaning on the frame of the door. He looks confused. 'What is this note? It was on the floor.'

He's holding the little white piece of paper Susie gave me. It was in my pocket. How . . . ?

'What note? I've not seen it before,' I stammer. For some reason, I feel like I have to lie.

'Okay. What a weird note,' he says flatly. He reaches around and takes a towel off the back of the door and throws it at the foot of the bath.

'Hurry up. I've got a surprise for you.'

CHAPTER 45

Eliza

That night Richard gets an emergency call from the unit. Swearing, he grabs his coat and leaves without much of an explanation. Before he goes, he points out the camera, and I nod. This is my window of opportunity, and I mustn't waste it. I'm going to make a chance dash. I must tell the police that George didn't do anything wrong. I abandoned Power after Richard shot her. If I don't stop this, I'm not much more than an accomplice.

I watch from our window as the car runs down the drive, lighting up trees in the distance. Richard must think he has me completely cornered. There are no mobile phones or landlines here. I don't have a computer or know Richard's password. There isn't a way I can call for help. He's cut me off from the possibility of Susie's for refuge, as they both hate me now.

Run. That is my only option. I'm not going to rot away here for a second longer. I'm going home to my mother. Surely once she sees Noah and Roxy's beautiful faces, she'll cave in.

I will gladly leave my precious children there and come back for my punishment if she still cannot stand the sight of me.

We've passed a petrol station a few times while out in the car. I think it's about three miles away. Maybe more. I will ask the person who works there to phone me a taxi and I will use the twenty-pound note I've squirrelled away to get to the train station. I'm not sure how I'll pay for the ticket, but maybe if I pretend to have lost my wallet, with two small children in tow, they'll take pity on me. Then once I'm home she'll understand what I've been through and help me call the police and explain. I close my eyes tightly and allow the sound of her laugh I've fought so hard to box away rush through me.

I wait patiently for an hour until I'm sure Richard has arrived at work and should be distracted by whatever crisis is happening there. Then I get out a rucksack from Richard's wardrobe and pack nappies and wipes, changes of clothes and loads of snacks. Avoiding the camera at all costs. Then I head to Noah's room. He's fast asleep. I shake him gently. 'We're going on a trip,' I whisper. He moans. 'Are there any special toys you want to bring? We'll have to come back for the rest another time.' I look around at all his things, his plastic dinosaurs and favourite books, and wonder if we'll ever see them again.

I prop Roxy's sleeping body to my chest and attach her with the baby carrier. She's heavy now, a little too big for it; my shoulders feel tight and for a moment I feel disheartened, as if this whole attempt is futile. But I must try. I put my coat on and she snuggles down. I struggle the backpack on and jump on the spot slightly, testing the weight. Noah rubs his eyes as he stands next to me. Before we go, I look up at the camera, but it seems languid this evening. Maybe Richard isn't watching. Maybe this will work. It's a good forty-five-minute drive back from the hospital, so even if he suspects something, that gives us a good head start.

We don't walk on the road, but to the side of it amongst the trees. Noah next to me holding my hand. If I was on my own, this would take about an hour, maybe less if I was running. With Noah's small steps it will take at least triple that. I pick him up occasionally and carry them both with a slight jog, but I can't cope for more than a few minutes. If I think of how far there is to go, I feel demoralised and hopeless. So, I just try to focus on each footstep. There are no street lights. Only the light of the moon. Noah trips, falling flat on his face in the mud. He begins to cry. It's hard to comfort him with everything that is holding me down. 'Shhh, shhh, it's okay. Nearly there,' I lie, hugging him until he recovers. Precious moments are lost.

Every time a car zooms past my stomach ties in knots, and adrenalin rushes as I ready myself to grab Noah and run into the depths of the forest. About an hour into our journey, I stop to give Noah a snack and some water and wait patiently for him to finish even though I'm desperate to hurry him. I look into my chest to see Roxy's eyes still closed in heavenly ignorance.

'Mummy I'm cold,' Noah moans softly.

I hug him to my side. 'I know, not long now.' My eyes jolt to the road as I hear the roar of a speeding car. A blur of blue rushes past and my shoulders relax. 'Come on, darling,' I whisper, trying to get him to chew just a tiny bit faster. Finally, we get up and trudge along again. He stops after a few minutes.

'No walk,' he says defiantly. Crossing him arms. 'Want to go bed. Tired, Mummy. Cold,' he moans.

I bite my lip. I swallow down a sob at what I'm forcing my child to do.

'It's okay, darling, we'll be there soon, I promise.' He bangs his feet on the floor and shakes his head. Oh God. How am I going to get him there?

My head spins around as I hear another vehicle. I hold my breath as I see the silver sheen of our car whizz past, and I cough in surprise. Richard knows. He's looking for us.

'Come on. I'll carry you.' I hold his limp body to one side, with Roxy on my front and the bag on my back. I am full of my most precious things, and I find strength I never knew I had. I jump forward with long, quick strides, hurtling past the trees. Twigs snap and leaves brush my face.

I hear a car again. It isn't racing like before. The eerie sound of the slow trundle that makes my insides freeze. Lights brighten the safe darkness and, feeling vulnerable, I scoop us behind a tree, gasping. Noah is quiet, he's scared. He doesn't even moan at me as I put my finger to my lips and say, 'Shhh.' I can try dressing this up all I want, but at the end of the day we are creeping through the woods in the dark, hiding and running. He must sense something is very badly wrong. I hope I'll be able to make him feel safe again once this is over.

Holding my breath, I hug him to me tightly, resisting the urge to squeeze my eyes shut; I watch as the headlights creep towards us. My breath scant, expecting the lights to stop and to hear a car door opening and closing. Footsteps getting closer. I will be no match for him under the weight of all of this.

The lights creep closer. The car moves from one side of the thick trunk. I turn my head in the hope I'll watch it pass through the other side and continue along its route. When it does, I let out a relieved sigh.

We stay there for what feels like hours, until I am sure he has gone.

After a while, I see it go back in the other direction towards the house, as though it has given up entirely.

Relief swells around my being and I allow a grin to unravel across my face.

Maybe, maybe we will get out of this.

CHAPTER 46

Lauren

As I get out the bath my naked body catches my attention in the mirror, and I stare. I think of the photograph of me with my friends and the black lycra dress I'm wearing. My hair is long in the photo; it now hangs it wet chunks just below my jawline. I spent so many months in hospital and at the unit, concentrating on the fundamentals of getting better, I hadn't given one jot of thought to how the lingering slumber would transfer to how I'd look at the end. I brush my thighs and my waistline and lament the fact they've lost that youthful snap. I have various scars around my body from the accident. I don't think I look very sexy these days. Paul would scorn me for saying that.

I narrow my eyes at my reflection. 'What a stupid thing to worry about,' I whisper, berating myself for the vanity. My body is amazing for what it survived. I'm proud of it for bringing me back to life.

My reoccurring dream comes to me in a flash. Blood. I quickly grab the towel and wrap it around myself.

Wandering into the bedroom, I go to the wardrobe and pull out the long black chiffon dress I bought online when we lived at the flat. Paul gave me his credit card and told me to 'go crazy' and treat myself to something special. I think of the surprise he mentioned and wonder if it would be presumptuous to wear it. Slipping it over my head, I walk to the dressing table to dry my hair. Then, I add some lipstick and mascara in the small oval mirror. I walk back to the bathroom and admire the new reflection. *That'll do, Lauren.* I get an excited shiver as I wonder what he could have in store for me.

The full floaty hem of the dress grazes my ankles as I tentatively walk down the stairs. Paul has opted for mood lighting in the living room. Dimmed with a candle on the kitchen counter reflecting onto a bottle of red and two glasses. 'You look amazing.' I turn to see him standing by the fire. It's been too hot to light it. Instead, he's placed a few candles on the sill of its door. He stands there blinking, and I blush. 'How are you feeling?' he asks, walking towards me. 'Hey, you're shaking.' He pulls his arms around me and moves me in a rocking motion in that way he does. It relieves some of the pressure instantly. 'Darling. I know you've had a tough month.'

'I'm sorry . . .' I begin, but he shakes his head.

'Please don't apologise, Lauren.' He sighs deeply. 'When you went out without a word it had a big impact. It made me question my behaviour, especially how I've neglected us.' I'm relieved my actions had the desired effect. 'The surprise – I . . . I thought we could try something to help us reset a bit.

'I know it's not easy with the kids. Especially with everything they've had to deal with. And I've used work as a coping mechanism to block out all my own trauma . . .' He peers over at me, thinking, his voice low and throaty. 'I miss those times when we'd talk for hours and there wasn't any baggage between us. No responsibilities. Just us.' He purses his lips and glances at me. 'I had an idea . . .' he says bashfully. 'But you'll think it's silly.' He scratches the back of his head, his cheeks flushed, and he can't look me. It's nice seeing him nervous and vulnerable like this.

'No, I won't,' I say, stepping into his arms. 'What is it?'

'I thought . . . that maybe we could have a session?'

I laugh a little, surprised. 'A session?'

'Yeah, like we used to . . . when we . . .' He's embarrassed. He clears his throat. 'Fell in love.'

The air becomes lucid, and I'm gripped with longing for all those feelings. 'Okay. Here?' I gesture to the sofa.

He shakes his head. 'Let's go into the study.' And I nod in agreement. I have so yearned for a way back to that time when we had that magnetic closeness which was impossible to ignore. He's right. If we go back to where we started, maybe we'll be able to find a way through this.

He wanders through to the kitchen and pours us a glass of wine each. Then he comes back, and gives me one. We hold hands, and our bodies knock as we wander through the hallway. I giggle. This is nice.

Once inside, he gestures to the chaise longue, and I sit down and lean my head back. I watch as he folds his legs and takes out a pencil and pad and I laugh at his faux professionalism.

'What do you want to know? How I'm feeling?' I ask, sarcastically.

He laughs. 'Well, that is always a good place to start.'

I watch as he removes his phone from his pocket and fiddles with it for a moment, laying it between us. 'Are you going to record this?' I ask, with a smirk.

'Well . . . we should make it authentic. Don't you think?' A cheeky glint in his eye. And I grin at him. He's right. We've lost each other amongst all this homemaking. I've been so desperate to get it right, I forgot the reason I'm here in the first place: us. We need to come back together again and reconnect the best way we know how.

'So, Lauren,' he says, trying to keep a straight face, 'tell me how you are.'

'I'm fine . . .' I glance at him, and he shakes his head. 'Okay – I can't say that.' I close my eyes and really try to centre myself. How am I feeling? I take a deep breath in through my nose and out through my mouth. This is a safe space. I can be honest with Paul, I remind myself. 'I guess I'm feeling a bit lost. As if I want to make this my home but something is stopping me,' I whisper, I wasn't sure what I was going to say until I uttered the words.

'Fear?' he asks.

I try to listen to myself, like he's taught me. 'Yes, there is some fear there.'

'It's okay, Lauren. I'm scared too.'

I open one of my eyes and peer back at him. 'You are?' I grin, finding it comforting that we are relating to each other.

He laughs. 'Of course. I've put everything on the line for you. My work. My kids. And now I feel like you're pushing me away. That's scary.'

I bite my lip. Maybe this whole time we've both been holding everything in. And because we haven't let it out, the pressure has just built up. I whisper, 'I suppose I'm scared that because I'm only half a person I don't deserve you.' It feels good to say that out loud. 'You deserve more. I screw up all the time. I forget things. I'm not a very good with Jesse or Margo.' I feel the weight lifting as I unload. He squeezes my shoulder and thrusts a tissue towards me. I take it.

He sighs, deeply. 'Do you still want to be with me, Lauren?'

'Of course I do . . .' I reply sincerely, meaning every syllable.

His voice changes then; gone is the lightness of touch and humour. 'Do you still want us to be a family? Or is it all just too much for you? Maybe you aren't ready for this big lifestyle change?'

My senses become alert at the change of gear. 'I'm ready. I told you. I love you – I love the kids.' His face has changed.

Come back. I want you back.

'I just need to know you're here, with us, one hundred per cent.'

'I am, you know I am.' I try to catch his eye.

'You're not planning to leave us and go back to your old life?' he asks, his jaw clenched.

I think of my message to Claudia and shake my head. 'No,'

I whisper. 'Of course not.' The heat of the lie rushes through my cheeks as he leans forward.

'I think we need to start from the very beginning,' he adds with a whisper. 'Like we used to.'

When I first started seeing him professionally, we'd pick over my past chronologically. The purpose was to immerse myself in it. Regurgitating what happened might make the memories fill in holes over time, he told me. I'm not sure it really worked, but I never felt I could admit that to him. 'Tell me. From the beginning.'

I close my eyes. These are words I have uttered many times. 'I grew up in a town called Kindling on the south coast. My parents . . . they died when I was four, and I was brought up by my aunt and uncle.' My mind feels foggy – the next line is lost for a moment . . . The memories zip and zap – I'm unable to find the right connection. 'I . . . I . . .'

'Lauren,' he says firmly. 'Tell me what you did again.'

I frown and look at him to assess what he means. He nods. He can't want me to go there tonight. The candle and the dimmed lighting lulled me into thinking this was going to be romantic somehow. He knows I hate having to say these words out loud. They feel wretched inside my mouth.

'With the car crash?' I whisper and he nods sadly. I grip my hands together. 'I was only small.'

'It wasn't your fault. I keep telling you, but you don't listen.'

My throat hurts. 'Do I have to?' I plead but he only continues his sympathetic nodding. 'It will make you feel better,' he adds. 'I promise.' He flaps his pencil between his fingers.

'Okay . . .' I stammer. I close my eyes and fight the words out. 'We were driving through the mountains. I wasn't paying much attention to the road. I was playing with my doll . . .' I sniff. 'Her name was Baby,' I explain. My words drift off – how this could ever make me better . . . Every time I recount it I've felt worse for days.

'Lauren,' he says softly. 'What happened?'

'I dropped Baby. And I started to cry . . . my dad reached back to collect it out of the footwell. And then . . . and then . . .' Not one cell wants to admit this part of me out loud.

'And then you crashed,' he says for me. 'Terrible. What an awful thing to go through.' He squeezes my shoulder. 'Again, Lauren. Tell me again.' And I repeat the words. The pain fills me up, and I hate myself all over again.

'I think that's enough for today,' Paul says. He helps me off the chair and hugs me. I feel numb with grief. Tears fall but I feel nothing. 'It's okay, Lauren, let it out. I'm here.' A few minutes later, he removes himself from the embrace. Tears have stained the shoulder of his shirt, along with the inky black wash of my mascara. 'Do you trust me, Lauren?' he asks.

I look up at him and stare. I've been so confused these last weeks. *Do you trust me?* The question echoes. *Are you scared?* Jesse's question lingers louder. 'Lauren,' he prompts firmly.

'Sorry, I . . .'

'I just sometimes feel like I'm over here, waving, waiting for you to fully be here with us. Do you want me? Do you really want *us*?'

My mouth gapes at the question. 'I moved here to be with you . . .'

'Lauren,' he repeats. I touch my head – it hurts. The pulsating is back. 'Lauren, do you think you might be self-sabotaging? I mean, for all I know you're messaging your friends working out how to get away from us.'

'What?' I ask meekly, feeling seen.

He continues: 'Then what will I be left with? Two children far more confused than when we started this.'

'I would never want to hurt them . . .' I try. Suddenly it's all mixed up. The girls' faces, my flat. The accident. I have a flash of my nightmare and all that blood.

'There is a theory I learnt about total trust,' he says, looking at me cautiously. 'I was thinking we could try it. It's quite an innovative method. I really think it will help you.'

'What is it?' I ask. I want to feel better, less dirty and wrong. I don't want to feel guilty all the time any more.

'It's like that game that you used to play as a kid. When you fell backwards and trusted someone to catch you. Would you . . . would you trust me to catch you, Lauren?'

I think of us, how everything made sense when we met. He's right – I must be trying to shake him off because I can't handle what I did. I killed my parents, so I must be stuck in some sort of belief system where I think I don't deserve to be happy, or be part of a family again. In case I destroy that too.

Paul has been trying to teach me how to get past all that. Of course I trust him. He's all I have. They are all I ever wanted. 'Yes,' I murmur.

'Come,' he says, taking my hand. We walk through the sitting room to the back doors. My trainers are already on the mat. He gestures for me to put them on.

'Where are we going? The kids . . .' I nod towards their rooms.

'Not far. They're fine. Asleep.'

He pushes open the door and we step down onto the patio and then the lawn. It is a cloudless, cool evening; the breeze catches my bare arms. For a moment I wonder if this is some sort of kinky outdoor sex thing. But Paul doesn't seem in that sort of mood. There is a detached determination to his movements, and once we get to the bushes at the bottom, he gets out his phone and turns on the torch.

'Paul,' I say softly.

'Come on, Lauren,' he replies, and we continue down to the path.

I've no pockets and didn't think to bring my phone. I look back towards the house, annoyed at the loss.

Once we get to the clearing where the shed is, we stop. He fiddles with his phone and opens the door. 'What are we doing?' I ask, breathless.

'You'll see.' He grins, stepping inside. 'Come on.' He gestures for me to follow. It smells damp, fetid. I look at him questioningly again. And he takes my hands. For one silly moment I think he's going to propose. 'This theory I was telling you about. It's about relinquishing control and the freedom that can give.' I nod, still unsure where he's going with this. A lot of the mindfulness mediations he's given me talk about handing over control. 'I thought maybe we could try it. See what happens. An experiment? You've been so unhappy and distant these last few weeks.'

'What?' I ask, still unsure what he actually wants me to do. Then he backs away towards the door and steps down onto the other side of the glass. 'Do you trust me, Lauren?'

I pause. *No*, my head screams, but my heart says, *surely I do*? I've come all this way, ignored so much advice. He's put so much on the line for me. 'Yes.'

'Do you trust me to do what's best for you?' And as I nod, he closes the door. I rush at the glass and put my hands against the cool surface. 'Paul?' I say, 'What . . . ?'

'I'll come get you later.'

'But . . . when?' I am filled with the urgent need to know.

'Trust me, darling,' he says, and I watch as the light goes back up the path. And I am alone in the darkness.

I blink. *Am I mad?* I wonder what my friends would think. Locked in a shed. They wouldn't understand. I think of Emma. Maybe this is something I can do to be as perfect as her. The anxiety I've felt to be flawless. And the simplicity of sitting here, knowing I'm doing something that makes him happy. It is strangely comforting. It is impossible to fail at this. Just sitting here is making him happy.

When I met Paul, and he started to piece it all together for me, the waves of grief were blurred by the waves of happiness I felt. It became a current pulling me away from the disaster I found myself in. How can something that made me feel so safe – so at home – be wrong? It must be *me* that's wrong. It must be.

I sit back on the cold concrete floor and close my eyes. For once I can barely think of anything. My busy mind is silent for the first time in a long time. The road is no longer complicated. It is simple.

I just have to stay here. And wait.

CHAPTER 47

Eliza

Finally, after another hour of slow trudging, I see the red blinking lights of the petrol station. Relief grips me and I grab Noah and run the rest of the way. My arms feel as though they're going to fall off as I hang on to him, whilst carrying Roxy and the backpack. He's exhausted and confused. 'Mummy,' he mutters into my shoulder, half asleep. Panting, we reach the forecourt, and I stop to catch my breath as my boots hit the tarmac. Composing myself, I imagine what we must look like. I lick my thumb and wipe a smudge of mud from Noah's cheek.

'You did it, darling. We're here.'

He looks a bit dismayed at our destination. 'Here?' is all he can muster.

The bell on the door dings as we enter, and bright strobing lights jar against the blackness we've been embedded within for the last few hours. It takes my eyes a moment to readjust. Everything has a heightened quality. The colours. The sounds.

The shop within is sparse with tired, dusty goods, and the man behind the counter stares, chewing gum. He is large with white stubble and floppy unwashed hair. His worn grey sweater has holes around the neckline, and a dirty stain on his shoulder and there's a freshly popped spot on his chin. His beady eyes watch us, as he stands there motionless. He must be wondering who this strange patron without a car is, muddy and laden with floppy children.

I walk to the counter, smiling. Trying to radiate normality. 'Excuse me, would you mind ordering me a taxi, please?'

He continues to stare without so much as a friendly smile. 'Are you lost?' he asks, between sloppy chews of gum. He peers out the glass at the forecourt. 'No car?'

'Would you mind? I need to get to the station . . .'

He takes out his phone. 'There aren't many round here. You usually have to prebook.'

I squeeze my teeth together and glance at the deserted road, trying not to let stress build. 'It's ringing,' he says. 'What are you doing out here on your own with the kiddies anyway?' I open my mouth to fill out the lie.

Ding! The bell goes.

I turn and see stars.

'Ah! There you are.' Richard. 'Goodness. You lot must be freezing.' He walks over and rubs my shoulders, smiling pleasantly. 'What a palaver. Don't worry, I fixed it.'

I look at the man; he seems relieved I'm no longer his problem. 'Looks like your mister's here.' I watch in horror as he hangs up the call and puts his phone in his pocket.

'Dada!' Roxy cries from the baby carrier. The lights must have woken her up.

'Come on – heating's on in the car. Told you I could sort the puncture. Ye of little faith!' He laughs.

I feel swept along down a stream towards a waterfall. He turns to the man. 'Nightmare – she thought she'd walk for help while I battled with it. Come on, darling.' Before I can get any footing in the situation, he picks Noah up and walks towards the door. 'I'll take him,' I say, rushing after them, not wanting Noah to be parted from me. But Richard opens the door – *ding!* – and strides outside towards our silver car which is parked chaotically across two spaces. I glance back at the man behind the counter. But he's already turned the other way.

I rush after them. Richard is already strapping Noah into his seat. He turns to me and forcefully clips Roxy out of the baby carrier, and she holds out her chubby arms to him. I'm frozen. What can I do? I watch as she too is inserted into the car. Both my babies.

'You coming?' he asks. He opens the passenger door and gestures for me to get in.

I really don't have a choice.

We drive back towards the house in silence. Staring out into the darkness, I realise how hidden and safe we were in the woods; I can't see a thing. All that way. For nothing. 'You know that was the last straw, right?' he says.

Part of me is glad it's over. The hope I was feeling was

painful to reconcile within. Imagining I might wake up somewhere one day and be safe. The longing bound up in that was hard to bear.

'I thought you'd like this fresh start, Eliza. Just us, happy in our perfect home. I thought we could put all that nonsense about you taking off behind us. But I can't trust you, can I? I lay all these traps and time and time again you fall for them.' He shakes his head. 'I won't ever be able to trust you, will I?' He tuts. 'Such a shame. I gave you everything, and you just chuck it back in my face.' I find myself nodding along to his monologue in surrender, barely listening to it. I wonder how it'll end. I hope it won't hurt.

Then I hear a beeping. *Beep, beep. Beep, beep.* All in quick succession. I sit up in my seat and turn to look behind us through the rear windscreen.

The white van. It's George. He has come for me.

PART FOUR

CHAPTER 48

It's funny when you have no measure of a length of time. It passes in waves of anxiety that crash with moments of raging despair. Thoughts are circular and unrelenting, a veritable washing machine rinsing through past, present and future. Overanalysing what is completely plain to see: I've been locked up by a man who says he loves me.

How did I get here? How have I made it okay to willingly let someone lock me up? I had a choice – didn't I?

Birds tweet. I lift my head, which I'd been cradling in my arms. I glance up at the dewy glass from my spot on the floor. Golden morning light leaks into the wooden box. I'm shaking. Goosebumps cover my legs and the fabric of my dress lies between my thighs on the dusty concrete floor. My teeth pressed together reverberating gingerly as I shiver.

I'm glad for the birdsong.

I hope he isn't too much longer.

A sob escapes and my hand grasps my mouth in anguish.

The shame.

I stand with a wobble. My bones ache from the pressure on

the hard surface. I take a few steps to the sink and lean over the basin, scooping up water into the palm of my hand, and sip. At least it's July. I'm chilly without a rug or a jacket but it's manageable. Tears swell in my eyes.

Will he come for me soon?

I feel as though my self-respect has crept away – like a friend embarrassed by another's behaviour on a night out. I think back to the happy journey from London. How Paul had rushed around the front of the car to help me out of the passenger seat. How we'd held hands over the gearstick, occasionally staring into each other's eyes basking in the joy of this new adventure. How long ago was that? A few months? How have we got here?

The soft light sneaks in further, and the birdsong becomes hysterical. A ray of sun pokes through the trees outside and a shard of light hits the back wall. I move myself into it, hoping for warmth. Glancing down, I notice something etched into the grain of the wood. I take a few steps towards it and crouch. My fingers brush the surface so it becomes legible.

E was here.

The air leaves me. 'Emma . . .' I whisper.

Before I can process it fully: a noise from outside. I turn. Paul is standing there smiling supportively. I hear a click and swallow. He opens the door and beckons me into his arms. I find myself not wanting to move.

He takes my hand and helps me onto the grass before throwing a blanket around my shoulders tenderly. 'You did so well,' he whispers, kissing my cheek.

I want to go home. But where is that? I wipe a tear away and sniff. 'I don't feel great,' I mutter.

'It's okay, it's still too raw. Once the clouds part you will see,' he whispers gently.

I nod, but I don't believe him.

Paul's arm is slung around my shoulders as we slowly progress up the path. The house looks incredible with the trees reflecting off it becoming part of its surroundings. He pushes back the doors and I mechanically wipe my trainers on the mat. He puts me on one of the kitchen stools and I rearrange the blanket and hug myself. Glancing at the clock on the wall, I realise it's seven a.m. and the children will be up any moment. I will have to put on a show. The smell of cinnamon and raisin fills the air as he toasts me a bagel. A hot cup of coffee is placed by my trembling hand. I watch him, trying to work it out. He seems so normal. So keen to please.

Is this some sort of pleasure–pain thing? Is this how my boyfriend really gets his kicks? I take a sip and the hot liquid cascades down my chilly insides, causing me to shiver. I say, 'Thank you.' My eyes drift around the room and come to rest on the crumpled pile of drawings on the dining table.

'You did so well,' he says, looking at me. 'I'm so proud of you. What did you think?'

I have no idea what he's talking about. 'Of what?' I croak.

'The experiment.'

I feel like crying. The experiment? Does he really think this is some sort of healing programme? I can't do anything but stare.

'Are you okay?' he asks.

'Yes,' I murmur.

We hear the cry of Margo waking. Paul dries his hands. 'I'll go.' And he puts the cooked bagel in front of me. I stare at the butter as it melts into the craters of the bread. Once he's gone, I slip off the stool and walk over to the pile of drawings on the dining table. There is one in particular I'd like to find. I couldn't quite decipher what it was before. Locating it, I stare. A brown box with pink flowers and trees either side and a pink circle floating in the middle. My finger follows the line of it. A face.

Emma. *E was here*. E . . . Eliza.

Richard and Eliza.

And then the memory of Jesse's voice as he twisted the handle of the door, repeating over and over, 'Get her out.' And what he'd said when we first arrived: 'Don't go in the shed.' And the family photograph.

The penny drops.

Everything that I've learnt the last few days comes into view. As though I'm in an art gallery with a vast collection of framed work on the wall, and I've been standing too close.

I've suddenly taken three steps back.

The photograph on the porch: they couldn't have been visiting Gloria and Jack, they didn't live here then. Eliza and Richard did. And if this couple had a baby and a toddler, they would be Margo and Jesse's age now. Exactly how they were in the photograph. There was never a twin. Paul lied.

I'm bitten by fear as the realisation dawns.

Jesse used to be called Noah.

And Paul used to be called Richard.

Emma was Eliza.

My hand slams down on the table to stop myself falling. I hear voices coming and my fingers fumble quickly, putting the drawings into one tidy pile. How will I hide the terror on my face? Because all I can think is: *where is she? Where is Eliza?* What if she didn't die of cancer, like Paul said Emma did? Maybe he changed their identities because he is hiding from something else.

Murder.

If he killed her, where is she? The thought pummels through me like an avalanche. The question lingers as I look out into the garden. The slabs of the patio, and the vast woods that surround us. The nature that will swallow you up. Is Eliza out there – in the woods?

Or the shed? That strange trapdoor with a juicy fat padlock. I swallow.

Margo comes running towards me still in pyjamas. Her pigtails skew-whiff.

'Looozzz!' she cries excitedly, and I open my arms as she runs into them. The smell of her sends a crashing weight through me and I want to weep.

Jesse wanders in next carrying a book. 'Lauren, can you read this to me? It's about bugs. There's a spider, but I know what page it's on, so don't worry.'

Nodding, I try not to sway. Everything is swinging around

as though I'm on a carousel. I can hear the music tinkering in the background.

My head screams, *Get out.*

The car – I'll take it as soon as he's preoccupied. Dump it at the station and get on the first train back to London. I'll phone Claudia and she'll meet me at Paddington. We'll go together to the police, and I'll report him.

I'll be in her flat drinking rosé and dissecting this awful mess in no time. She can say 'I told you so' a million times, I won't care a jot.

Margo hugs my legs and Jesse grabs at my hand, pulling me to the sofa so I'll read to them. *They're not your kids. You can just leave.* But how can I leave them alone for a moment with a man like this? Numbly, I sit on the sofa, and Jesse thrusts the book into my hands. Margo joins. My voice quivers as I slowly read. Sporadically looking up at the hallway, as I wait for him to return.

Once the book is finished, I set them up at the dining table with their breakfast and put the telly on. 'Come and get me if you need anything, okay?' I tell Jesse who nods, already engrossed in the cartoon.

With my heart banging loudly I rush through the hallway. Stopping to listen for him, I realise the shower is on upstairs. As quietly as possible I creep up, needing to locate my phone. I can see his body through the opaque panel. He's whistling happily. My phone is still on the bedside table from yesterday. Phew. Grabbing it, I make my way back downstairs and pull up Claudia's number. It rings and rings. 'Please, Claudia, pick up, pick up,' I say under my breath. I debate leaving a message, but then decide to try again.

I begin to look for the car key in Paul's coat pocket, but it's not there. Biting my thumbnail, I pace the hallway, intermittently checking for the sound of the shower.

Then, as I walk past Paul's study I hear a grating sound, as if something is vibrating on a surface. I pause at the open door, trying to find where the sound is coming from. Claudia's voicemail kicks in again, and my hand falls to my side. Stepping inside the study, I realise the vibrating has stopped. I decide to try Claudia just once more. I press the button and the ringing begins again.

So does the vibrating.

My vision hones in on his desk drawers and I stumble forward, falling to my knees, jerking each open with messy haste. The call goes to voicemail and the vibrating stops again. Holding my breath, I look down at the home screen and press call. To my horror the vibrating continues and I yank open another drawer. There, I find a small metal box, like one of those petty cash tins. Shaking, I pick it up and it vibrates in my hand until the call goes to voicemail again.

Heart racing, I check to hear the shower. Thankfully it's still running. The key. Where is the key? I stand and pivot around a few times looking, before I stop at the framed photograph of his mother. My fingers charge at it and fumble around the four corners. I press my cheek to the wall and pull the picture away from the hook, to look at the back. There is a small metal key stuck on with Blu-Tack. I rip it off and fall to the floor, jutting it into the lock. Twisting the key, the box flaps open dramatically with the force.

The contents scatters on the oriental rug.

Four mobile phones. I pick one up and turn it over. In sharpie pen an 'A' is written, and then on the others a 'C', an 'A' and an 'F' – I wonder what they mean. They are turned off apart from the one labelled 'C' which has four missed calls.

I recognise the number: it's mine.

Reality stops and turns in on itself. So, Claudia never got my messages? And I've been sending them to Paul? The secrets I have been unburdening onto her have gone straight to him?

He knew I was thinking of leaving this whole time. He must have been using these messages to gauge how I was feeling about our relationship. The timings – as I began to voice my concerns to Claudia, Paul became more controlling.

He knew I was thinking of leaving him.

The sound of water gushing from the upstairs bathroom stops. I quickly drop the phones back into the tin and lock it. Then I jam the box back in the drawer. Jumping to my feet, I put the key back behind the frame.

Rushing into the hallway, the realisation hits me. Claudia isn't waiting for me. No one is. They don't even know where I am.

Paul comes downstairs in jeans and a T-shirt. His hair is wet. 'There you are!' he beams.

CHAPTER 49

Paul doesn't leave my side all day. I can't move without him hovering around me. Sucked down by danger and sickening dread, my head conspires against me, pounding in an awful nauseating way. Distorting my vision and making me shaky and weak. I try to act as normally as possible as I look after the children. I do some washing and clean the kitchen floor. As I go through these motions, my head rushes with new insight.

The man I've been living with, having sex with, cooking and cleaning for, whose children I've been caring for. The man I trusted to build a whole new life with – is a killer.

I pelted sympathy on him. *Oh, the poor widower*, I thought, and put him on a pedestal so high, I couldn't see him for who he really was. All the red flags I dismissed, so wanting the fantasy to be true.

I can't process the intricacies of it all. He fabricated reams of messages from my friends. There must have been thousands in our group chat. They were constant. Is that what he's been doing in that room all this time? Sitting there creating a real-time narrative journey for my friends. Because of the black holes in my memory, a lot of the time private jokes just went over my head, or talk of old boyfriends didn't quite land. He knew that vulnerability, and he used it to create a fucked-up script to get me all on my own. And I fell for it. Hook, line and sinker.

But if Paul has been pretending to be them this whole time, where do my friends think I've gone? I realise I've called Claudia a few times and spoken to her, very briefly. Each time she cut me off and moved our communication over to the messaging service. Because of my memory I don't remember the sound of her voice. There must be an app that can distort or mimic. There seems to be one for everything these days.

He must have seen me in hospital and read my notes – memory loss and distant relatives. *Perfect*, he must have thought. He came along with a version of the future I wanted so urgently, at a time I felt so lost. I took it. No questions asked.

The girls tried to make me see sense.

I laugh out loud. It wasn't the girls, I realise. It was him. I remember now. My phone was lost during the accident, the nurses told me. And I was given a new one with a new number. The girls talked about their visit to see me, on our group chat. I had cards left by them, and flowers. And I chatted away afterwards thanking them, explaining how much I appreciated them coming. When secretly, I couldn't remember them coming at all. I was so mixed up in those early days – my memory didn't always stick. The doctors told me that was normal at the beginning. I was embarrassed by it, and nodded along with information sometimes, even if I couldn't place it. Especially if my counsellor, Paul, had something to say.

But the 'girls' all tried to put me off Paul. Why would he do that? Was it a test of how far I'd go for him? Who I was prepared to shun for him?

I suppose having a bust-up with them meant I was removed from their lives and wouldn't expect to spend time with them once I was discharged. It gave me a reason to 'other' them and fall into his arms, harder and with more loyalty than ever.

After tucking the children into bed, we walk through to the living area. My face hurts from all the fake smiles. As soon as Paul is asleep I'm going to put on my trainers and run out that door and call the police. I'm not going to let what happened to her happen to me.

Paul rests back and sips a glass of wine, watching TV. He's enjoying a comedy and laughs occasionally. I have closed my eyes, trying not to think of the danger I am in.

All I can think of is Eliza. She left behind all these clues. The note. The scratch in the shed. She wants me to find her. I can feel her. She must still be here – somewhere. But will I escape before he gets me? Maybe he'll bury me next to her in a shallow grave in the woods? Under the patio perhaps? A flash of Jesse's drawing of the shed. Maybe Paul didn't even touch her. Maybe he just left her to rot in there by simply locking the door and walking away. I think of the ghastly sound the bolt makes.

A blast of anger. I was so vulnerable. This man in a position of authority – hiding in plain sight. I wonder how many times he's done this before. Overcome with hatred, I can't seem to hold it down as I watch him calmly take a sip of his drink and laugh out loud at another joke. How dare he be so untarnished by any of this. He glances across at me, having felt my intense stare.

'Emma,' I say. His smile freezes on his lips as I utter the word. 'Can I see her photograph?'

He shifts. 'Why?' He gestures his glass to the telly. 'Why now? Can't you see I'm enjoying this?'

'I just want to see what she looked like,' I persist. 'Don't you think it would be good for the children to remember her? Talk about her? We could frame a photo and put it up on the wall.' I can't help it – I'm angry. What he did to Emma – Eliza – and my poor little Margo and Jesse. How could he?

'Can't you just leave it? Come on. We're having a lovely evening.'

'It's not healthy,' I push.

He sighs and pauses the show, before turning to face me. 'I'm sorry, Lauren, but I just don't think this is any of your business. I really thought – I hoped – that all this work we've done this week was going to help you . . . but I was wrong, it seems.' He stops and waits, as though he is expecting me to apologise for my outburst.

He's trying to push me into submission, I see that now. I shake my head. And his tact changes. 'God, those children have lost so much.' His voice trembles. My hate for him rages. How could he do this to those gorgeous children of his? Doesn't he know how lucky he is? He killed their mother and hoped they'd grow up thinking she succumbed to some terrible illness. Tears swell as I think of Margo's confused face when she wakes up in the morning and I am gone.

Will she walk around with her stuffed cat under arm calling my name. *Lozzz, where are you?* And Jesse will sit at the window looking down at the drive waiting for me to return. My actions reinforcing the idea that everyone leaves him.

How can I do that? How can I bear it?

'Did you ever play that trust game with her? Did you ever lock her up?' I ask, my words measured and quiet.

He laughs, and shakes his head dismissively. 'No. I told you. It was an experiment. We won't do it again if you didn't enjoy it.'

Enjoy it? I want to smack him in the face. I know that was the first step in an escalation of behaviour that I'm not going to stick around to see through.

'Which hospital did she die in?'

He coughs into his glass. 'Why all this sudden interest in my ex-wife?' He studies my features. 'Lauren, you don't look well. Why don't I make you a bath?'

I shake my head. 'Where is she buried?'

'What?' he croaks.

'Her grave. Where is it? Don't you want to visit sometimes?'

He gets up and takes his empty glass to the kitchen. 'How I deal with my family's grief is nothing to do with you . . .'

'Where is she, Paul?' I ask again. Finding confidence I'm sure I'll later regret. I think of the crumpled white note and feel a stabbing pain in my chest. *SOS*. She must have been so desperate, and it kills me that the help she asked for never came.

I clear my throat. 'I was thinking maybe we could go and visit my parents' grave. Leave them some flowers. I'd like to,' I whisper. 'But I can't remember where they're buried. Can you help me find out?'

He nods and shifts uncomfortably. 'Sure. You've just never seemed interested before.' He comes over and strokes my hair. 'Let me make you a bath, darling, you look so tired.'

A tear falls. I feel his breath on my cheek. I shake my head. And even though I've never felt so terrified, I ask, 'Where is she?'

'Who?'

I stare up at him. I'm going to say her name. I have to. She is screaming for me to. 'Eliza,' I whisper.

His soft eyes become dark and defined. And then a small sadistic smile creeps across his lips, like a shadow.

CHAPTER 50

It's strange now to think I wanted to be just like Emma. It seems I was right to see her as a mystical creature – she never did exist. Not in the way I imagined her anyway. I almost hated her I was so intimidated. But now, all I feel is love and a deep understanding. What did he put her through before he finally did it?

I hope I'm not about to find out.

He shoves me and I stumble. As I recover I look up at the full moon before ducking my head into the passageway. The light of his phone flicks on as he juts me forward in silence.

I do not know the man behind me any more.

We stop outside the shed. He presses his phone and the door clicks, before slowly opening. 'Are you going to lock me away again?' I ask.

Paul grins and scratches his beard in a hasty, agitated way. 'I thought you wanted to meet her.'

My heart thuds. 'What?' I stammer, turning to look over at the structure. 'Eliza?' I whisper. Is it true? Could she be alive? All those times I saw him trooping down the garden in this direction. Could there . . . could there be a basement underneath? I stare down at my bare feet, covered in wet grass, and wonder what could be below.

'You couldn't have,' I whisper thickly.

He didn't kill her after all. This whole time I was homemaking, gardening and mothering her kids – she's been here. Stuck. Even when we were in London Paul disappeared off on work trips. He must have been bringing her food. Maybe she was in the shed, and then when we arrived, he moved her to the room below the hatch, which is why he needed that heavy-duty new padlock.

How long? Years. God knows what state she'll be in. Half dead, a jabbering wreck. Solitary confinement can do that to a person. I was there one night and feel irreversibly changed. It is the ultimate control. Food, water – freedom. I can't believe I was so brainwashed by him that I willingly let him lock me in there too.

Eliza and I were so close for those twelve hours. 'You're sick,' I spit.

He grins, pleased. 'Go in. You can meet her if you want?' I shake my head and take a step back and he laughs. 'I thought you were desperate to meet her? That's all you've whined on about this whole time. Emma, Emma, Emma.' He jumps from side to side as he says it. 'Fuck me, Lauren. Talk about obsessed. Have some self-respect, woman!' He laughs, throwing his head back. 'Come on, get in there. You said you wanted to know where she is.' He smirks. 'Well, this is your opportunity.'

I shake my head and he stalks towards me. I step back.

He grabs my wrist and pulls me towards the shed. 'No!' I shriek as he drags me closer. 'No!' I cry. As he pulls me to the door, making an attempt at pushing me across the threshold. 'Please . . . I don't want to go in there,' I moan, clinging to the door frame, trying not to lose my footing. I want to help her get out, not be trapped down there too. Panting, I lash out, scratching his face. He shouts and lets go, and momentarily, I am free.

I dart away but he comes back for me, his yellowing eyes afire with venom. His fingers curl around my sweater, holding me back. 'Don't you ever think you can get away. You can never get away from me.' His spit shoots in my face as he marches me backwards and flings me onto the concrete floor. With a wild grin he begins to shut the door as I watch in desolation.

But the door never contacts the frame. Instead, Paul groans and hits the ground.

CHAPTER 51

I slowly remove my face from behind my hands. There, standing in place of Paul, is Susie. She has the same look of horror that must be plastered on my own face. In her hands is a large rock. She looks down at it in dismay and drops it on the floor. Thud. 'Come on, love, come on,' she beckons, glancing at Paul's crumpled body nervously. He could stir at any moment.

I take a few steps towards her and pause, looking at the fat padlock on the hatch. I can't leave her. It could have easily been me down there. I owe it to her to get her out. On all fours I crawl to the spot and begin to bang. 'Eliza. Eliza!' I cry, 'I'm going to get you out. I'm not going to leave you here.'

'Come on, love, let's go.' Susie steps forward, stretching out her hand, not wanting to fully enter the room.

'Hello,' I shout. 'Hello!' I bang on the hatch and pull at the lock, sobbing. Tears and snot career down my face as I crash down on the wood. My fingers scratch until they're bloody. But it's impossible. 'Eliza!' I call again, thudding with all my might. 'Eliza!' My fingers dig into the wood painfully as I try to pry it open. 'I'm going to get you out!' I sob, looking around for anything that might help.

'Love. Come on, love,' Susie's says quietly.

I sniff, wiping the snot from my nose, and blink at her, frustrated she's just standing there, not helping. But then I realise she doesn't understand the urgency. 'She's locked down there,' I ramble. 'We need to help her.'

Susie nods. 'It's okay, dear. Let's call the police and get some help.' I sit back and think. She's right. We can't do this on our own without the code. We'll get help and come back. 'Come on, love, come on. It's time to go,' she says gently. I sniff and nod, relenting.

'I'll come back for you,' I whisper to Eliza. Taking Susie's hand, I let her help me out onto the grass. 'I don't have any sodding reception down here,' Susie mutters as we begin to walk towards the lower passageway.

'How did you . . . how did you know to come?' I ask.

She sighs and shakes the phone in her hand. 'Yesterday, I was feeling nostalgic after our chat and began to look through the old riding school phone at George's photos.' She looks across at me, in a peculiar way. 'Love, I don't know what happened to you but . . .' I snatch it to see. She must have a photograph of Eliza.

'You fucking bitch.' Paul is back. He hovers over Susie. I scream as he grabs onto her head and smashes it against a tree. She collapses like a rag doll. I'm in shock as he yanks my arm back towards the shed. 'Come on. Let me make my introductions.'

I push and fight but I'm no match for him. I drop my resistance, surrendering to whatever the future has in store. Maybe it's always been my destiny to join her.

'Come on, you're so desperate to see what's down there.'

I sob as he jerks me again. My wrist aches from the pressure of his grip.

He lines up the numerical code on the padlock, and he then looks back at me. 'Ready?' he asks, enjoying this. I shake my head. I'll never be, but my eyes don't budge from the spot. He opens the metal flap and begins to lift the hatch. Underneath is another door, which he unlocks with a regular key.

My lips part as he opens it – expecting to see steps down to a dark room and a ghostly white face.

But all that's there, in a shallow pit, is a blue plastic storage tub. I frown. My shoulders fall. Where is Eliza?

'Here she is, Lauren.' He removes the box and drops it onto the concrete floor. I look at him curiously. Then my eyes fall back on the box. 'Is she . . . in there?' It would barely fit a few bones. Ashes maybe? I stare at it, trying to process what's happening. He's taking much delight at my confusion. 'You were so sure you'd worked it out, weren't you?' He smirks and yanks me over. 'It's a real shame that I'm going to have to end this before you find out.' He pushes me to the floor, and I give in to it.

Then I hear a small cry I recognise. Peering over, I see the two children standing with their jackets on, and their rucksacks on their backs. They both look terrified.

Margo is holding her cat and Jesse is holding the BB gun I saw in the garage.

I watch Paul's face flip as it registers. Gone are his harsh, twisted features, replaced by a friendly concerned facade. 'Jesse – give that to Daddy,' Paul says, but Jesse shakes his head sombrely and BANG the gun goes off. Jesse falls back, startled. I'm not sure he even meant to set it off. I dive for the gun at the same time as Paul. My fingers slip around it first, and I thrust it in Paul's face and without thinking, BANG, I pull the trigger. He roars backwards holding on to his bloody eye, writhing around on the floor. Gasping for breath, I stare as he begins to slacken, and stillness finds him.

Panting, I hurry to the children. Jesse is shielding his sister from the view. 'It's okay, darling,' I whisper as I pick her up and hold Jesse's hand.

'I woke up and heard you fighting,' Jesse whispers, his eyes wide in shock at what has just happened.

'It's okay, darling, don't worry about anything right now. Let's just get out of here.'

I stop at Susie, and put Margo down. Leaning over, I shake her, but she's out cold. Whimpering, I feel her chest, mouth, wrist for signs of life. But there is none. Not Susie. No. I think of her regrets. She said she couldn't save her sister, or George, or Eliza. Did she come here tonight to save me? Poor Susie. I'm devastated.

I pick up her phone and hold it up to the sky but she's right, there isn't any service. 'Come on,' I whisper, gathering Margo back up. Jesse is being particularly stoic and pulls my hand forward. I decide to go down instead of up – as I'm sure the lane on the other side of the cottage is far shorter than our mile-long drive, and we'll get to a public road quickly and I'll flag down the first car we see.

We appear out the other side of the tunnel. I look up at the moonlit starry night and think of Paul lying there. He was dead, wasn't he? There is no way he could survive that, surely? The doubt circling my mind keeps me on high alert.

We trudge through the long grass quickly. 'Horse!' cries Margo and I follow her pointed finger to the woods to the left of us. She's right. Following our trajectory on the other side of the fence is the wild horse I've seen a few times. It must be the one that was left behind, that Susie spoke of – what had she called it? Power.

'The horse, Lauren,' Jesse says excitedly. 'Why don't we ride it?'

I shake my head, dismissing the ridiculous idea. 'I can't . . . I can't ride,' I say breathlessly. I turn again to check the dark, sinister entrance to the passageway in case Paul has emerged. Even half blinded he will try to get to us. The horse snorts as it positions itself on the other side of the stile, as if trying to gain our attention.

I freeze, hearing Paul's voice echo from within the trees. Birds flutter out of the canopy and into the sky at the shock of the noise.

'Okay. Come on,' I say, diverting our route quickly. A new-found urgency in my step. I help them both up as we get to the stile. Power sidles up and turns to one side, as if expecting us to use the platform to climb onto her back.

'Come on, darling,' I whisper to Jesse, and I help him up.

The horse is huge and for a moment I stall – am I putting them in more danger? I'm not sure I'll be able to manoeuvre this creature to safety. I don't know the first thing about riding. Am I crazy? I hear Paul again and realise I don't have much choice.

'Come on, Lauren,' Jesse says, waving his hand trying to get us to hurry.

'Me too! Me too!' Margo says.

I clamber on next and then lift her up and put her between my legs, wrapping an arm around her. I feel Jesse grip my sides from behind. 'Hold on tightly, okay?' I whisper to him, and I feel his head nod into my back. The fingers on my free hand tangle into the horse's mane to stop us falling, and I instinctively squeeze my calves as an indication for her to go.

I gasp as my body rises and falls in an easy motion along with hers. And to my relief I don't feel unsteady at all. In fact, I feel anchored to her safely.

Before I know it, we are darting quickly through the woods with air rushing through my hair. It all just flows, and I realise – I can ride. I have ridden before.

Tears begin to pour down my face as we weave through the trees, and Paul's voice gets quieter and quieter in the distance.

And I remember who I am.

I'm finally free.

CHAPTER 52

Sitting in the back of an ambulance with a silver foil blanket over my shoulders and a child hunched under each arm, now the chaos and confusion has died down a little, I reach for the phone in my pocket. I want to see the photograph Susie was trying to show me. I'm a jumble of half-truths and realisations. Full up and empty all at once. The password is simple. One, two, three, four. I click on the photo app and am taken straight through to the last viewed. I hold a sob in my mouth and my chin buckles.

A version of me I don't recognise. I'm standing on top of Power's saddle, balancing with my arms out either side, as if I'm flying. A big grin on my face and my jaw high and proud. My hair long and swept back. I swallow thickly at the confirmation, and look down at the two children nestled into me. I know now the reason I felt so strongly in my gut for these two souls is because they were always mine.

That first moment I saw Margo in hospital, I felt so drawn to her. An inner yank was pulled that was so primal, I knew I needed her, more than she could ever need me. And Jesse – I blink at a memory. My lips move as I remember the line: *Best boy, you are my best boy.* The way he tugged at the handle of the back door, grappling in confusion at his mother's disappearance, when actually, I was there the whole time.

A few days later Detective Chief Inspector Glennon, who is in charge of the investigation, turns up at the hotel. We're in a family suite which sounds posh but, believe me, isn't. The place is on the new side of shabby, and I like the bedded-in quality of the carpet and the cracking paint above the sink. I like how a hundred different people have slept in this bed and have laid back naked in the bath. I can hear the couple in the room next door talking through the paper-thin walls. There is something comforting about my proximity to other people, even though I'm not quite sure how to be around them yet.

My liaison officer, Detective Sergeant Ahearn, lets her in. She gives me that sympathetic smile I've been universally greeted with over the last few days. 'Lauren . . . are you still happy for us to call you that? We know all this is very confusing.'

I shrug. It's the last thing I'm bothered by right now.

'Do you mind if we have a conversation? There are a few things we'd like to run past you.'

I nod. 'Can we do it in the other room?' I ask, nodding at the children who are splayed on top of each other on the sofa watching television.

'Of course,' says DCI Glennon. She has short blonde hair and must be about fifty. She looks sturdy, as though nothing could spook her. I immediately felt safe with her. I think. But . . . then I look at the floor. Will I ever trust myself again?

I check on the children. I don't like them out of my sight for a second, and leave a wide gap in the door before turning to join the detectives at the seating area by the window in the adjoining room.

'I wanted to personally come and speak to you about your husband. And what we've uncovered so far. Hoping it may connect a few dots for you. We want to remind you this is a very complex case, and we are doing our best to piece it together, but it's still early in the investigation.'

I nod. I've barely slept. 'Do I need my lawyer?' I whisper. I feel exhausted by the prospect of more questions. DCI Glennon shakes her head. 'We're not here to question you today, there are just some things we wanted to update you on regarding Mr Bloom, and what happened to you over the last six years.'

I nod, wiping my dry face, my eyes twitching, adrenalin the only thing keeping me vaguely functioning. At night, my nightmares come for me. And more formed things, which must be memories, knock on the door, wanting to come back in.

The lies he used to repress them were the only thing holding them down. They now float freely through me, all muddled, like a puzzle when you first shake out the pieces. Happiness collides with despair as I realise what my children have gone through. What I have gone through.

With trepidation I sit down. DCI Glennon brings a photograph out from a manilla envelope and lays it on the glass coffee table. I recognise Paul instantly. He looks about sixteen. I nearly scoff. He has a short buzz cut and is wearing a holey white vest and skinny jeans with a chain hanging from belt to pocket. 'Richard Duncan was his name then. He changed to Bloom later – I'll come to that.'

She lays an article next to the photograph. The headline says: *Dr Wonderful*. I pick up the flimsy paper, recognising the glass house in the background. It's a profile of a doctor and his family. The doctor is wearing a shirt and a sweater vest and gold-rimmed glasses. Remarkably like Paul's usual attire. The woman standing next to him has long brown hair, and she bears a striking resemblance to . . . me actually. There are two children, a little boy and girl, a few years older than Margo and Jesse. They're standing in exactly the same position as the photograph I found on Richard's phone.

'Is this the family who lived in the house years ago?' I ask, remembering what Susie told me about the lovely doctor. DCI Glennon nods. 'Fifteen years ago. He's an eminent psychologist. They had a young student live with them for a term. It was Richard.' I glance up in surprise. 'He lived there . . . before?'

She nods. 'The doctor saw the house on a news report and phoned in. It seems after Richard left Scotland, he stayed there for four months. At first the doctor was impressed with this intelligent young man and wanted to help give him a leg-up. But Paul changed. He'd become obsessed with some of the research he was doing into neuro-linguistic programming,' she reads from her notebook. 'It's a type of psychotherapy that attempts to change patterns of behaviour. A lot of hypnotists are trained in it. We're still getting up to date on all of this too,' she says, noting my confused face. 'We spoke to another specialist and in the wrong hands it can be very dangerous. It can be used to implant suggestive thoughts and control people.'

I think of Paul in the hospital, how during the sessions I often felt as though I was zoning out. Hours felt like minutes. 'The doctor tells us Paul had an affair with his wife and she went downhill mentally very quickly. She began to display some very worrying behaviours. He cottoned on and threw Richard out, but he stalked them for over a year. Hiding in the woods, waiting for her. Popping up when she least expected it. In the end, they decided to move somewhere less isolated.'

I look down at the family photo. 'He always said he wanted the perfect family.' I think of a young Richard turning up on Dr Wonderful's doorstep and wanting it all for himself. So, in the end, he tried to recreate it.

'Richard moved to Cardiff and began a psychology degree and became . . .' – she lifts out another picture of Richard wearing a university cap – '. . . Richard Bloom.' I swallow.

'After training he worked in psychotherapy for over a decade. Towards the end of his career there were various misdemeanours filed regarding his behaviour towards female patients. It seems these were never connected. We're sorry to say in some cases the aggrieved party wasn't believed because of their medical history. But his last position, in London, while you were in a relationship with him, as Eliza . . .' She pauses for breath. 'Do tell me to stop at any point, Lauren, this is a lot to take in.'

I shake my head for her to continue. I want to know everything.

'His contract was terminated. He managed to get out of any of the serious allegations, but he certainly wasn't going to find gainful employment anytime soon. It's at this point he moved you to the glass house for the first time.'

I think back to all the work he did from home in the study. 'He didn't have a job?'

'He had a couple of private clients he'd managed to string along. But even when he was with Eliza at the house, he was unemployed. No one would touch him. He'd flown too close to the sun. As it were. We think he used his time watching you on the CCTV or with his clients. We've tracked them down, they're quite distressed as I'm sure you can imagine – some of them are in quite a bad way. He also spent a considerable amount of time continuing the charade with your backstory.'

I bite my lip, half scared to ask. 'How did I change? The accident?'

DCI Glennon sighs. 'Do you want to take a break? Have a drink or something?'

I shake my head. 'I'm getting all of these memories,' I reply. I think of the dream with all the blood; it must be from the attack. The memory has been trying to come back to me for months. 'I need to know what he did to me.'

'Before the incident, it seems there was some sort of breakdown of your relationship, and Richard felt it was beyond repair. We're still trying to find out more, but we attended the property a few times during the period. We believe this could be connected to an accusation made about the deceased, Susie Sampson's nephew. A young man called George . . . umm . . .' She checks the detail. 'George Cooper, that was later dropped, and a car crash he was involved with – a collision with a tree. We're still trawling through the CCTV footage from the house to build a fuller picture.' She swallows. 'Some of it will be hard to digest, I'm afraid.' I nod, knowing it will be. Feeling it deep inside.

She picks up the large brown padded envelope she brought with her. 'It's all been bagged up, but we thought you may want to have a look before we store it.' I frown, questioning what it could be. 'This is what was in the box you told us about in the shed. It has been very helpful in piecing together your history.'

I sit back full of fear. 'We don't need to do this now,' she says. My hand shakes as I carefully remove the artefacts. A photo of us – must be from the beginning of our relationship as Paul looks younger, less grey and tired. I lift out another clear baggie holding a scrap of fabric – I blink at an image of a floaty summer dress, a hand on my round stomach. 'He kept memories – trophies possibly – of things from when you were Eliza.' My fingers trace around a baby band from hospital. I find a picture where I'm pregnant; my eyes are tired and haunted. I wonder what he was doing to me then. Had he started his programme of coercion? I was already so stuck, I wish I could reach into the photograph and shake me.

'How did I end up in the hospital?' I whisper.

DCI Glennon puts her hand on my arm. 'Lauren. He tried to kill you.' I try not to buckle. 'He brought you back to London and attacked you, making it look as though you were mugged, and left you for dead.' I heave a sob. My nightmare, that must be what I've been remembering, surely? 'You were found by a stranger and brought to hospital where you were put into an induced coma as your body recovered. Paul was your next of kin and keeping a close eye on you. When you woke up with amnesia he realised there was an opportunity to start afresh. He visited, the nurses knew he was your husband, but to you . . . he pretended to be your counsellor. He told the staff that you never liked the name Eliza, and always went by your middle name, Lauren. Speaking to neighbours and old colleagues of Richard's, you used the Bloom name, but it seems you never got around to formally changing it from Jones to Bloom after you were married, so you still had different surnames on the system,' She clears her throat. 'I spoke to someone who worked there this morning. Your memory was much worse at the beginning. Day-to-day things would evaporate into thin air. Richard charmed them. He was your next of kin – they were understaffed. When you called Richard Paul, and thought he was your therapist, they assumed you were confused – because he was a therapist, after all. Sometimes they even went along with it so you wouldn't get upset.

Then when you were discharged into the unit and got slightly better, he had a clear field to take you home to the flat he'd been renting with the children.'

'The children,' I mutter. 'How did he . . . ?' My voice dies away as I think how little they were when it happened. It's not their fault they forgot about me.

'He told them you'd died from an illness. And then began calling them by different names, even officially changing them. You came back into their lives around two years since they'd seen you. Sadly, he brainwashed them too. They didn't stand a chance against his manipulation.'

Poor Jesse . . . Noah. My poor, poor baby.

'But why did he go to all that trouble? Why not just keep me as Eliza and just start afresh with me? I wouldn't have remembered how terrible our relationship was . . . would I?'

DCI Glennon nods. 'A hypothesis we are working towards is that he knew you could remember at any point. By removing your real backstory, he could keep you away from a past he never wanted you to remember. After all, he'd spent his relationship with you, when you were Eliza, isolating you from your relatives and friends. Your mother desperately tried to reconnect with you on many occasions. She believes he took your old number and replaced it with another. You replied to her messages and unanswered calls telling her to stay away, but she thinks that was probably Richard, pretending to be you. It is safe to presume Richard was controlling both ends of the communication. A similar tactic to what he was doing with your friends' fake numbers. The move, and the new names . . . it was Richard's way of getting you away from your loved ones and isolating you for good.'

'The ultimate fresh start,' I mutter. Looking up, I realise what she said. 'My mother?' I whisper. Tears flood my eyes. 'My mother is dead?' The detective shakes her head.

'Your mother is waiting for you downstairs. She'd love to come up and say hello. If you're ready.'

'I . . . I didn't kill them?' The image of the dolly in the footwell flashes in my mind.

'We've been going through his recordings. We understand many of them were earmarked for blackmail – when you were Eliza – taken under duress. The ones in which we've heard you talking about this accident, as Lauren, in Greece . . . pure fabrication.'

She takes out my scrapbook and places it in front of me. 'None of this is true, Lauren. Your aunt and uncle never existed. Richard was corresponding with you via email, and paying a student using a freelancer website in Australia to send postcards. You have these friends here,' she says, pointing to the photo of the group of us on a night out. 'But these names are incorrect. During your sessions at the hospital, he built up false memories using your old photographs and asking leading questions. A colour-by-numbers past if you will. We are still waiting for the toxicology report, but we think some sort of sedative could account for the intermittent memory loss you were experiencing. Although, that could be down to the NLP or hypnosis, we're not sure at present. I'm so sorry.'

I flick the pages, in awe at the depth of his deception. 'Shall we . . . shall we tell her to come up?' DCI Glennon asks.

I nod quickly. 'Yes.' And DS Ahearn makes a call.

A few minutes later there's a knock. I stand with my hands over my mouth, waiting, as it is opened. Finally, when I feel as though I'm going to burst, a woman in her sixties comes through and rushes towards me sobbing with happiness, relief and despair.

And before I know it, I am being held. I recognise her from the photograph in my scrapbook. There is something about her smell and the sound of her voice that overwhelms me. 'I thought you didn't want to know. I tried to reach out to you so many times. I thought I'd lost you,' the woman keeps repeating. 'I never stopped looking for you. I never stopped looking for my precious little girl.'

'Can we go home?' I ask. 'I want to take the children home.' She nods and cradles my face, and her eyes shine. And I know deep down that I love her.

The nightmare takes hold of me once more. The pain – hard, thrashing and gut-wrenching. I feel as though I am being cut in two or exploded from the inside out. It's gnawing, grating, and goes right through me and back again, as if I'll never be free from it. My teeth gnash and I drool, reaching out for a hand to hold. Stop it. Make it stop.

And then – whoosh – it does.

And the relief.

And the light.

The serene light.

And the doctor hands me my baby. And I'm in pure bliss.

EPILOGUE

A year later

Bright pink rhododendrons clutter the pale blue front door. I poke my head out and grab the glass milk bottle off the step below and turn back into the house. A waft of Kate Bush leaks from the living room and I lean inside. Mum is writing at her desk in the corner. A cram of books surround her haphazardly on shelves which bend at the centre, threatening collapse.

'Mum,' I call over the music.

She turns around and smiles. 'Never heard so much crashing around and babble in my life!' she cries, with laughter in her voice, looking up towards the ceiling. 'Honestly, those two.'

I grin. 'They're pirates today.' I explain the tearing around on the threadbare floorboards upstairs. 'Cup of tea?' I offer.

'No, I'm fine, darling. Are you taking him to the stables? Want me to have little Margo?'

I nod. 'That would be great, if you don't mind?'

She throws down her pen. 'I've been sitting here waiting for you to ask me all morning!'

Noah and I drive five minutes down the road to our local stables. He decided to keep his original name in the end. I think he was always trying to fight his way back to it. Margo has stuck, but she doesn't remember ever being called anything else.

I pull up outside the gate and am transported back twenty years. I'm waiting for my mum to pick me up. I must have just got back from a show jumping competition as my shiny hair is plaited tightly, and I have a ribbon on my chest that I can't help staring at proudly.

Memories come to me often now, and I trust them in a way I never did the shaky lies from before. They appear naturally, just from being here with my mum. And my children. I still get that same dream, but it's no longer a nightmare. I now know it was never my mind trying to uncover my attacker; it was trying to show me something else entirely.

I don't feel sad that he's dead. They tried their best to save him, but the blank lodged too deep and a millimetre in the wrong spot. There is a sense of relief at the finality of it. That I will never have to see him again. And that my children will never have the burden of a father like that left behind somewhere, in the shadows.

Another car parks next to mine. I look across to see Cleo, my old school friend from the photograph, who I thought was Claudia. She waves at me enthusiastically through the window before helping her daughter down from the passenger seat. Noah rushes over to join her, and they chat happily and begin dawdling inside together. Cleo hugs me. 'Hello, darling.' Then she clutches my arm, 'Oh, watch out,' she says, looking over my shoulder. I turn to see George walk from one of the stables, denim sleeves rolled up. 'So you got him a job here?' she asks.

I nod. 'It was the least I could do after what happened to Susie,' I sigh, thinking of her. 'Never mind the fact he totalled his van, was nearly decapitated, and then basically run out of his hometown trying to help me.'

'Yes, how very charitable of you,' Cleo says dryly. Sarcasm dripping from every syllable.

'It's not like that. We're friends,' I try.

But she laughs. 'Right. Yeah, "friends". I wonder how long that's going to last.'

The kids begin to throw straw at one another, laughing hysterically. George catches my eye, and we grin. And then I look up to the top field to see Power gallop across it. All the precious things I've manage to salvage, after leaving them behind.

ACKNOWLEDGEMENTS

I wrote the first draft of this novel during the winter lockdown of 2020/21.

I want to thank my incredible editorial team at Quercus Books – Stefanie Bierwerth and Kat Burdon – for understanding what I was trying to achieve and helping me refine the story with such thoughtful and creative suggestions. This novel is so much better for them. Thank you to my agent Teresa Chris. I wouldn't have carried on without your passion for my writing and stoic belief that I could do this.

Thank you Joe Christie, Ellie Nightingale and David Murphy for all your hard work publicising, marketing and selling this novel; Lorraine Green for your excellent copyediting skills; Lisa Brewster for the gorgeous cover design. There is a plethora more people that I don't come into contact with who work tirelessly towards taking a book to market so thank you to everyone who has had a hand in this one.

I have more cousins than you can shake a stick at, eighteen at last count, spanning a colourful array of professions. This proved handy when I needed to firm up details convincingly that I completely winged during the first draft. Thank you to my day one, Jessica Penney, for reading parts of this with professional eyes. And to Jennifer Kinderman for not refusing to answer round after round of random questions – I really appreciate it. Any mistakes are my own.

Thank you to my sister, Juliet Freud, who was so encouraging in her feedback early on. Mum and Dad's scrupulous eyes for detail and enthusiastic suggestions. Also – I know you are slightly concerned about my wellbeing after reading this novel, and I just want to assure you that I am fine!

Thank you to Kathie and Celia Child-Villers for taking my horse-mad son riding that lockdown summer when restrictions eased. From his excited babbling sprung equestrian ideas, for which I am truly grateful. Celia standing on top of her horse, Pip, is a sight to behold!

As always, my closest friends – Lucy Francis, Candice O'Brien, Sophie Nevin and Bridie Woodward. The most supportive, funny, smart and insane group of women I know. Thank you. Writer friends, old and new – Katie Khan, Jane Lythell, Kate Maxwell and Charlotte Philby – thank you for all your support, over messenger and coffees, while I was in a neurotic worry-haze as I plotted my way through writing this book.

Big massive huge thanks to all the book bloggers, you are amazing and a hidden joy of a burgeoning writing career has been connecting with you all.

I've dedicated this book to my firstborn, Jude, because he made me a mother, the most challenging endeavour of my life. I'm so proud of you. Thank you also to my hilarious little girl, Lola. You both helped me write this book, two years apart and both under five.

Thank you to my husband, Dan, my first reader. I always say that I married you because you are better at spelling and cooking than I am, and I still think it is one of the better decisions I've made in my life. Thank you for taking my calls, when you're clearly very busy, to decipher words that have escaped me. I would have gone mad over the last two years without you.

Lastly, I hope you enjoyed this book and I'd love to hear from you. You can find me on Instagram or Twitter – do come and say hello!